Pe

THE ROSE NOTES

Andrea Mayes was born in the north of England in 1955 and emigrated to Melbourne in 1979. She has written stories and poetry since she was a child. Her writing has won awards and commendations and has been published on-line and in literary magazines, anthologies, newspapers, and broadcast by the ABC. This is her first novel.

ANDREA MAYES

THE
ROSE
NOTES

A novel

Penguin Books

For Ben and Ant
(for all the love and light)

PENGUIN BOOKS

Published by the Penguin Group
Penguin Group (Australia)
250 Camberwell Road, Camberwell, Victoria 3124, Australia
(a division of Pearson Australia Group Pty Ltd)
Penguin Group (USA) Inc.
375 Hudson Street, New York, New York 10014, USA
Penguin Group (Canada)
10 Alcorn Avenue, Toronto, Ontario, Canada M4V 3B2
(a division of Pearson Penguin Canada Inc.)
Penguin Books Ltd
80 Strand, London WC2R 0RL, England
Penguin Ireland
25 St Stephen's Green, Dublin 2, Ireland
(a division of Penguin Books Ltd)
Penguin Books India Pvt Ltd
11 Community Centre, Panchsheel Park, New Delhi – 110 017, India
Penguin Group (NZ)
Cnr Airborne and Rosedale Roads, Albany, Auckland, New Zealand
(a division of Pearson New Zealand Ltd)
Penguin Books (South Africa) (Pty) Ltd
24 Sturdee Avenue, Rosebank, Johannesburg 2196, South Africa

Penguin Books Ltd, Registered Offices: 80 Strand, London, WC2R 0RL, England

First published by Penguin Group (Australia),
a division of Pearson Australia Group Pty Ltd, 2005

1 3 5 7 9 10 8 6 4 2

Text copyright © Andrea Mayes 2005

The moral right of the author has been asserted

Cover and text design by Marina Messiha © Penguin Group (Australia)
Typeset in 11/15.5 pt Stempel Garamond by Post Pre-press Group, Brisbane, Queensland
Printed in Australia by McPherson's Printing Group, Maryborough, Victoria

National Library of Australia
Cataloguing-in-Publication data:

Mayes, Andrea.
The rose notes.

ISBN 0 14 300317 8.

1. Fathers and daughters – Fiction. 2. Farmers – Fiction.
3. Roses – Varieties – Fiction. I. Title.

A823.4

www.penguin.com.au

'Territory, you see, is not necessarily the place you feed in. It's the place in which you stay . . . where you know every nook and cranny . . . where you know by heart every refuge . . . where you are invincible to the pursuer. I've even measured it with sticklebacks.'

Konrad Lorenz

(comment made to Bruce Chatwin, published in *The Songlines*)

Rose is a rose is a rose is a rose
Gertrude Stein

Just when we are safest, there's a sunset-touch,
A fancy from a flower-bell, some one's death,
A chorus-ending from Euripides, –
And that's enough for fifty hopes and fears
As old and new at once as nature's self,
To rap and knock and enter in our soul . . .
Robert Browning

(from *Bishop Blougram's Apology*)

AUTHOR NOTE

The region of Coolabarradin with its outlying farms, including Mamerbrook, is a fictional place, modelled on the southern Riverina in New South Wales, Australia. All of the characters in the book, with the exception of the Southern Bell Frog and the Plains Wanderer, are fictional and bear no relation to any person, living or dead.

PROLOGUE

1955

It is a quarter to eleven on December 31, 1954.

Henry Hearne writes *Yours sincerely* at the bottom of the letter he has just finished and looks across at his wife, Nora. She is snoring gently in the rocking chair, knitting needles and yarn fallen in her lap. The *Women's Weekly* knitting pattern with its picture of a laughing toddler has slipped to the floor. She'd warned him she wouldn't make it to midnight. Looks like she's right.

Nora's face betrays an exhaustion as much emotional as physical. She seems older than her thirty years. Older than *his* thirty years. More mother than wife. Older and wiser and wary of happiness. Life has made her that way, and joy seldom visits the wary. Henry knows this, but what can you do?

The boys, Robert, aged three, and Thomas, fifteen months, are sleeping in the back room. Through the open window a chorus of frogs and crickets declares amatory intentions and territorial rights. The air in the living room trembles with the fragrance of five hundred blossoming roses. Their nearest neighbour, three miles distant, smiles to himself when the wind carries the scent across his fields. It is the aroma of happiness.

The rose nursery is Henry's dream, not Nora's. There's a price to pay for living someone else's dream. Just ask Nora. There's a price to pay for binding someone to your own dreams, too. Even if it's done with the best of intentions. We all have our cross to bear, Nora says, matter-of-fact. Whatever you have to believe to get by, Henry thinks, but sometimes he feels that he'll never reach her again. He would have scattered her path with rose petals for the rest of her life, to see the spark of a smile in that face.

The Westinghouse refrigerator whirrs into action and Nora stirs, opening her eyes. He looks for a sign. He's got a bottle of advocaat tucked away, to help bring the New Year in. He's hoping she'll have a drop with some lemonade in it. A snowball, they call it. Sweet stuff. With a bit of luck, she'll have a couple of them. She yawns and lifts her head, running a hand through her permed fair hair. It has flattened on one side, tangled on the other, giving her a dissolute look. She groans and stretches, arching her back that aches so, from carrying babies and buckets of nappies.

Henry watches her hungrily, the heavy curves of her body beneath the full blue cotton skirt, the cream blouse with its lace-edged collar, her legs, splayed and bare under the skirt. In his mind, he strokes the inside of her thigh delicately with one finger, just above the knee. In his mind, she curls towards him, kissing him and . . . ah, Nora.

'What time is it?'

He tells her.

'Told you I wouldn't make it to midnight.'

'Glass of the sweet stuff will perk you up a bit. What do you think?'

'Don't think I have it in me. Sorry, love,' she says and hope rises in him, comes gambolling at the tenderness in her voice. 'You'll have to see this year in by yourself.'

Again.

He moves the writing pad from his knees, laying it on the table beside him, on one of the crocheted doilies that Nora's mother sends out from England every Christmas. A doily a year for every year they've been here. What does that say? Old Mrs Dugan in her rocking chair, with her cottons and her crochet hook flashing in and out, in and out of a web of yearning for her only child, the daughter she lost to Henry Hearne and Australia. Seven doilies. And when they stop coming? More grief for Nora. He wonders how many doilies they'll have by then.

'Not enough, is it? Everything I do? You want a song-and-dance act as well? I can't help it if I'm exhausted.' The sudden rancid note in her voice brings his head up sharply. She's misinterpreted his silence.

'Nora, love . . .' But he doesn't finish the protest. What reassurance can he offer? The same old words, the same old promises. But life goes on. You have to take what you can and make the best of it. He wants to make it right. The need is like a knife behind his rib

3

cage. Sometimes, just for a moment when she wakes, there'll be the old burr of affection in her voice. It gets him every time. And then, every time, she remembers. Her baby girl. Four months and miscarried. She's given birth to Thomas since then, a nervous baby with grave, far-seeing eyes that shake the balance in Henry, make him want to throw a look over his shoulder, just in case there's something . . . He's not at all like little Robbie. Nora's baby, this one. But Thomas hasn't helped her over the grief. You can hear it in her voice. You can see it in her eyes, in her trembling, reddened fingers. Grief for the one who didn't make it.

'I want to go home, Henry,' she says to him now. 'I want this to be the year I . . . we . . . go back to England. There's a New Year's resolution for you.'

Here we go again. This is what Nora believes will make everything right; this is how they will become the people they once were, innocent, not without fear, but full of hope. Despite himself, he glances at their wedding photograph on the mantlepiece.

'This is home, Nora,' he says quietly.

'You know what I mean.'

The circle of their words tightens around his throat. Will she never tire of it? It can only end, as it always does, with Nora crying into her pillow. He is a mild man who will look for a way to soothe, for words to charm and cajole. He will not abandon her to grief and bitterness but neither will he go back to a land he'd fled without a backward glance. The middle child of strict

Baptist Yorkshire parents, Henry felt the need to escape at an early age, long before he had any understanding of what drove him to it. Climbing the bare hillsides behind the squat house, scaling dry-stone walls, stirring the grey sheep that watched him with calm, incurious eyes. He ran away from the need to conform, to oblige; he ran towards the strength he drew from solitude. It was his conscience that always brought him back.

The family decided, after his elder brother William had forsaken them for the merchant navy, that Henry should take over the management of the family's grocery shop in Cudworth. But Henry didn't take over. Henry took off once and for all. What fuelled this flight? A tender dream. A pocketful of petals.

Roses! they cried. What kind of a living can you expect to make from roses? How are you going to keep a wife and raise children, on roses?

He ran until he got to the point where if he'd run any further, he'd have been running back. Australia. And he brought Nora with him. By now his heart has spread far deeper than the roots of roses into this land of light and wide spaces. He won't give it up. His children have been born here. Here, he has forced his budding dreams out into the real world with blistering hands. Safety lies here. Salvation is with him. Close. Close enough. If only Nora . . .

'Nora. Let's not do this again. Not tonight, lass. It's New Year's Eve. Let's have a drink together. Come on, sit over here beside me. We ought to be looking forward to the future. You know how business is picking up, and we have two marvellous healthy boys, our own home, so much to be thankful for, eh?'

'When are you going off on your next trip?' she asks, distracted, eyeing the letter he's written and ignoring his words.

No hope of winning her round now, Henry.

'In about three weeks.'

'And how long will you be away this time?'

'About the same. Three weeks or so. I'm just trying to sign up a few more appointments. I'll make the trip as quick as I can.'

'Like last time?'

'Last time brought us some good business.'

'I'm going to bed.'

'Nora . . .' He puts out a hand to detain her, knowing that with every plea of his that she rejects, she feels a little stronger, a little less helpless.

There's a rising wail from the back room. Thomas. A fretful baby, waking frequently at night. Nora bears the brunt of the sleeplessness but they are both anxious about the boy.

'It's his age, that's all. He'll grow out of it,' Henry reassures her, wondering privately if the child is drinking his mother's grief along with her milk. Perhaps if he could give her a girl next time, things might look up? But it has been a long time since Nora allowed him to get close, shying away if he even tries to put an arm around her. She goes into the boys' room. He can hear her murmuring to the little one – the softness in her voice sears him. Shrugging off self-pity, he pours himself a beer and stands by the window, whistling soundlessly between his teeth to raise his spirits. It's a new song he's heard on the radio, a catchy tune. *Oh, I can't see the roos for the roses, and I can't see the sheep for your smile. For the rose in your cheek and the smile in your eye, I'll come running the four-minute mile.*

We just need to see what's here, in front of our eyes, he thinks. What we have. There's things you want and things you need, and we have everything we need, right here, me and Nora, and the boys.

But she wants to go home, Henry.

Home?

Home is a place to grow in, a place to sally out from, a place where courage and the heart lie. And home is here, isn't it? In this good earth, surrounded by Henry's roses. One day, she'll see it. She'll come to her senses. And one day, he'll show them all. He'll breed a rose of such exquisite perfection that the whole world will want it.

The scent of roses washes over him, calming the little chirrup of guilt awakened by his eagerness to load up the Morris Minor and hit the road with his catalogues of roses, his list of addresses and his gift of the gab. It's like taking a deep breath of fresh air, to drive off into the sunshine, free and alone, knowing that you'll always be coming home to the roses, and Nora. It's the boy in him.

She'd have him praying for forgiveness, if she knew how happy it made him. On the whole, he thinks, Catholics, like Baptists, aren't too good at happiness. But it isn't hard to be happy. It doesn't mean that you don't grieve, or that you don't care. It's just that anything else is a waste. Sacrilege. He doesn't have Nora's consoling faith in priests and hymns and heaven. He doesn't believe that everything will be rosy in the next life if your heart breaks in this one. Heaven? Heaven would be nice, but it's not an idea you can hang your hat on, is it? You're only here once. One chance, that's all.

Across the garden, rows and rows of nappies hanging on the washing line flash white in the moonlight. His little blue car is shining under the stars, beckoning him. Think of the opportunities that await. All the talk about roses there'll be! A new customer, perhaps? Maybe he'll even find an old rose he hasn't seen before, waiting for him in a forgotten corner of someone's garden? A chat with a stranger in a country pub. The chance to swap stories with someone he might never see again, to tell them about his boys, and learn a few things. Time to be alone, time to dream.

He'd like to make it better for her. Really, he would. He loves her. And that's why he has to go away. Not just for the business, not just for the roses, but so that he can be happy for a while, restore himself, and come back and keep on loving her until she heals.

He picks up the letter he's written and scans it quickly.

Dear Mrs Kinnear,

I do enjoy receiving your letters – always so inform-ative! I was interested to read your assessment of the seven shrubs. In our cooler climate and different soil conditions, we get many variations that complicate the business of isolating certain characteristics, as you say. But the world would be a dull place if everything turned out as we'd anticipated . . .

. . . let me say that it would be marvellous if you could see your way to inviting me to have a look at your place when I travel north. Particularly as I would like some budwood of the varieties which I am no longer hold-ing. Would you be so kind? I would greatly appreciate the opportunity to meet you face to face, and to see your roses.

It will do. He's been writing to Mrs Kinnear for almost three years, since she first ordered roses from his cata-logue. They share an intimacy of roses – tips, gleanings, anecdotes, hopes, worries and several minor miracles. He keeps folders of letters from rose-growers, nurseries and customers around the country, all filed by region for easy access when he plans his trips. Alice Kinnear's letters are in the folder marked 'Southern Riverina'. It's a long way to the southern Riverina but there's plenty of work he can do there. Every region is a land of oppor-tunity, for Henry. He knows nothing about her life, beyond the fact that she's a farmer's wife, and a prosper-ous one at that. It will be their first meeting and he can't

9

wait to see her garden. Wonders if he should take her a gift in return for the budwood he wants. What does he have that she might need?

He scribbles a signature on the letter, smiling in expectation of her reply. The clock on the mantlepiece chimes twelve. Henry raises his glass to the night sky, to the future, and the future of his children, born and unborn. May they all love roses.

It is New Year's Day, 1955.

1

January, 2004

Who is that, slipping like a shadow past the water tank, bending under the branches of the white cedar trees so that their leaves brush the top of his hat? It's Dobie Kinnear, moving at a fair clip too, for his seventy-eight years. Blackleg stalks him, nosing at his heels.

'Get away with you!' hisses Dobie. 'Go on. Be off! Stop following me. Wait for my whistle.'

The dog stops, pricks his ears, raises an inquiring face. Dobie points, arm outstretched towards the homestead.

'Home!' he whispers.

Home?

If dogs could shrug . . .

Dobie skirts the farmhouse in a half-crouch, keeping well out of sight of the windows and avoiding the main garden in case his daughter, Pearl, is working there. As long as she can see the dogs hanging round the back door, she'll assume he's in the house. If the phone rings for him, she'll go calling his name, looking for him, and she won't find him.

Round the back of the chookpen he goes, then the long way around the dam, scattering the little black marsh hens that scoot and swerve like roadrunners in front of him.

'Shhhh!' he says, but they've already vanished.

It's easy for him to disappear when it suits him, and reappear too, now that most of the real farm work has been delegated to younger, stronger men. He likes to catch people unawares. It gives him an edge. It annoys the hell out of Pearl. He's a one-man resistance movement, Dobie Kinnear. Pushing through the tangle of his years, wearing the camouflage of innocence. Feeling his way along familiar paths like a man whose sight has grown suddenly dim, determined to hide the fact from everyone.

In the vegetable garden where the earth is soft and black, Dobie lowers himself cautiously to his knees with a silent prayer that he'll be able to get up again. No guarantees. He sorts and sifts the dirt, letting it slip through stiff fingers, keeping in his palms the fat worms, pink and brown, seething and speckled with soil. When the worm can is half full, he stows it in the back of the ute with his fishing tackle and a couple of big buckets. Optimistic, that.

Now he's ready. Where are those dogs? He whistles softly and Blackleg is instantly quivering at his side. *What's the game, boss?* No sign of the old one. Blackleg leaps into the back. Dobie whistles again, eyes scanning the long grass for Mutt's dark shape. No? Found something better to do, has she? He rolls the ute down the track oh so gently in first gear. You'd hardly know he was there.

Fishing's a good way to soothe the spirit, and his old spirit needs a fair bit of soothing, now that the world is moving faster than he can. Years back, he'd go up to the high country and follow the trout streams. Nights of swag and stars with a sleek fish on the embers. Takes some beating, fly-fishing. The sweet ritual of choosing from a box of lures. None of your gaudy plastic stuff, but the delicate magic of wood, hand-carved and hand-painted, and all the bright feathers. The muscles of Dobie's arm twitch in sympathy with the remembered rhythm of the cast and his thighs on the ute's seat brace against the force of moving water. His rheumy eyes squint at the memory of sun-glare on wild river shallows and he wonders how a passion like that ever gets to be too much trouble.

This old river meandering across a corner of Mamerbrook Farm is as far as he goes now. Massive river red gums twisting and muscling along the banks, skin of ochre and russet, smooth cream and silver. Bird calls dropping into still air. The sounds of slow-moving water. The peace of it swallows you up.

Look at him, sitting on the steep clay bank with one rod pressed against his knee and another set further along, propped against tree roots. Dobie Kinnear, in his dull green shirt and brown trousers with an old Akubra low on his head, drowsing, as carp break the water surface with insatiable yellow mouths and thousands of insects dance unaware in the air above them. There's little enough here to betray his place on the mazy trail of human life, or to show what he's gained, and what he's lost. He's just a man fishing, touched by the only god he needs.

The river is low today. The water controllers aren't sending so much interstate right now. Building up reserves for the irrigators. It's a channel, this river, from reservoir to reservoir, from state to state, carrying an asset, not a gift. It used to flood with the seasons and according to its own cycles, its stories told and sung, marking boundaries of time. Now it flows as directed and floods only on command. Dobie watches the dark ripples, picturing the hidden life lurking beneath them, crooning in his mind for a fat Murray cod to take the bait.

It's not a sudden tautness of the fishing line that rouses him. It's a soft thud – plock! – on his hat.

Shit, he thinks.

That'd be right.

There's a heavy beating of wings low behind him, a draught of air as the bird comes around, and a cry of dreadful yearning. Crow. Another bird swoops past him, fast and close. It settles on a low bough over the river. Magpie. Dobie looks nervously over his shoulder. Any more where they came from? He takes off his hat. His head with its sparse white curls is suddenly, shockingly vulnerable, as if all his authority resides in the Akubra. Without the softening shade of its brim, his cheeks sag, the grooves in his face deepen and his eyes are already watering in the sunlight. He blinks. Stares in surprise. There's a piece of meat on his hat. It's been torn from the innards of some creature. Rabbit maybe. Or a joey? That old crow must be pretty cheesed off.

He picks up the morsel, pinching it between a grimy finger and thumb. If he knew what he had there, grief would slice his heart. Not knowing? You can be lucky that way. Sometimes.

What are the odds of having a piece of meat land on your hat? He pictures himself telling the story to Ted Figgit at Elders. *You wouldn't credit it, Ted* . . . But Ted's not the audience he used to be. Always looking over his shoulder, rubbing at the mark on his cheek where they took out the skin cancer.

Pearl would be amazed but she'd manage to say something sarcastic and spoil it. Anything to get back at him. God knows what he's done to deserve it. Only given her a comfortable home. And a purpose in life. Don't forget that. Where would she be without him to look after? All this time and still no man within cooee for her. Not that she's put much effort into it. Likes her own company too much. How many men have come sniffing around her over the years? He reckons he could count them on the fingers of one hand. It's suited him all right, keeping her here. Made life easier. But there's no question now. She's missed the boat. You can't have everything, can you? He sighs, looks over at the dog. The dog looks at the meat, hopefully.

Once there was someone who listened to his stories. Someone warm and funny and quick – a mind that made him dizzy and a body to match. The one perfect thing in his life. And he wasn't surprised at all, you see, when they confirmed her cancer. He'd always known there'd be something. You have to pay for that degree of happiness, sooner or later. In his case, it was soon. Too soon. Thirty-five years since she died and the memory of her still sears his mind and makes his balls ache with loneliness. Alice. Dearly beloved wife of Dobie Kinnear, mother of Pearl. Here she comes.

'It's a sign,' she says. 'An omen. It's amazing. Of all the hats . . .'

'But what do you think it means?'

'Whatever you want it to mean, Dobie my love.'

Isn't that the truth.

Dobie looks for signs in the same way that he searches the skies for a weather pattern. Signs of treachery. Signs of deceit. Signs of what's coming. You never know, do you, when the world will pounce? You have to keep your wits about you. Stay on top of things. Top of the pile. King of the castle. Responsible for the wellbeing of family and employees, temporary guardian of the land, as his father Alistair had been, and his father before him, and his father before him, and . . .

. . . who will come after?

Pearl?

Is that it?

Heaven help us and save us.

'I could do with a good sign, Alice. A good omen,' he whispers, but Alice has gone.

Blackleg is lying quietly with his head on his paws, perfectly still except for those yellow eyes that have followed every movement of the meat since the second before it landed on the hat.

'Well,' says Dobie to the dog, 'at least I caught something. Here.' He tosses the meat. Blackleg snaps it up and pads over to him in case there's another miracle in the offing.

'Where's the old girl got to?' Dobie asks, giving him a rough pat on the head. 'Where's your mate Mutt?'

Time to go home. He turns on the steeply sloping river bank so that he can push himself to his feet with the flat of his hands. There – oops! – made it. No fish for dinner. What's Pearl going to dish up? Her cooking hasn't been up to much lately. It's not like she's rushed off her feet with anything else. She does the paperwork once a month or so and takes care of the housework. Hardly a full-time job. You'd think she could get a decent meal together for a working man, wouldn't you?

He packs up his gear, stows it next to the empty buckets in the back of the ute and drives off, a bit stiff, a bit rickety in his old age, but with all his beliefs intact.

Makes you wonder about things though, when something like that happens to you, out of the blue.

Makes you glad you've got a hat on.

2

My name is Henry Hearne and this recording was made over a period of several days just before my death. (Pause) No. I can't say that. It doesn't even sound like me.

   – It's true though.

   – Yes, but it won't do. How do you wind this thing back? (Click) Never mind. I can manage.

   This recording was made over a period of several days at Mt Solomon Private Hospital by me, Henry Hearne, for my son Thomas. How did that sound?

   – It sounds fine. Carry on.

   – Well toddle off then. I need a bit of peace and quiet to do this.

   – You'll fall asleep again.

   – And no wonder, the noise they make in this bloody place every night.

   – You're still recording, you know. When you've got your thumb on that button, just remember it's picking up everything you say.

Ah, she's gone now. She's a grand lass. Don't know how they do it. Don't know how they manage to stay so bloody cheerful. Wait for the moments of lucidity, she said. There'll be times like this when everything is clear. Moments when you understand everything that's happening around you. That'll be a first, I told her.

Truth is, I can't tell where I am half the time, so I'm going to keep my finger on this button and keep talking. And you'd better listen, Thomas. Sort out the sense from the waffling. No doubt you can do that. You've always been the smart one of the family. In some ways. Your mother was so proud of you. A son of hers going to the university. She never stopped bragging about you. Thomas? Are you listening? I have a job for you. Better late than never, this one. I think so. Yes.

She put the recorder right into my hand, that nurse. It isn't very big. Marvellous thing. There you are, she said. Talk into that, when you feel like yourself. She meant, when the pain isn't too bad, when the dreams aren't too strong, when I know who I am. But every time I close my eyes, I'm home again. In a place I haven't called home for sixty years. Is it the morphine, do you think, that's tidying my life into a loop? Am I making sense?

I'm going home, Thomas. I'm going home and I can't stop it. It drags at my stomach and teases my knocking old heart. I can hear your mother telling me, Better late than never. Poor Nora. She always thought heaven would look like Yorkshire. I wonder if that's where I'm going? I'm afraid, you know. We're all afraid. Be careful, Thomas. It's so easy to damage the innocent . . .

Wait three months after I go, lass. That's what Henry told her. It's been more than three months. A few days more, because she's been ringing the number that Henry gave her but no one answers. It's a weighty responsibility, carrying the words of a dead man. She'd like to have done with it. You don't know what you're setting in motion. No control and no recourse; Henry has gone. It's against all her principles, this degree of involvement. But he'd had such a way about him. They might have been friends, given time.

'What's your accent?' she'd asked him, that first day, looking for a way to break through the dread that they all feel when they come here, to this ward. Some patients talk to her nonstop, filling their heads with sound so they can't hear the fear. Some are angry and looking for a target. Others are obsessive about details, as though a cup of tea at the right temperature might keep reality at bay. The truth is, no matter what you do, you can never make it up to any of them for the simple fact that they are dying. But you can try.

Henry had been determined to enjoy whatever there was to be enjoyed for as long as he drew breath.

'South African,' he answered.

'Go on with you! It is not. You sound just like my gran used to, and she was from Yorkshire, in England.'

'Why'd you ask then?'

'Just being polite. Didn't want to put my foot in it. Like when you ask a Scotsman what part of Ireland he's from.'

'I've lived here most of my life. I should sound like an Aussie.'

'You don't.'

'No.' He grinned at her.

She'd been straightening the bedclothes as she chatted and she asked him to raise his upper body slightly so she could freshen his pillows. He tried but he couldn't manage it. She saw how it bothered him, the weakness displayed.

'Come on, I'll give you a hand.'

'No, no. Don't fret yourself. I'm settled enough. The pillows are fine.'

'But are you sure you're comfy, love?' she asked.

'Now you sound like your gran.'

'My gran would have said: "Here, let me do it – you shap like a wet hen."'

'Oh yes,' he said, delighted, 'so would mine,' and he closed his eyes and went time-travelling. Sheila Mulraney has grown accustomed to patients who do this. She understands their preference for a time when they stood straight and went about the business of living. She is comfortable if they call her by the names of their wives and daughters. When they speak, she takes a moment to gauge the time in which their clock is ticking, and then her conversation slips right along with them, easing their stories, gilding their dreams.

With Henry, it was the broad accent and the humour that gave them a way through to each other and access to the comfort of ordinary conversation. It was something they shared, as well as the business of dying. It was why she'd agreed to help him, despite her misgivings. It was why she was stuck with this tape.

Henry had two grown sons, Robert, the elder, and Thomas. He had a job for Thomas to do. Something mysterious. It was moithering him, he said. At first he'd tried to write it down but the effort of shaping thought into legible shapes and coherent sentences exhausted him.

'I suppose I could write it for you?' she said doubtfully. 'You could tell me and I could write it down, if you like.'

But that didn't suit Henry. It had to be private at this stage, he explained, apologetic. No third party. Just him and Thomas. Well, she was happy with that. But curious. Who wouldn't be?

'Why don't you talk to him? Just tell him, when he comes to see you?' she'd asked.

'Ah, but then there'd be questions. Questions I have no right to answer. There's someone else involved, you see. I don't know if . . . Oh, there must be a way.'

She found a way. She brought him a little box, so neat you could hold it in just one hand. A tape recorder. He held it on his chest, where he could speak into it whenever a thought occurred to him and turn it off easily when he was done. They had a few trial runs. She thought it remarkable, how clearly you could hear Henry's hoarse whispers on the tape. The astonishing insistence of his old heart played a moody bass to his words.

'It's going to be fine,' she told him.

Sometimes, she came in and found him sleeping, the tape whirring away by itself, recording the burbles and snorts of his breathing. She'd take it and wind it back to the point where he'd last spoken, leaving it within his reach for when he woke. Beyond that, she didn't interfere, though she wondered how anyone would make sense of what he was saying.

It was six days before he told her.

'That's it. I think that's it. I'm pretty sure I've got it all down. He just has to find Alice. Can't be that hard.'

But she wasn't in the clear. Not yet. He didn't want to give the tape to Thomas right away. No one was to know about it but her.

'I think it's important that it doesn't come hot on the heels of my funeral, so to speak. Give him time. He may feel more inclined then, after the first shock of it, when it really starts to come home to him that I am dead. And some good may come of it for him. I hope so. It's time someone understood what's what. If that's possible.'

She saw Thomas on one of his visits to the hospital and she paid attention, noticing how he behaved around Henry. How polite he was. How uncomfortable. A lanky, sandy-haired man with a straggly ginger beard and moustache and a worried frown. The other son, Robert, looked like a younger Henry, a Henry with muscle and flesh on him, but Thomas was tall, much taller than Henry would have been in his prime. Hazel eyes that skittered away from hers when she greeted him. A loner, she thought.

'Look here,' said Henry, 'that was Thomas, my youngest, who just went out. He's a good boy but he's never been able to make his mind up to do anything without a boot up the backside. Unless it concerns frogs. Always messing about with frogs. He's a herpetologist. A scientist.' He paused, as if after all these years the fact still bewildered him. 'I want you to wait three months after I go, lass, and then give him this tape.'

It was too late to pull out. It was too late to protest. She could only promise to do as he asked.

Henry died the following night.

3

Pearl is ripping out weeds and grass from her rose beds as though she's tearing the hair from someone's head. Rip! And . . . rip! That's fixed you. The work is tough and repetitious. Rose by rose she works, occasionally murmuring the odd endearment, addressing the shrubs by name. Double Delight. Moon Flight. Peace. Fragrant Clouds. She moves along the curving beds, merciless with aphids and earwigs, leaving tidy pyramids of earth and broken plants on the grass, ready to collect later when she brings the wheelbarrow through.

What's that buzzing? Blowflies? After a while, still hearing it, she wonders. Better go and check it out. As she stoops under the bough of the crepe myrtle, two crows depart with heavy wingbeats, a sullen gleam of dark feathers. The blowflies rise in a fierce, dense cloud, then settle again.

Oh Christ.

That's torn it.

One dead dog. Dobie's old darling. And you'll have to tell him.

Shit.

They've grown old together, her father and this kelpie. They've slowed down together and stiffened up. They've yawned in secret unison and taken to sneaking naps in the sun. For the last couple of years it's been odds on as to which one of them would go first, man or dog. Pearl fans a couple of blowflies away from her hot face. She'd asked him to shoot the dog months ago.

'She's like the walking dead, for heaven's sake. If you're not going to shoot her, get her to the vet then. He might be able to give her something for that arthritis.'

'No call for that kind of talk, Pearlie. You'll come good, won't you, girl?' said Dobie, leaning down and scratching Mutt beneath her jaw, whispering tender words that were not for Pearl, who knew exactly what the vet would say. As did Dobie.

Well, she won't come good this time. He'll want the dog buried properly, not thrown into the tip for the crows to pick over. She'll have to see if Pete can spare a man. God! if it's not one thing, it's another. She takes another look. The pale tongue is shredded, the eyeballs gone – black ants massing in the empty sockets. The belly is slashed open, trailing innards. Damn crows.

Hell's bells, she thinks, I could have done without this. Halfway down the track to the manager's cottage, cramp curls tight in her stomach. Guilt or fear? Not that it matters. Or is it her period? Probably not. It's been five months. She's ordered books about menopause over the Internet, unable to find the courage to ask for them in the gossip-ridden town of Coolabarradin, fifty miles away. So far, two books have arrived, wrapped securely in brown paper and addressed to Miss Pearl Kinnear. She kept them on the table all through dinner one night, anonymous in their wrapping, knowing how Dobie was dying to ask about them and knowing he wouldn't. She still hasn't unwrapped them, fearing any further investigation might confirm a sinister and incurable collaboration between her own ageing and this pervasive sense of failure. She doubles over, pressing a hand beneath her rib cage, then straightens and breathes in deeply. It's just a dog, Pearl. Just a dog. Wanting to be rid of it isn't a crime. It's not necessarily the beginning of the end. Is it?

The low white gate creaks when she pushes it, and a dark face appears at a window. The door opens and Bel waits, sunlit, framed by the shadows beyond. She's wearing a loose blue dress with a tiny yellow floral design. Her black hair is pulled back, showing broad streaks of grey, and caught in a thick knot at the nape of her neck. Her feet are bare, toes spread and comfortable on the floorboards. This is her territory. You meet trouble at the front door, and Bel has no doubt that this is trouble. The expectation of it is there in her eyes, in the line of her lips that might be a smile, but isn't. Pearl Kinnear wouldn't be dropping by for a cup of tea and a chat.

Pearl, shiny and red-faced, grimy from the weeding, feels her body protesting against the waistband of her pink pedal-pushers that had seemed neither so pink nor so tight when she'd tried them in the shop. She smiles a greeting, feels herself swelling under Bel's calm gaze to cow-like proportions with grass breath, beseeching eyes and a drone of flies around her enormous rump.

'Any idea where Pete is, Bel?'

'Did you try the radio? I heard him on channel not five minutes ago. Said he was heading down to the river pump to fix something.'

Pearl pushes back her hair with a dirty hand.

'Mutt's dead. Dad won't be back for a while. I didn't want her lying out there in this heat, with the crows lining up on the fence. Didn't want him to see her like that.' She wrinkles her nose. 'Wouldn't be right for him to hear about it over the radio.'

'Ah. It'll be strange seeing Dobie around the place without old Mutt limping at his heels. But she was over-due for it, the old girl,' says Bel. 'It won't come as much of a shock to him.'

Won't come as much of a shock to him? What does she know?

'Expecting it is one thing, dealing with the reality of it is another thing altogether,' Pearl says crisply and immediately wishes she hadn't. 'If you could just ask Pete to send someone over, please? No need to say what it's for. She's lying under the big crepe myrtle, behind the homestead.'

'There are worse places to die.'

A breath of the cool space beneath those grey branches

comes whispering into Pearl's mind. If you were to lie on your back and look up, the delicate green and rose tints of the crepe myrtle leaves would trace such patterns in the blue of the sky that you might well become absorbed by them, enchanted, until something like sleep comes stealing over you . . .

Oh, for some peace.

Get a grip, Pearl.

'He'll be looking for a pup, will he? To train up?' Bel asks.

'God, no. He's still got the three year-old, Blackleg. Remember the trouble we had with that one when we first got him? Tearing up plants all over my garden and howling every night like a heart-broken wolf.

(He just wants his mother, Dobie had said, when she'd threatened to use the pup for target practice.)

'No, a pup is the last thing I need. Blackleg will . . . do.'

She'd almost said, *Blackleg will see him out*, and feels the unspoken words reach Bel, whose expression doesn't change. Pearl, guilty Pearl, scents reproach and stiffens against it as she turns to the gate.

'Your roses look fine,' she calls gaily over her shoulder, to show that all is well and if it isn't, she couldn't give a damn.

The only two women on twenty thousand acres, and this is how it is with them. Some things, never aired, never heal.

It was Bel who'd declined with shy dignity the offer of housekeeping work on the day she and Pete first came

29

to the farm, when everyone knows that the manager's wife helps out at the homestead. It's understood, isn't it? Someone to clean out the chookhouse, wash all the windows and take on the eternal battle with the brown paddock dust that blows through the house all summer. Oh, how Pearl had been longing for that.

Dobie hadn't helped. 'Don't go upsetting them,' he cautioned Pearl. 'I think that young fellow's going to work out fine. She doesn't want to clean for you, so what? Can't have a black woman cleaning the house anyway. Wouldn't look right. And besides, what else are you going to do with your time?'

Spun between the peculiar slant of his prejudice and her outrage at his suggestion that she had nothing better to do, Pearl had found no words, and no housekeeper either. And Bel? Bel keeps her life separate and safe as she can. She's been doing that for the seventeen years they've been here on the property and Pearl will never forgive her for it. Bel, who doesn't even own the land beneath her feet or the roof over her head, still has the right to say no. Bel, who has nothing, and everything.

Pete doesn't send a man over but comes himself. Pearl watches as he bends to cradle the dog, hugging the animal close so nothing will spill from the body. The blue shirt tightens across his back. He's built lean as a post-hole digger and never seems to tire. Beneath the battered hat, his head is shaved. It's cooler that way. She'd thought them an unlikely couple when they first came to the farm – the Irishman and the Aboriginal woman – but they've raised two children here and let them loose in the world and still seem happy together, he and Bel. Happy enough to spit at, sometimes.

Pete lays Mutt down on a piece of sacking in the back of his ute, elbowing aside a couple of shovels, some fence posts and a loose tangle of orange nylon rope.

'Want to come along?'

'No thanks, Pete. I must get on.'

'No problem,' he says, swinging himself into the ute with the ease of a twenty year old. He drives out towards the paddocks, the old dog and her shroud of blowflies rising and falling at every bump and rut. When he finds the place where the earth is soft, a sand-ridge running out to the north, he takes a shovel and digs deep so he can bury her where she won't be disturbed by crow or eagle, fox or dog.

'You were a good dog, Mutt,' he says, easing her off the sacking into the hole. A gentle epitaph. A country benediction. Forty years away from the land of his birth, you can still hear the Irish in Pete Jenkins. He pats down the last spadeful of dirt over Dobie's dog and wipes the sweat from his forehead with the back of one hand. A magpie, hidden in a black box tree, bursts into song.

At dinner that night, Pearl drinks her wine quickly and refills her glass, fretting under the burden of her news. Somehow, sooner or later, she'll carry the blame for it. She'll be the one who pays. Have another glass, Pearl. And another. Not that she's expecting a scene. Oh no.

He'll acknowledge the dog's death with a monosyllable and seal up any emotion safe from Pearl's hungry eyes. Love is a weakness. Unavoidable and shameful as tears. Pearl is weak. Brimming with unspent love and forever spilling tears. She can feel them now, all the little lost griefs, tightening her throat.

Look at him! He doesn't know anything is wrong. How can he not see it in her eyes? She tries out the words in her head.

Dad, Mutt's dead.

No. Not yet. Wait a while longer. Just a little while longer. She can't bring herself to eat but the wine is going down a treat.

'Where'd the carrots come from?' asks Dobie, noisily sucking back a fragment from his lower lip.

'Bel's garden. She brought them round yesterday.'

'Sweet.'

He's thinking about fly-fishing again, about that box of lures. He used to have a lure with a cluster of tiny, blue, rosella feathers. Magic, it was. His father, Alistair, made it for him. Where is that box? It must be around somewhere.

Pearl is drifting on a wave of shiraz. Bloody dogs. Look at the attention they get. Safe, isn't it, to love, when the object of your affection is in a state of unambiguous dependency. It's a good deal, for a dog. Look at Celia, at the hairdresser's. Always going on about her Pomeranian, Betsy. A paragon of a dog. Faithful, loyal and true. More than you could say for Celia's husband when he was alive.

And who am I to talk, thinks Pearl miserably.

'So she's pregnant,' Celia had said that day (was it really a year ago?), 'and everyone knows it wasn't her limp stick of a husband. That loser! The only thing he ever kisses goodnight is the neck of a beer bottle.'

Everyone knows, thought Pearl. So sad.

It was time for her to make a comment, to reaffirm their pact of righteousness, but something caught in her and the pause lengthened, two beats, three beats, time enough to look at yourself and through yourself. She sighed. Celia raised the pencilled arches of her eyebrows and met Pearl's eyes in the mirror.

'Oh, I don't know,' said Pearl. 'Sometimes, you wonder, you know, about the lives people have. Women. If she was lonely . . . if she was caught up in a situation she couldn't escape . . .' *If her life was pure shit.* 'Well, you can understand it, can't you?'

'Oh yes, you can understand it,' said Celia. 'Understanding it isn't the problem at all, but . . .' and again her eyes met Pearl's, in significant unspoken comment.

She's married, thought Pearl. The Holy Grail. The sisterhood of the put-upon and the martyrs, the misunderstood and the mistreated. How dare she enjoy herself? And with someone else too. So difficult to avoid becoming a focus for gossip in a town where people gather in judgement if you're half an hour late hanging out the washing.

'Perhaps she just had to reach out, Celia?' *Or break out.* 'Perhaps she saw a chance and grabbed it. Can you blame her, really?'

She stopped herself, horrified. The scissors were poised, motionless, above her head.

'We all have times when we feel like that,' said Celia, 'but we don't all go around throwing ourselves at the nearest available, do we? And her a teacher too!'

Pearl hadn't noticed before how often Celia pursed her lips, as if sipping a soured yearning. She checked her own mouth in the mirror.

'Look at me,' Celia continued. 'Seven years since Bill died and that great big house full of spaces every night. But then I got my little Betsy.' She eyed Pearl critically. 'You should get a dog, Pearl. Keeps you sane. What about a poodle? I can see you with a poodle. Very intelligent, poodles are. Good company. I'm telling you, you won't know yourself.'

If I don't get out of here right now, Pearl thought, I'll be howling like a dog myself.

At home, she'd studied her haircut. It was the same. It was always the same.

'Poodle?' she asked the face in the mirror. 'Is that what it's come to? I'm poodle material now, am I?'

She had called him at work, dialling the number with trembling hands before she could change her mind, accepting his offer, a standing offer – it had been standing so long it might have grown stale . . . please god it hasn't grown stale. He was married, of course. A stock and station agent she often saw at the Rural Supplies Office and at the sheep sales. The nearest available.

Tuesday, she'd told him, in a voice over-bright with

fear. Dad's going to a clearing sale up north. Come Tuesday, Dan, for lunch.

Yes, he'd said, after a moment of surprise. I can get away Tuesday. I'll be there. Great! he'd said, as an afterthought. Good onya, Pearlie.

'Poodle?' she told the face in the mirror. 'I don't think so.'

But in the space of a phone call, the face had changed, the eyes grown furtive, and a sly, shy smile quivered at the corners of her mouth.

'Good pork,' says Dobie, working a bit of crackling between his teeth, sucking the fat from it with audible relish.

Pearl blinks.

He licks his fingers thoughtfully. Look at her. She's miles away. Something going on in that head of hers.

'Have a whisky?' He watches the consciousness return to her eyes.

'No thanks, Dad. I'll stick with the wine.'

'Well I'll be off then. 'Night.' He skids his chair across the slate tiles and levers himself to his feet, glass in hand, making his escape.

How long has it been since he pulled anything but carp out of that river? What happened to all the redfin and yellow-belly perch, the little silver bream and sweet Murray cod that he used to bring home, trophies for Alice? In his mind, the fast-flowing streams of the high country sparkle and beckon. I can go again, he thinks.

I'm not too old for the swag. Not if I take it easy and don't try anything stupid. It's not too late.

The top of the old mahogany wardrobe is piled with boxes. All the personal stuff he doesn't use and never will, but can't bring himself to throw away. Bits and pieces that escaped the great clearing out after Alice died are stored there too, pushed out of sight, out of mind. Somewhere up there is the fly-fishing box. He's sure of it.

He climbs up on the bedroom chair to get a better look at the boxes stacked towards the back. God knows what's in them. Tons of rubbish, covered in dust. He can see the edge of the wooden chess set that Alice loved. He'd tried to teach Pearl once, a long time ago, but she hadn't the instinct for it. She'd rather be out there muttering to her roses or walking the paddocks than take on any real challenge. And the game had brought back too many memories for him. He'd put the chess set away again. Ah! there's the marquetry jewel box that had belonged to Hannah Dobie, his mother, handed down to her from her grandmother and then passed on to Alice. It's a beautiful piece of work. His eyes flicker past it hopefully. Where's that tackle box?

He's stretching with his arms up over his head to move a box to one side, wanting to see what's behind it. The chair isn't high enough and he's up on his toes when the whole wardrobe sways to the right and then back again with a sickening, impossible curving of solid wood. He's scrabbling at the heavy frame that runs around the top, a storm-ridden sailor clutching at a spar. It takes a few moments, an age, before everything steadies. When he's sure that the wardrobe isn't going to move again, he steps down from the chair, feeling his way to the corner of the bed where he sits down, breathing the dust he's dislodged. That wasn't much fun.

There's a slithering noise, then a light whoomph! as something lands on the floor. The hairs rise on the back of his neck, even though he knows that it's only one of the smaller boxes falling. Must have unbalanced things up there. His breathing should be steadier than this. Can't be a good sign to have your heart jumping out of your chest. He turns around. It wasn't a box falling. It's a scrapbook of some kind. Loose papers and yellowing newspaper articles have spilled from its pages. More rubbish. His hand gropes for the whisky that he'd put down on the bedside table. He takes a gulp. Nothing to panic about. Just a spot of dizziness. No reason at all for this crawling suspicion that things, perfectly solid things, like wardrobes, can no longer be relied upon to behave as they should. That beneath the surface reflections lie other darker shapes, fast and fluid, offering no certainty, nothing you can rest your weight against with any confidence.

After a while he puts on his pyjamas, rolls over and pulls the bedclothes up to his chin. At the foot of the bed lies the scrapbook, its title handwritten in neat black capital letters on the front: *ALICE'S ROSE BOOK.*

4

Thomas Hearne wakes to the harsh squawks of a wattle-bird in the melaleuca tree outside his window and checks the bedside clock. It's after ten but he can't think of a reason to get out of bed. More accurately, he knows, there are lots of reasons, alighting one after another on the branch of his brain that is sternly labelled 'Responsibilities'. Missed deadlines for papers, lectures postponed, research deferred, conferences avoided . . . He rolls over and pulls the doona up around his ears. It's been three months since his father died.

The transition from son to middle-aged orphan had caught Thomas in a sharp storm of grief, soon abated. The prodding finger of regret kept him sleepless for several nights. He ought to have made more of an effort to see his father, especially after Mum died, but there was his work to consider, and the travelling time. It wasn't always possible to drop everything and drive all the way to the coast just because his father was . . . what? Lonely? The basic human condition when all was said and done. But there in the hospital, Thomas had the odd conviction that he'd made his farewells years ago, and moved out of the orbit of Henry's life.

Frogs! What kind of a living can you expect to make from frogs? How can you expect to keep a wife and pay for your children's education if all you do is play around with frogs?

But Thomas, at fourteen, a foot taller than other boys his age, silent to hide his stutter, stooping to attempt invisibility, had no dreams of wife and children. Saw himself roaming through marshes and bush landscapes, solitary, safe from the raucous boys who were a perfect embodiment of the mysterious art of having fun. And if, at times, a wood-nymph seemed to beckon, Thomas had no illusions that she was calling to him. With Nora's favour fluttering atop his lance, he worked and studied hard, burnishing the shield that kept the world and its ridicule at bay.

By the time he reached twenty, he had completely mastered his slight stutter at the price of an occasionally overbearing tone of voice and the odd outbreak of a bright pink rash on his neck and face, a reddening and itching of the skin, an overt blossoming of excitement or anxiety.

At forty, the lance had crumbled, Nora's favour a mere wisp of memory, but the shield was as strong as ever. Thomas had decided that the world would know him as a solitary eccentric, and he played to the gallery until the role fitted him like a second skin, until he no longer knew that he played. The quiet paths he'd chosen so long ago led him into a land of academic camouflage, the dubious shade of eucalyptus leaves and a risible chorus of frogs. He had achieved a measure of control over his life, a basic contentment that swelled at rare moments into private jubilation. His work had begun to be mentioned in international circles. Some had hinted that he was a man to watch, on his way up in the world of frogs. It was balm to those old wounds, salve to his loneliness. And life had been satisfactory. Much as expected. Much as he had planned. Until his father died.

Robert and Mel had come over for the funeral. They stayed for a couple of days but they're long gone now, back to Kerrimuir. Back, safe, in their own world with their two children and the rose nursery. It's only Thomas who can't seem to get back on track. Mel had rung a couple of times to see how he was but, receiving only the answering machine, she seemed to have given up.

When Nora had died seven years earlier there had been tears, yes. Weeping at her graveside. Unbearable pity. The kind of pity to turn your back on and run from, fast as you can. A cold touch on his heart at the knowledge that he would never now be able to make it up to her for anything at all. But afterwards, his life had continued along familiar paths. And when he thinks about Nora, she is still there, at Kerrimuir, peering through the orange cafe curtains to see what Henry is up to with his roses. Still there, turning out vast dinners of roast beef and Yorkshire puddings on the promise of a rare visit from Thomas. Still there, fussing about some small grievance and hugging close all the sins and travesties by which the world, and her own family, had confirmed her expectations that life is a vale of tears.

In reality, Henry and Nora had left the nursery in Robert's care and moved to a cottage on the coast several years before Nora died. The roast beef didn't ever taste the same, after that. It is his childhood that Thomas visits when he thinks of Nora. He watches them all – Dad, Mum, Robert, the footballer, Robert, the cricketer, Robert, *a right one with the girls*, Robert, his big brother, a god in the eyes of all, including . . . yes, there he is, little Thomas, the baby of the family. The quiet one.

Why, now, should he disintegrate?

Father dies. You're fifty-one years old. It's time to take stock.

Fair enough.

Except that this doesn't feel like taking stock. Aimlessness pins him down as surely as a heavy stack of blankets. An awareness of futility isn't a thin cold blade slicing through illusions, silently stripping away self-deceit and self-esteem. For Thomas, there is no grand despair or tearing anguish; just an enormous boredom. Every single thing is as pointless as the next.

He moves as little as possible, performing only those tasks that can't be avoided; any effort requires a concentration of will that exhausts him. You might be forgiven for thinking him almost comatose, so little vitality lights his features or flickers across his gaze. And in the inner recesses of his mind, the frightened child who is Thomas flutters above the landscape of his life with no sense of direction, like a moth without the moon.

Dad?

What the hell is going on?

It won't be the last time he asks that question.

He drifts off into a light doze, vaguely aware of the sounds of the world around him. An hour or so passes and he hears another squawk of protest. It's not a bird this time. Someone is opening his gate. Creak. Shutting it. Light, quick footsteps move up the path and the doorbell rings. He has no intention of answering it. Whoever it is, whatever they want, he doesn't want to know.

The bell rings again.

Pushy.

He levers himself up onto an elbow, parts two slats of the venetian blinds with his fingers and sees a woman standing at the front door with her back towards him. Slim. Short brown hair. He has no idea who she is. She turns quickly, too quickly for him. He withdraws his fingers but he knows she's seen a movement at the blinds.

What now, Thomas?

Eventually, because it's the only way to get her finger off the doorbell, he answers the door in his pyjamas.

'We have met,' she tells him. 'In the hospital. Just before Henry...your father...died. Sheila Mulraney.'

Thomas, blinking in the sunlight, steps back automatically when she walks down the hall as though he'd invited her in.

'You were watching me through the blinds,' she tells him, over her shoulder.

'Yes.'

'I could have left this in the letterbox. I might have done, if I hadn't seen you there. But I think Henry meant for me to actually hand it to you. And I couldn't be absolutely sure, if I left it somewhere, that you'd ever receive it. It's best to be sure, in these circumstances. Why don't you answer your phone? Or get an answering machine?'

'I . . .'

He's got one; he's turned it off. Avoiding the obligations it presents.

'You don't remember me, do you?'

'No, I'm sorry, I . . .'

'We look different in uniform.'

Uniform? She's wearing blue jeans, a cream cotton shirt worn loose over them. She sits down at the kitchen table, holding on to a yellow envelope as though it isn't quite the right time yet, to hand it over. As though she isn't convinced that she has his full attention. She smiles up at him and he becomes suddenly conscious of his baggy, stale pyjamas, his hair, matted almost to dreadlocks. What an inspiring sight. His fingers go to his neck unconsciously, rubbing at the itching skin, a blush rising from his collarbone. What is it, in the envelope? Something from Henry. Thomas wants to crawl back under the covers into the succouring warmth of his bed. He can't pick up the knack of interaction so quickly.

His father used to say, *Our Thomas hasn't got the gift of the gab* – his way of excusing the boy's stutter.

Sheila notices Thomas scratching at his neck and beard and, considering the dirty room, his unkempt appearance, wonders about fleas. They look at each other and silence sways between them, unthreatening, scented faintly with curiosity and gentle, mutual distaste. Thomas edges behind the breakfast bench, stifles a yawn, sees his face, fat and bear-like in the kettle's curved steel. An idea hits him with the force of revelation. Coffee!

'Ah . . . do you want a coffee?'

'That would be nice. Perhaps I could get the coffee and you might . . .' She gives the slightest nod of her head in the direction of his night attire.

'Oh. Yes. All right. Ah . . . kettle here, coffee in that cupboard, mugs over there.'

'Over there' being the sink, piled high with unwashed crockery.

'You might have to rinse a couple out.'

'No problem.'

No, thinks Thomas, unable to imagine anything that might present a problem for this alarming woman. When he returns in jeans and a sweatshirt, his feet still bare, she's sitting at the table again, two steaming mugs of black coffee in front of her.

'I couldn't find any milk.'

'I've run out. Sorry. I've pretty well run out of everything, actually.'

She takes a sip of her coffee, sets the mug down.

'Henry made a tape for you. An audio tape. I don't know what's on it. I don't know anything about it. And I don't want to know. He asked me to bring it to you three months after his death, so here I am and here it is and that's all I can tell you.' She gives the envelope a little push towards him with one finger.

Thomas doesn't make a move. A tape? For him? Shouldn't it have gone to Robert? Just about everything else did. He doesn't know what to say. He is suddenly certain that the envelope holds the potential to dissolve the cocoon he is growing around himself. Things might get tricky. He might have to do something.

'He was a lovely man, your dad. Brave. Funny too. Never complained unless he could make a joke out of it. We had some laughs when I was looking after him.'

Ah! This is Henry's 'grand lass'. The nurse he used to comment on in stage whispers that she calmly ignored.

'Thomas,' she begins, and pauses, choosing her words, 'whatever is on this tape, you must understand that it was really important to Henry. OK? No matter how . . . er . . . confusing it might seem. No one else knows about it. Not even the other members of your family. He told me that. It was the last thing he did, Thomas, and he did it for you.'

So don't bugger it up.

She doesn't say that but he hears it anyway. He looks at the envelope. This is too weird. It feels like a dream. Is he going to open the envelope, play the tape and discover that Henry is not his real father and that he, Thomas, is about to inherit an enormous estate in Provence, or Guernsey, or the Seychelles? A vast cattle ranch in the Northern Territory, perhaps? He looks at her from behind the shield of his face and cannot think of anything to say.

'Look, if you need to talk about it, you can reach me at the hospital. Leave a message anytime and I'll get back to you when I can.'

Now why did you have to go and say that, Sheila?

Well look at him. Hopeless.

'Thank you,' says Thomas.

'So what's my name?'

'Sorry?'

'What's my name? I introduced myself on your doorstep.'

'No idea.' He hopes his grin is apologetic and is immediately irritated by his desire to placate her. He wants her to go. He wants to be left in peace but, yes, there it is, uncurling, strengthening minute by minute, the desire to know what Henry has put on that tape.

Sheila Mulraney. That's her name. She finds a scrap of paper in her pocket, a pen in her bag, and writes it down for him. Sheila Mulraney. Mt Solomon Private Hospital. If you need me, she said. For Henry's sake.

5

Dobie Kinnear shifts in his sleep, his left shoulder twitching. No peace for the wicked. There's a scratching of claws, a whispering, scrabbling presence. He twitches his shoulder again. Can't shake it off. When he turns his head, Mary Brecken is there, turkey neck bobbling above the buttoned black misery of her cardigan. She sits back, folds her hands in her lap and regards him.

What is she doing here? He should have stuck a sign on the door: No Stepmothers Beyond This Point. Especially dead ones. What has she come for, the old gloom-carrier? Harbinger of miseries. Foreteller of failings. She's skinnier than he remembers. Sad little eyes, still despairing of him. Thin lips in a straight line above a pointed chin. That delicate, venomous face. She's tried to arrange her wisps of hair to hide the indecency of her naked scalp. There's a bold, baby-like innocence about those patches of pale skin. A confronting fragility. He stares at her head until she lifts a nervous hand and rearranges a strand of grey. Then she leans forward, pursing her lips to whisper to him. Her voice, bursting from that thin chest, is not a whisper, is not even her voice but that of a raucous cockney, thrilling with energy, sanguine in all its expectations.

'You wouldn't be dead for quids, would you?' she says, and tightens her lips to prevent any further obscene exuberance. Eyes popping in surprise.

Dobie feels a rumble of laughter deep in his belly.

You are old, Mary Brecken. Old, old, old.

You are old and you are dead and I am not.

'Don't count your chickens . . .' she says, her voice now as he remembers it from his youth. Hateful.

'You're dead,' he says.

She shrugs.

Whatever you have to believe, to get by.

He bares his teeth, menaces her with a low growl so that she rears back, stricken, looks over her shoulder.

Dobie can feel bubbles of laughter rising, struggles to stop them, and then he's roaring with it, tears on his face, rolling and helpless with laughter, because life's a battle and he's a winner and everything in his world, right at that moment, is good and sweet and as it should be.

There are worse things to wake a man than laughter. Dobie squints at his bedside clock. Four in the morning. Too early for breakfast. He slides out of bed. Notices the scrapbook and spilled papers lying on the floor and edges them under the bed with his foot, out of sight. Whatever it is, it will keep.

Tiptoeing through the dark house he can feel the

night, still and quiet as though the whole farm is sleeping. No birds stirring yet. No foxes barking or dogs yelping. No owls calling. He's often awake at this time and the peace of it comes down to him like the stroke of a soft, worn hand on his cheek.

Even as a young man he used to go outside in the deep of the night and walk with his head tipped back until he grew dizzy, a tiny figure under the wide sweep of the stars. Back then, he didn't have to contend with the ghosts of fear and failure rustling around his feet like fallen poplar leaves. He didn't have the eager dead tapping him on the shoulder, filled with expectations. The dead kept to themselves. The nights are more populated these days. But it's still a grand thing, to be standing in your own doorway, breathing in the moonlight, having the night sky all to yourself.

He's got an appointment with Dr Mac tomorrow. Time for the quarterly injection that helps to keep his prostate cancer at bay. She'll fix him up. On the whole, he thinks, he's got this old age stuff pretty well under control, except for the odd flutter of panic and the seductive vitality of his dreams.

He listens. Everything's quiet at Pearl's end of the house. He helps himself to a big piece of sponge cake, wanders off licking jam from his thumb. Starlight illuminates his pyjama stripes as he pads towards his bedroom, leaving a crumb trail so he can always find his way back.

At seven o'clock, Dobie is shaking muesli into his

breakfast bowl, scattering it over the bench-top. Pearl, still in her dressing-gown, sees the mess he's made and clenches her teeth. She grabs a dishcloth and wipes around his bowl, lifting the milk carton to get all the spilt grain. Dobie takes the carton out of her hand and pours milk over his cereal. Neither has greeted the other but this is not a sign of unusual hostility.

He munches, standing by the window, bowl in one hand, spoon in the other. Only three clouds up there. Not much of a showing. Another hot one on its way. The Merc tractor fires up. That'll be Pete. They have to move the ewes and lambs through from the river pasture today, to the other side of the levee bank. Be a tricky job too, with that break in the irrigation channel. Water all over the place and they'll have to keep the sheep dry because the shearers are coming. He wonders if they'll try to bring the mob around on the east side, through the lignum. They'll have trouble if they do. Ewes and lambs losing sight of each other in the scrub. Stopping and calling to each other and doubling back. They'll have a fine old time of it. Almost a pity to miss it. Not that they'd take his advice. He's seen the glances flit from face to face. Watched the eyelids droop. Ten years ago it was a different matter. Five years ago. He'd like to save them the trouble of getting things wrong, or going all the way around the mulberry bush, but who wants to listen? It's as if for each visible sign of his ageing – the fading hair, the stiffening joints, the wrinkles – there has been a corresponding reduction in his credibility. He knows he's still got what it takes but it's not something you can challenge head-on, is it? So he watches them with patient stealth, out in the paddocks. All those hours, apparently dozing in his chair, he's eavesdropping on their conversations on the UHF radio. He bides his time until they make a mistake and then he points out, very gently, how it might have been done better.

The slam and clatter of crockery breaks in upon his thoughts. Pearl's in a snitch about something again.

'It's not as if we can't afford it. It's just your bloody-mindedness. All I do is clean up after you, like a servant. You tramp mud through the house all day long. Never dream of taking your boots off. You leave trails of crumbs from the bread bin and the biscuit tin all over the bench-tops and the floor. The thought of rinsing a cup or washing a plate wouldn't even cross your mind.'

Well of course not. Why have a dog and bark yourself? Dobie sighs, prudently keeping his thoughts to himself.

'Do you think the place cleans itself? Do you think your food cooks itself? Do you think the washing machine turns out your clothes clean and pressed every day? Do you?'

Does he? No. He doesn't think about it at all.

'I'm sick of it, Dad. There's absolutely no reason why we can't have a housekeeper. I'm not going to . . .'

Her voice rises dangerously, wobbles, drifts out through the kitchen past the door left open when Dobie went through it. He's heard it all before. No way is he hiring a housekeeper. He shudders as the face of Mary Brecken swims up from memory. The Brecken, who had kept house for them and kept his father's bed warm too, after Dobie's mother died when he was just six years old. (Six years old!) And after Alice died, another brief procession of housekeepers. He'd kept as far away from them as he could. Pearl had her schooling to finish but when she came home for good, there was no need for housekeepers anymore. Bloody nuisances. The liberties they take. Throwing out your old underwear. Putting your clothes in the wash just when you want to wear them again. Checking up on what you're eating and tutting at the ice-cream, the chocolate, the line of empty Scotch bottles. You lift up your head from easing off your boots after a long hard day and there they are, one after another, smiling at you, offering tea and sympathy with eyes as soft as quicksand. Step this way and you're stuck forever. No, thank you very much. No, and no, and no again. A man of seventy-eight is entitled to do what he likes with his life. While he can. And if you can't count on your only child to take care of you, well, what's the good of anything?

Pearl, alone in the kitchen, has stopped mid-sentence, the air around her still quivering with the frustration she's unleashed. Where did all that come from? Wasn't she supposed to be telling him about the dead dog this morning? It was the spilled muesli that set her off. A person can only take so much mess, when the mess is of someone else's making. She can feel tears swelling behind her eyes, a quivering in her bottom lip.

I'm a wreck, she thinks. I'm falling apart here, and who's to notice?

She has sleepless nights over shopping lists. Vertigo, peering into the chasm of what to prepare for lunch. How can she explain this to her father, who believes that if you can walk, there's nothing much wrong with you? She would like to spend all her days in the garden, at war with the weeds, in the company of birds and roses. No bluffing there. No pretending you understand why you've done something, when you don't. Or that everything's all right, when it isn't. Or that you know who you are, when you only know who you've been, and to look any further makes your heart race and your hands shake, and your skin grow clammy with fear.

She ought to write a shopping list. Dobie's got that doctor's appointment in town today. He might as well pick up a few things on his way back. She finds a pad and pencil. Chicken might be nice. Or fish? They haven't had fish for a while. No, better not leave the fish to Dobie. He won't think to check how fresh it is. Chicken then. Or veal? That might make a change. And we need tomatoes too, she thinks. A disgrace to be buying tomatoes at this time of year, but their own are blotched with scaly patches and queer knobbly excrescences, the fruit hanging from yellowing plants scarcely able to support them. Once, she would have found the cause and treated it, or if it was a virus, cleared the bed and burned the plants. Always, at this time of year, they've had good crops of tomatoes, carrots, parsley and basil, with onions drying off on the wooden trestle and three or four types of beans curling vigorously up the frames. This year, six vegetable beds lie fallow, given over to weeds and grasses.

'Not putting the beans in?' he'd asked her, almost plaintively.

Will you put up the trellises and spray the leaves for pests? Will you water and tend them and pick them? she thought.

'No,' she said.

Later she'd seen him, bending down awkwardly in the vegetable garden. She watched as he made six holes with his thick index finger, putting three beans into each hole, covering them with soil. He was down there for a while, on his knees. She came closer to see why, but he seemed to be thinking about something, his big hand moving lightly, stroking the surface of the soil. She was gone before he raised his head but took care to soak the beans with kerosene the next day and cover them over again. *As if I haven't got enough to do!* He looked, whenever he passed the vegetable garden, to see if they were sprouting.

She sits down heavily, leaning her arms on the dining table and resting her heavy breasts on them. At the loose V of her dressing-gown, her flesh jumps in tiny shivers at the heart's juddering protest. A flush has spread from her cheeks down over her double chin, her neck, and across her chest. She'll have a heart attack one of these days, but not yet.

Strong morning sunshine sprays filtered light onto her skin from the round stained-glass feature above the main window. Alice had brought it with her when she came here as a bride. It had been the devil of a job, as Dobie had told Pearl many, many times, to set it into such a thick load-bearing wall. But whatever Alice wanted, Alice got. And there it is. A perfect round of bubbled glass with black leadlighting and, set into it, a single dark bird, black wings spread and a white crescent of tail feathers. Currawong. Black magpies, Alice called them. There are no currawongs here. Plenty of crows, plenty of white- and black-backed magpies, butcher birds and white-winged choughs, but no currawongs. Alice had loved the calls that had woken her throughout her childhood, and missed them.

Pearl, pointing sticky fingers. 'Look, Mummy, it's the moon.'

Alice laughing, bending down to her, warm breath on Pearl's cheek.

'Why, so it is. What a clever girl. Our very own magpie moon.'

The bird had entered Pearl's dreams. The great dark wings lent gentle shadows, brought intimations of comfort, shelter and peace to the child.

She forces herself to breathe deeply, slowly. She sniffs the air, focuses on the play of light on the cut-glass fruit bowl. Two shrivelled apples, a lemon, two over-ripe bananas. It's the bananas she can smell. He tells her to buy bananas and then they just sit there going brown. Every week of her life she throws out bananas.

A sudden blaring of ABC radio startles her. Dobie has turned the volume up full blast so he can hear it in the bathroom. She looks at the pencil still clasped in her hand. What was she going to do with that? She lets it fall, pushes herself to her feet, hands at the table edge. Hold on to that scream, Pearl. Keep it inside, deep inside, where only you can hear it. Hold tight to all the frayed edges of your self. That's it. Pull them all together, and carry on.

Dobie is lathering up his chin for a shave. In the mirror, his eyes are mean and thoughtful. There'd been real anger under her words. Usually it's more of a whine, in the mornings. Now what has Pearl to be angry about? He can't think of anything he's done to bring it on. Is she hiding something? Feeling guilty? He leans in closer, pressing his big belly against the edge of the vanity unit, baggy grey underpants hitched over his buttocks. The radio's on but he's only half listening. She's got some plan. He's sure of it. Housekeeper? Or keeper? Is that it? A bloody nursemaid for him. A starched candidate ready to spring into action. Someone to mash his food and wipe the dribble from his chin. Is that it? Well, Pearlie. We'll see about that.

He squares his shoulders, chin up and facing his own image in the mirror, but fear hits him with a sneaky low one and all the fight goes out of him on a breath. It's the nightmare again. The image of himself, dependent and conciliatory, wheedling for small indulgences.

Get a grip now, Dobie.

He lifts his nose with one finger and strokes the razor under it, troubled that, despite all the years, all the hurt and all the effort, it should be so difficult for a man to get his own way.

A kelpie starts barking frantically. He hears it over the noise of the radio as he's getting into his town clothes. Mutt and Blackleg still on their chains. Pearl's forgotten them again. It's past eight already. He wanders out to them on his way to the ute, stopping by the chook-house to help himself to an egg. The old black hen is in one of the nesting boxes, nothing beneath her but a golf ball. She'll have been there all night again. He gives her a shove off the straw and she squawks mournfully, ruffling her feathers and pecking at his hand. Clucky old thing.

'Get out of there. Go on.'

Mutt isn't at the kennels, and Blackleg, released, streaks away down the dirt track to the river, head in line with his spine, arrow-straight. Dobie gives a low whistle. Where's the old girl got to? Come to think of it, she wasn't there last night for her feed, but he doesn't tie her up every night. Not these days. Some nights she curls up on an old sack outside the back door. Pearl hates that because the dog's bladder is weak and the sack stinks of dribbled urine. For Dobie, an occasional whiff is a slight cross to bear for such proof of devotion.

Mutt? he sings out, in his mind. *Don't go too far away. Make sure you can get home again. Don't go worrying any sheep, except in your dreams. Don't let your old bones get cold.*

She'll be dozing somewhere, he thinks, in a patch of soft grass and morning sunshine. The egg, a little breakfast treat he'd planned for her, is warm in his palm. He rolls it gently into her food bowl, where Blackleg finds and devours it before the sun is over the poplars.

In the kitchen, Pearl hears Dobie's ute heading down the driveway. Tension flows out from her shoulders, her neck, her jaw, as the sound of the vehicle recedes. Gone! Slowly she unclenches her hands and begins to clear up the breakfast things. Everything is lighter when he leaves.

She's doing the floors when the head of the vacuum cleaner nudges against the scrapbook beneath Dobie's bed, the suction tube choking on a piece of old newspaper. She rescues the paper, and reads: 'Put Those Roses In Now!' Pulling out the book, she sees her mother's name on the front, and can't believe what she's found. All the designs for Alice's rose beds. All her rose notes.

But why is it hidden here, under his bed? It wasn't there the last time she vacuumed.

She starts to flick through the book but stops. It is fragile, coming apart. Papers pasted on to faded pages have come loose. Why has he kept it from her all these years? He must know how she would value it. Had he been looking at it, remembering? Perhaps he had meant to surprise her with it, and then forgotten? It seems unlikely. He doesn't share his memories of her mother. He's avoided mention of Alice for so long that it has become a habit for both of them.

But under the bed? Is it a sign? Is his mind beginning to wander? Sometimes, when she's looking for him, she has the strongest feeling that he's in the house, hiding. It's absurd, she knows. You're paranoid, Pearl, she tells herself, even as he appears silently, emerging from a room that she's already looked in, or seated in a chair that had been empty moments before. At other times, she's seen him creeping around the perimeter of the garden, all stealth and subterfuge, like a geriatric guerrilla fighter. Who is he stalking? Who is he hiding from? And what can she do except watch him and try to take care of him? As she has done all of her adult life. For Alice, who asked the impossible, and got it.

Take good care of your father, my darling. Stay with him. He needs you.

Pearl looks at the book.

'To hell with it,' she says aloud, picking up Dobie's reading glasses and putting them carefully in the top drawer beneath his underwear where he'll never think of looking for them. That should keep him busy for a while. He'll have to come and ask her if she's seen them. He'll have to ask her nicely. And the scrapbook? She's keeping it. He probably won't even notice that it's missing. She puts it away safely in her old mahogany dressing-table, the same dressing-table where Alice had sat in the years before Pearl, combing her hair at the mirror, watching the face that would never grow old.

What other treasures has Dobie got stashed away? It will all be mine one day, she thinks, and banishes the thought quickly, before she can breathe in and throw her arms wide in all that space, spreading her fingers, reaching and turning and dancing into her own future. What's left of it.

Oh yes, put that thought away, Pearl. As far away as possible. Lock it up tight in the little box at the back of all the other boxes in the farthest corner of your mind. You know how fickle the gods can be.

She's a farmer's daughter, isn't she? Spent too many hours praying for rain that comes after you've given up all hope, when you're looking the other way, when it's too late. Spent too many hours waiting for the prince, who doesn't come at all, not even when you're looking the other way. And it's definitely too late. Plenty of frogs around here, but their transformation lasts only as long as a champagne bubble. Sometimes less. Still, she reasons, a decision can be better than a whinge. A frog can be better than a poodle.

6

'Bury the dog, did you, Pete?' Bel asks.

'Yes. Don't see why she couldn't let him bury his own dog. He's not senile. He's lost working dogs before – three of them that I can name. What's she frightened of?'

'I don't think that woman knows what she's frightened of. That's half her problem. Don't think she's ever known.'

You have to learn your fears, don't you, Bel? Square up to them every morning, tick them off, see them for what they are and judge the shadows they cast.

'Mollycoddling him,' says Pete. 'Making him old before his time.'

'He is old.'

'Still doing a fair day's work out there. Not many of those buggers do more.'

She loves this loyalty in him, born of the long hours working the land in all weathers, side by side with Dobie Kinnear. The shared triumph when a good crop comes through or a gamble with the water pays off. The difficulties, the worries over drought, hail, rust, locusts . . . How many nights has she sat by this window watching the tractor lights shine through the darkness making decreasing circles across the hundred-acre paddock? Their voices carrying from the plant shed at nine, ten, eleven o'clock at night, weary but satisfied at a job done as well as it can be done and the rest in the lap of the gods. They are a good team, Dobie and his manager, despite everything. And when it comes time to mark the lambs, everyone's in there, all hands pulling together, Bel and the children, Pearl too. Jokes crackling and fatigue pushed aside as the little woolly creatures are passed along the line, a jab here, a snip, a band tied tight . . . then turn your back on all the terror and the bleating, the bloodied wool where the punch slipped on an ear – here are scones and jam, chicken sandwiches, lemonade and beer!

Yes, they will all pull together for the farm; anything to keep Mamerbrook afloat. Pete's loyalty is as much to the land as to Dobie, and it runs deep, but he doesn't have much time for Pearl. Dobie will sit there in Bel's kitchen, having a yarn and a beer. Has done many times, though not so often in recent years, but it's never been good enough for his daughter.

Bel sets their meals down, quelling the impulse to call out for Daniel and Sara to come to the table. Daniel is working on a farm down Ballarat way. Sara is doing agri-cultural studies in Albury. It is all good, all as it should be and, one day, she might even grow accustomed to their absence.

'It'd be different if Pearl had someone else to care for,' she says.

'She won't get that with Dan Woods. The man's a disgrace. He talks about her in the pub, you know, when he's got a few pints in him. Telling stories, giving everyone a good laugh. Life and soul of the party he is. She ought to have more bloody pride in her than to take up with someone like that.'

'She never goes out except to sheep sales with Dobie, or the supermarket. How's she going to meet anyone? She doesn't even have friends. You have to want friends, I suppose. You have to make time for them.'

'And trust them. I don't think she knows how. God knows what she'll do with herself when her old man finally kicks the bucket.'

'Oh, let's not worry about Pearl Kinnear,' Bel says suddenly, a shiver touching her.

'Wonder if she's told him yet?'

'What?'

'About the dog.'

'That's another thing; you just reminded me. She says Dobie won't want a pup to train up.'

'Of course he will.'

'That's what I thought. Tricia Finnegan told me yesterday morning that their Nutmeg had a litter a while back. You might drop a word to Dobie about it?'

'I'll tell him tomorrow sometime. He's in town today. There's a big sheep sale coming up soon, Bel. You coming in with us?'

'No, you know how I like to have the place to myself.'

'I'll have Alex working up at Top End, if you need him. Oh – and don't you go giving all the cherry tomatoes to the Kinnears. I could eat a bushful myself. Sweetest I've ever tasted, this year. Don't see why you have to give them our vegetables anyway,' he grumbles, but Bel laughs.

'We have more than we need and more than we can freeze with both children living away. Besides, have you seen their vegetable garden? She's let it all go to grass. There's nothing coming up at all except a bit of self-sown parsley. I don't know what she's thinking of. All the time she spends on those roses. Nice, they are, but you can't eat roses, can you? It's like she's stopped trying.'

'Can't do that here,' says Pete. 'Not on a farm.'

'Poor woman,' says Bel compulsively, and grasps Pete's hand.

'Don't you go doing their vegetable garden,' he warns her, mock-stern. 'They won't thank you for it.'

'I hate to see good earth going to waste, but you're right. Hey, want to go fishing at the weekend? Can you get a few hours off? Jamie Finnegan got a Murray cod last week – a whopper. Fed the whole family on it.'

'I'll see how we go – we've got a bit on right now but I might be able to wangle it. Wouldn't set your hopes on a Murray cod though.'

'Ah, I wouldn't be there for the fish, Pete Jenkins,'

she says, leaning over and winding both arms around his neck.

They had met on a river bank, many miles from here. It was by a river that he courted her. Under river gums he first made love to her one late afternoon in spring whilst fish ate his bait and tugged at his lines unseen. A few years after that, they had come here to Mamerbrook, the baby Sara in her arms, and two-year-old Daniel clutching at the hem of her yellow dress.

What do you think, Bel? Shall I take the job?

And she had looked at the cottage with its shabby weatherboards and untended garden and beyond, a magnificent backdrop of those big old river gums, and he could see it in her eyes right there that she wasn't going anywhere ever again.

'And just how am I supposed to catch a fish, with you there?' he asks, kissing her warmly and making a silent promise to himself to arrange to have a few hours free. She doesn't ask for much, Bel, believing as she does that she has more bounty than anyone could ask for, and more luck than anyone has a right to.

Touch wood, Bel.

Rub that smooth old river-gum timber under your plate with one finger when you think he isn't looking.

Touch wood and keep them all safe.

7

Thomas reaches over and presses the play button again. The tape hisses into life:

Go on then, lass. Leave me be. I've got the hang of it again.

A sharp noise. His father trying to clear his throat.

Well, Thomas, it's me, your dad. There's something...

A cough. A loud click as the machine is turned off. Then the hoarse voice reaches Thomas again and he feels the prick of tears behind his eyes.

... there's something I want you to do for me. I ought to have done it myself. Nearly did, once or twice, but I couldn't decide if I'd be doing more harm than good. Better that you do it, now that I'm out of the way, but go softly, Thomas. By the time you listen to this, I'll have been pushing up daisies for three months, if that nurse got it right. She's a grand lass.

He crosses his hands on the cushion behind his head and stares at the opposite wall, willing a memory of Henry – solid, peaceful, cheerful, never seeing much

66

further than the end of his nose, or his roses. Who is this stranger spilling words and images on to a tape? Was the cancer affecting his central nervous system? Or was it the drugs they gave him? What *is* this story about a farm and a rose and a woman named Alice, interwoven with memories of his childhood in England? Ancient history, all of it. The sadness that Thomas feels is suddenly all for himself. There's no one left to explain anything to him. He is alone, webbed about by Henry's hopes, Henry's visions, a life lived and gone.

He listens again. What does it mean when he says, '. . . doing more harm than good'? And what's all that about damaging the innocent? Who is innocent? Did his father really expect him to drop everything and go haring around the countryside to find this woman?

Drop what? You haven't done anything for months.

Okay, okay.

But why wait three months? And why give it to a total stranger? That nurse? Why not hand over the tape while he was still around to answer some damn questions? If it comes to that: why the tape at all? Why not just talk about it, man to man, father to son? It's all too ridiculous, Thomas decides. I have papers to write, studies to share, lectures to give, frogs to consider. How can I be expected to trace someone my father met years and years ago? Irritation whirrs in his head. Thomas is waking up.

Perhaps that nurse knows something that might make sense of it all? He blows his nose, shuffles into the kitchen, rings Mt Solomon Private Hospital and asks for Sheila Mulraney.

The following day, with tiny bubbles of anticipation fizzing in his bloodstream, Thomas decides to clean the house. It will pass the time until Sheila Mulraney arrives.

He strides through rooms that seem withered and shabby, with shadows crowding the corners and stale air. Haphazard accumulations of crockery with well-established fungal patches. A foetid, feral den of a bedroom, the sheets grey from over-use. This is his cocoon? His sanctuary? He flings open windows and the scent of eucalypts spreads through the house on beams of sunlight, generating swirls of dust-motes and causing several complacent spiders to suddenly scurry for cover.

In four hours he has the place spick-and-span. Long lines of washing drying in the garden. A clean kitchen at last. He falls on to his bed, tired as if he'd run a marathon, and sleeps until woken once again by that peremptory summons to his door.

He searches her face for a sign that she's noticed the change in him, in his surroundings.

A sign of approval, Thomas?

He sees nothing but masked irritation. She doesn't want to be here. She's doing this for Henry. A promise to a dead man. He dismisses his first thought of an informal chat around the kitchen table and shows her into the office, indicating a comfortable chair by a low table.

'Would you like a coffee? I have real coffee this time. And milk.'

'Thanks, that'd be good. White with one, please.'

Oh.

'No sugar, sorry.'

'No problem.'

He disappears. Sheila smiles and allows herself to relax. The room smells of furniture polish and lemons. There are tidy stacks of typed paper and periodicals. The wall to the left of the large desk is shelved from floor to ceiling with books. She can feel the pull of them but stays in her chair. Behind the desk, on a large corkboard fixed to the wall, there are many bright pictures and photographs of frogs, newspaper clippings pinned here and there, some of them older and yellowing. Two-drawer filing cabinets at the other side of the desk. A laptop computer connected to a printer. An air of orderliness and control in here that she finds soothing. In the bottom left-hand corner of the corkboard, peeping around another pinned article, there is a cartoon tree frog. Its colours are faded but the touch of whimsy in those bulbous eyes is still strong. Sheila listens for sounds of approach. Nothing. Quickly, she examines the frog. It is sitting on a real twig, wood pasted onto cardboard, the front page of a greeting card. She lifts the flap. Inside someone has written in ink. Red ink, she thinks, though now it is closer to brown:

Thomas, where the hell are you? Julie.

She wonders if he'd pinned it there, long ago, as a

reminder to call the woman, or simply because he liked the frog.

'So Henry's tape was a bit of a surprise?' she says, when Thomas returns with two coffees and a plate of assorted biscuits.

'Yes. It is . . . er . . . very peculiar. Hard to know what he means.'

'I think I told you, Henry didn't talk to me about it. He said it was private. He indicated that there was someone else involved, said he didn't have the right . . . I don't know what he meant by that.'

'Someone else?' That will be the woman he wants me to find, Thomas thinks. 'You don't think it's all . . . hallucinatory?'

Sheila shrugs. How can anyone be sure, now?

'Parents,' she says. 'You think you know them. They're beside you in one way or another, in fact or in fiction, for your whole life. You'd think the least they could do would be to leave you at peace with your own impressions of them when they die.'

Her words have stirred a recent memory. Robert, immediately after Henry's funeral, reminiscing about their mother and the 'snowball' – a drink of advocaat and lemonade – that used to make her giggle and blush at Christmas dinner every year. Henry, the old rogue, he said, always tried to persuade her to drink two of them, but she never had. Thomas had laughed along with him, but had no memory of this woman who giggled, and was left with the disconcerting impression that Robert had experienced quite a different mother, in the same place, at the same time.

Is that all there is left? Selective memories chosen by a too-busy brain? A few facets of Henry's character catching the light as they spin past? What chance does Thomas have of unravelling even a tiny part of Henry's story, now? And if he discovers something, will that be another version of Henry to add to the confusion?

'After my father died,' Sheila says, drawing his attention back, 'eight years ago, I found I was unable to relate to things, familiar things, habits even. It was like losing the rhythm of living, falling out of step. And a dreadful lethargy. Overwhelming, really. It took a long time to get over it, but I did. Is that how it is with you?'

'It has been a strange few months,' he admits reluctantly, but then, 'He was a good father to me, you know.' The avowal bursts from him with a fervour that surprises them both.

'He was a good man,' she says.

'I just don't have the knack for relationships, you see. Something missing up here.' He taps his forehead, grins.

She waits.

'I seemed to be on the outside of things somehow, most of the time. Always tugging at him for attention, tapping on the glass for him to notice me and let me through. Or out?' He pauses. 'I don't know what it was. Robert didn't have a problem with him, and Mum, well . . . she's dead too.'

He stops, aghast, on the verge of tears. Swallowing,

he scratches at his neck. Sheila sees the flush, the spreading rash. Rosacea, she thinks. Not fleas.

'Robert, the eldest?'

'Yes, my brother. He took over my father's business, the rose nursery.'

'Were you close to your mother?'

Thomas avoids her eyes, embarrassed now.

'Yes. Yes I was.'

You were her knight, Thomas. You went into battle for her again and again, with dragons, with giants. But it didn't do any good, did it?

He takes a moment. Draws a deep breath to calm himself. 'She's the reason I'm a scientist. She was the one who pushed and encouraged me. Enough people in this family messing about with roses, she used to say.'

'So you set off on your own path, carved out your own life. Most of us do.'

'But the tape . . . Henry's request. I have to find a woman and present her with a rose that he's grown, to thank her. A perfect rose, the only one of its kind, grown especially for her.'

'Quest,' she corrects him. 'It sounds like a quest to me. And what are you waiting for?'

'I don't know who this woman is. I don't know anything about her. I don't know if she's alive or dead. Or if she ever existed. Why does he want me to do this? I don't know . . .'

'You don't know who he is anymore, do you? You see? Fathers aren't supposed to surprise their offspring.

72

Particularly irritating of him to do it post-mortem too.'

'I don't know,' says Thomas, feeling his way carefully amongst the minefield of his thoughts, 'why he'd be cultivating the perfect rose for someone I've never heard of, while my mother was still alive. He didn't . . . he didn't . . .'

Oh Henry, she thinks, why did you do this? If life is trotting along steadily, you don't whip the horses.

But for Thomas, life wasn't trotting along steadily. It had come to a full stop.

'Where do you start your search for this woman?' she asks.

'Last seen somewhere in the southern Riverina,' he tells her wryly.

'Southern Riverina. That must be irrigation country. Very good for frogs, I'd imagine.'

She's right. Somewhere, in a far dark corner of his brain, a synapse flashes briefly, a decision is made, a moth spies the moon.

Sheila looks at her watch.

'I'm sorry, I did warn you I wouldn't be of much use.'

'No, no. I feel much better for having talked to you. Thank you.'

'It's none of my business, of course, but I think you should do what Henry has asked you to do. I think you should begin your journey. And forgive him his realities, Thomas. That's my advice to you.'

Saying goodbye to Thomas at the door, Sheila also

bids Henry a silent farewell. She has done what he asked of her. The rest is not her affair. Everyone has their stories. Some, perhaps most, remain forever unheard; others reach out beyond the confines of a single lifetime. With a little luck. With a little help.

Thomas, carefully clipping his moustache with nail scissors the next morning, becomes aware of the list in his head – tent, torch, tarp, snake gaiters – and realises that he's going. First to Robert, to see what he knows about this rose business, and then on to the southern Riverina on Henry's quest. Suddenly, it's all so simple. The Southern Bell Frog! Endangered. Small populations known to exist in the southern Riverina. He can tie it all in with some fieldwork. He can get back to his frogs. This is already beginning to feel less of an obligation and more of an adventure.

If you don't go, Thomas, you'll always be wondering.

'I'm going on a quest,' he says to his mirrored face, pushing up an imaginary knightly visor with the back of his hand. Sir Wait-a-While, Sir Put-it-Off, Sir Stay-in-Bed. Not any more. He snips off a lock of his beard, feeling light-hearted for the first time since Henry died.

Too methodical to leave a list in his head, he writes it all out and soon has a neat line of ticks beside the items and a large pile of gear standing by the back door ready to be stowed in the station wagon. He fills a water bottle – it's a long drive. He dithers. What else? He's sent emails to colleagues at CSIRO and the University of

Canberra about his proposed field studies. He's checked the Internet for the most recently published data. He's turned off the hot water. There's a thermos of black coffee in case he needs it during the night drive. His mobile phone is charged and he can pick up any landline calls by remote. Not that's he's expecting any. Everyone's given up.

He loads the car, suddenly discovering that he's ravenous. Appetite returns, he notes. I'm getting over it all. I'm coming back to myself. He calls in at a fish and chip shop for takeaway, so that he can eat and drive.

There he is, zipping along at a fair pace, groping with his left hand for a chip or two, a strong, pleasing scent of brown vinegar in the car. He's caught the tail end of peak traffic but it doesn't worry him. Soon the city will be far behind him with a long empty highway ahead and several hours of daylight yet. I'm doing this for Dad, he thinks. And for the Southern Bell Frog. I'm making something happen. I'm in control again.

Whatever you have to believe . . .

He passes a large green signpost but doesn't look. He knows the road.

This way salvation lies.

That way, madness.

Henry knew it too.

8

Doctor Macnulty's surgery is in a white weatherboard house. A couple of tall eucalypts throw dancing shadows on the green tin roof. A high paling fence surrounds the garden and they've installed a child-proof gate that usually keeps Dobie busy for a while.

The certainty of Dr Mac's sympathetic attention gives him a rush of contentment. Every three months, she injects him with the chemicals that keep his prostate cancer in check. He gives her all the credit for this. Wonderful woman! You go in there, a patient waiting for a cancer shot, and you come out two feet taller. Respect, that's the key to it. That's what Dr Macnulty understands. Respect for who you are, for the life you've had, for what you've tried to achieve. It's a comfort on the low days when you can't help asking yourself, what's it all been for?

Gillian's on the desk today. Gillian, with her orange hair and large, black-rimmed eyes. Dobie feels more comfortable with Margaret, a calm middle-aged woman who has nursing qualifications, but Margaret is nowhere in sight. Gillian alarms him. Minions can make life difficult. You have to get them on side. He produces his most charming smile, with a calculated hint of helplessness about it. Her eyes are bloodshot. She stifles a yawn.

'Late night?' he asks sympathetically.

'Oh yes,' she groans. 'Twenty-first party. You know how it is.'

Dobie can't even begin to imagine how it is.

'Congratulations,' he says, politely.

'Not *my* twenty-first,' she says scornfully. 'God! I'm not that old.'

The phone rings on her desk. Dobie escapes into the waiting room where green venetian blinds are angled to keep out the sunlight. The atmosphere is whisper-inducing and scented faintly with disinfectant. The walls, at some stage, have been given a pale blue rag wash. The uneven application of the paint always reminds Dobie of a child's picture of the sea. It needs a red bucket, a sandcastle or two, triangles of white sails under a spiky yellow sun. He knows just where he'd put them too. He spends a lot of time looking at this wall, avoiding the eyes of other patients. Even with an appointment, you have to wait. Sometimes for an hour. Sitting here next to weary women with their fat, smeared babies, or plump brown girls bursting from flimsy singlets and hunched boys with hooded sleepy eyes. Dobie stares at the sea wall and tries not to breathe too deeply.

'Mr Kinnear?'

A short, dark-haired man with a green folder in his hands has come into the room. Chinese, by the look of him. His eyes range hopefully over the waiting patients.

'Mr Dobie Kinnear?'

Oh. 'Yes?'

'This way please.'

The room they enter is Dr Mac's sanctuary.

'Have a seat please, Mr Kinnear.'

Must be some foreign trainee she's taken under her wing, he thinks.

'Er, I'm sorry. There's been some mistake. Dr Macnulty takes care of me, you know. Has done for years. If you don't mind, I'll wait until she's free. No offence, of course.'

'No offence taken,' says the man, 'but please, won't you sit down, Mr Kinnear? I am Dr Li. Dr Macnulty has had to leave her practice. I am familiar with your medical history so –'

'Leave her practice?' He's panicking. 'What do you mean, leave her practice? Isn't she coming back?'

'Ah. That I cannot say. It may be that she will return in several months. Now, if you'll roll up your sleeve please, we'll take a look at your blood pressure. How are you feeling? Any problems?'

Any problems? Any *problems*? Apart from the prostate cancer? Apart from the fact that she's abandoned him without a word?

Aloud, he says: 'Well, I don't buy green bananas anymore.'

'I see,' says Dr Li, fitting the blood pressure cuff to his arm.

Straight through to the keeper with that one.

How could she have gone away without warning him, as though he was just another patient? Easy now, he cautions himself. She might have had a family emergency. No time to let anyone know. He rallies a little, thinking this. Still . . .

Dr Li tightens the pressure around Dobie's arm and takes the reading, frowning. 'Hmm. Are you experiencing any unusual stress in your life?'

Jesus! Dobie manages a weak smile and a head-shake, not trusting himself to speak.

'Would you pop up here for me? And if you'd just loosen those? That's it. Any problems here? Any tenderness?' His quick hands move about Dobie's body, testing, probing.

'Thigh or buttock?' he asks, needle at the ready.

'Thigh,' says Dobie.

Oh! The pain is an outrage, swelling into self-pity. What is this man – a bloody apprentice or something? It never hurts like that when Dr Mac does it. But Dr Mac has gone, Dobie. Dr Mac has left you. And now there's a bitter taste in his mouth; loneliness thickens his tongue and there's a treacherous sting of tears behind his eyes. He wants to explain. He wants to be heard. He wants to sit down with this stranger and tell him how his mother died when he was six years old. Six years old! He wants to tell him how the coming of Mary

Brecken turned his father's face from him. How his own dear wife Alice died without giving him a son. How Pearl's missed the boat and that's an end of it. The end of the line. He should be made to understand, before he judges Dobie Kinnear, that there is a great deal to be forgiven.

Dobie fastens his clothes in silence.

Dr Li stands by the door, smiling.

'Take good care of yourself. Let me know if you have any reactions to the shot. Any discomfort at all. Goodbye. Goodbye.'

Like he's shooing geese, thinks Dobie, limping savagely towards his ute. Chink doctors! Dead stepmothers. Housekeepers with their creeping and sweeping. For Christ's sake, what kind of a day is this?

'Anything else?' he says, craning up at the empty sky.

He heads out of town, flooring the accelerator. To either side of him, a flat land of floodplains and pasture rolls right out to the sky, a distant horizon broken here and there by the soft fuzz of black box trees, red gum and saltbush scrub. Like his own twenty thousand acres, the farms hereabout grow wheat and barley, irrigate the soil for rice crops, and provide grazing land for thousands of sheep.

The town is far behind him now. Dobie hasn't slackened his speed. He races over a dry creek bed, trees and scrub suddenly clustered on each side. A crow flies up from the roadside, cawing harshly, veers into his path and away again, just in time. Dobie operates on a 'no brake for birds' rule. Has done for years.

A kangaroo the size of a yeti turns its head and braces for the jump that will carry it right into the path of the ute. In a split second Dobie gauges the distance, the speed, the road, the trees at either side, knows as the sweat breaks out on his face that there's no way he can avoid it . . .

. . . but then he's passed it somehow and he's speeding down the long straight road with the sun overhead. Phew! Luck's running with him now. He checks the rearview mirror. No sign of the brute. It's shaken him. He's going to die with his boots on all right, but one day, not today, and not from bouncing off a bloody roo, thank you very much. He feels queer, cold all over but his skin is damp and his hands and thighs have got the shakes. He wipes his face with his sleeve, tries to breathe steadily.

'That's enough now,' he says, to the universe in general, in case anybody's listening. 'That'll do.'

Sorry, Dobie, it's only just beginning.

He slows to take the bend at the approach to the single-lane bridge over Pretty Ruby Creek and she's there, waiting on his side of the road by the white bridge palings.

She's wearing a tight dress in a leopardskin pattern, a short red jacket with the sleeves pushed up. From her left hand, outstretched and pointing down the road, dangles a high-heeled red sandal. Her hair is a fluffy blonde cloud and her whole face is smiling right at him.

He can't believe his eyes. He scans the countryside for some clue as to how she got there. Nothing. The shape she makes against the backdrop of sky and paddocks is unnervingly out of context. He pulls up. She walks over, barefoot, and leans in at his passenger window. He can see now that she's well over thirty, closer to forty maybe, and tired-looking round the eyes. Her arms are pale and plump with light-brown freckles. He thinks of toffee, spun and sweet. She produces the red shoe, flips it so that he can see how the thin heel has been wrenched away from the sole. There are so many questions tumbling through his mind that he can only manage the obvious.

'Where're you heading?'

'Anywhere that way.' She nods her head down the road.

'Swan Hill do you?'

'Swan Hill'd be great. Thanks.'

Swan Hill? Dobie? What do you think you're doing?

She climbs in, throwing the red sandals under the dash and tossing a soft black leather backpack into the space behind their seats. Dobie watches her long bare legs fold themselves into place, the rounded knees pressed together. Notes how her breasts push against the low-cut neckline of the dress. Filling it. Squashed in there. It's enough to bring a tear to your eye.

'Been walking long, have you?'

She laughs, an easy sound that Dobie melts into. Bit

82

of an adventure this, eh, Dobie? Feeling sparky. Daring. He wants someone to see them, sitting here together. He wants someone to notice and jump to all the wrong conclusions.

'I've been walking since I decided I needed a change of company,' she says, and shrugs off the red jacket, releasing the odours of her skin – a light perspiration and something citrusy. Lime, is it? Dobie breathes in deeply, quietly.

They drive for almost half an hour and Dobie can see the gateway of his farm. She scans the miles of flat land to either side of them with an eager energy, eating it all up. Dobie drives past his own gate, saying nothing. The day has skidded out of control. Swan Hill is another seventy-five miles past the boundary of his own farm – an extra hundred and fifty mile round journey.

No fool like an old fool.

And what would Pearlie say, if she could see him now?

The miles speed by. He's amazed and enjoying it. It's as though he's been given the chance to retrieve something of the day. Of himself.

'Great country round here,' says his hitchhiker.

Dobie shrugs, pretending nonchalance. 'I'm used to it, I suppose. I farm here.' He knows the colours, rhythms and cycles of this land better than his own heart.

'Such a huge sky,' she murmurs. 'I felt so small, waiting out there. And the light is golden. The horizon's so far away. Like the sea. Must be amazing at night. All the stars and no light pollution.'

He tells her how the moon is so bright sometimes, you can read a paper out on the porch at two in the morning.

'No!'

'Sure as I'm sitting here driving you to Swan Hill,' he says with a grin, thinking, she's not a country girl. He wants to know her name but doesn't know how to ask. She turns excitedly when she sees a brown falcon sitting on a fence post and Dobie slides another look at her bare legs. The stirring in his penis is as much use as the twitch in a phantom limb.

When they get to Swan Hill, she asks him where he's headed and for a moment he can't think what she means.

'Town centre?'

'Oh – no problem. I can drop you there.' He already knows how dull the car will be when she leaves him. Stupid. And stupid to feel that something else ought to be happening.

'Got people here, have you?' he asks. 'Are you staying in Swan Hill?'

'No. I'm not sure how long I'll be around for. It depends on work, you know. And how much I like it.'

She turns to get her bag from the back just as Dobie leans forward to pick up her shoes for her. Her bare shoulder, warm, brushes against his chin and he rears back, shocked speechless. It doesn't look as though she's noticed. She's got her bag. She has her hand on the door handle.

Go on. Go on. For god's sake. Get a move on!

'What sort of work are you after?'

'Oh, anything really. Cooking, cleaning, gardening, you know. Board and lodging type stuff. Don't really want to be stuck in a shop or an office though. I can turn my hand to lots of things. I'll be fine.'

And then she's leaning in at the window again, thanking him, and he's grabbing at an old Mitre 10 docket on the dashboard, scrabbling around for a pen. He writes his number down, and then his name, and the name of the farm: Mamerbrook.

'Give me a call if you like,' he tells her. 'We're looking for a housekeeper.'

9

Pearl is thinking about dinner, about all the dinners, all the days, all the weeks and months ahead, season after season rolling on, all the same. It makes her mind curl in upon itself, a hard ball, spines outwards.

She's going to make a chicken curry and serve it with rice. Easy. Her hands chop and dice, mix and stir. She is in urgent need of distraction. A very particular distraction. It's time to see Dan Woods again. This isn't a conscious decision; it's her body's insistence. Time to be touched again, Pearl. Time to be handled and fondled. Funny that the need should grow stronger, the older she gets. And alarming. It wouldn't do to grow too dependent upon a shaky source of reassurance like Dan Woods. It isn't an appetite that she's proud of. The circumstances are not as she would wish, not as she has dreamed them. Beggars can't be choosers. And why is it always me who has to call him, she wonders? Rehearsing what I'm going to say for two days beforehand. Trying to think of something that will amuse him and make me sound more interesting, less pathetic. Why doesn't he ever ring me?

You knows why, Pearl. He doesn't need to.

'Don't expect me to fall in love with you,' she told him once, when she knew what to expect from him. 'I'm not eighteen. I'm no fool.'

It sounded good. She almost had herself convinced. And Dan? Dan had grinned, accepting what was offered and enjoying it without understanding at all.

It's fine, she tells herself each time he leaves. It's better than nothing. And then her mind sets to work, caressing the memory, warming her body and supplying the tender gesture, the affectionate nuance that she hungers for.

She scoops up the chopped onion and lets it fall into the hot oil. She gives the curry mixture another quick stir and slices carrots, mushrooms, cauliflower. Laying out cutlery for dinner, she considers the table. That's where it happened, the first time, followed by many weeks of delicious shivers, thinking about him, replaying it (the enhanced version), and waiting in vain for him to call her. Right there, on the table, underneath the magpie moon. How bold she was. How terrified.

She'd rung and invited him to lunch and – oh! she was so nervous that she'd had a drink at eleven in the morning, and then another. One for courage. One for luck. He smelled it on her breath.

'You a bit tiddly are you, Pearlie? Got one for me, have you?'

What had she expected? A chat?

But how did it happen that his hand was suddenly inside her shirt, taking the weight of a breast and squeezing it hard? How did it happen that her zip was undone, his tongue filling her mouth? That she was bent over the table with knickers drooping around her fat knees, rough hands parting her, thick fingers exploring between her legs? He leaned over her, muttering in her ear.

'Ah, Pearlie, you're a bit of a surprise, you are. Who'd have thought it? A real dark horse, aren't you?'

Am I? she thought. He is not kind, and this is not about me. But it was too late. The lace tablecloth was rough beneath her cheek. Crumbs lay scattered on its surface, directly in her line of vision. Light from the window whitened facets of the glass fruit bowl and gave the three green apples an unreal lustre. The daylight, the grass, the poplar trees by the dam, Blackleg scratching himself at the back gate, a blue wren on the concrete path, all these things she could see until he entered her and the shock of it brought sudden tears to her eyes.

'Oh, Pearlie,' he groaned.

Don't call me Pearlie, she thought. Then she said it aloud, panicking.

'Don't call me Pearlie, please!'

Dan gave a shout of laughter. 'All-right-Miss-Kinnear,' he said, emphasising each word with a thrust of his penis.

Oh, Miss Kinnear. Oh, Pearl. What are you doing to yourself?

And then it was over. He'd buttoned himself back into his jeans, thanking her with a smirk and an awkward pat on the shoulder. Long before the dust of his passing had settled on the long driveway, Pearl had tidied away her hopes and humiliation and was already wondering how she might buy condoms without exciting the gossip of the town.

'What's this?' says Dobie, dubiously, poking at the food with his fork. ' Some sort of cauliflower curry?'

'No. It's . . .'

Chicken curry?

But it isn't, is it, Pearl? You've forgotten to put the chicken in.

'Vegetable curry,' she says. 'If you don't like it, get yourself something else.'

'Didn't say I didn't like it,' he says mildly. 'Bit unusual, that's all.'

Soon, he's thinking, his lovely hitchhiker will come and there'll be no more strange vegetable curries, but roast chickens and steak-and-kidney puddings and apple and rhubarb pies with thick custard. He has no doubt about it.

'Cauliflower isn't good for prostate cancer,' he says.

'That so?' Pearl is unable to muster suitable indignation.

'Heard it on Radio National the other day.' He's lying blithely but she won't rise to the bait. He gives up. Opts for fantasy again.

And how the hell are you going to explain it to Pearl when your new housekeeper turns up on the doorstep, sweet and ripe in her leopardskin dress and her jacket red as pomegranates? There's mischief and there's trouble, Dobie. This might well be trouble. Anticipation broke his sleep last night, kept him running through anxious dreams, hiding and ducking for cover in thorny scrub and rank tangles of vines, pursued by raucous voices and incoherent abuse. Oh, but how she glows in his mind, burnished by sly whispers of desire, stirring a part of him that has slept for a hundred years. Those plump, round knees. Those soft, freckled arms. Those breasts . . . those breasts. Just to look at her would be gift enough. Just to see her in his kitchen, leaning over the table, or reaching up to that cupboard with her cosy body and easy laugh. He wouldn't ask for more. Will she call? He should have signed her up there and then but you can't let them see that you're needy, can you? Doesn't he deserve a break? Doesn't he? A little cheer in his life, considering everything?

There's no answer to that.

Pearl can't eat. It's taken the edge off her appetite, the chicken business. Tilted things sideways again. Can't she get anything right? And Dan won't ring. She knows that. If she doesn't call him, he'll wait, maybe wonder a little, but it will be just one more shrug in a long day's sunshine, for him. It's always on offer somewhere out there, for a man like Dan Woods. All he has to do is let a woman know that he sees her, let her know with his eyes that she's not too old, not too fat, not too tired, and not, contrary to almost every other indicator of her life, not invisible after all.

The curry can't be that bad, Pearl thinks, watching Dobie shovel it in. He speaks through a mouthful of it.

'Seen Mutt anywhere today? She hasn't been in for her food the last night or two.'

He's concentrating on his own food when he asks the question but when she doesn't answer he looks up into her face, sees the colour drain out of it, the awful expression in her eyes.

'Pearlie, what's happened? What have you done?'

The dog. The bloody dog. She's forgotten to tell him. Forgotten all about it. Before she can speak, her tears are falling, fast as a blessing and just as much use.

10

Pearl goes over the bridge in a great rush, sending up hoards of screeching cockatoos and corellas, the morning falling in shards around her, the devil at her heels.

'I'm the one losing my mind,' she tells the river gums, breathlessly. 'It's me that's going crazy. Not him.'

She pushes through lignum and saplings until the paddock opens out before her and then she stands perfectly still, absorbing the scene, waiting for it to calm her as it always does. Dotted around the paddock in the middle distance are dark stumps. Her grandfather cleared this paddock of its river red gums and black box, years ago. He left three majestic trees in a diagonal line, not just to provide shade for the sheep, but as a reminder of what had been here.

Pearl watches, waiting, breathing in the smell of the earth and the river behind her. She takes one more step, just one, and the paddock comes alive. All of the tree stumps straighten, lengthen and turn towards her for a quivering moment that dissolves as fifty, sixty kangaroos leap to safety. She scans the far side of the paddock and the line of trees that marks the right-hand boundary but they've vanished. She's been coming here to this spot and waking the tree stumps since she was a little girl. Unlike just about everything else in her life, she would like this part of it never to change.

She takes a swig of water from the bottle in her bag. Jesus, it's quiet here when the cockies settle down. It's the only place where she feels whole. And safe. Forgetfulness? Panic attacks? To have or not to have Dan Woods? To be or not to be her father's housekeeper? What do these things matter, here at the heart of Mamerbrook?

She pulls the brim of her sunhat lower to keep the light from her eyes, reducing her vision to about three feet in front of her. Now she can see the grasses, and occasional starbursts of flowers, white paper daisies and yellow billy buttons, and her own feet moving one after another on the trail. She plays this game across paddocks so large you can't see where they end. The single-file trails, worn by sheep and kangaroos, crisscross and weave their way at random over the pastures. They loop and curve back upon themselves like vast unravelled skeins of wool. They might fade out by a gate or at the river bank, only to begin again close by. They'll run parallel to a boundary fence for miles and then suddenly spiral across the great spaces of a paddock, or twine through low shrubs and over the spreading roots of ancient trees that shelter a thousand rabbit holes.

Pearl picks up a trail and follows it. She'll take this

fork or that, on a whim, never able to see more than a few feet in front of her. Sometimes she'll come full circle. Sometimes she'll end up a long way from where she started. Occasionally she'll come across sheep, staring at her, braced and ready to trot away. When she does lift her head, there's a startling moment as she studies the landmarks to work out where she is. The surprise of it. That's the idea. A taste of the unpredictable. And then, having walked off her worries and exhausted herself, she'll be ready to come home.

In late spring and summer, the trails are speckled with the bright blue of Wahlenbergia flowers. After rain, the ground is slashed by parallel slots where the kangaroos have jumped. Today, on baked and cracking clay, the main thing to watch out for is a snake. Tiger snakes, brown snakes, copperheads and red-bellied black snakes. She's too close to the river to take it easy on this account. If you've got water out here, you've got snakes. She plods on, one foot after another, trying to empty herself of every thought, every image, every shame. Breathing steadily.

An image comes to mind, unbidden. Her mother's scrapbook of roses. She still hasn't had a good look at it; a reluctance stemming from sadness at the sight of that handwriting and the thought of Alice making garden plans all those years ago, as though she had a long life ahead of her and all the time in the world to watch her roses grow. Pearl makes a promise to herself. That's what she'll do when she gets home. Curl up on the sofa with her mother's rose notes. A sad haven but a safe one, and a passion shared.

Dobie has parked so that the truck is hidden from the road, on the far side of a dense patch of shrubs – needle-wood, lignum, old man saltbush and tumbled cooba branches. It's one of his snooze spots. The air vibrates with a sweet high twittering of invisible birds. Through the insect-splattered, dusty windscreen, rye and wild oats, white-top and plains grasses stir in a light breeze. Not a sheep in sight. They'll be over in the east, he thinks. They'll be feeding into this wind. The sun-warmed air folds around him. He rests his arms on the steering wheel, leaning forward over them, trying not to look for Mutt, trying to stop himself from scanning the ground as though he might conjure her dark, loping shape in the pale gold of the grasses. Grief pricks at him like a grass seed in his sock.

A magpie carols from the scrub and is answered by another two. The sound forms a triangle around the truck, webbing the air long after the song has finished. Somebody told him once – was it Bel? Or was it one of those dreamtime stories on the radio? – an old Aboriginal story about how the magpie created the heavens, pushing up the sky bit by bit, with sticks in its beak. Must have given one hell of a push in these parts, that old magpie. No bigger sky anywhere than this one. It can give a man the need for company, for some kind of a rejoinder. For chocks, to stop you flying off into all that space.

One of the birds flies down on to a patch of cropped grass. Dirty great beak they have, for all their pretty singing. The magpie struts around, looking this way and that, head tipped on one side, then the other, studying the grass. Then the head bobs swiftly and comes up swallowing. A few more steps, looking, looking, then the quick down and up, the swallowing.

Wouldn't like to be a beetle, thinks Dobie, or a slow fat worm. Wouldn't have much chance with that cruel beak hanging over you. He pictures all the wriggling, slithering, running, crawling creatures making their way through grass blades high as forest trees. And the magpie, too enormous, too terrible for comprehension except as a shadow, like a storm cloud passing overhead, or a god stalking on sure, delicate legs. One minute you're there, wondering what's for lunch, whether it'll be a good year for tomatoes, and why on earth the electricity bill is so high, and the next minute – peck! – you're a magpie's breakfast.

Peck! and there goes Hannah Dobie, my mother.

Peck! and there goes Alistair Kinnear, my father.

Peck! and there goes Mary Brecken, my stepmother.

Peck! and there goes Alice Kinnear, my wife . . .

. . . and Mutt, poor Mutt, my friend.

And soon it will be, peck! and there goes Dobie Kinnear.

But not yet, you bugger. Not yet.

He starts the engine, just for the satisfaction of seeing the bird fly off.

That's fixed him.

He should really head off and see what those sheep are up to. Just about snooze temperature in the truck though. Shame to waste a good moment. He flicks the ignition off again and drops his head on to his arms, just for a minute or two, an hour or two. The radio crackles into cryptic communication and his half-sleeping brain deciphers it. No need to stir. Into the settling silence around the vehicle, the magpies circle, one, two, three, looking for breakfast.

Alice's rose book has a thin scarlet cover, almost ready to disintegrate between Pearl's fingers. 'Scrap Book' is printed on the front in a large, black cursive script with Alice's handwriting underneath it. The pages inside are thickened and stiff with all the things she has pasted. There are articles that she has cut from magazines and newspapers – all of them about roses. And pictures upon pictures of roses. Other pages contain lists, columns, comments in a crabbed, untidy hand. Names, colours, perfumes, information about how well the various plants survived and other codes that Pearl can only guess at. Some of the pages have come loose from the covers. All are yellowing with age. Odd scraps of paper, with notes and lists scribbled on them, have been tucked in amongst drawings and articles. Pearl picks up an envelope. On the back of it is scrawled:

Perfumed Roses

pink	Ophelia	gorgeous
crimson	Papa Meilland	marvellous
coral red	Fragrant Cloud	amazing
yellow/pink	Golden Melody	astonishing
pink	Amelia	v/sweet
white	Iceberg	apple subtle
blue	Blue Moon	good
pale pink	Souvenir de la Malmaison	cinnamon – nice

Double page plans have been pasted in, garden beds sketched and filled in with the names of roses in their positions. Ena Harkness, Cécile Brunner, Avon, Peace, Golden Dawn, Diamond Jubilee, First Love, Elizabeth Arden, Folklore, King's Ransom, Pascale, Princess Margaret, Montezuma, Bluebird, Honeymoon, Grandpa Dickson, Edith Cavell and Viridiflora, the green rose.

Pearl murmurs the names aloud like an incantation. Many of them are familiar to her. Some of these roses she has planted herself, in more recent times. What she'd give, to be able to sit and talk this over with her mother. At the thought, something begins to soften in her and lighten. Imperceptibly, her body is no longer braced for defence.

Towards the end of the scrapbook, the first of the letters appears. Its tone is tentative, appreciative. A touch of the salesman perhaps, but with evidence of genuine passion.

Dear Mrs Kinnear, it begins, *it is to people like your-self that I owe a huge debt of gratitude . . .*

The rose-grower, from whom Alice ordered stock, goes on for three small, tightly written pages, discussing varieties and the conditions they require, treatment of pests, grafting and so on, answering the queries that Alice wrote to him so long ago. Pearl imagines her mother's excitement when rose catalogues and letters from growers arrived with the mail. There are many letters, all written by the same hand. She flicks through them – every word is about caring for and cultivating roses. What a treasure trove she's found! The last letter is dated December 31, 1954. Pearl skims it.

Dear Mrs Kinnear,

I do enjoy receiving your letters – always so inform-ative! I was interested to read your assessment of the seven shrubs. In our cooler climate and different soil conditions, we get many variations that complicate the business of isolating certain characteristics, as you say. But the world would be a dull place if everything turned out as we'd anticipated.

Now then, with regard to roses on their own roots. It is my opinion that it is logically unsound to believe that plants on their own roots are as good as grafted plants. Not everyone agrees with me, I know, but there it is . . .

What a pity about the sheep getting at the roses, but they'll come again – the roses, I mean (and no doubt the sheep will too) . . .

. . . Unfortunately, Mrs Hearne won't be coming with me on my northern tour. As things are, it's impossible for her to get away . . .

. . . Well, I think I've responded to all your comments. Now let me say that it would be marvellous if you could see your way to inviting me to have a look at your place when I travel north, particularly as I would like some budwood of the varieties which I am no longer holding. Would you be so kind? I would greatly appreciate the opportunity to meet you face to face, and to see your roses.'

It is signed, *Yours sincerely, Henry Hearne.*

You think you know what's going to happen, don't you?
We all do.

11

At the saleyards on the outskirts of Coolabarradin, men
call harshly to dogs and sheep, harrying animals along
the ramp off the transport. Dust rises, coating hair and
hats and shoulders, sticking to the inside of mouths and
noses, smarting in your eyes. Dust stirred up by thousands of dainty hooves tap-tapping on the dry ground.
The carrier, a local man, climbs into the cabin and waves
an arm to Dobie, giving the nod that he's about to move
off. Dobie is pleased that someone remembers who's
the boss. It's eleven in the morning and it's going to be
a hot one.

A lean young kelpie crosses from one sheep-pen to
another, scrambling on the backs of sheep in response
to someone's whistled command. It reminds Dobie
that he still hasn't done anything about getting a pup
to replace Mutt. If you've only got one dog, he's sure to
go and run under a truck, and then you have no old dog
to bring a young one on. He digs a piece of paper and a
stub of pencil from his shirt pocket, scribbles himself a
note and stuffs it back into the pocket.

At Mamerbrook you can find these jottings everywhere. Scraps of paper, torn edgings of newspaper, advertising brochures, the backs of used envelopes. They pile up on shelves and fall out of books. They rustle under cushions. Pearl finds them on Dobie's bedside table and under his mattress, on the mantlepiece in the living room and wedged into the corners of picture frames. They fall from his pockets when she turns them inside out for the wash. They waft out from behind the tea-bag jar, littering the kitchen bench. They are pinned beneath the fruit bowl on the dining table and stuffed into the cutlery drawer. They lie, scattered across the dashboard of the ute and accumulate unseen under its seats, like blown leaves. Pearl, unable to decipher the scribbled notes and figures, often throws them away. There's malice in the act. He knows.

When Tolly Breardon had rung with those freight prices a few weeks ago, Dobie wrote them down, but when Pete asked about them, the note had disappeared. Dobie searched for it, shifting things from table to floor, from chairs to table, emptying containers, rearranging shelves and turning the house upside down until Pearl exploded, as he'd known she would.

'What the hell are you looking for? What are you doing? Give me that! There's nothing in there but Visa receipts.'

She grabbed the box from him, shuffled the spread newspapers back into a pile and gathered them up from the floor.

'It's those freight figures,' he told her. 'Thought I'd stuck them on the mantlepiece. Just there.' He watched her. Saw her colour come up. Aha! So that's it. 'If you've got a moment, Pearlie, you might give me a hand?'

And Pearl, guilty Pearl, had to pretend to look for the note she'd thrown away.

Eventually she said, 'Do you want me to call Tolly and get the prices again?'

'Oh, that won't look good, Pearlie. Don't know about that. Can't have him thinking we don't know what we're doing.'

'I . . . I'll say you wrote the figures down and I threw them away, by mistake. Something like that?'

He waited. It was coming.

'And I'll tell him how sorry I am, for the nuisance of it. I'll tell him it was my fault, shall I?'

If that was all he was going to get, it was sweet enough.

Long after Dobie has stopped writing notes to himself or to anybody else, Pearl still discovers them. The scribbles have become hallowed, hieroglyphic, an indecipherable record of the ordinary that she is quite unable now to throw away. She stores them in an empty tin she finds. An old, round cake tin with roses on the lid. It's where Alice used to put them too, but by then there's no one left to tell Pearl this.

The heat packs a solid blow in the glare between the shade of desert ash trees. The metal piping around the pens scorches your hand, burns through the cloth of your trousers when you brush against it. The air, no longer gas but powdered earth, seals your nose and scours your lungs.

Dobie makes his way around the yard, sweat running from under his hatband. It's a poor showing today. The Mamerbrook sheep, clean and plump, stand out from the other animals. There's nothing else here to help drive up the prices or cause any excitement. With any luck, he thinks, his lot will be up for sale early to mid-proceedings. The impetus will die soon. He's got four hundred cross-breed ewe lambs in here and believes, without evident justification, that his presence will guarantee him a higher price. Pearl believes that her presence will guard against him spending all the proceeds on more merinos. It won't. He'll do what he wants to do, as always, but it's good to have a woman to sharpen your wits on. Even Pearl. And it's a chance to see and be seen. The Kinnears. They are a team, in this.

In the whole sea of hats he can see just two women. The other one's scrawny and straight-backed, seventy if she's a day. Pearl's got those navy slacks on with her cream blouse. Her straw hat is dark blue with a cream band. She looks well, thinks Dobie, watching her from across the yard. She looks a real Kinnear. She's chatting to Dan Woods, a stock and station agent.

Dan gives a loud laugh at something Pearl says. She turns her body towards him, away from the sheep they've been studying. He puts one foot up on the rails next to her and tips his hat low over his eyes. He's standing very close to her. Dobie can't see her face. She won't be wasting time on any romantic thoughts. Not at her age. She's got more sense than that. She'll be getting all the information she can from Dan, finding out what he knows about the stock and the buyers, who's looking for what, and the price they can expect. But just in case, Dobie touches a finger to his hat brim and offers a benign smile when Dan Woods glances his way. It's enough to make the big man pull back slightly, bringing his foot down from the rail. It's always enough.

There's quite a crowd by their yard already. An agent has hopped over the fence and is holding open the mouth of a ewe lamb, showing the teeth. The other sheep startle and begin to gallop around in a tight circle, little hooves drumming up clouds of fine dust. Dobie wanders over to check out the merinos before the call starts. Pearl's right though. They don't need more merinos right now. A poor lot anyway. He won't be buying. A large ram with enormous curling horns challenges him, stamping its forefoot. Dobie leans into the enclosure and gives the animal a secret smile.

'Won't be long before you're back in the paddocks with your harem.'

Profits and offspring, he thinks. Offspring and profits. The ram stares back, defiant, holding his gaze. For a second, until the auctioneer's shout reaches Dobie's ears, the world narrows to a shining crossbeam of mutual incomprehension.

Bidding has started from the south end, two rows across. He elbows his way through to the area, standing back from the action but taking in every nuance, casting the odd glance around for Pearlie, who seems to have disappeared.

After the sheep sale, they call in at the supermarket. Pearl has a bit of a glow about her. When Dobie moves to get out of the car, she tells him no.

'You stay here. We only need a few bits and pieces. I won't be more than a minute or two.'

She just couldn't bear it, to drag around the aisles with him now, when she's feeling so light, so separate. He'll argue about the necessity, or price, of every item she picks up. He'll insist on pushing the trolley and then he'll wander off with it so that she's stuck with an armful of shopping, looking for him up and down the aisles, like an idiot. He does it every time they come here, without fail. It's his supermarket party trick. Well, not today. Shoulders back and head up, she watches her reflection approach the double glass doors, adjusting her stride to allow for the fraction of a second when they part before her. Watch out, people. Pearl Kinnear is here.

Very keen, Dan had been, to get her away from the crowds and into the little office he had a key for. To get her, as he put it, all to himself for a while. As soon as he got the door closed, he couldn't keep his hands off her. She can't help but see herself from the perspective of the risk he was taking, his eager attentions. She is a woman desired. Menopause? Ha!

There is a confidential voice in her head, whispering asides. *You know, she practically runs that farm on her own. Looks after her father too. I don't know how she does it. A fine woman, Pearl Kinnear.* She gives a small, satisfied sigh and picks up a bunch of bananas. They are too ripe and bruised. He never eats them anyway. No more bananas. She strolls over to the avocados and inspects one critically, giving a business-like tweak to the stem end. Two of them don't meet her requirements; a third one goes into her basket. She lingers over the hair colours, chooses a new shade of blonde that promises a youthful shine, great body and glowing natural colour, and she wonders if it will work on the rest of her. She flicks through a magazine that offers 'Sizzling Summer Salads' and hints on 'How to Smoulder in Under Five Minutes!' It, too, goes into the basket. Dan, Dan, Elders Agent. The packed round brown-ness of his arms, his height, leaning in to her. The sly suggestion in his eyes that makes her hands tremble. His teeth are tobacco stained and his breath tastes of stale smoke.

You could do a lot better, Pearl.

I could do a lot worse.

She picks up bread and orange juice, smiling to herself. She can't remember the last time she felt like this. Visible. All the way through the checkouts, she's smiling.

Nodding in the car, in the heat, Dobie slips away, loses a few decades, finds himself, eight years old, face screwed up with the effort of trying to move a sandbag as big as himself. All around, the paddocks are filled with floodwater, pale brown and delicate under a clear sky, and the air carries the sounds of the past. His father's boots thump down the verandah steps. The screen door squeals as it swings shut behind Mary Brecken. Oh, that voice. It would peel paint.

'Come here, you! See, you need to get these out of here before they start to smell in this heat.'

She leans over to show him, gathered in her apron, the tumbled, silky-grey bodies of mice from the traps that she's set four times a day since the water started rising. He's been feeding the mice in his bedroom, leaving winding trails of crumbs around the skirting boards, making tunnels amongst his sheets, staying awake to feel them moving across his bed. They are his friends. Does she know everything then? Does she see through walls like a witch? Does she see through his innocent eyes to the place where his anger stirs, quick as a snake?

He dumps the sandbag and approaches her. With one hand, she grabs at and untucks his shirt, motioning him to make a pouch of the front of it. He obeys her slowly, stupidly, knowing how to infuriate her. Eyes downcast, he glares at her feet, willing the verandah boards to crack and splinter beneath her, the waters to take her down, the cold grey mud to fill her awful mouth and stop her eyes forever. Holding out the thin stuff of his shirt, he receives the tiny bodies. A cool burden. Scarcely any weight. An armful of ghosts, that's all.

'I expect there'll be another load of them before your father's ready with the boat,' she sighs.

'Bloody old cow,' says the eight-year-old, under his breath. He tips the bodies into the bottom of the dinghy that his father has tied up to the verandah post.

'The sandbag's no use like that, boy. Set it straight like I showed you.'

His father gives an exasperated shake of his head. Dobie, scarlet to his ears, goes back to work on the sandbag. Alistair is looking out over the shining acres of water that came two days ago, creeping quicksilver around the homestead on its patch of raised ground.

'It won't go away in a hurry, this one, Mary. Never seen a flood as bad as this in these parts. It beggars belief,' he says.

'It beggars belief,' whispers Dobie, to himself, in the carpark.

Pearl loads the shopping and slams the back door of the car, jerking Dobie upright in his seat, shell-shocked. She climbs up heavily into the driver's seat. Can't she do anything quietly? Big lump of a girl. She's putting weight on. Can't be good for her. Even the Brecken had a waist. And Alice . . . well, better not think of that. Look at those dirty smudges on the front of her shirt. Like she's been pawed. No pride in herself, that's the trouble.

Pearl fires up the car, flings her straw hat to the back where it falls amongst the bags of shopping. He can feel the odd energy coming off her, and he doesn't like it.

Soon the town is far behind them and wide farms open out on either side of the road, green rice shoots, bare, turned earth, golden stubble, bleached pasture and, in the distance but always perceptible, the curving lines of river gums that follow two rivers across this part of the country.

'Wasn't a bad result, the sale,' says Pearl.

'Could have been worse,' Dobie agrees. 'I'd have been happier with it up around the eighty-dollar mark but it was never going to happen with that lot.'

He's thinking about the pup he'll have to find and train up. Thinking about Mutt too, years ago, a tiny black pup with tan socks and more love in her eyes than anyone had a right to expect.

'Merinos weren't up to much,' she says.

'No. Bad bloodlines and old stock. Nothing there for us,' he agrees, aware of a confidence in her that's shutting him out, making an irrelevance of him.

'Oh, Dad, while I think of it, I found a scrapbook when I was cleaning your room. It was Mum's. Her rose notes.'

He remembers a scrapbook falling from the top of the wardrobe, remembers that he'd almost fallen too, from a chair, and wonders what he was doing up there.

'I took it,' she says. 'I didn't think you'd mind. It's just roses.'

He hears a challenge in her voice. She's got him on the back foot. Alice's rose book? Pearlie should have had it long before this. Alice would have wanted that.

'I'd forgotten I had it,' he grunts. The road ahead melts in a mirror pool of heat, blurring the horizon. He shifts his focus to objects of greater certainty. A shrub. A fence line. A splayed roo carcass at the roadside. What's she going on about now? How wonderful it is to have something that belonged to her mother. How important it is for her to have links with the past.

Pearl knows she's treading in delicate territory. She softens her voice when she asks him, 'Have you anything else that was Mum's? Anything else like the scrapbook, that I could see?'

But he can't face the memories, the inevitable questions about Alice. Not even after all these years. His reticence has grown armour-plating. Lift it now and you tear his skin.

'No,' he says. 'There's nothing else. Anyway, it's not like you've got anyone to pass things on to, is it?'

He can't resist sliding a look at her to see the effect of his venom. She's gazing straight ahead. Her expression hasn't changed but her hands are gripping the steering wheel so tightly that her knuckles have whitened and the air around her face has petrified.

12

Thomas kicks at a piece of the gravel that makes up the dividing paths between the rose beds and the propagation sheds. In the distance, he can see his brother turning over the soil with a long-handled spade. Robert hasn't seen him yet. Doesn't know he's here. Thomas waits, watching. The sturdy figure working the earth might be Henry, and himself a child again.

He drove for five hours last night, slept curled and cramped in the car for two hours, then drove on to arrive at his brother's place at seven-thirty in the morning. He'd seen it in Mel's face when she opened the door, that he'd done the wrong thing again.

'Thomas! Why didn't you call? What's happened?'

But he'd had to do it this way. If he'd stayed at home another minute, if he'd telephoned and tried to explain, if he'd allowed a voice to express doubt or beg a few days' delay, or even if he'd waited till morning, he would have lost both courage and momentum. He would have gone back to bed.

Mel had given him a hug, invited him in, satisfied

112

herself that there was no disaster, no broken bones, nothing she could mend, and then she'd made him coffee, and eggs on toast, and gone to rouse her two children for school.

'Robert's already at work down the back,' she said. 'Wander out there when you're ready.'

Even through his distraction, Thomas noticed how tired she looked. An ageing fatigue that could lead you to believe she and Robert were of an age when in fact she was nine years younger. He inquired gently how things were with her.

'Oh, you know,' she laughed, 'two teenage boys – what can you do? There just never seems to be enough time for anything.' She ran a hand through her brown curls as she paused in the doorway, a brief touchdown only.

Ah, the chaotic results of procreation.

Well, someone has to do the dirty work, Thomas.

'I got your phone messages,' he said. 'Thank you for thinking of me. I'm afraid I just couldn't . . . I wasn't . . .'

'Hey, that's all right, Thomas. It's a bad time, when your father goes. No matter how prepared you think you are. We all have our own ways of dealing with it. I wish Robert would. Seems to me he's got Henry's death filed away somewhere, like something he'll take a look at when he's got the time. Bit of a worry. Much better to let it out, talk about it, and allow yourself to grieve, don't you think? He loved Henry so much. Well, we all did, didn't we?'

With a quick pat on his shoulder, she whirled away and a few seconds later Thomas heard the washing machine churning. He had eaten his eggs alone in the kitchen where he'd grown up. Not quite the same kitchen. Now there's a dishwasher tucked under the bench-top and slanted beechwood blinds hanging where the ruffled orange cafe curtains used to be. A sense of disorientation pursues him, like he's almost made it to the right place, but not quite. It's his home, but not anymore; his childhood, overlaid with anachronisms. It has grown, changed, gone on without him. Mel's voice reached him from the bedrooms and the protesting boyish groan that answered her might have been his own, once. You can never go back to the same place.

Robert, after the first grunt of surprise, hands him a spade. Together, they turn over one of the garden beds.

'Business good?' asks Thomas.

'Could be better.'

'And the kids?'

'Kids are fine. Driving Mel crazy. Tony's been selected for the cricket team. Makings of a good batsman, so they tell me. And Charlie never has his nose out of a book. Bit like you used to be. But minus the frogs, thank god.'

Thomas grins.

Robert sprinkles the clods of earth with white powder from a blue plastic bucket.

'You back at work yet?' he asks, after a while.

'On my way to do a field study right now, as a matter

of fact. An endangered species in southern New South Wales.'

'Oh. Right.'

'It's the Southern Bell Frog. CSIRO are keen to have an update on regional populations. Thought I'd drop in here on the way, and say hello. Catch up with you and Mel, and the kids.'

'You're all right then?'

'Of course I am. Everything's fine.' Except the weeks of leave without pay, the university lectures booked but not delivered, the frantic emails for papers due and deadlines passed, the queer passivity of his life since his father died. 'And you?'

'Me? Never been better.'

'Thing is, Robbie, something odd happened, a couple of weeks ago.'

Thomas isn't aware that he's used the childhood name, but Robert hears it. He puts down the bucket and feels around in the pockets of his overalls for his cigarettes.

'I got an audio tape from Dad. A nurse brought it round. She told me he made the tape just before he died and asked her to give it to me three months after his death. I have to deliver a rose to someone.'

'Shit!' says Robert. 'I was hoping the old man had forgotten about that.'

'So you know about it? What the hell is going on?'

'Steady on, mate. You've no cause to go snapping at me. I just looked after a rose, that's all. Prop yourself over here and I'll tell you what I know.'

They sit, side by side on a low stone wall, pale smoke from Robert's cigarette eddying in the still air. Currawongs and a single butcher bird call from the trees behind them. Thomas is sharply aware of the ripples of dislocated time, the liquid notes of the birds, the odour of tobacco cutting through the fragrance of the roses, the feel of rough-hewn stone beneath his jeans, the lumps of brown clay sticking to his boots. This moment will stay with him, caught on the keen point of a quickening excitement.

Robert exhales a long stream of smoke, his eyes on the middle distance. 'When I took over the nursery it was a pretty drawn-out process, you remember. Dad kept giving me last instructions as though I might forget something vital, even though I'd been working alongside him for over seven years by then. It was so hard for him to give up control and let go. At first I thought the business about the specially bred rose was just a part of that whole thing, but then he said that on this matter, his instructions were to be followed to the letter. He said that my inheriting the business depended on it. He was deadly serious.'

Thomas is incredulous. 'You've never mentioned this before.'

'No. And if you hadn't brought it up, I probably never would have. I gave him my word. Anyway, eventually he and Mum moved up the coast and he swapped roses for tomatoes and broad beans. I always thought it was odd that he gave up so completely on the roses but I suppose it was his way of making a clean break, once he'd got my promise. Mum was happy about it, of course. She'd waited long enough for her little cottage by the sea. It was either that or she was going to leave him and go back to England, she said.'

'What!'

'Oh, it would never have happened. She'd been away from her beloved England so long I reckon she was too scared to go back, even if Dad had agreed to come with her. And that was about as likely as hell freezing over.'

And where was I, thinks Thomas, when all this was being played out?

In a swamp somewhere.

'And the rose?' he prompts.

'Ah, yes. It's a white rose, petals tipped with carmine. A real beauty. A rambler with masses of single blooms. Has this sweet, long-lasting lemony-rose fragrance. It took him years and years to get it to this stage. I don't know . . .'

Robert looks down at his grimy hands.

'. . . I don't have his patience. He had a real gift for roses, old Henry did. It'd be a winner internationally if we promoted it. Worth a few bucks. But he told me it had been developed for someone else. I was to say nothing to anyone about it. Mel knows, of course, but no one else. He said I was to care for it until the day that he came to collect it. After he died, I thought, well, there's no need to talk about it now. I'm the one who's looked after it all this time. It's mine, isn't it? Comes to me with the rest of the nursery.'

117

'Apparently not. He's asked me to find someone. A woman. Name of Alice Kinnear. He wants me to give her the rose. On the tape he said, "Tell her it's for the budwood."'

'Alice Kinnear? Never heard of her. Who is she?'

'Haven't a clue. Some farmer's wife who lives in the southern Riverina. Or did. She might have moved. She might be dead by now. It's half a century ago.'

'Sounds bloody ridiculous to me. Thomas, we're talking real money here. Mel and I could do with it, you know. He was a sick old man. Probably out of his mind on drugs for the pain. You can't take this seriously. I've already made inquiries about releasing the rose.'

'What am I supposed to do? Ignore his deathbed wishes? Would you do that? He left what money he had to the two of us and there'll be more when the sale of the cottage comes through. You know that.' He pauses. 'It's a rose, Robert – a specially created rose. In your own words, it's a real beauty. What does that say to you?'

'It says money, publicity for the nursery and for my name,' says Robert, exasperated. 'I don't see why it should go to a complete stranger.'

'But that's my point. Dad must have had his reasons. Don't you want to know? Aren't you the least bit curious?'

'It's ridiculous,' Robert repeats, ignoring him. 'And there are several of them of course. Not just the one plant. I suppose he means for her to take them all, this Kinnear woman? Take over the rose completely. You realise she might not release it? It might be lost to the world.'

'It's what he wanted,' said Thomas stubbornly. 'It has some special significance for him. We may never know what that is but I have to do this for him. I won't sleep easy again if I don't try. I can't take the rose with me though. It might take me a while to track her down. I doubt it would survive a field study in the Riverina.'

'So we're not going to get this sorted overnight?'

'I don't think so.'

'Why don't you take out an advertisement in the paper? Put a deadline in. Say that if she doesn't contact us by a certain date, the rose stays put.'

'I can't. Because of something Henry said in the tape – it was a very peculiar and confused recording. He said I was to "go softly". He said that it's easy to damage the innocent. I don't think he'd want it all over the papers.'

'Oh, mate, this is just unbelievable.'

'My thoughts exactly. Look, when I get back, I'll send you the tape. You can see for yourself.'

'You've made up your mind then?'

'Yes. I want to find out who she is and why Dad wants to give her a gift like this after so many years. I want to know why I have to "go softly". I want to know what the mystery is. Don't you?'

'The mystery was all in his head, I tell you. And what if this woman's dead? What then? Did Dad's instructions cover that too?'

119

'No. Perhaps he didn't want to consider the fact that he might have left it too late.'

'Aw, this is just crap, Thomas. I can't believe it.'

'If she's dead we can talk about it then. Decide what's for the best. But I have to try. You never know, if I find her, I might be able to persuade her to sell you the rights to the rose.'

'Sell them! They're already mine.'

'No, Robert, they aren't.'

'Give her a damn rose. Don't give her the rights, Thomas. She doesn't have to know, for Christ's sake.'

'You don't mean that.'

'I bloody well do.'

'If I find her, I'll explain. I'll do my best for you. I promise. Anyway, what's budwood? I remember the word.'

'Budwood is a cutting taken from new growth. It's a way of propagating the rose. If it's good stock, you can use it as a strong base for developing your own lines. Sounds like that's what's happened here.' Robert grinds out his cigarette underfoot and tucks the butt into his pocket.

'Do you think Mum knew anything about this?'

'What? The rose? If she did, she didn't hear it from me. And I doubt it. Dad only told me at the last moment because he had no choice, because he was leaving. I can tell you, I'm not happy about this.'

Looking at Thomas, intending to persuade, maybe even intimidate a little, he sees the boy behind the man's face and senses his brother's need to atone. For what, he wonders? He has never understood Thomas but he recognises the set of that mouth. Thomas has made up his mind. And something else. A hint of . . . what is it? Satisfaction? Smugness? Dad left the tape to Thomas. Delirious or not, there's business to be done here between a father and his youngest son. Pull back, Robert. As Henry would have said, let the lad sort it out for himself. It will all come out eventually, he thinks. Chances are, she's dead anyway, like Henry, like Nora.

'What's her name again? Kinnear? Can't be too many of those around, I suppose. And it's for budwood, he said? She must have helped him to build up the nursery or something.'

Or something, thinks Thomas.

'Well, if you're going, you're going. Let me know what you find out. Come on now, we'd better get inside and let Mel know what's going on. She'll think we're all crazy, not just Henry,' Robert warns. 'Doesn't have much faith in men or mysteries, my Mel. I've often wondered if she isn't the real reason Dad finally allowed me to run things here without him. *"There's more to life than cricket, you know."*' Delivered in Henry's broad accent. He forces a grin, gives Thomas a friendly punch in the arm to show that everything is fine, but he's angry and they both know it.

121

13

A mopoke calls out, soft and clear through the stillness. The sky is a brilliant layering of stars, a fine shoal in a moonless sky. Orion is low in the west and the Milky Way flows right over Mamerbrook Farm.

The first call of the mopoke is unheard by all but Dobie, tired out of his brain and still awake at 2 a.m., casting for sleep with a long snaking line over the dark ripples of the night, tickling for sleep amongst the smooth grey river stones and tangled weeds of his mind. Mopoke, he thinks, and listens to the rhythm of the call, hungry for a few hours of oblivion. Mo-poke. Mo-poke. Tic-toc. Tic-toc. At five o'clock he'll allow himself to listen to the news on the radio and day will begin for him, but till then . . .

At the second call of the mopoke, Bel stirs and moves in closer to the curve of Pete's hard body, guarding his back as only she can against all the dangers of the world. Her two children are out there, making their own shapes in the air that the wind will shift and toss regardless of their designs; they are building their lives without her now. She calls to them in her mind, consciously. Take care. Keep safe. Be happy.

Mo-poke. Mo-poke.

Change coming, she thinks, registering the bird's call, sinking down into dreams again.

At 4.20 a.m. a third call peels away sleep from Pearl who opens her eyes and glares at the clock. What is it? What's woken her? She closes her eyes and sinks back into a darkness pulsing with the rhythm of her thudding head. When she wakes again, there's a bird in her hair. It scrabbles at her scalp, desperate to be free of her. She can feel its nasty little claws. Unclean. A thousand parasites making the move from its feathers to her head. The bird panics. Pearl panics, sitting up, uttering little screams, hands flapping wildly about her head. She opens her eyes. No bird. With a shudder she tries to burrow back down under the bedclothes but the sudden awakening has made her feel queasy. Her exploding head is demanding painkillers. Getting to her feet is a progression of pain.

Hunched against the daylight, she pads slowly up the corridor to the bathroom where her bare feet leave dark moist shapes on the grey slate floor. When she lifts her nightdress over her head, she's disgusted by her own stale flesh. In the shower, she runs cool water over her head and lets it splash onto her shoulders. The scent of her tangerine soap rises into the air. She's in there for a long time but she can't wash the mud from her mind.

When she steps out of the shower and dries herself,

heat moves around her in a humid wrap. She looks at the pale blur of her face in the mirror. Fool! she whispers, staring into bloodshot eyes. *Who've you got to pass things on to?* Anger leaps in her mind but fades quickly with no energy to sustain it. Her body is already warm and clammy again. She feels a drip run from beneath her right breast down over her stomach, disappearing into her pubic hair like some quick nestling creature. The slate tiles are cool beneath the soles of her feet. Another drip forms at her hairline and slips down her forehead and temple. The face in the mirror has nothing to say. She rolls the towel into a soft pad for her head and lies down. Her stomach slides stickily on the slate, flesh retracting briefly from its cold, unyielding surface. Her big breasts flatten against it, cooling, cooling. She turns her knees to the side, curling her legs. Her arms are curved around her towel cushion, their undersides touching the floor. Head on one side, she can see how precisely the fine coating of dust clings to the white skirting board. It is the only thing she wants to think about. It is enough.

14

It's that slow-creeping, never-ending slide towards chaos that you have to keep your eye on if you want to stay ahead of the game. You have to fight to keep things the way you want them. Stay alert, read the signs, keep your guard up, leave nothing undone. Always, the struggle. He's a fighter, all right. He's fought the land and fought the weather. He's fought the gods and lost, but only once. He's taken on all comers and he's still there in his corner, Dobie Kinnear, sagging a little, tiring more quickly, but still bouncing, still skipping and throwing punches at the air.

This morning he's been quizzing Pete about his work schedule instead of letting the man get on with it. After that, he went out spying on the farmhands to see if they were slacking off. They weren't, and Pete has everything under control as usual, but Dobie can feel it, tantalising as the scent of rain on the wind but far less welcome. Something's coming and he doesn't think it's his new housekeeper. He's given up on that one, except in his dreams.

He's arranged to pick up a kelpie pup this afternoon. Ian Finnegan, a neighbour, has a litter on his hands.

'Are you sure you want a pup?' Pearl had asked.

At your age?

'If we lose Blackleg,' he said, 'where will we be then? No old dog to bring a young dog on. You've got to have one that knows the tricks and one to learn them. That's the way it goes, my girl.'

He's thinking about Pearl when he turns onto the highway towards the Finnegan place. Whatever's biting her, she needs to get over it. Moody. Likely to bite your head off over nothing. And drinking way too much for a woman. Into the vodka now, though she thinks he hasn't noticed. She's rarely out of bed these days when he leaves in the morning. And that expression on her face when she thinks she's alone, as though something inside her has given way. It's starting to get on his nerves. He's read about people getting depressed. Is that what's wrong with her? Depression? That's all I need, he thinks. Aren't there tablets she can take for that?

Ten minutes down the road, the ute coughs to a halt.

Leave nothing undone, eh, Dobie?

What is it now?

Diesel, damn it.

He knows someone will come along soon, he's not worried about that, but he hates the way it looks. If you're forty and you run out of fuel, there might be a bit of good-humoured joshing but they'll assume you were too busy to look. At his age, it's different. *Poor old guy,*

Dobie Kinnear, found him sitting at the roadside, out of fuel. Shame. Shouldn't be allowed to drive. Shouldn't be allowed out on his own. Shouldn't be allowed.

Get a grip, Dobie.

It's Ian Finnegan, the very man he was on his way to see, who pulls over to help.

'Can happen to anyone,' says Ian cheerfully. 'Ran out of diesel myself last week. Bloody pain in the arse, it is. Always happens when you're in a rush to get somewhere, too. You want to hop in here and we'll go and get that pup for you and come back with a couple of cans of diesel?'

As they drive, Ian chats about fuel prices, wool prices, water allocations for the rice, what kind of a year they can expect. He's planning to try a chickpea crop for the first time. The projections look good. Did a few acres of corn along with the usual stuff last year, he says.

'Good harvest but a thirsty old crop. You should try it, if you've got the water.'

Dobie prefers to stick to what he knows. These farmers with their spreadsheets and forecasts. Throw in a low rainfall year and what good is your spreadsheet then? Nothing but kindling. And can he talk! Dobie can't get a word in edgeways.

They've just got the pup tied up when Tricia, Ian's wife, comes on the radio to tell him someone's turned up to see him.

'I can wait,' says Dobie, embarrassed to be a nuisance.

'No, no. I'll get our Sam to drive you over to your

127

ute. It's no problem. Hope the pup works out well for you. He's from good stock.'

Ian heads off towards the homestead with a wave of his arm and here is Sam, seventeen years old, six feet tall and built to last, with Ian's red hair and fair freckled skin. He shakes Dobie's hand.

'Mr Kinnear.'

'Sam.' This boy scarcely came up to his shoulder the last time Dobie saw him, and just look at him now. Doing Ian Finnegan proud. One of four as well. Four sons. God rot him.

'We can go now, if that's all right with you?' says Sam, shyly.

'Fine. It's good of you to go to all this trouble.'

Sam tosses the diesel into the back and climbs into the truck. He waits, watching, as Dobie struggles up into the passenger seat and Dobie, gritting his teeth, knows the boy is wondering if he should lend him a hand. He is ancient, from Sam's perspective. Crumbling. Creaking. In my time, he thinks, I'd have run rings around you and your father too. It doesn't help. He grows sour and shrinks a little more, answering Sam's polite attempts at conversation with monosyllables. Eventually Sam gives up. By the time they've transferred the diesel to Dobie's ute, they part with a wave of the hand, heads turned homewards.

It's growing dark when Dobie finally pulls into the homestead at Mamerbrook. Across two hundred yards of lawn, the windows of the old house shine soft and golden. Backlit, Alice's magpie moon is sharply defined. That damn bird. Why couldn't she have chosen something pretty? Something cheerful with a bit more colour? A rosella, say? Or a galah?

There's Pearl, laying the table for dinner. Right scene. Wrong woman.

'Doesn't look after you the way I used to, does she?' says Mary Brecken, looking back at him over her shoulder, her strong wiry arms pummelling bread dough at the kitchen table.

He shudders, blows her from his mind like a puff of flour.

'Doesn't look after you the way I used to, does she?' says Alice, reaching out pale arms from her sickbed. *'But it wasn't my fault, Dobie. Oh, it wasn't my fault.'*

Dobie turns his back on the window and the ghosts. A creamy three-quarter moon hangs low and the Southern Cross is brightening by the minute. The big leaves of the poplars by the dam create a black mosaic against a sky fast draining of light and colour. Tiny bats flit past him, intent on their prey, swift and dainty as dark-winged fairies. Pete has pulled the stops out on the irrigation channel during the day and flooded the orchard to give the trees some deep drinking. There, in the stillness of evening, the black trunks and leafy branches of apple, pear and almond trees rise from limpid pale-blue pools. The water has drawn all the remaining radiance of the day and concentrated its essence into lakes of blue milk, leaving them holy.

He stands at peace amidst the darkening shadows until a low mournful howl rouses him. The pup's still tied up in the back of the ute. He whistles for Blackleg and gives the two dogs time for a bit of a growl and a sniff at each other before he ties up the pup at Mutt's kennel and puts Blackleg on his chain. He's bone tired. It's been a long day, with one thing and another.

At dinner, he says nothing to Pearl about where he's been, and she doesn't ask. Time enough to tell her about the pup tomorrow. A vacant, half smile on her face makes him suspect that the opened bottle of wine isn't her first drink of the day, but he prefers it to the times when her eyes are full of a pain he doesn't know how to ease and questions he can't answer. Yes! Drink up everyone! And cheer up, for god's sake. You're a long time dead. He pours himself a generous whisky.

Pearl looks at Dobie, sees an old man shrinking and wrinkling, losing all his substance, his mind far away. What is he thinking about? What decade is he moving through? She searches herself for feelings of pity, or something approaching it, and finds none.

'No bananas. You forgot the bananas,' he grunts. A sliver of fish escapes from his mouth and comes to rest beside his glass.

'Yes,' she says. 'Sorry.' She recalls a woman, poised and confident, rejecting bananas in an aura of light. Who was that woman?

You'll go to hell, Pearl, hating your father. It's not nice.

They eat in silence after this, Pearl's mind turning slowly in search of the last glimpses of her self-esteem, and Dobie, wandering through the paddocks of his memory, looking for his hitchhiker, with her hair like a halo, her dress of leopardskin and her jacket red as pomegranates.

15

Thomas makes his first stop at Coolabarradin, a southern Riverina catchment of ten thousand souls, flanking a great curve of the Murray River and its tributary, the Ada. On the main street of Coola, as the locals call it, there are four banks, three hair salons and six pubs, though the town has eight pubs in all, if you count the RSL. It has an airport and sale yards, a gun club and a golf club. It has a large open-air swimming pool and a racing track with roses as fine as those at Flemington when they run the Melbourne Cup. The town has its own newspaper, the *Coola Standard*. There is a Post Office, an Amateur Dramatic Society, a Quilting Society, a Family History Society and a Society for the Preservation of the Plains Wanderer, a small brown, quail-like bird teetering on the edge of extinction. The predicament of this creature arouses curiously strong passions, particularly now that the Society has acquired the authority to forbid the farming of any land where nests have been found. Sightings of the bird are down.

As befits an irrigation capital, or not, depending on

your perspective, water is the first thing that meets your eye when you enter the town. Water is everywhere, drawn from the Ada River that feeds into the Murray-Darling system. There are creeks and lagoons where several varieties of duck float and feed, and black swans pose regally. Twenty miles from here, less, they are target practice. There are fountains too, and not your drip-and-bubble type but real bursts of shining water, ten, twelve feet high, and rolling lawns, vividly green, green as the acres of rice paddies quilting the farms to the north. It is all very pleasant to the eye, with an air of lush relaxation that some might call hubris, in a land where thirteen inches of rain falls in a good year.

The broad main street of Coola is shaded by parallel lines of jacaranda trees and the beauty of their massed blue flowers would make any heart more prone to gladness, but Thomas sees little evidence of this as he walks the length of the main street. One of the booklets that he's picked up from the information centre mentions council plans for the eventual removal of the jacarandas and the installation of low maintenance native trees with low water requirements. Very sensible. Very politically correct. I could have missed all this, thinks Thomas, squinting up at sunlight through a grace of leaf and blossom as his feet move through the lavender-blue of fallen petals.

From Coola, he plans to gradually work his way through the Riverina. For frogs, it's a great place to start. For Kinnears, who knows? He returns to the station wagon and locates a sprawling supermarket complex on the outskirts of town, its carpark filled with dusty utes and mud-splattered four-wheel drives. Time to pick up some supplies. He has his list ready.

Inside the supermarket, there is a moment of disorientation. It is all so familiar – the long aisles of produce and diffuse lighting, the horrible music playing in an endless loop. He could be anywhere, in any town. His senses quicken and begin to filter environmental clues.

At the delicatessen counter, three Aboriginal women are gathered around two trolleys. One of them, the eldest, he guesses, is wearing a pale blue top and short black skirt, a black straw hat and shiny black sandals. A younger woman, in a loose, full-length dark dress worn low on her shoulders, points at something in the trolley, laughing. He can't catch what she's saying. The third woman, in jeans and a black T-shirt, picks it up, wrinkles her nose incredulously. The older woman grabs it from her hands and puts it back with the rest of the shopping, laughing. He can't see what it is, the package, but the warmth of their communication spreads around him delightfully as he stands next to them, unnoticed.

A large woman in a red-and-white check uniform, her blonde hair stuffed untidily into a net, calls out from behind the counter, 'Number forty-two. Number forty-two, please?' She waits.

Thomas, watching with interest, sees how her face tightens and her gaze slides to the middle distance when the woman in the black straw hat presents her ticket. Number forty-two.

When his turn comes, he receives a wide-lipped smile beneath a quick, curious glance. She knows I'm a stranger here, he thinks, and wonders what gives him away? He usually strives for a discreet camouflage. You see more, that way.

The aisles are difficult to negotiate; fat people everywhere. Why are there so many fat people here? That waddling walk, coming towards you with an awful determination. Momentum is the goal. *You'd better get out of the way, mate, because otherwise I'm going to roll right over the top of you.* Sometimes, it is difficult to get out of the way. Sometimes, retreat is the only sensible option. It takes Thomas quite a while to gather the items on his list.

At the checkout he's third in line behind a woman with the sucked-in, prematurely old face that tells of poor dental work. She's wearing an orange T-shirt with baggy blue-and-white shorts. Big hips and full breasts but a scrawny neck. Spindly legs on high-heeled white sandals. Her bleached blonde hair is held high in a ponytail with an elastic band. She has a nose like a toucan above which her pale eyes flit ceaselessly, alighting nervously on this and that, as though she's expecting the pounce of an invisible cat. Thomas is fascinated. She doesn't blink. Not once. How does she do that? Her partner, waiting to load the goods into the trolley, is over six feet tall, all bulk and muscle, built like a river red gum. His blue singlet is the same colour as the tattoos all down his thick brown arms. His low-slung blue jeans are filthy with dark stains that look like oil. His face is bearded, his brown eyes hooded and blank. A great tub of a belly hangs over the rim of his jeans. Neither of them can be much over thirty years old.

A message is called out over the public address system. The rhythmic sing-song syllables are repeated three times. The words are completely incomprehensible. Thomas is a visitor in an alien world. He hands over his goods for the tallying, and leaves.

'You need to get out more,' he mutters to himself.

As he waits for a break in the traffic, two brown and lanky teenage boys cross in front of his car. They are tall and bare-armed, both wearing singlets with long dark shorts and enormous shoes. One of them gives a brief nod in acknowledgement of his letting them pass. Thomas experiences an odd moment of gratitude. We are the same species, he reminds himself, not for the first time.

He takes a room at a pub called The Grebe, choosing it because there isn't a gaming machine in sight and the name pleases him. Grebes are his favourite waterbirds, despite their appetite for small frogs and tadpoles.

Inside, the sunlight is muted. There are a couple of lads at the pool table and three men sitting at the bar. All five of them turn to look at him when he comes in. He tries a weak G'day to break the atmosphere. Just another bloke.

'G'day,' says one of the men at the bar, and then yells, 'Bob! Get your arse out here. You've got a customer.' He turns back to Thomas. 'He won't be long. He's out the back getting the beer in. New in town?'

'Yes,' says Thomas, 'I am.' Not wishing to be unfriendly but not knowing what else to say, he goes over to a large corkboard at the side of the bar and studies it. The room sinks back into its former rhythms except for the listening ears. The board carries business cards, advertisements and printed notes about town functions. *Southern Riverina Worm Farm – Business For Sale (p.o.a.). Angel Air Services for all your Sowing, Spraying and Top-Dressing. Jerry Piscano – Broadacre Channels, Spot Spraying, Weed Control Services, Seven Days a Week. The Coola Rodeo Committee invites you to sign up for the Pub Steer Ride, $50 prize to anyone who makes it past the eight second hooter!*

The Bindy Bad Boys are playing at The Grebe on Saturday nights this month. There are dates and locations of matches for the Coola Darts Team, Volunteers Wanted by the CFA, and handwritten notes: Rooms to Let, Help Needed, Ironing Done.

Apart from the thock thock of the pool balls and the low drone from the television fixed high at one corner of the bar, it's quiet in here and the odours of beer, cigarettes and wood polish are a stimulating signal of new territory, but Thomas can't shake the faint resonance of unreality. Displacement anxiety, he thinks. I've been in bed for too long.

'You thinking of signing up for the Pub Steer Ride, are you?'

The voice belongs to a man behind the bar. He's pink-faced, short, with corrugations of ginger hair. The manager? Snorts and laughter from the other patrons greet his sally. There's no friendliness in this man's smile, just a hard, bright curiosity with the shadow of a sneer. Thomas laughs along with them, shaking his head. All good fun, isn't it?

His room is a surprise, shabby with a worn floral carpet and cigarette-scarred wooden furnishings but clean and light. Its second floor position overlooks the street from a large corner window. Squinting, with his nose pressed to the glass, he even gets a glimpse of the river. Fat people stroll beneath the jacarandas. Two fat women pass, each with a fat baby in a stroller. Fat children. Fat teenagers sitting on the low wall beneath the clock tower, passing a cigarette amongst themselves. Is it something in the water? Thomas quickly calculates the percentage of visible non-fat people and deduces from the sample that there aren't sufficient numbers to ensure survival. It is a population doomed to extinction in these parts. He sighs. It's not his field. Frogs are so much more rewarding.

He surveys the large room with a growing sense of achievement and satisfaction. He's here. He's taking control of his life again in the best way he knows. The only way he knows. Frogs. He has his tent and his field gear, and the station wagon, not so white after hours of country driving, is full of supplies. He's quietly excited. All those peaceful hours of field work to look forward to. A surprise under every log. It's been a long time since he's felt so motivated. But first, the Kinnear woman.

The regional phone directory is on a low shelf next to the bed. He takes it over to the table under the window, with a chicken sandwich that he picked up at Dee's Bakehouse, and a cup of coffee that he's made right here in his room, heating the water in the small electric jug. It's Sunday. Ought to be a good time to catch people at home. He flicks through the pages for 'K'.

16

On Sundays, Dobie's rarely in a good mood. To start with, all the farmhands down tools on Sundays. You can't get anyone to work unless it's a real, no-doubt-about-it, jobs-in-the-balance, life-and-death type of emergency. Even then, it's usually only Pete you can count on. In Dobie's view, it's just plain crazy. What? Do they all go off to church on Sundays? Not likely. Do the requirements of a farm – the crops and the animals – stop because it's Sunday? Of course not. Ridiculous. All the Sundays he's had, and he still can't settle down to this thought.

Another problem with Sundays is that it's his second day without newspapers. The weekend papers aren't delivered until the afternoon run on Mondays, by which time they're not news at all. The time between meals passes more slowly without them and he misses his crosswords but it's unthinkable to make the 100 mile round trip to town just for newspapers. Pearl doesn't like shopping at the weekends. Too many people in the supermarket. Long queues at the checkouts. So – no papers.

The only good thing about Sunday, is Sunday lunch. No sandwiches or cold meat salads on a Sunday. It's a proper fry-up. Sausages and bacon, eggs and tomatoes, mushrooms and fried bread with tomato sauce on top. Worth expending a bit of energy on a Sunday morning to whet the appetite for a spread like that. Driving around the paddocks all morning, the only vehicle stirring for miles, he's daydreaming about it, hoping she'll get the eggs right – soft and runny – and the bacon crisp and slightly burnt.

He pushes open the kitchen door eagerly and stops. No clatter of plates. No smell of bacon. No sound of spitting fat from the hotplate. A rising tide of disbelief carries him into the room. Nothing's ready. No food prepared. No table set. He turns the radio on to full volume and waits for a wail of complaint. Nothing. He stomps down the corridor to Pearl's end of the house.

'Pearl? You there, Pearlie?'

There's no answer to his knock at her bedroom door. He pushes it open, cautiously, and sees her bed rumpled, sheets in a tangle. Where is she? And more importantly, who the hell is going to get his lunch?

Back in the kitchen, he turns off the radio and sets about preparing it himself. Three eggs in the pan, four rashers of bacon and four pork sausages under the grill with the halved tomatoes. A separate frying pan, sizzling with canola oil, ready for the bread. All the time that he's cooking, he's waiting for her to walk in, imagining her apologies, rehearsing his cool displeasure. He pours tomato sauce over a mountain of food and sprinkles it with salt and pepper. He's managed to scatter breadcrumbs and splatter fat over every available surface. He leaves the dirty frying pans on the stove. The raw egg that he accidentally dropped on the bench top remains there, spread and congealing.

Satisfied by this declaration of his grievances, he takes himself off to watch the cricket in his sitting room, from where he can see the approach to the house across the lawn, and keep an ear cocked for any shrieks of horror. But by the time he's finished eating, there's still no sign of her. He's feeling more uneasy now than peevish. Sunday lunch is sacred. He can't recall her ever missing it before. What if she's had an accident? Jesus! He might have to clear up that mess in the kitchen all by himself. Guilt makes his heart knock hard. He starts to feel slightly sick, sitting there, watching and waiting.

It's quiet for so long that when the phone rings he nearly jumps out of his skin. At first he assumes that it's Pearl ringing but when he hears a man's voice, he knows instantly that there's been an accident.

'Mr Kinnear?'

'Where is she?' he barks.

'I . . . is that Mr Kinnear?'

'Well, who is it? What do you want?'

'Sorry to disturb you, Mr Kinnear. If you could just spare me a few minutes of your time? My name's Thomas Hearne . . .'

Dobie bangs the phone down. Bloody people selling

things on Sundays. Ought to be a law against it. Where on earth is she? The car. He goes to the window to check. Her car's still there. She must have gone for a walk. But at lunchtime? This might be serious. Either she's hurt herself, maybe twisted an ankle and lying out there in a paddock, or she's deliberately making him suffer. And what about dinner? He can't see anything prepared or thawing. Is he going to have to make his own dinner too? Would she take things that far? There'd be no going back after something like that. Is it time, perhaps, for a serious gesture of reconciliation? But it wouldn't do to give the impression that he's weakening. I'll give her another half an hour, he decides, before I go looking. Ten minutes later, he's hurrying towards the ute, in search of his daughter.

Thomas stares at the phone in his hand. What was that all about?

Where is she?

That was my line, he thinks, bewildered.

Was that a Kinnear or not? Why would someone answer the phone in that way? Crazy.

Well, I can't call him back, he thinks. Not after having the phone slammed in my ear.

The regional phone book covers a broad area but lists only four Kinnears. Three of the listings are in Riverina towns with street names and numbers. Not farms. He'd rung them anyway and found that two of the families were related to each other but not to an Alice Kinnear. They hadn't heard of her. His third call, to a J. Kinnear in a town some distance away, went unanswered. Only one Kinnear is listed at a farm address. D. Kinnear, the book says, Mamerbrook Farm, Coolabarradin. Thomas had been quite hopeful, making the call. Now he's beginning to feel more apprehensive. He'd only managed to say his name before the connection was cut. What kind of a reaction can he expect when he delivers Henry's gift? Will it be welcome? Will he be welcome? Perhaps telephoning to introduce himself isn't such a good idea. A letter might be safer. In a letter he can describe the situation with more delicacy. What was it his father had said? *Be careful, Thomas. It's so easy to damage the innocent.* Yes, he thinks, I'll write to her. To Alice. To see if she's at Mamerbrook. And I'll put my mobile phone number in the letter. When all's said and done, it's a gift I'm bringing. It's not as if I'm trying to take something from anyone. He thinks uneasily for a moment about Robert. Chances are it will all come to nothing and Robert will get to keep the rose. Fair enough, in a way, but a deflating thought, isn't it, Thomas? How long has it been since Henry asked for your help? How long since he stopped asking?

Daylight beckons. He decides to go for a walk to clear his head. He can write the letter when he gets back, post it tomorrow. If they haven't heard of Alice Kinnear at Mamerbrook Farm, he'll move on into the next region after a few days here with the frogs. And now? A wander around some of those lagoons behind the winding Ada River.

17

When Pearl finally does come home, she's walked herself out of her hangover but she's almost staggering with exhaustion. Her legs are heavy and her feet ache. Her shoulders are slumped and her fingers are puffy and tingling. Every physical instinct she possesses, every fibre, every nerve end, is telling her to lie down, close her eyes, take it easy. Must stay closer to home next time I go walking, she decides, wondering if her iron is low, or if she needs a B12 shot. Maybe she's coming down with a virus? No reduction of the vodka intake is planned. We can only operate according to the wisdom we have at the time, and Pearl's current store of wisdom tells her that vodka heals, vodka is her friend. She can handle anything with vodka. Even Dobie.

She's sneaking through the rose garden towards her door when she hears voices. Dobie, outside the shed, talking to a young man beside a shiny red ute with bright chrome pipes crossing the cabin roof, and serious spotlights. There's a black and tan kelpie tied in the back of the truck. Dobie's got his hands on his hips; he's shaking his head slowly.

'You can't go shooting pig in there. I've got 1500 wethers in that paddock. And besides, you've got a dog there. Looks like a young 'un too.'

The dog, yellow-eyed and panting, pricks up his ears. *Come on! What's the hold-up? Let's go, boys!*

'Ah, that dog only chases pigs. He wouldn't ever chase sheep, not that one. He's a real good dog. Aren't you, mate?'

'Oh yes, we know, nobody's dog ever chases sheep, but you're still not shooting pig over there. Sorry, mate. Better try up the road a bit. About seven miles on the left, you'll see the gate for Winnar Holdings. Maybe you'll have better luck there.'

'Okay. No worries. See you around.'

Dobie watches him off the property. Better keep an eye open for that one. Okay-no-worries? Ha! He's going to shoot round here somewhere, whether he gets permission or not. And there's Pearl, at last. What on earth is she doing, creeping around the side of the house like that?

Pearl makes a direct line for her pillow, falls asleep as soon as her head hits it, swimming straight into a dark dream. She's imprisoned in a small barred cage. She can only lie down by curling herself up on the floor. The cage is one of many, fixed to the interior walls of a moving semi-trailer. The darkness inside the trailer is dense and tangible as a black fog. You can push it away at one point and it swirls in at you from another, black on black, billowing. The trailer stops and a back door is thrown open. She blinks, eyes watering at the sudden light, but when they adjust, she sees that the other cages are occupied by silent, mournful forms. As if in a slow dance, these people straighten up and turn towards the front, grasping the bars with both hands. As one, they raise their eyes to her and all of the faces are her own. Pearl. Pearl. Pearl. Pearl. Pearl . . .

Ooooh! What a horror. Awful! She drags herself off the bed and hurries to the kitchen to settle her nerves with a cup of tea. In the doorway, she stops, her mouth falling open in astonishment. Dear god. How is it possible for one man to make so much mess? What is this? A temper tantrum because for once in his life he's had to get his own lunch? (She really had forgotten the time, absorbed in her own miseries.) Does he think he can get away with anything? Her anger mounts until she can hear it, drumming in her ears. She can almost see, almost touch, the bars of her cage, strobing in front of her eyes. It can bloody well stay like this, she thinks, and see how he likes getting his own dinner too.

She makes a pot of tea and carries it into the dining room, away from the disaster area. On the dining table is a wooden box, the size of a shoe box, its top inlaid with small, precisely cut pieces of timber of different shades. She stares at it, still holding the teapot, and an image floats to the surface of her mind, scented with lavender. The image of this box, sitting on top of her mother's dressing table. It's Alice's jewellery box. Pearl opens the lid. There's a half-tray at the top that you can slide across or lift out, and three compartments lie beneath it, all lined in green felt. In one of these is a piece of paper torn from the back of an envelope. *This belonged to my mother, then to your mother. Yours now. Dad.*

Oh!

The old bastard.

So it is that by Sunday evening, a truce has been declared between Pearl and Dobie, and Monday's bright dawn peels away the night, with never a wink or a hint of what is in the wind and blowing towards them.

Peter Jenkins cups a mug of tea between his hands and blows gently on the surface of the liquid. Bel busies herself rinsing their plates and tidying away the breakfast things.

'Grass fire over at Reg Wallace's place last night,' he tells her. 'They reckon it was some idiot doing wheelies in the long grass. He was probably after the wild pigs or roos. Might have been his catalytic converter. That or a cigarette.'

'That's bad,' says Bel, thankful that he hadn't been called out during the night to fight the fire.

'Reg didn't even know there was a stranger on the property. One of the farmhands spotted him but didn't think to mention it at the time. Thought Reg must've given him the nod. Burnt itself out anyway, the fire. Lucky the wind was in the right direction.

'Lucky,' Bel agrees. 'Will they catch him?'

'Won't try, I shouldn't think. Didn't get a number plate. Some kind of ute. Red. Lots of red utes around. Reg said he might put a warning over the radio but I doubt he'll bother. Not much you can do really.' He shrugs.

'Wonder if he knew?'

'Knew he'd started it? Might have. Wouldn't be smouldering for long. It's tinder-dry up there. It would have gone up like kindling. You think he'd have smelled the smoke. Unless he was drunk. Might have been drunk. Bloody maniacs. If I caught anyone turning their backs on a fire, I'd shoot the bastard.'

'Pete . . . about that other business?'

He looks up at her. 'I know, I know. I'll talk to Pearl today. I will. It's just . . . I've been busy. I'll tell her. I promise.'

He gets to his feet and kisses her on the lips before leaving, as he always does, whether he's going off to work, or just going out into the garden. She watches from the window as he folds his long legs into the ute, follows his dust trail with her eyes, right across the paddock, before turning back to her tasks.

18

Dobie goes out early to let the dogs off but there's only Blackleg, squirming and jumping in excitement at the farthest extent of his chain.

Dammit! Where's that pup got to? Must have had the collar too loose. He's slipped it. Dobie releases the older dog. He tries a whistle. Nothing. He turns slowly in a full circle, looking for the pup, knowing that it's useless – the animal could be anywhere. A great bustle and commotion and cackling of hens rises into the air. The chookhouse! But not his chookhouse. That noise is coming from Bel's place. Might be the pup. Or there might be a snake in there. Either way, it doesn't look like anyone's checking it out.

But when he arrives, the hens crowd around the wire gate to greet him, expecting scraps. There's no disturbance now, no sign of fear in them, and no pup. Funny that Bel didn't come to take a look. Is she out somewhere? He can see her washing hanging on the clothes hoist at the side of the house. A nightdress of some cream silky stuff with a lace border. A pair of faded jeans. A blue dress with flowers. A line of thick wool socks, paired and all pointing in the same direction. Very precise. The clothes hang still in the sunlight. There's not a breath of wind today. He wanders across to the house, thinking he'll ask Bel to keep an eye open for the pup. He gives a knock at the front door, pushes it open and calls out.

'Bel. You there?'

No answer. He closes the door. She might be out the back. He walks around the side of the house. His father built this house and the adjoining, smaller one that has stood empty for years. The paintwork on the old weatherboards is peeling. Time Pete did something about that. Vegetable garden looks good. A riot of beans and thriving tomato plants with lots of fruit on them. Bel's got her herbs in there too – sage, parsley, rosemary, basil, thyme. A great little patch. Not an inch of ground gone to waste. He plucks a cherry tomato and chews it, thinking about his own empty vegetable garden. Blighted. Even his beans didn't come up. He ducks under a bra, stirs the nightdress softly with a callused hand.

'Bel?'

The back door is ajar but the flywire is closed. He climbs the back steps and calls again. There's no one around. He pushes open the door and stops, his senses assaulted by a fragrance. Lavender, is it? Everything is clean and orderly. Even the ancient brown linoleum has been scrubbed to a soft gleam and there's a colourful rag rug by the hearth. Crisp black-and-white gingham curtains hang at the kitchen windows. Dobie's thinking fondly of women and homes, the little touches . . . his eye falls on his dirty boots. Can't go in with those on.

Going in, are you?

Looks like it.

He levers them off, toe to heel, and places them just outside the back door. There. No tell-tale dirt on the floor. He tiptoes across the room in his wool socks, a caricature of a burglar, except he isn't going to steal anything, is he? He's just come to have a look. A little snoop while he has the chance. Got to keep the upper hand, haven't you? Never know what you might find.

It's a habit of his, and one that will bring him undone. But not yet. Not for a while.

Pearl has found the pup.

'Drop that, you mongrel!' she roars.

The pup streaks across the lawn with a brown hen between his jaws and an outraged Pearl panting in pursuit. He's found a way into Pearl's chookhouse, having discovered that Bel's is very well fox-proofed. He drops the stunned hen in a swirl of brown feathers and disappears into the shrubbery, emerging with another one. He stops a little way off from Pearl, tail held high and wagging. This is good fun. Pearl retrieves the first hen and stomps over to the chookyard with it. How did that dog manage to get through the fence? She unlatches the gate and lets the hen fly free, shaken but unhurt. Hens rush up, bustling and clucking around her legs: *Oooh! look what's happened, just look what's happened, you won't believe what he's gone and done, oooh, you won't, come and see, come and see . . .* Pearl counts them. There are seven, including two squashed together inside one laying-box, terrified. The old black hen is lying on her side in the far corner playing dead but when Pearl approaches she gets to her feet quickly enough and makes a dash for it. They're all very put out. Bet they won't lay today, she thinks. There are feathers everywhere but no dead hens. And the only one missing is the one he's got out there now. But where is the damned creature getting in? She stands there, puzzled. The kelpie watches her quizzically from outside the fence, head on one side, drooping hen in his mouth: *Well, you're in there. Shall I come in too? We can play together. Can we? Can we?* But Pearl is not in a playful mood. She finds the gap between fence and ground where the pup has dug a hole big enough to squirm through. She blocks it and pegs it, backing a wooden crate up against it for good measure. The pup watches her. When she comes out, he takes off again, still carrying the hen, looking over his shoulder to see if she's following. She isn't. She's gone for the .22 calibre rifle that's locked in the gun cabinet in the laundry.

Run, pup. Run!

Where are you, Dobie?
Up to no good.

Why should he squirm? He has every right to enter the cottage. He owns it, doesn't he? He's been inside the house many times.

But not in here, you haven't. Not in this room.

What of it? He could easily be taking a look around to see what repairs need doing.

In their bedroom, Dobie? Without asking?

The light is soft behind partly drawn blinds. The room smells of sleep and warmed flesh and – yes, it is lavender – there's a blue jug filled with lavender flowers on the dressing table. Alice used to love lavender. He closes his eyes for a moment, inhaling it. Bel's old double bed has a plain cream doona with stacked pillows at the head. The pillows are plain too, except for one that is smaller and embroidered with sprigs of lilac. On one side of the bed is a straight-backed wooden chair with a blue T-shirt thrown across it. Pete's. A lamp with a cream shade stands on the bedside table. There's a little silver clock, ticking. A tube of something lies beside it. He'd like to know what it is but doesn't dare cross the room to see. To move would be to break the spell. He is jolted out of his fantasies by the sound of a gunshot. When his heart stops leaping, he knows it will be Pete or one of the men, taking down a roo. Nothing unusual about a gunshot round here. Must be close by though. The next thing he hears is a high, sweet whistling of an old song: *Oh, I can't see the roos for the roses, and I can't see the sheep for your smile . . .*

It's very close.

It stops abruptly.

Dobie freezes, listening, waiting for the inevitable. What can he offer as an excuse? White ants? Warped floorboards? But nothing happens. There's no tread on the step. No one calls out. Everything's gone quiet again. Quiet, but not easy. It's a waiting quiet. And Dobie's not the only one waiting.

He drops to his hands and knees – no easy task, but necessary if you want to check out the enemy without being seen through the windows. He crawls to a place where he can take a look at the back garden, buggering his knees in the process. He can't see anyone out there. He crawls back, wanting to slip out of the front door, away from the direction of the whistler, but then he remembers – his boots are on the back step. He sighs. The back door is a long way off, for a man on his knees. What a ridiculous situation. Stand up, man! But he daren't. Better to suffer bruised knees than whipped pride. He can just imagine Pete's face. He crawls slowly to the kitchen again and peeps out. No one.

Carefully, unable to stifle a groan, he levers himself to his feet. The flywire door creaks a little when he pushes it open. Keeping his eyes on the garden for any sign of Bel or Pete, he reaches a hand down for his boots. Then his eyes go to his hand. The boots are gone.

Dobie stays fixed in a half stoop. Did he or didn't he leave his boots here?

(He did.)

Did he or didn't he hear a whistle?

There's no answer to that.

Dobie walks right around the outside of the cottage looking for his boots. Nothing. Eventually, with a shrug that he can't quite carry off, he goes down the track towards the homestead, wincing and dancing as the gravel pierces his feet.

He can't get that song out of his head and finds a memory of Alice, in the kitchen with her back to him, doing the washing up. She was singing softly to herself . . . *and I can't see the sheep for your smile. For the rose in your cheek and the smile in your eye, I'll come running the four-minute mile.* He'd just got back from a long drive. Four days he'd been away, buying merinos. He'd come up behind her and given her a squeeze.

Oh! Dobie!

In the garden, Bel and Pearl stop talking to each other and turn their attention towards him.

Too late to hide, Dobie. They've seen you.

They watch him approach in silence. Pearl has the rifle under her arm, pointing at the ground. He remembers the gunshot.

'I came over to see if she'd shot you,' Bel says with a grin. 'Your pup's been at the hens, Dobie.'

Shot me? His eyes go from her face to the rifle that Pearl holds so casually. Not the pup! Oh sweet Christ, she hasn't shot the pup, has she?

Pearl's face is grim. She's not giving anything away.

'He took off like a rocket when she fired,' says Bel. 'Took the hen with him.'

'Why did you have to go and shoot at him?' Dobie yells, hopping mad. 'I'm trying to train him. We won't see him for dust now.'

And Pearl replies calmly, 'Why are you walking around in your socks?'

There's no answer to that, either.

19

Pearl, splashing vodka into a yellow coffee mug to hide the fact that she's drinking in the afternoon, hopes the pup has gone for good. Hasn't she got enough to do around here without chasing dogs and rounding up hens? And what on earth was that business with Dobie in his socks? Excruciating. Bel had noticed. It would have been hard not to. There he was, right in front of them, his big toe sticking through a hole in his sock. Bel hadn't commented. Dobie hadn't offered an explanation. Pearl sips the vodka reflectively.

She's taken to nipping into town on her own more often, and comes back with cardboard boxes that clink when she moves them. She knows that Dobie's seen her unload these boxes, her private supplies, but he's never mentioned them. She might forget the bread, or the chook feed, or the tomatoes for his lunch, but she doesn't forget the boxes. They do not appear in the main part of the house; they stay with Pearl, tucked away in her cupboards and her wardrobe. She can't bear the thought of running out. Their contents are measured out inch by inch, often too much, never too little. It's a maintenance program to keep all the loneliness and confusion at arm's length, where she can look at it and acknowledge it, but not drown in it. That is what she tells herself. In fact, she's drowning a little every day.

She settles herself in a low garden chair, a good measure of vodka still in the bottom of her mug. She's thinking about Dan, Dan the Elders' man, and her bottled maintenance program softens the edges of those thoughts, airbrushing their hasty couplings and colouring them with a pale-pink wash of romance.

'Anybody home?'

'Round here, Pete.' She jumps guiltily, setting the mug down in the grass, knowing that her face has reddened. Can you smell vodka on a person's breath? Should she get up? Maybe not. He stands in front of her, one thumb hooked into his belt, one hand waving flies away from under the brim of his hat. She tilts her face towards him and squints into the sunglare.

'Dobie around?' he asks.

'I don't know,' she says, puzzled. 'Did you try the back door? Or he might be over at the sheds. Is the ute there?'

His crotch is at her eye level. Don't you love the way old jeans wrinkle and fade and define a man's body? Somebody else's prince, Pearl. The hand hooked into the belt loop is brown and capable, the nails dirty.

'Fact is,' he's saying, 'I wanted a word with you. Alone.'

159

Steady, Pearl. Focus.

'There's a bit of a problem you see.'

'So what's new?' she grins up at him, trying to ignore a tiny coil of panic tightening in her stomach. Problem?

He's staring at his mud-caked boots. Won't meet her eyes.

'It's like this, Pearl. A few days ago, four or five, I'm guessing, your father moved three hundred ewes over into Bent Post Paddock.'

'Yes, he mentioned it. Said the feed was good after those sprinkles of rain we had. Said it was going to waste.'

'Well now, that might be so . . . but see, I've been working on the rice with the men and, well, he left them shut in there. The ewes. In the paddock. And . . .'

'There's no water,' breathed Pearl.

'Exactly. He should have opened the far gate to give them access to the dam, but it was shut. I've moved them over to Woolshed Paddock. We'll need to keep an eye on them for a day or so. They're in a poor way. Some of them have miscarried and there'll be more of those. It'll take its toll on the wool too, and I doubt we'll be joining them with the rams again this season. Thing is, Pearl, he's never done anything like that before. Not in all the years I've worked for him. He's always so careful with the stock. So I was just wondering, you know, if he's all right?'

She hears it and doesn't like it. This is her father he's talking about. *Is he all right? Is he losing it? Are there kangaroos loose in the old top paddock?* But what can she say? Has Pete, too, seen Dobie wandering around in his socks?

'Thank you, Pete,' she says firmly. 'I'll have a word with him. Don't you worry about it. I'm sure everything will be fine.'

'You'll tell him, will you? Why I moved 'em? I wouldn't want to have to explain . . .'

'Of course. Don't worry about it.'

She wants him to go. She wants to hide from his news, from the sight of his worried face. She wants to get back to the view of her roses, and drink and drink until this cloud of encroaching catastrophe dissolves. It's bad. Very bad. We might have had three hundred dead sheep out there. He could die from the shame of it. He's not managing. Oh Christ . . . it's beginning, isn't it? She can feel it, gathering momentum. The slow drift downwards, the slip, the sudden uncontrollable rush, the end.

And then what?

Pete is still talking, still not looking at her.

'Well I do, you know. Worry about it. Got my work cut out here without . . .'

'Without having to babysit my father? I know, Pete. We appreciate what you do. I'll speak to him. We'll . . . we'll sort something out.'

She gets to her feet as he leaves. Sort out what? What's to be done? He can't be left on his own with jobs any more. If Pete left us, she thinks, we'd be lost. How can she tell Dobie that his carelessness almost killed three hundred ewes and their lambs, born and unborn? It's unimaginable. She tries the conversation out in her head. It falters at every turn. She can picture herself telling someone else. Anyone else. Dobie doesn't make mistakes. Not ones that you can pin him down on anyway. We're the ones who make mistakes and are taken to task for them. How can they leave the stock management to him now? How can they not? It's all he has left. She sits down again suddenly and wraps both arms around her body as if she's holding it together, eyes looking inward to a future where nothing can be depended upon except the increasing weight of responsibilities, and where, day by day, she grows older and more alone.

20

Dobie – thinking about his missing boots, his missing pup and his missing hen, with that stupid song ... *I'll come running the four-minute mile* ... going round and round in his head – swings the ute out in a wide curve on to the Coolabarradin road and doesn't see the white station wagon coming at him until he straightens the wheel. By then it's too late to do anything but breathe a word, half obscenity, half prayer.

The oncoming driver hits the horn; the sound screams in Dobie's head as the station wagon swerves sharply, passing him on his left and veering off, wheels skidding in the roadside dirt. The car bounces wildly over the rough ground and pulls up inches from a fence post in a great cloud of dust.

Jesus!

Dobie's in a sweat. Can't believe he's still sitting there at the wheel, not hit. Not dead. If he needed any proof that his number isn't up yet, this has to be it.

He can see the other driver moving but still seated. Probably in shock. Dobie's afraid to confront him.

Never had an accident in all these years of driving. He didn't look. He knows he didn't look. He just pulled out wide, taking up the wrong side of the road. What's happening to him? He gets out of the ute stiffly and hobbles over to the car as quickly as he can. His town boots are pinching his toes; they haven't developed the soft pouches that his workboots had. Thank god there wasn't anyone here to see what happened. If word got around, they could probably take his licence away, at his age. His bowels dissolve at the thought. Shame.

Then he realises – no witnesses. His word against this fellow's. That's good, that is. That's better.

The stranger sees Dobie approach and swings out his legs but stays seated. His face is white but he manages a grin of sorts.

Looks like a bloody hippie type, thinks Dobie suspiciously. With that beard and long hair. Might be one of those homosexuals. His car's packed to the roof. Could be full of that marijuana stuff. Proceed with caution.

'Bit close,' says Dobie.

'It certainly was. You okay?'

'Yup. You?'

'Fine. Bit shaky, that's all. It was a rough landing.'

No accusations then. No anger coming his way. Dobie decides to seize the initiative.

'You were coming down there at a fair clip. Didn't you see me?'

The man looks up at him, surprised, but says nothing.

'You could have caused a nasty accident, driving

like that. You get farm vehicles all along this road, you know. Stock too. You not from round here?'

'No.'

Dobie sniffs the air and smells triumph. They both know what's happened but there isn't going to be any trouble. He can sense this fellow's resignation.

'Well, take a bit more care when you get back on the road, eh? We'll say no more about it.'

The man gives Dobie a brief nod.

Better get out while the going's good, Dobie thinks. He sets off down the road towards his ute then looks around again. 'You'll be all right?'

'Fine,' says the stranger, ducking back into his car and starting the engine. He pulls back on to the roadside and stops again.

Dobie speeds away, wanting as many miles as possible between him and the station wagon. Bloody ridiculous, he thinks, the way some people drive! Shouldn't be allowed on the roads. Shouldn't be allowed behind a wheel. Might have killed him, driving like that.

Thomas, however, can't drive. Not yet. His hands are shaking from his body's chemical reaction to the near miss, his face and neck aflame with the prickly rash. He relives the giddy moment when the steering wheel was wrenched from his hands and he lost control of the car, the rush of anger that rose in response to his fear. Bloody idiot might have killed him, swinging out on to the wrong side of the road like that, and not a word of apology. Acting as though it was all Thomas's fault. How fast had he been going when the old guy pulled out in front of him? Not unusually fast for country roads. If he'd been driving any faster, they'd both be dead. Him and the old one. Too bloody close for comfort, that was.

Thomas had set out after lunch, eager to get the feel of the countryside and to find a likely spot for his field studies. Once out of town, the river runs through farmland for miles and miles as his map had predicted. All private property. He'll need the goodwill of the farmers if he's to set up camp and start work. And that might be tricky.

He gets out of the car to shake the shivers from his legs, and walks towards the driveway that the old man had turned out of. Silence falls upon his shoulders, muffling his agitation, spreading out and around him in seemingly infinite space and sunlight. He breathes in deeply and looks up. Behind him and in front of him, the road runs straight to the horizon without a living soul in sight. Beside the driveway, a rusty oil drum is suspended by chains from a bent steel post, for mail deliveries. A wide straight dirt track with pasture on each side leads up to a thick group of poplar trees, probably shielding the main homestead from the road, he decides, and providing some shade. To the left of them he can see a large roof, silver in the sunshine. Work shed. Wool or machinery. There are some smaller buildings too. An unbroken line of huge old river red gums and black box trees some distance away shows him where the river runs, right through the property.

Thoughts of the river remind him that he is standing here in the dust and the heat without a hat, when he might be moving through dappled shade, searching for still pools and marshes and listening for his frogs. He's about to turn back to the car when a sign burnt into the wooden fence behind the mailbox catches his eye. Mamerbrook Farm.

D. Kinnear, Mamerbrook Farm, Coolabarradin. That's what it said in the phone book! Coolabarradin covers a lot of territory. He grins to himself, feels as though he's been led here. Hell of a way to get him to stop though. He wonders if he should pay a visit to the homestead right now, before the old lunatic comes back. He's sure, now he comes to think of it, that the crazy driver was the same man who'd answered the phone and hung up on him. Same voice. Yes, much better to try his luck at the farm now. He might learn something useful. Who knows, he might even find Alice at home and bring the quest to a triumphant end today?

By the time Dobie gets to Bent Post Paddock, he's almost convinced himself that he's been the victim of a drugged, poofter hippie and lucky to have got away with his life.

'Damn lucky I didn't have the rifle with me,' he mutters to himself as he opens the gate. 'Bloody outrage, it is.' It will make a good story to tell Ted on the next trip to town. *There I was, driving along, minding my own business, when this character comes up in a white car, going like a bat out of hell – on the wrong side of the road, Ted! What can you do?*

He drives the ute through the gate and gets out again to close it because there are three hundred ewes in this paddock. Can't see so much as a wool curl right now, but they're here somewhere. He heads off diagonally across the paddock on old wheel tracks towards a stand of low trees and shrubs. Hmm. Not there, eh? Cutting around slowly over bumpy ground, he veers left and goes to the fence line. Nothing. Coming back around the other side, he traverses the paddock again on the other diagonal. Next, he follows the fence line right around the entire paddock. Then he crosses from mid-point to mid-point at each side. Nothing.

He drives very slowly around the paddock again, starting from the boundary fences and moving in gradually, in ever-decreasing circles. When he reaches dead-centre of the paddock, he gets out of the ute, climbs up into the tray at the back and standing as tall as he can, with his hat pushed back, he turns around slowly, gazing in every direction, scratching his head in disbelief. Where are the bloody sheep?

Pearl clips sharply at a branch of pink oleander that's obscuring the view of the driveway from the house. She misses it and tries again. There's a car approaching. She waits, listening, thinking it will turn off in the direction of Bel's place. She's not expecting anyone. But the car doesn't turn off. She steps in amongst the shrubbery and peers through the leaves. The car moves cautiously along the dirt track, almost comes to a full stop at the cattle grid. A white station wagon with a light icing of brown country dust. She doesn't recognise it. The driver pulls up at the house but Pearl, safe in the leaves, doesn't move.

A man gets out. Tall and lean with sandy hair. No hat. He stretches his arms above his head, looking around at the garden, the paddocks, the big gum trees over by the river, and then he tips his head back as if to receive the sunshine and the sky.

He's not in a rush, at any rate, thinks Pearl.

He goes up to the door and knocks.

He should yell, she thinks. Not knock like that. Tap-tap. Very polite. Very city. This is a farmhouse. He should call out.

She knows there's no one inside the house. She saw Dobie drive off in the ute. The stranger knocks again but she doesn't move, wondering what he'll do next. There's something about that knock. She doesn't like it. He doesn't look as though he's about to ask permission to shoot pig or duck or do a bit of spotlighting with the roos. Not even with the gear she can see piled in the back of the car. Might be after some fishing, but there are better places on the river than this. Why come here? No. Not the fishing then.

The man peers through a window, leaning in close

with a hand cupped at the glass to keep the glare off. Nosy bugger, she thinks. He knocks again. Stands there. Looks around. When he gets back into his car and drives away, she realises she's been frozen to the spot, arms still upraised with the shears. She clips once, twice, and ducks away from the shower of twigs and poisonous pink blossoms. If it was something important, he'll be back. If it was trouble, he'll be back. Sufficient unto the day is the evil thereof, and so on.

21

Dobie's been driving around the farm in a state of increasing anxiety and decreasing hope for quite a while. He's been back to Bent Post Paddock twice because he simply cannot believe that the ewes aren't there, blending into the dusty landscape, still as saltbush on a hot summer day. This time they'll be there, he thinks. This time. This time they'll be there and it will all be right as rain.

Won't it?

Please?

He brought them down just the other day to take advantage of the underlying flush of green that those showers had brought on. Three hundred of them. Did he do it, or did he dream it?

If he did it, where the hell are the ewes?

And if he dreamed it, where the hell are the ewes?

But he didn't dream it. He knows he didn't. He got them down here along the road, by himself, driving the ute very slowly behind them, urging them on, with Blackleg running ahead of him and to the side, keeping them tidy. He remembers. He definitely remembers. So what's going on? There's no break in the fence line. No gates open. He's covered every inch of the paddock, even checking amongst the scrub and the black box trees. Is he going to have to drive around the whole damn farm looking for them? It's not exactly the sort of thing you can ask someone, is it?

'Excuse me, I left three hundred ewes in this paddock and they seem to have gone walkabout. Any idea where they've got to?'

Oh Dobie, Little Bo-peep's got nothing on this one.

Bel is wandering in the back country staying on vehicle tracks where the snakes are easier to spot, and always within cooee of the river and its birds. She likes to walk by the water. Sulphur-crested cockatoos and shrieking corellas, swerving multitudes of pink and grey galahs flash in the hot bright air above her. Something's upsetting them, something other than Bel's quiet steps. The low shrubs and flowers, saplings and lignum, the clumps of white paper daisies are all alive with tiny chattering birds, fairy wrens, diamond-backed finches, thornbills the size of butterflies. Forty feet away from her, deep in the paddock grass, three huge wedge-tailed eagles rise at her approach, one of them trailing strands of gut from the fresh kangaroo carcass on which they'd been feeding. Shocked into stillness, Bel watches as they spiral over her head, higher and higher until they are completely invisible, but she knows they're still up there, still watching her. As soon as she's gone, they'll return. So that's what was upsetting the other birds. Eagles. Coming over the old bridge she hears a duck fly up with a clatter of wings but she doesn't look up in case she trips or puts a foot through one of the gaps between the planks. By the time you've turned your head, the duck's long gone and all you see are the ripples of its wingbeats on the surface of the water. Wild ducks don't take much scaring up. Not in these parts.

Once over the river, she sees Dobie straight away. The ute is parked in the middle of a paddock. He's sitting at the wheel and she can tell from the angle of his head that he's not napping. What's he up to then? She changes her direction so that she moves into his line of vision and waits for him to start up the vehicle and come towards her, but he doesn't. She's close, close enough to lean in at the driver's window and touch his shoulder, when she sees the look on his face.

'Get that inside you,' Bel says, handing Dobie a cup of strong sweet tea. They are sitting in her little kitchen, with the black and white gingham curtains blowing at the windows and sunlight falling on the rainbow rag rug on the floor.

'You okay now?'

His eyes settle on her and she sees how long it takes him to process her question.

'Bel,' he says, his hands spread in front of him, palms up, empty of answers, 'I can't find the ewes. The lambing ewes. I don't remember moving them again. I don't think I did. This head of mine!' He knocks on his forehead with a closed fist. 'Do you think we've had sheep rustlers on the property?'

'They're all right,' she says, softly. He thinks he's forgotten that he moved them. He's worried that he's forgotten where he put them. She's so sorry for him, that worse news is to come.

'Pete moved 'em,' she says, and tells him straight how he left the animals with the far gate shut, with no access to water. How Pete's man found them just in time and how they brought them up to Woolshed Paddock, where they could keep an eye on them for a day or two, before moving them back to wider pastures.

'The gate was shut?' he says. 'But, I couldn't have . . . I couldn't have left them there with the gate shut. They need access to the bottom dam. I couldn't have, Bel. You know that.'

He looks at her fiercely, demanding her concurrence, and in his mind he sees again the gate that he checked not half an hour ago, closed.

'They're coming good,' she says. 'No real harm done. They were in good condition to begin with. Another week or so and you won't be able to see any difference.'

He says nothing, doesn't move. He feels her arms go round his stiff old body and for one second he allows himself to accept her comfort before he curls his heart up tight and pushes her away. This is totally inappropriate. Ridiculous. But the tears won't stop running down the side of his nose and dripping off his chin.

'It's the shock of it, that's all,' she says. 'Drink your tea.'

He sips at the hot liquid until his legs feel stronger. The moments tick away under the white wall clock. She's standing, leaning one hip against the cupboards. She won't crowd him now. I have to get out of here, he thinks. She'll be wanting to get the dinner on before Pete comes home. Pete mustn't see him like this.

She leads him to the gate and across the track to the ute, holding his arm. It makes him feel like an invalid, but her arm is a warm and steady thing in this world and he doesn't shake her off.

'Well, thanks, Bel,' he says awkwardly.

'If we can't look out for each other after all these years . . .' she says.

He finds the ewes in the small paddock behind the woolshed, just as she'd told him. It's land that has direct access to the irrigation channel and decent feed, not too rich for them. He gets out and leans on the fence. The ewes look at him reproachfully.

Pete cleans the worst of the dust from himself and waits until they're sitting at the table with dinner in front of them. He can see that something's upset her.

'What is it, Bel?'

She smiles for him, then shrugs. 'Not sure yet.'

Is it the pity that she feels for the old man? Is that what's unsettling her? She feels as though she's been exposed to something dangerous, but she can't see it. Not yet.

'I had to explain to Dobie this afternoon, about the sheep you moved. I expect that's what it is.'

'You explained? I saw Pearl today. She was going to tell him about it. It's not something you should have had to do.' He's irritated that she's had to wear this, for the Kinnears.

'He was just . . . there, when I came by. He seemed so lost. He thought he'd moved them and then forgotten about it. He couldn't find the sheep, Pete.'

Imagine, her eyes are telling him. Imagine how that felt to him. Not knowing what he'd done. Imagine the horror of it.

'Yes, well, it's sad when things get to that stage for an old farmer. No doubt it will happen to me one day. Will you follow me round, Bel, counting my sheep?' He's teasing, trying to lift her spirits, but she frowns.

'Things are going to change around here, Pete.'

'They sure are. I'll need at least one more man, for a start, if I'm to manage the livestock as well as the crops. And I've been thinking. It might not be such a bad thing if Dobie's not interfering so much, sitting in judgement all the time, like he does these days. Could be just the change I need. Might be able to squeeze a bit more money out of them too, what do you think?'

'I wouldn't hold your breath,' she says. A tight-fisted pair, the Kinnears, but that's not why she says it. And then, because she still can't put into words the dark feeling she has, she gives him the plate of lamb chops that she's unable to eat and, standing behind him with her hands on

176

his shoulders, she places a kiss on the bare skin of his head with such tenderness that he understands she is afraid.

Back in his room at The Grebe, Thomas reflects on the day. A non-event at Mamerbrook, if a near-death experience can be called a non-event. He hasn't made any headway with the quest. He still doesn't know if there's any connection with Alice Kinnear but at least he knows where the farm is. And he knows one inhabitant he wouldn't care to run into again. He doesn't need to worry about another cold call though. He posted the letter to Alice Kinnear earlier today. He had to write five versions before he was satisfied that he'd got it right.

Dear Mrs Kinnear,
    You don't know me, but I think you knew my father, Henry Hearne. He was a rose-grower. Many years ago, I think you may have met him, and helped him in some way. I'm sorry to have to tell you that he died earlier this year. I have a gift for you, from him. He said to tell you that it was for the budwood, though whether that will mean anything to you after all this time, I cannot say. Would you permit me to visit you? I am staying in the area and you can reach me anytime on my mobile phone . . .
    With kind regards,
    Thomas Hearne

That covered it nicely. All he has to do now, is wait.

Bel was right. The ewes will pull through. They may lose some more of their lambs and the wool will be stressed, poor quality and breaking easily, but the sheep will recover. But that gate? Dobie cannot bring himself to believe that he left the gate shut. Yet he'd seen the evidence with his own eyes. Why would he shut it? He knew they had to have access to water. He's never in all his life put a farm animal at risk. No. The only possible explanation is that someone else closed it. By mistake? Or something more sinister? Is someone playing games with him? Was it Pete, or one of his men? Either way, Pete is responsible. And the other thing is down to Pete too. The thing he won't ever forget or forgive – those humiliating hours of searching for the sheep. Why hadn't Pete told him that the sheep had been moved? Did they know he was looking for them? Was it a great big joke? But with the memory of himself driving round and round that hundred acre paddock comes the understanding. It was the embarrassment of it. That's why Pete didn't speak up. Not cruelty then, but the treachery of pity.

He'll have to be careful with his timing. Can't do it before the rice is in and those acres of hay have been baled. He's already sold the hay. Got someone coming up in the next week or so to cart it over to Todmorden. It will have to be straight after the baling then, which doesn't leave a lot of time. I'll write up an advertisement for the newspaper tonight, after dinner, he thinks, and I'll get it in the mail tomorrow. He'll have to be discreet, interviewing the applicants. He'll have to talk to Pearl about it. And what a lurch his stomach gives at the thought of that! Well, it's a shame, really it is. He'll miss them too. They've got used to each other's ways. There are bound to be difficulties, being without Bel and Pete, but unthinkable that they should remain here, after this.

22

Pearl has found a heavy round tin of beeswax with lin-
seed oil, in the cupboard where the cleaning materials
crowd and accumulate. It is old. Not like something
you'd find in the shops today. On the faded label is a
kookaburra that looks hand-drawn and watercoloured.
When she removes the tight-fitting lid, thinking to find
the wax dried out and cracked, she smells Sunday school
and Christmas cards and sees herself, seven years old in
white knee socks, shiny black shoes and a red dress with
a border of white puppies. Just a flash, then it's gone.

The wax is still usable. On the table is a pile of soft
white cloths that she's cut from an old sheet. She takes
a cloth, smears it with beeswax and applies it to the
top of the jewellery box, rubbing gently in tiny circles,
nourishing the old marquetry timbers that have been
neglected for so long. Think of Alice, laying out her
treasures in here. Brooches, maybe. A necklace or two?
Earrings for a special occasion? Where are they now?

There are fine cracks and gaps at the joins where
the wood has dried out. Pearl fills them with beeswax,

rubbing and rubbing. She's promised herself that she'll do this once a week, every week, until the lustre is restored. She finishes the top and all around the outside and then opens the box to see if there's any exposed wood. The lining of green felt covers everything except the inside of the lid so she waxes that too.

The felt on the right-hand side is coming away from the top edge of the box. Some of the tiny brass tacks are missing. I can fix that with glue, she thinks. There isn't any. Have to put it on the list. Smoothing the felt into place, she feels the slight outline of something and draws out a little photograph. It's a fading black-and-white shot, barely two inches square, of a thick-set man. He's wearing wide pressed trousers in a pale colour, a light shirt and an open check waistcoat. His shirt-sleeves are rolled back. Looks like he's wearing his Sunday best, but in a relaxed way. His cheekbones are broad and flat in a round face and his hair is fair, flopping onto his forehead, in need of a trim. He's smiling at the person who's taking the picture. Smiling out of another age, at Pearl.

Behind the man is this house. Dobie's house. Pearl's home. Set against the wall of the house, rising on a trellis that no longer exists, is a white climbing rose with masses of clustered white blooms. There's a name on the back of the photograph, but it isn't a man's name. Henry's White Rambler, it says. And then in neat capitals, the word BUDWOOD. Her mother, Alice, has written this. The man is probably incidental, thinks Pearl. Some visitor. Alice has taken a photograph of the rose. And budwood is a way of propagating a rose from softwood cuttings taken in spring or summer. She checks in her rose reference book, the Moody and Harkness *What Rose is That?* It lists over a thousand roses, but not this one. She searches for Henry's White Rambler in the index and then by flicking through the pages, as though that might change things, but it doesn't. The rose isn't there.

She puts the beeswax and the cloths away and tucks the photograph into one of the pages of Alice's rose book, where she is sure it belongs. Leaning down to set the box on the old dressing table, she catches a sideways glimpse of herself in the mirror and sees Alice, leaning, setting the box down, just so. She smiles.

23

Bugger of a mailman's late again. Dobie's been sitting there for forty steaming minutes in the ute, batting flies back through the open window. No point turning round and going back now. Hell, it's three o'clock in the afternoon and the mail's supposed to be here by one. He's got to be here soon.

The last few years, they haven't had much luck with the mail deliveries. There was that woman, Gladys what's-her-name. Built like a mallee bull. Some days, she used to skip your mailbox altogether, newspapers and everything. Once or twice he'd been actually parked by the mailbox, waiting, and still she'd driven straight past. He'd complained; everyone did. Turned out she had a lover, over in Darranoon. Another woman. A lesbian. Imagine. Everyone in town had stories about it, or wanted them. Dobie just wanted his newspapers.

The mailman before this one was a disaster too. Drinking himself closer to oblivion day by day, after his wife left him. Deliveries became sporadic. Often, a week's worth of mail and papers would be jammed into the oil drum all on the same day. When a representative from Australia Post finally tracked down their errant contractor and sacked him, nine bulging sacks of mail were discovered in his house. Seven boxes, full, in the garage. He admitted that he'd destroyed several full sacks when he got too far behind with things. Burned them. It seemed to be the simplest way of dealing with it, he told the horrified young man from regional head-quarters, who told his girlfriend, who told the town.

Sweat dribbles from beneath Dobie's Akubra and he wipes an arm across his face. The moisture is cool on his skin, salty on his lips. He feels completely drained of energy. And that horrid dream last night – a real corker that was. Pearl doing some strange knees-up kind of dance in an enormous pair of boots – but they were his boots, the boots that disappeared. She was keeping time with rifle shots aimed at a group of startled ewes and bloody just-dropped lambs, and the pup's head peered out of a hen's laying-box, cackling like a kookaburra. Dobie shudders at the memory of it. He's desperate for sleep now but too wary to go into his bedroom in the afternoon without the visible excuse of the newspaper. He has to keep his guard up. You never know who's watching. There must be no more slip-ups.

He still hasn't spoken to Pearl about his plans to sack Pete and hire a new operations manager. He wants to. He needs her on side but he can't find the right words. It's clear enough in his mind. Somebody has to pay. It's only right. But she'll be very emotional about it. She'll fly off at him. You need a cool head when Pearl loses her temper. He's thinking maybe he'll break it to her at dinner tonight, when she's had a drink or three. But where's the sweetener for Pearl? How can he balance the scales for this one?

He's written out an advertisement for the local paper. Operations manager, live in. The envelope's right there on the dashboard, waiting for the mailman. He can't look at it squarely, the enormity of what he's planning. But he sees that poor creature – *not Dobie Kinnear, it couldn't be!* – crying like a baby in Bel's arms and he knows he won't be whole again until they go.

His eyes are fixed on the straight strip of road. A wobbling dark shape emerges from the waves of heat, gradually defining itself as the mailman's black Pajero. Dobie has parked so that they can make a pass, driver to driver, through the windows, mail in, mail out.

'G'day, Dobie.'

'Hugh.'

'Fair sort of day.'

'Warmish.'

Dobie receives the mail and newspapers through his window and picks up the envelope addressed to the newspaper. Fear rises inside him with an irresistible pressure, until he thinks it must be visible in his eyes and he hides them in the shadow of his hat brim. There's a moment, a split second, when he can still withdraw the envelope, succumb to the kicks and tricks of the world, but then it's gone. Sweat runs down his face and his heart knocks hard against the wall of his chest as though it's trying to tell him something.

(It is.)

'Better get on. Bit behind today.'

Hugh touches a finger to his Akubra and with a spin of wheels on the gravel he's off to the next farm. Dobie turns the ute around and takes it back to the house, trying to keep his mind focused on the day's newspaper and his bed, but his brain is worm-ridden, seething and niggling. God, it's hot. A man needs to make up his mind and get on with things. A man needs to get some rest.

He parks the ute and walks slowly across the lawn towards the house with the newspapers tucked under his arm. *The Australian*'s here, and the *Coola Standard*. He flicks through the mail, noticing that his hands are trembling badly. He's dizzy too. Fear tightens his throat, thin and acid, like a thread of vomit. Probably wasn't all that smart sitting in the hot truck for the best part of an hour. Here's the electricity bill. And a bill from Rural Supplies. A statement from Coola Cellars. That'll be a big one no doubt. Unless Pearl's been sticking the contents of her cardboard boxes on her credit card as well. Murray Irrigation. That'll be the water figures. Fertiliser pamphlets. A Harvey Norman brochure . . . and suddenly he stops, right there in the middle of the lawn, so that Blackleg, running with nose to Dobie's heels, has to make a quick sidestep. It's a plain white envelope. Blue ballpoint. Precisely formed handwriting. But the address. It's addressed to Mrs Alice Kinnear. There's no sender's address on the other side. He squints at the postmark. It's local. How can that be? Everyone around here knows that Alice . . . that Alice . . .

The shock of it comes upon him like a slow wave rising, towering, curling through him, all green and curving tension, an imminence of white water. It roars in his ears. It fills his eyes so that all he can see are the tumbling spectres of memory, and all he can feel is the dead weight of it, pressing down on his heart.

24

Thomas is at last making some headway, frogs-wise. He's got permission to camp, from a farm close to Mamerbrook. It took some doing. They're a cautious lot round here. Less suspicious if you have a gun, but Thomas couldn't show them one. He produced his CSIRO credentials.

'You one of those greenies, are you?' The voice was friendly, the eyes less so.

Thomas reassured them that he wasn't a greenie, in that sense. He just wanted to count frogs for a report he was putting together. He might have gone on, in his eagerness, to tell them about the endangered Southern Bell Frog but it was as well that he didn't. The word 'endangered' doesn't sit too well with these people, unless it applies to themselves. As it was, they interrupted him, father and son in unison.

'Frogs?' they'd said. Incredulous.

'Frogs, eh?' said the son with a smirk. 'Plenty of those around here.'

'What about Aboriginal remains?' asked the father. 'You interested in those, are you?'

'Not in the slightest,' said Thomas. 'Just frogs.'

'But if you do happen to come across, say, one of them mounds, like? One of the big oven mounds they used to make thousands of years ago, down by the river. Or a canoe tree, where they cut into the bark of a big river gum. You know what they look like? You'd be sure to tell someone about that, wouldn't you?'

The questions had a curious undertone.

'Oh, I'm sure I won't see any of those,' said Thomas, very definitely. 'Don't have a clue about that sort of stuff.'

'And are you interested in birds, as well as frogs?' It was the son.

'Well, I . . .'

'Birds like that Plains Wanderer, say. Lot of people get excited about that one. It's very rare. Bet you'd like to see one of those, wouldn't you? Be a lucky farmer that found those Wanderers nesting on his property.'

But Thomas had done his reading. He had their measure now.

'Wouldn't know one if it flew up and hit me on the nose,' he assured them.

'They don't fly that high,' said the son, and caught a slashing nudge from his father's elbow.

'I'm strictly a frog man,' said Thomas. 'Don't know a thing about birds.'

They looked at each other, father and son.

'Will we get a mention then? In your book?' asked the father.

'An acknowledgement in the report? Would you like that?'

The father hesitated, sensing a rare moment of fame. It was the son who answered.

'No,' he said firmly. 'Best not.'

So Thomas promised in accordance with all of their requirements, spoken and unspoken, and they gave him the boundary details and permission, at his own risk, to camp on the land.

'Take care now,' said the son. 'If we find you with a broken leg or something, we'll bring out the dozer and finish the job properly. No one will ever find you out there. Haven't the time for insurance claims and liability and all that.'

He's joking, Thomas told himself.

The spot where he decides to set up camp is not far from the Kinnear farm. The river is fine here, not very wide but a slow steady flow with plenty of evidence of old changes in its course that have resulted in areas of swamp and lagoons. He's seen three snakes already, one tiger snake and two red-bellied black snakes. Both big frog eaters. This will be a good area for research.

And why so close to Mamerbrook? He's rung, he's visited, he's been driven off the road and almost killed, but he still hasn't made satisfactory contact with anyone there. He has a feeling about the place. It might just be the roses. There were roses everywhere, clustered around the homestead. Might as well hang around for a while, get on with his fieldwork and see what happens.

Will Alice ring him when she gets his letter? Is she here at Mamerbrook? Or somewhere else? Or nowhere at all? Would she even remember Henry after all these years? Had he been important to her, or merely a passing visitor? It's possible, thinks Thomas, that Alice Kinnear won't have the faintest idea who Henry Hearne is.

Was.

Would it be a fair thing, then, to give her the rose? Wouldn't it be better, in that case, for the rose to go to Robert and Mel? And what would Henry think of that? His father is trusting him to do this thing. Him. Sir Wait-a-while. Not Robert. It could have been Robert. Why wasn't it Robert? Because Robert wants the rose? Or did Henry think it would be easier for Thomas to get away, unencumbered by children? Was that it? It doesn't feel so simple.

(It never is.)

He finds a glade with no overhead branches that might come crashing down on him when the wind blows up, but the ground frustrates him. The clay has baked so hard that he can't drive the tent pegs in. He looks around for any rocks that he might use either as a hammer or just to stabilise the tent. Poor Thomas, there isn't a rock within fifty miles of this place. He has to make do with ropes. After a couple of tries, he gets the double half hitch knot right and secures the tent on long lines between tree trunks. It's not the best job but it will have to do. He's worked up a sweat, getting this done, and here he is, right next to a river. Perfect.

He looks down into the brown water flecked with blue sky, silvered trunks and grey-green leaves, as the sprawling river red gums are reflected from the banks. The river is slow and lazy. He scans the surface thinking of all the fish, turtles, eels, yabbies, grubs, all the teeming invisible life, but this isn't just idle contemplation; he's also looking for snakes. A snake in water can move much faster than a human being. He's not going for a dip if the water is full of tiger snakes. He crouches close, looking for signs, head tilted to one side to cut the reflections.

Between the river gums, the banks are a chaos of fallen trees half in the water. There are broken boughs and strewn branches. Growing up through them are saplings with slender trunks and round, blue-green leaves. Lignum is pervasive and everything is adorned with dangling bark strips and downy white curling feathers. He was lucky to find such a good spot for the tent. High above him in the gum trees, unseen by Thomas, hundreds of sulphur-crested cockatoos perch still as blossoms, waiting for something interesting to happen. It would be a mistake to take peace for granted here. It would be a mistake to take anything at face value.

There's a bit of a beach on his side of the river but on the other side of the curve the water is deep and cool and the bank is steep. He splashes around here for a while in the shadow of the big gums, kicking up enough white water to keep snakes away. You can't really strike out and swim any distance because of the snags, all the fallen trees and branches. Floating, keeping himself in position with one arm hooked around a branch, watching the play of sunlight on the ripples and the reflected sky, he is suddenly, deeply happy. Think of all the frogs he will find here! The detailed notes he will make. He's fifty-one years old, still single, and the only thought on his mind when happiness comes tapping, is frogs; the only dream he still holds dear, is that the world will leave him alone.

But Henry won't.

Thomas sees the two willie wagtails first, his eye drawn by their flickering dance, a sharpness of black and white in a low tree at the water's edge. It isn't until the other bird moves that he understands the cause of their agitation. A small owl, disturbed in its roost. Dark rings around its eyes, like spectacles. A mopoke. The owl swivels its head but otherwise makes no move to avoid the wagtails' harassment. Then, as he watches, it swoops from the tree. A single heavy wingflap, a low curving flight taking it over the water and out of his perspective. He is left with an image of broad, brown-grey mottled wings – the solid reality of it against pale silver tree trunks and sky-shining water. Owl. Symbol of death, symbol of wisdom. He closes his eyes, lulled by the movement of water against his body and the sounds and scents of the bush all around him. It's a physical shock to him, bringing him upright, wide-eyed and gasping in the river, when over his head the cockatoos take flight with a sound like a great wave crashing.

25

It's Pearl who finds Dobie sprawled on the grass.

She runs across the lawn to him, shrieking, 'Dad! Dad!'

Quivering with shameful excitement. She can see herself. Heavy legs thudding one after another, arms ridiculously outstretched in front of her as though she's running to greet him, or catch him.

So this is what it feels like.

She drops to her knees by the body.

It's happening. This is it.

'Dad?' she says tentatively.

He's pale as a corpse but he's still breathing. She can hear it, like a little snore on the inhale. He's fallen awkwardly. You aren't supposed to move them, are you? But she can't leave him here like this. She looks around wildly, as though a solution may be found in amongst the white cedar trees, or over by the chookhouse. There's only the wheelbarrow. It's not big enough.

'Get away from there! Stupid dog!'

It's Blackleg, who's progressed from licking Dobie's curled and empty hand, to licking his ear.

I should get an ambulance, she thinks. And keep him warm or something. He looks so small, so innocent, lying there with his hat knocked off, and one leg of his trousers rucked up by the fall, so that anyone can see he's got odd socks on. Is he all right, lying on his back like that? Shouldn't he be on his side? I must go and get help.

But she discovers that she's quite unable to let go of his hand.

Bel has heard Pearl's cries and guessed their urgency, understanding at last how she's been waiting for something like this to happen. Catastrophe. She has already alerted her husband by radio.

'Pete'll be here in a minute,' she tells Pearl. 'We can get your dad inside and make him comfortable. Did you see what happened? Is it his heart?'

Pearl looks at her, hearing a rush of words but unable to push a response through her mind.

Bel gives her a brief hug. 'He'll be all right, Pearl. He's a tough old bird. I'll get the ambulance, shall I? You stay with him.'

She goes into the house to make the call, and when Pete arrives the three of them stagger inside carrying Dobie, who is no lightweight.

'We shouldn't jolt him around too much. Better put him down right here on the floor,' Pete says.

'I was wondering if we shouldn't put him in one of the cars and go to meet the ambulance?' Bel asks him.

He's on his knees, two fingers pressing the side of Dobie's neck.

'No, I don't think so. His pulse is weak but it's regular enough, and his breathing seems steady. I think we should wait.'

Pearl slips a cushion under Dobie's head and covers him with a blanket of crocheted wool squares, even though the day is warm and sunlight is pouring though the windows.

'You have to keep them warm,' she mutters to herself.

Bel throws a glance at Pete, who nods, takes down an old jacket from the back of the door and drapes it around Pearl's shoulders.

Pearl doesn't notice.

They wait.

And wait.

In the darkness behind his eyelids, his brain swollen with water, his chest heaving with it, his ears and eyes bursting with it, his nose and mouth streaming with it, Dobie hears someone hum a few bars of a tune. *Oh, I can't see the roos for the roses . . .* and then the humming ceases abruptly, mid-line. Who was humming? He must know who was humming. He can't remember why this is so important. He hears the clink of mugs being set down on the table. They're having a cup of tea. Nice for them! He stirs suddenly but he can't open his eyes. He gives a feeble groan.

'Wonder what it was that brought him down,' says Bel.

He hears her. It was the water, he tries to tell her. The water! He's been caught and rolled by the wave, and dumped, blind and spewing, heaving for breath, but he can't make anyone understand this.

'What do you think he's saying?' It's Pearl now, leaning over him.

'It's the water!' he croaks, coughing up phlegm.

This time, they all hear him.

'The water?' asks Bel.

'Oh my god, it's those sheep. Leaving the sheep without water. I knew it. It's broken his heart.' Pearl sets down her mug and kneels at his side, stroking his forehead.

Sheep?

Two ambulance men arrive in a great flurry and test Dobie's vital signs. He's still present, fighting the darkness and the water that fills him, but unable to rise above it into full consciousness. They lift him onto a stretcher.

'Hold on a minute,' says Pearl. 'I'm going with him. I'll just get my bag.'

Hold on a minute? I'm dying here, Pearl.

'Follow us in your own car,' says the paramedic. 'Get some things together for him. Pyjamas and so on. He'll be fine with us.'

'I'll drive you in, Pearl,' says Bel, 'in case the shock, you know . . .'

Pearl's still operating with a split-level brain, watching herself demur even as she accepts the sensible offer of assistance.

So Dobie is tucked away in the back of the ambulance, and Bel and Pearl pack a bag of necessities for him and follow in Pearl's car. Pete goes back to work leaving the cushion and blanket still on the floor and the mugs on the table. After all the commotion, the farmhouse is empty.

The mail – newspapers, bills, advertising brochures, and the handwritten letter to Alice Kinnear – lies forgotten on the grass. The letter is sniffed at and spurned by Blackleg, criss-crossed by ants, bleached and stiffened by the late-afternoon sun and made finally, irrevocably illegible by a persisting shower of rain that night. Later, Pearl will gather it all up, toss the newspapers and brochures into the bin and prop up the rest of the soggy bundle against the accounts shoe box to dry out.

When Dobie comes back to himself, he has no memory of the letter, or the great wave that rolled him and dumped him in his own backyard, the oldest and loneliest surfer in the world.

26

Dobie is sitting in a little hut at a workbench piled with old, worn shoes. There are navy-blue ones and brown, black ones, cream, red, tan and white. They are all women's shoes. Lace-ups and court shoes, sling-backs with pointed toes and stiletto heels, tooled leather sandals and flat slip-ons, all moulded intimately by the feet of women. A great jumble of shoes reaching halfway up the dusty, cobwebbed window. He's wearing a thick leather apron with metal tools in the wide front pocket. He can feel the comfortable weight of these in his lap. He really looks the part, he knows, but he hasn't a clue what he's doing here.

He picks up a fine, red leather sandal with a broken heel. It's the same sandal that his hitchhiker held out to him that day on the road to Swan Hill. How hard can it be to repair shoes? The mystery of it is at the forefront of his mind; the knowledge lies behind it, definite and inaccessible. He presses the wrenched heel against the sole and dreams the ankle that rises from it, the mouth-watering swell of a shapely leg. An indistinct shape looms at the thick glass of the little window and moves past. Someone's coming to the door.

Dobie's mother, plain and gentle, brown-eyed Hannah Dobie, who died when he was only six years old (six years old!) pops her head round the door of the hut and asks him how long he'll be, fixing her sandal. It's the one he's holding. The red one.

'Oh, it won't be ready today,' he says, knowing suddenly that he can have it done in an hour, good as new. But as soon as her sandal is fixed, she'll go. She'll leave him again. She cannot leave until he mends it.

Hurry up, Dobie. I've been waiting such a long time. Hurry . . .

'Come on, now. I need to take that reading.'

It's the nurse, wanting to take his temperature again. Dobie, fighting to stay asleep, shakes her hand off, keeping his eyes closed. He wants to remain inside the hut for a few minutes longer. He's striving to imprint the features of his mother's face on his memory, but it fades, like it always does. He only ever sees her in his dreams.

'How are we today?' says the nurse, persisting. She sticks a thermometer into his mouth and pegs a white clip to the end of his index finger.

So many gadgets. They don't explain anything.

'Sick,' he says, with his eyes still closed.

'Tell me about it. Twelve hours, I was, when I had my hysterectomy. Twelve hours of vomiting. Sick? Do I know sick. They gave me everything they had, all the anti-nausea drugs, and nothing worked. There wasn't a shred of anything left in my stomach. You know what that feels like? Throwing up for twelve hours on an empty stomach? Don't tell me about sick.'

He's so surprised that he opens his eyes.

'Bedpan?' she asks.

'No, thank you,' he mumbles past the thermometer. Christ! Everyone in the building can hear her. How could anyone use a bedpan after that? He's managing without them. Tottering down the draughty corridor, wheeling his drip. What's in this drip anyway? Glucose? Saline? Drugs? Who knows? He's not going to ask. He's not going to complain. He's just going to do what he's told and smile and smile. What else can you do in here? The power they have.

He watches her. From the shape of her body and the way she moves, he'd guess she's around fifty, but her face is older, heavily lined under the make-up. Dyed hair, the colour of rust. She's slender, with quick hands and a quiet ferocity. *Don't even think about it!* her eyes flash, before anyone has a chance to draw breath. *Don't even think about giving me trouble.* Her lips are pursed, guarded, and look like they've been that way for a long time. A smile now and again wouldn't hurt, he thinks.

Pearlie's coming this afternoon. He's pretty sure it will be this afternoon. She's promised to come every second day, if she can. She's the only visitor he's had. Not that she adds much to the experience. She'd fallen asleep in the chair beside his bed. He studied her as she sat there, fat and rumpled, a light sheen of sweat on her face. She gave

201

a rumbling snore and her head bounced up and drooped again. She's really letting herself go, he thought, banishing a brief spasm of guilt. What has he to feel guilty about? He watched for a while to see if she'd open her eyes, but couldn't bring himself to wake her and soon fell asleep again himself. When he woke, she was gone. He's pretty sure that wasn't yesterday, so she must be coming in today.

He's been in here for almost a week and they still haven't managed to work out what caused his collapse. They're running tests and awaiting results. So they say. Nothing to panic about at this stage, the doctor told him.

At this stage? thought Dobie. What does he mean, at this stage?

They don't always tell you, do they? And they don't always know. You'd think they'd know, with all these beeps and buzzers and flashing lights, but they don't. To tell the truth, he feels better than he has in ages but that's no guarantee of anything. His dream comes back to him, with the yeasty sweat of old shoe leather. That big leather apron he was wearing. And his mother, bless her, saying, *Hurry up, Dobie . . .*

Somehow, it doesn't sound so comforting now. What else did she say?

I've been waiting such a long time.

The hairs go up on his arms. It doesn't sound as though she was talking about the red sandal. It sounds like she's expecting him. Perhaps he's sicker than he feels? They don't tell you. It's enough to put the fear of God into anyone. The nurse is checking the contents of the drip. Frowning, she makes an adjustment to a valve, then writes something onto the chart at the foot of his bed.

What is it? Am I getting worse? Can I be dying and feel like this?

Should I ask her?

Dying? Tell me about it. Twelve hours I was, dying. They gave me everything they had but it didn't do any good . . .

Maybe not.

Later that day, another elderly man is admitted to his ward. There is a suitcase. Is he planning on a long stay? Dobie lies listening as the man unpacks, opening and closing the drawers. He hears him put on his pyjamas and climb into the bed next to Dobie's with the curtains drawn but the nurse swishes them back when she checks in on them both a few minutes later.

When they are alone again, Dobie looks over, cautiously. The man gives him a brief nod, then leans towards him, speaking in a hoarse whisper.

'I think I've got perforated intestines. Rotting from the inside out, I am. Not long for this world.'

'That right?' says Dobie, with an unmistakeable lack of interest, and hides himself in the newspaper.

It is quite by chance that he notices his advertisement in the Classifieds. 'Operations Manager – Live In.' So his letter made the deadline! It looks good. Very professional. That should bring some quick results, he thinks, well pleased with himself.

27

Pearl's going to enjoy some peace before they let Dobie out. And she's decided to develop a get-fit program, having frightened herself half to death yesterday when she realised that she had just poured vodka into her breakfast mug and drunk it with her cereal. She never feels good in the mornings – it takes her a long time to come back to her body after sleeping. It was the fact that she felt so optimistic, so cheerful over the cornflakes, that made her see what she'd done. No vodka before tea-time, she's vowed, seeing spectres of herself, fat and fifty with grey straggly hair, blood-shot eyes and a permanent hangover. It's up to you Pearl, she tells herself. Who else is going to save her? But she's jumpy as hell and no matter what she does or where she turns, there is the vodka bottle. I can do it, you bastard, she tells the bottle.

She puts the washing out on the line and works amongst her roses for a couple of hours. Now, she thinks, a cup of tea, a cheese and ham sandwich, a piece of Sara Lee chocolate cake and an hour or so of sitting in the garden with Alice's rose book.

She settles in her garden chair between the sun-warmed wall and the first curving flush of roses, delighted that so many of the ones she's planted here are named on these old lists in her mother's scrapbook. A slight breeze carries the scent of roses. The rose beds fan out in alternating and overlapping curves, set at a comfortable width for the ride-on mower to pass through. There is no direct path to Pearl's door. To reach it, you must meander a little.

On one of the pages, she finds a design that Alice had drawn up – a garden bed intended for the front of the French windows in Pearl's bedroom. No rose bed grows there now. In the design, Alice has included two roses of the same variety – both climbers. Why, thinks Pearl, would you put climbers directly in front of French windows that offer a view right to the horizon? You could run them up the wall and frame the windows very prettily, but that isn't how Alice has drawn it. Pearl knows that rose. Emily Gray. A brilliant yellow with semi-double blooms. It's gorgeous, but would easily grow to fifteen feet or so. Alice would have needed a lattice to put them there. Why would she do that?

Pearl wonders if her mother had begun to feel safer behind screens and walls. It happens to some people. One minute, they're fine, and the next, they can't take the space any more, the far-seeing, the dangerous weight of all that sky. So they move to town, to snug brick houses where they grow tomatoes in little gardens behind high fences. Outwardly, they might seem comforted by these narrow parameters, even happy, but watch them. They hunch against the light; they cannot look up. And if you cannot look up, you are lost indeed, and without land-marks. And the sky goes with you anyway, inside your head, wherever you go.

You're thinking about what it would be like to leave Mamerbrook, aren't you, Pearl?

She wants to leave; she can't leave. She wants to stay; she can't stay. It's been that way for almost as long as she can remember.

She tries to concentrate on the page of roses. Alice's design is dated with the year of Pearl's birth. Pearl pic-tures her mother there, hands firming the soil around the new plants, her baby girl in a netted bassinet at her side and life, all the generous days, stretching endlessly before them. The vodka need bubbles up again. She banishes it.

There's no sign in the garden that Alice's rose bed ever existed by those windows and Pearl has no mem-ory of it at all. She follows the sequence of roses with her fingers, seeing with her mind's eye their colours and shapes. Honorine de Brabant. Oh, that's a lovely old rose – pale pink with a delicate purple stripe. Pearl's had no luck with it here. Then Emily Gray, the climber. Nuits de Young, with those lovely dark maroon petals and Rosa Mundi. Next to them is Yolande d'Aragon and then Souvenir de la Malmaison. Alice had drawn in a pathway at the spot where the French windows open, and the next rose is Peace. Always so reliable, thinks

Pearl, who grows several of them. Then comes Emily Gray, the climber, again. Then Amelia. She doesn't know that one. Then Reine des Violettes – Pearl has lost two of these beauties in the hot, dry summers. Finally there is Louise Odier, rose-pink with a hint of lilac, according to her mother's pencilled note.

So what's the colour scheme? Pink/purple, yellow, dark maroon, pink/white, pink, pale pink, yellow/pink, yellow, pink, red/violet, pink/lilac. Not really a harmonious mixture. Perhaps it worked when you saw them all together. Festive? According to the notes, some are fragrant; some are not. Pearl feels a faint stirring of irritation. She tries, but can't quite shake the irreverent thought that it would have looked a bit of a mess, really. It's not what she would have chosen for a plot outside her bedroom window. Just as well that Alice's plans didn't bear fruit in this case, she thinks, and stretches lazily. Closing her eyes, she breathes in deeply the fragrance of her own roses and happiness, a sweet bliss, strokes her cheek, kisses her brow and blows away.

She wakes a little later with the vodka bottle humming inside her head. I'll go for a long walk, she thinks. The first few days will be the worst. And I only have to make it to six o'clock. That's all. Not long.

Passing the manager's cottage, she can see Bel bent double in the vegetable garden and calls out to her cheerfully. Their help, when Dobie collapsed, really brought it home to her how much she needs them. And how much she takes them for granted. How would she have coped if they hadn't been here? She hadn't even had to ask. They were on the scene immediately, doing everything that was needed. Caring for Dobie, caring for herself in the way (she hesitates over the word) *friends* would help. Certainly, their actions were above and beyond the call of duty, as Dobie would say. They'll have to think of an appropriate way to thank them both. Not a pay rise though. The mere thought of that would be enough to put Dobie back in hospital again.

Bel straightens when she hears Pearl's voice. Pearl half-turns towards the gate, prepared for a little chat, but something about Bel's face and the tension in her stance warns her off. Correcting her course, she carries on past the cottage down to the bridge. Bel hadn't spoken. She didn't ask how Dobie is getting on. Didn't even say hello. Just that unwavering black stare. It's enough to give you the willies. Pearl shudders. What's wrong with the woman? Perhaps she's had a row with her beloved Irishman, she thinks, and finds a great deal of satisfaction in the thought. But Bel's gaze chills a spot between her shoulder blades and Pearl quickens her pace.

Dobie will be coming home soon. It's nothing serious, they said. Bit of a short circuit, they think. Whatever that means. They've told her he'll be just the same as he was before it happened. That's one of the things she's afraid of. The other thing is that he won't be. He'll be worse. And then what?

One foot after the other, Pearl. One foot after the other. Just keep moving and don't look too far ahead and the world will hold together. Keep your eyes down. If you look up now, you'll be able to see where you're heading, and you don't want to do that, Pearl, do you? No surprises there.

But looking up one time, she sees, with a dreamy sense of wonder, the paddock shining like a lake before her, where the heat haze has turned the dry grasses to silver. Her feet veer onto a trail that seems as though it might head in that direction but the lake neither changes, nor comes within reach.

Passing beneath a black box tree, she registers with part of her mind the fallen branches, piles of dead wood. Snake hidey-holes. She crackles through twigs. Her eyes continually scan the ground for any sudden movement, for a stirring or a quick slithering, for the stick that grows scales and takes on breath, blood, and venom.

Pearl, it's not the snake you see that you have to worry about; it's the snake you don't.

The bite comes straight through the thin cotton of her trousers. For a second, she thinks she's caught her leg on the jagged end of a twig but then she's confronted with the rearing, hissing head, neck flattened and spread in cobra-style outrage.

Not a twig then, she thinks, freezing on the spot.

Full realisation trickles down her spine and panic begins to beat wild wings against the dumb cage of her body. No. Not a twig.

Pearl stands as still as the tree. The snake departs.

Think, Pearl, think.

She's doing her best but there's not a soul in sight. With Dobie in hospital, there's no one at the homestead to raise the alarm when she doesn't come home and here she is with a tiger-snake bite low on her calf. It has to be said – things aren't looking too good. Will Bel notice if the lights don't go on at the homestead tonight? Will she wonder where I am? Will she knock to see if I'm all right? Will she send Pete out to look for me? It's a chance, she thinks. A slim one, but it's a chance. How long till dark?

Too long, Pearl.

She takes the opposite direction to the snake, very, very slowly, each movement made with minimal effort. She's heading for the vehicle track.

You have a little time, Pearl.

You'd have more if you'd carried a snake bandage.

Movement pushes the venom around the lymph system. She must move as little as possible. She looks at the vehicle track over by the river. She can make it that far, but could she go further? It would be the shortest way back to a house, a telephone. Should she risk it? No. She wouldn't make it. It's too far. And the effort would wipe out any chance she has. Get to the track, girl. Do what you know you have to do. Before she leaves the shade of the tree, she picks up four long, thin sticks.

Out here on the vehicle track, she's in full sun, but at least she will be visible, if there's anyone to see. Her leg is beginning to tingle and her toes feel cold. Is it imagination? How quickly does the body respond to the toxin?

She unfastens her trousers and steps out of them. Lowering herself to the dusty earth of the track, she winds them in a clumsy bandage up the leg from the snake bite to her thigh. She fastens it with her belt, firmly but not too tightly. She's concentrating hard. Sweat breaks out on her forehead and runs into her eyes, stinging. She takes off her shirt and spreads it over the other leg to keep the sun off her skin. Her red T-shirt will protect the upper body to some extent. Sunburn is the least of her problems but she's trying to give herself the best chance she can. You can't just give up.

Breaking up the sticks she collected, she lays out the word TIGER on the flat track. If anyone does happen to come along and find her, they'll know immediately what the problem is. Or was. She wonders how long she's got. Reactions to tiger-snake bites are highly individual, she knows. She's already dehydrated from last night's alcohol. There's an inch, no more, left in her water bottle. She drains it and lies down, pulling her hat over her face and hearing Dobie's words from a long time ago.

'If a tiger snake gets you and you can't reach help, lie down and keep still. After four hours you'll gradually begin to recover your strength. Or you'll be dead. Either way, you'll be through the worst of it.'

Not funny now, is it?

Tears prickle behind her eyelids. Can she weep the poison away? Waves of nausea roll over her. She feels clammy, and she's shivering a little. Stay calm, Pearl. Keep still. There's a thick cold rolling and curdling of her stomach and bowels. Is it fear, or venom? From somewhere over by the river comes the sound of a kookaburra's echoing hysterics.

She discovers that she cannot move. She cannot even will a movement of her little finger. Consciousness has retracted to a pinpoint, a space of quiet astonishment in a body without boundaries.

Someone is whispering.

Don't let me die, oh don't let me die, oh please, don't let me die . . .

Who is that, pleading?

I cannot open my eyes, she thinks.

Over and over again, the dry whispers come, like a breeze through sorghum.

Danger. Everywhere. They will never find me here. See! Nothing. My face is fractured clay, my hair a pale tangle of sun-bleached grasses. The tumbled mounds of my body are blown tussocks of saltbush shrouded in dust. My limbs are dead wood, lying this way and that, making shadows for sleek death dealers. They will not find me; I am part of the plains. I am already gone.

A copper-tailed skink moves swiftly, delicately, over her discarded boot. It disappears beneath the battered leather tongue, emerges from the laces and is lost again. The sun moves on. Flies drone and crawl upon her but she is not there. A roaring fills her ears; the wind of it brushes unbearably over her body and through it comes a rush of whispers and the faint scent of onions.

28

Bel puts the plate down in front of Pete, saying nothing. What can she say? It's as if they've both been struck dumb. As if they are moving inside separate, sealed clouds of misery. The ticking of the clock is abnormally loud. The repeated cawing of a crow startles her and she looks round, expecting to see it inside the room. Ah, the marrow-deep sadness in the bird's call. She's tempted to go outside and frighten the creature away; the noise is plucking at her fear, stirring up a terrible grief and anger. What is Pete going to do?

To see it in the newspaper like that. His job advertised. After all these years. She can't think straight; doesn't know how best to help him. And the children. They'll have to be told. It's like a crazy dream. Could it all be a mistake? Sometimes her imaginings veer in this direction and everyone is laughing and apologising and the world rights itself. But in reality she knows it wouldn't make any difference now. Mistake or not, he'll not forget it. Nothing will ever be the same.

He won't talk to her. Hasn't said a word since she gave

a little cry and passed the local paper to him with shaking hands. Not one word. I must call Daniel, she thinks. And Sara. They'll be able to reach him. They'll be able to separate him from this anger tearing at him from inside his own belly. The children must come home.

Home?

And that damn woman, Pearl, calling out 'hello' as though nothing is wrong. She must know. Even he wouldn't do something like this without telling his daughter.

How could they do it?

And why?

Once again all coherent thought stops here and a wave of darkness descends like a spread eagle over entrails. It's all torn. Torn beyond repair.

Pete eats his lunch. She can eat nothing. He pushes his plate away and goes out. She hears the door slam, the ute engine start up. He'll go into town, to the pub. The farmhands will take off, drift away, one after another. It will be a slack afternoon for them. Have they heard? Are they wondering? She can see, as if she's there, all the eager faces over coffee mugs, tea cups, beer glasses, all over town. All the hungry ears. Have you heard? The passing of the word. The telling of the story. But they won't ask Pete. They'll wait, as she is waiting, for him to speak first. And today, because of this, he will put his life and the lives of others on the line, driving home god knows when, drunk on beer and fury.

Home?

214

For how long?

The floor dips, sways and dips again beneath her feet as though the earth itself is heaving in outrage. She grasps at the table to keep herself upright. And then this woman, who has moved from task to task all her life, looks around her home and can't think of what to do next, where to set foot, what to turn her hand to. What does it matter, now?

It's the first time since they were married that he's left the house without kissing her.

29

When Pearl comes to, she is in a hospital bed connected to a drip and experiencing the most dreadful headache of her life. And that's saying something. There is an angry octopus in full battle armour banging around inside her skull, trying to get out.

'No,' she croaks aloud, as another tentacle slams into the back of her eyeball. And another. Oh god.

Waves of nausea wash over her leaving little tears at the corners of her eyes. Her mouth is dry, her throat constricted. Why has she been left here on her own? What happens if she throws up?

Oh-oh, don't think about that, Pearl.

When the nausea subsides for a moment, she locates a buzzer by her bedside and presses it. Someone must know what's going on.

A young woman in pale blue overalls comes in and examines the chart at the end of her bed. She takes Pearl's temperature and checks her heart rate.

'Headache?' she murmurs sympathetically.

'Yes,' says Pearl, but it comes out as a groan, not a word.

'I'll get you something for that. You're all right, you know.'

All right? This is all right? Dying seems a sweet option.

'Very lucky, you are. Some people don't rally so well after a tiger-snake bite. Some people don't rally at all. You've been blessed with a strong constitution. We'll keep you in here overnight to get your fluids up and help your kidneys get over the shock but you'll be right as rain by tomorrow.'

She stops what she's doing and looks into Pearl's doubting eyes.

'I promise, you will. Now, there's a gentleman waiting outside. He's very keen to know how you are. Would you like to see him for just a moment? Wouldn't that cheer you up?'

Another groan from Pearl. It's her father. Who else? What are the odds? Two Kinnears in a country hospital at the same time. They'll probably write it up in the local rag. Photos, anyone? Smile please. She gives a ferocious grimace.

'I'll tell him to come back later, shall I?' says the nurse hastily. 'When you're feeling better.'

Pearl beckons the nurse. The octopus protests vigorously. The young woman bends close to hear Pearl's whisper.

'I . . . think sssnakes . . . should be . . . like bees . . . and die . . . after they get you.'

Not fair, is it, Pearl? That they should slither off to

take their snakey pleasure elsewhere after causing such agony. After attempted murder.

The nurse laughs. She gives Pearl two white tablets and a paper cup of water. Pearl accepts them gratefully and closes her eyes on the strobing room.

Three hours later, she wakes feeling much stronger; the octopus has departed. She moves her body slightly, cautiously. The nausea has gone too. And come to think of it, she's hungry. That must be a good sign. How long is it till mealtime? She isn't wearing her watch, looks around for a clock and finds a huge man sitting by her bed, reading a paper. Shoulders like a bear. She's never seen him before in her life. She tries for her voice. Finds it.

'Hello?'

He lifts his head, a large round head with fair curls and a reddish, moon face split by a wide smile.

'You're awake! I'm the onion man,' he says, quite inexplicably, and starts shaking her hand as though utterly thrilled to meet her.

He is.

He saved her life.

It takes a while for the story to penetrate because she has difficulty focusing on more than one thing at a time inside her head. She wants to listen, she wants to know what happened, but she wants to look at him too. Such a big man! All those curls. Big hands clasping the brim of his hat on his knees. And she can't help thinking about food. She is so hungry.

Her saviour has a soft, slow voice, a leisurely way of shaping his words that's almost a drawl, yet his delight is palpable. He'd come to Mamerbrook, he explains, to collect the first load of hay bales for his brother, but when he got there, he couldn't raise anyone, and couldn't find the hay either.

'I thought to myself, I can't go all that way back without it. It must be around here somewhere. Can't be easy to hide sixty great bales of hay. Most probably stacked in the paddock where they were cut. I'll just take a tootle round the place, I thought, and see what I can find.'

And tootle he did, in his rickety old truck, through gates, across paddocks, between buildings and sheds, sticking his head out of the window every now and then to call cooee! Until she'd answered him, he tells her.

'I most certainly did not,' says Pearl, who has never said cooee in her life.

'Oh, but you did. I heard you. Faint but definite: cooee. I turned the truck in that direction and pretty soon I spotted the bright red of your T-shirt. That was a good thought, writing TIGER with those twigs. You're quick. I brought you here,' he says proudly. 'Faster than any ambulance could have reached you.'

She's quiet thinking about this, the incredible fact that he should be there, on the farm, just at that time. Odd that he hadn't come across Pete, or one of the farm-hands, or that Bel hadn't heard him sing out. If he'd met any one of them, he'd have collected his hay and left, and I might have died, she thinks, wondering what sound it was that he'd heard, that brought him to her.

'Did you find the hay?' she asks.

'Nope, but there's plenty of time to sort that out,' he says. 'I'd better be going now and leave you to get your rest. I'll have to make a few trips for the hay. I'm delivering it to my brother's farm in Todmorden. I do a bit of work for him on the side. They tell me you'll be going home tomorrow morning. Would it be all right with you, if I come and say hello sometime? At the farm? When I come to get the hay, I mean?'

'Oh yes, of course. You must,' she says. 'You saved my life.'

'That's true,' he says, complacently, settling his hat on top of his curls. 'I'll tell the nurse you're awake, shall I? On my way out?'

'Yes please. You can tell her I'm starving too. One thing . . .' she stops, puzzled, wondering if she'd heard correctly or dreamt it.

He knows what she's thinking.

'Yes, I'm the onion man,' he says with a grin as he turns to go. 'Shalom.'

Shalom? She sinks back on to her piled pillows. It's all too much. But rather nice? Yes, definitely. And he's coming to see her again. If she wasn't so weak, she'd probably have a warm fuzzy feeling just thinking about that.

Well, well, well. The onion man.

And again she thinks how close she came to death,

and wonders why there was no one to answer his calls at the farm.

He's left his newspaper folded on the chair beside the bed. It's the local paper. She reaches for it and gasps as the drip needle twists savagely in the back of her left hand. I can do without that, she thinks, keeping her finger on the buzzer until the nurse comes. It's a different nurse this time, with a sour face and rusty-coloured hair.

'Spasm, is it?' she asks.

'Sorry? What?'

'Your finger gone into a spasm, has it? On the buzzer? I can give you an enema that will fix that.'

'Sorry,' says Pearl, horrified. Are they allowed to talk to patients that way?

'I tried to reach over for the newspaper but this thing in the back of my hand hurt like hell. And when can I have some food? I don't mean to be a nuisance, but I'm just so hungry. Also, I need to go to the toilet. Do you have one of those bedpans handy?'

'You don't need a bedpan. Not much wrong with you.'

'But what about all these tubes and things?' She waves the drip line in a panic.

'You gather it up like this. That's it. Now put your arm around my shoulders and pull yourself up. That's right. Now swing your legs over the side. That's the way. Good. How do you feel? Not dizzy?'

Not dizzy at all, and flushed with success.

'Good girl. That's the way. The more you do for yourself, the faster you'll be out of here. Now, you just wheel it ahead of you like this. And don't get the lines caught in your gown. I'll come with you. Don't try to go too fast. Just be sure of your balance. You might want to hold that gown closed at the back before we go into the corridor.'

'Oh!' says Pearl, and clutching the gown with one hand, pushing the drip stand with the other, she takes one tottery step after another until she gets to the bathroom.

'All right from here?'

'Yes, thank you,' says Pearl, meekly.

'I'll see what I can do about a cup of tea and some food for you. It's a couple of hours till the next meal, but I'm sure I'll find something. Not choosy, are you?'

'No. Anything will do. Anything at all. Thank you so much,' says Pearl. She makes it back to bed without too much trouble, though her hand still hurts. She's settled under the sheets before she remembers that she'd meant to look at her leg where the snake got her. She can't feel any pain at all from there. She rubs at it with one foot. They've got some kind of a dressing on it. She presses tentatively with her big toe. No. No pain. A little tenderness, that's all. Like a mild burn or a scald. The nurse bustles in with a tray that holds a cup of tea and a ham sandwich.

'Headache?' she asks.

'No,' says Pearl. 'My head feels just fine but my voice is so croaky. Why is that?'

'Just the way it takes you sometimes. One of the side effects.' She arranges the tray and puts the newspaper within reach. 'Anything else?'

'Oh no, this is wonderful. Thank you.'

'No more spasms?'

'No more spasms.'

There are two other beds in this room but both are empty. Pearl has the place to herself. Her bed-curtains are drawn back and the room is filled with sunshine. Beyond the bubble-glass window there is greenery of some kind, and blue sky and she can hear birds twittering. Wrens and sparrows. It is just so nice to be here in bed, alone, with clean sheets that someone else has to wash, and food that someone else has to make, and a cup of tea that someone else provides.

She folds the paper so she can see it as she eats, reading the stories of local happenings, scanning the faces to see if there's anyone she knows. The sandwich is delicious, the tea soon gone. She'd like another but daren't push her luck. What did the nurse say? Two hours to the next meal? I can hold out, she thinks. She turns the pages, relaxing happily, and checks out the classified advertisements from habit.

One . . . two . . . three . . .

and whoosh! Her blood pressure goes into orbit.

'Operations Manager – Live In.' And there's the Mamerbrook mailbox number and their phone number, plain as day. No way is this a misprint. They couldn't have misprinted an entire ad. What the hell is going on?

Is Pete leaving? But why didn't Dobie tell her? Why didn't Pete tell her? They wouldn't quit without a word after all these years. Not unless something was very, very wrong. Is that why Bel was giving her black looks the other day?

That look.

That dreadful look.

It is with a sick horror that Pearl realises there's a very good chance nobody told Bel and Pete about the advertisement either.

The bloody old bastard!

The bloody buggering bollocks of an old bastard!

I'll have him committed for this.

I have to get home, she thinks. I have to fix this. I'll deal with him later.

Gritting her teeth, she pulls out the needle in her hand and disconnects the drip. Finger on the buzzer again.

'I have to go today. Right now,' she explains to the doctor whom the nurse summoned when she found Pearl dressing herself.

'It's an emergency. On the farm. There's no one at home. As you know, my father (she almost spits the word) is in here too. Having tests.'

She sees them exchange glances.

'You haven't told him I'm in here, have you?'

'No,' says the doctor. 'We didn't want to worry him unnecessarily. We thought we'd leave it up to you.'

Worry him? I'll worry him all right, she thinks.

'Well, I'm going home.'

'We don't advise that you leave until tomorrow morning, but—'

'If you think my blood pressure's bad now, wait till you see what happens if you try to keep me in here!'

In fifteen minutes she is dressed and in a taxi, heading home at top speed and unheard of expense, to Bel and Pete. Have they seen the paper yet? Will she be able to salvage something, anything, from this mess?

30

At home, Pearl showers and changes her clothes then makes a cup of strong sweet tea. The kitchen is exactly as she'd left it before the snake bite. Wind it back, she prays. Let everything be as it was before I went for that walk. No, before that. Before Dobie . . .

Wind it back to when, Pearl?

When did it all start?

I'll just have another cup of tea, she thinks, putting off the moment when she has to face them. Voices come and go over the UHF radio, but Pete's isn't among them.

It's a long way to the cottage today, but not far enough. Pearl squares her shoulders and lifts her head, feeling the feather touch of spies and whispers all around her. No one in sight. When she raises her hand to knock, Pete opens the door and leans against the frame, looking at her, saying nothing.

Oh god.

'Pete . . .'

He laughs then. A blast of whisky breath hits her in the face.

'Miss Kinnear,' he says, with a jeering familiarity, and steps aside to let her through.

Pearl, blushing scarlet, is saved from a near faint by Bel's arm. She guides Pearl to a chair but doesn't sit down herself.

'You sick or something?' Bel's voice is hard.

'No, just a bit wobbly. Had a run-in with a tiger snake. But I'm fine, really.'

The outlook for a sympathy vote seems bleak.

'Please,' says Pearl, gesturing helplessly to the chairs beside her. 'We have to talk. My father is . . . not himself. You've seen the advertisement, I take it? Yes, of course you have.'

She stands up again, steadying herself on the chair-back. She needs to look them in the eyes.

'Please. I'm so sorry that this has happened, but you must try to ignore it. I'll sort things out with my father. You know how we need you here. You're as much a part of Mamerbrook as I am. It is unthinkable, simply unthinkable that you'd leave. It's not what I want and I'm sure it's not really what my father wants. He's . . . he's not been well. You know that. He's old. He gets . . . anxious about things.' She stops.

No one speaks.

She doesn't have to force the tears. They come swiftly, furiously, and they are all for herself.

'Oh for goodness sake, sit down,' says Bel. 'I'll make us some tea. Pete! You too. Sit down before you fall down. You're scaring the woman half to death.'

227

Pearl smiles at her, weak with gratitude, but Bel ignores that and goes into the kitchen.

'So, Miss Kinnear,' says Pete, 'you'd like us to behave as though nothing has happened, would you?'

The insolence in his tone confuses her. Why is he saying that: *Miss Kinnear*? There is a knowingness about it, sharp as a blade.

'Had any visitors lately, Miss Kinnear?'

'Pete!' Bel yells a warning from the kitchen and in the same instant Pearl understands that Pete knows about Dan Woods.

I can die right now, she thinks.

'Pay no attention to him, Pearl, he's drunk and he's angry and you can't blame him for either, can you? He's talking rubbish. Stop calling her Miss Kinnear, Pete. It's made him feel lowly, what's happened,' she explains. 'It's made him feel worthless. And you have the power to do that, see? To send us away. It's the difference between you and us that he's feeling. That's what it is.' Her words are all the more chilling, delivered in a reasonable tone of voice.

Pearl grasps at this, willing it to be true, wanting to be convinced that no one knows, that Dan wouldn't . . . but of course Dan wouldn't betray her secret to anybody else. What was she thinking? He's married. He wouldn't talk about her. He wouldn't.

Whatever you have to believe, to get by.

'Listen to me, Bel. I promise you, both of you, we'll make it up to you. And Pete, you've got to hire another farmhand to help with the workload, not just while

Dad's in hospital, but for good. Will you do that?'

Will you ever be able to put this behind you, she wonders? Will we all, any of us, be able to move on from this, unscathed?

Pete doesn't answer her. He leans towards her for a precarious moment and then turns and goes out of the house, leaving the door wide open behind him. They hear the ute start up.

'He's driving?' says Pearl.

'He's hurting,' says Bel, rubbing her finger on the tabletop.

Don't hit a tree, Pete. Don't hit a roo. Don't roll the ute into the irrigation channel. Don't take it onto the road, Pete. Be safe. Be safe. Come home.

'I know how upset you both must be,' Pearl says, desperately.

'What do you know, Pearl Kinnear? Anybody ever ripped the floor out from under your feet? Torn the roof from over your head?' she hisses. 'What do you know about how that feels? Nobody's going to take your home away from you. What's yours is yours. Mamerbrook. Not ours. Being a part of it for so long, you know, you come to think ... Well,' she says, looking down at her hands, 'you better go now, Pearl.'

Pearl, turning once on her way down the garden path, another entreaty rising to her lips, sees that Bel still hasn't moved. For a second, she imagines herself walking back up the path and into the house, putting her arms around this woman, to comfort her.

If only it were possible.

31

Dobie is bored. He's not getting the sympathy he deserves. Pearl didn't bother to visit yesterday. (He won't forget that.) And they can't find anything wrong with him that they didn't already know about. Hell of an anticlimax.

'Time I went home,' he says to the nurse. 'I don't know how they'll be managing without me at the farm. They've never had to before.' I'm the one who knows everything, he thinks. About the land, the crops, the plant, the history of it all. I'm the one who knows. They don't understand.

'Now don't you go disturbing yourself about that. Doctor will tell you when you can go home. The farm isn't going to fall apart for another couple of days, is it? You've got a manager out there, haven't you?'

Yes, he has. And you're doing something about that, aren't you, Dobie?

She fusses with his pillows and leaves him. He's done both crosswords. He'd like to put the television on and sneaks a look at his neighbour to see if he's sleeping. He is. It's all he ever does. You'd think if he was that close to dying he'd want to stay awake a bit more before he goes. Dobie presses the remote and the room fills with sound. Hurriedly he fumbles for the volume switch but drops the remote. A weary groan issues from the next bed.

Got it! Dobie flicks the television off and drops his head as though he's snoozing.

His neighbour raises himself on one elbow. 'Do you have to have that thing on so loudly? Is it too much to ask, that I can sleep?'

'What thing?' says Dobie. 'Don't know what you're talking about.'

'The television! You just woke me with the television.'

'I did not. I think you must be dreaming, mate.'

Speechless, the man stares at Dobie. Dobie looks back at him, a picture of innocence. 'You should get some rest,' he says. 'You're not looking too good.'

But this little piece of fun is rudely interrupted by Pearl who storms into the ward in a billowing fury. She flings the curtains close around Dobie's bed, after a brief, fierce glance in the direction of the other patient who shrinks down under the bedclothes out of harm's way.

She waves an envelope in Dobie's face.

'Eh? What's the matter with you?' he says. 'What's that then?'

'You've got a letter, Father.'

She's holding it in front of his eyes, too close for him to focus.

'Remember? Don't you want to see what it says?'

A letter? Remember?

No, he doesn't want to remember. He won't remember. His head fills with a great, clanging fear, a juddering nervousness runs right through him. *Alice, Alice, Alice . . .*

What does she mean, a letter? What is she so excited about?

Pearl throws down the letter on the bedcovers. He looks at it, refusing to touch it. She drags a copy of the *Coola Standard* from her shoulderbag and slams it down across his legs.

'Steady on, Pearlie. What's got into you? You'll have the nurse in here, carrying on like that.' He keeps his voice mild, but he's worried. He hasn't a clue what's wrong but it's coming. Oh, it's coming. He looks down at the paper. It is folded at the Employment page, a blue ring drawn around an advertisement for an 'Operations Manager'. His advertisement.

Oh! So that's all it is.

He reads the letter.

'Dear Sir, in response to your advertisement for a Manager, I would like to . . .'

Already! An application here and the paper only out this week. That's better than he'd expected. But he reads on.

'. . . draw your attention to the fact that the Bega River Times *has a readership of . . . covering the regions of . . .'*

What's this? Someone trying to get him to place the advertisement in their paper too? Oh well.

'Pity,' he says.

Not exactly the reaction Pearl is expecting.

'Pity?' she says. 'Pity? Did you give them a thought, Bel and Pete? Do you even *begin* to understand what you've done to those people? Did you think about what it would mean for them to leave their home, after all these years? They could sue us over this, you know. They could ruin us. There are laws against treating employees this way. What did you think? That they don't read newspapers? That they wouldn't find out until you were ready? Until you'd hired someone else? Is that when you intended to tell them? Is that when you intended to tell me? You . . . you . . . How dare you do this!'

Ah. Now he's got the picture. He's forgotten to tell Pearl about his decision to sack Pete. Forgotten to tell her about the advertisement too. Shit! What a mess! Has she talked to Pete? Has he seen the paper? Is he already packing, with Dobie stuck here in hospital? How can he make her understand that there was no other way? They left him with no option. He tries to find words to explain the perfidy of Pete Jenkins, of Bel bearing witness to his own weakness, but the half-formed excuses swirl and dissolve in the terrible vortex of Pearl's anger.

And then suddenly, he's inspired.

'I'm sorry you're upset about it, Pearlie. No, wait. Let me finish. I couldn't find you. I looked, but I couldn't find you, so I wrote you a note, but then, what with my

233

heart attack, and ending up in here . . . everything went to pot. Didn't you find my note?'

Brilliant, Dobie. But you'd better remember to plant that note somewhere when you get home.

'A note? A note! And just where did you leave this note? How could you do this?'

Her voice would do credit to a cobra.

A wise man knows when to bide his time and when to make his point. Dobie stays quiet, eyes downcast.

She continues. 'Well, you listen to me. I've told them to ignore it. I've told them that you're not in your right mind, since it's the only explanation I can come up with.'

He winces.

'You hear me, Dad? I've told them that you are no longer responsible for decisions on the farm and that they're to stay put and help me run the place. I've told Pete he can hire another man. I've told him to do it straight away. I've promised him that we'll make it up to him – and I can tell you, that will cost you! Do you understand me? I'm making the decisions from now on. And you – you can just stay out of bloody trouble and out of my way. So help me god, if I hear another word about their leaving, I'll pack up and go myself. Don't think I won't!'

'Excuse me, if I might just . . .'

It's the man from the other bed.

Pearl leaps to her feet and switches the curtain back, incredulous at this interruption.

'I just wanted to point out . . . you're obviously

angry ... but surely this isn't the time or the place? Whatever he's done. You're making a great deal of noise. I really need to sleep.'

Livid, embarrassed, Pearl manages a high-voiced apology. Dobie is feeling pressure rising within himself, filling his skin to bursting point. It's bad enough that she speaks to him this way, threatening him, but to have someone else listening! Judging them both. It will be all over town by tomorrow. Anger is leaking out of his ears, his nose, flashing from his eyes. He can't stop it. He cannot hear his thoughts, or her voice, over the whip-cracking surges of rage. It takes every ounce of strength that he has, to try to keep it all inside his head. It takes superhuman energy. He holds and holds until the rage drains away, taking with it all the juice, all the crunch, and leaving him feeling like a stick of celery that's been too long cut and out in the air.

She pushes back her chair and he jerks his legs defensively, away from her. The letter and the newspaper slide off the bedcovers onto the floor. They look down and see, in the same moment, that Pearl is wearing odd shoes. Both slip-ons, it's true, but the left one is blue with tooled patterns worked into the leather, and the right one is brown and plain. He raises his eyes to hers.

This is the woman who is going to make all the decisions?

This is the woman who is going to run his farm?

Heaven help us and save us.

32

'Pearl? It's Dan here.'

'Who?'

'It's me, Pearl. Dan. Dan Woods.'

'Oh! Dan, I'm so sorry. I didn't recognise your voice. Things have been a bit . . .'

The world has turned. Dan, ringing her. Whatever next? She wants to pour her heart out to him. Oh, to feel his arms around her and have the luxury of sobbing into a strong shoulder. No one has time for Pearl's troubles. I was bitten by a snake! I almost died out there in the paddock! Sometimes she wants to scream it at the sky.

Might as well, Pearl. No one is listening.

But now here is Dan, ringing her. Is it surprising that she feels this rush of girlish relief? How long has it been since she's given him a thought?

'I heard your old man was in hospital,' he's saying. 'Bad that. Be okay, will he?'

'Yes, I think so. He had a bit of a turn. Collapsed in the garden. They kept him in for a while, tests and so on. I'm bringing him home tomorrow.'

'Lucky then. Still, he's running down, isn't he? It was the same with my old man before he went. You have to face it. Anyway, how are you managing out there? Pete Jenkins still looking after things, is he?'

Now why would he ... oh Christ! He's seen the advertisement. It will be all over town by now. Everyone knows. She isn't sure that Pete has been persuaded. She isn't sure she's got him settled.

'Pete does a great job for us, Dan. Always has. Nothing to worry about there.'

'So you don't need an extra hand, Pearlie? I've got a bit of spare time up my sleeve. I could pop round.'

What a darling he is!

'Oh, Dan, that would be great. They're a bit pressed, with Dad not here. He usually takes care of the paddock runs and keeps an eye on the stock. If you could fit one or two of those in, just till he's back on his feet again?'

'Actually, it wasn't that kind of extra hand I meant.'

He's amused, surprised.

'Oh.'

How stupid can you get, Pearl? Imagining that he gives a damn about how you're coping. Whatever are you thinking of? Not sex, that's for sure.

She feels foolish and then, quickly, angry.

'Dan, I really haven't time to worry about that sort of thing at the moment. Thanks for the call though.'

Before he can speak, before she can weaken, she puts the phone down with a shaking hand.

Now you've done it.

He's going to be rushing round here with flowers and chocolates for you now, isn't he? That's the end of it, that is, and only yourself to blame.

She leans against the door, looking out over the rose garden. He wasn't much to lose, she thinks. He wasn't much at all. He wasn't even mine.

He was all you had.

If I had a choice, I wouldn't have given him the time of day.

No, but . . .

She knows what she wants. She's never expected the impossible, just someone she can invent a love with, share a life with, plan a garden. He wasn't around when she was twenty and in with a chance, this 'someone'. He wasn't around when she was thirty and beginning to count the years. He's certainly not going to pop up now, is he?

Well, there's always the onion man.

Oh, get back in your box! He'll be married with five children. And I'm too old for fairy stories and happy endings.

Or not old enough.

She's still not herself. Not quite. Dizzy if she stands up too quickly and by the end of the day, when she's tiring, her legs go to jelly. She hasn't had a drink since the snake bite. Not that she's sworn off it forever though. None of that Oh-Lord-if-you-save-me-I'll-never-drink-again for our Pearl. No. She just wants to feel well. The structure of her world seems suddenly terribly fragile. More and more often she finds herself thinking about her mother and wondering. Alice had known these same routines, the days and days of never-changing, never-ending chores. Were they a curse to her? A blessing? Or both. And how she must have yearned for the ability to do them when sickness put them forever beyond her reach.

You're alive one minute, dead the next. There's nothing like a snake bite to teach you to appreciate life's little certainties. Look around, Pearl. Walls are transparent and may not be relied upon. The bars of your cage flicker and bend like a prism over water, and disappear.

And then what?

The old dread illusion of all her tomorrows rolling on, season after season, all the same?

Gone. Anything can happen.

No wonder she's dizzy. No wonder she puts a hand out, now and again, to grasp a support that isn't there.

For one more day, she has the place to herself. Not on alert for the slam of the door when he comes in. Not having to decide what to set out for his lunch, cook for his dinner. No need to follow him around, cleaning up his mess. No need to sit at the table and listen to him chewing his food. Is this how it will feel, to live here without him? But he's in every crack and crumb of the place, every nook and cranny. She'll never be without him, here.

33

Thomas, still in the area, moving around between several sites, has no idea that there's been a crisis at the farm. He's having a crisis of his own. He can't find any trace of the Southern Bell Frog, *Litoria raniformis*. He's gone from a state of mild jubilation at the stimulation of fieldwork, to a growing sense of panic. There's been rain recently, just a few brief showers, but enough. Many frogs are active and calling, but not that one. Not the one that he's come for.

This is one of the last regions known to have a population of Southern Bell Frogs. He'd expected to be monitoring them, studying behaviour and building information about a vulnerable species. Instead he's recording no sightings in prime habitat. Is it going to be the same all the way down the Murray River to South Australia? Is he going to have to testify to an extinction? Is that how science will remember him?

He knows it's not a question of the environmental health of this region. Frogs are a good indicator of that, and there are frogs everywhere. The habitat is perfect –

irrigation, farm dams, permanent lagoons, marshes, the periphery of rivers with dense corridors of native vegetation. He's recorded brown froglets, pobblebonks, tree frogs and marsh frogs amongst others. He has seen red-bellied black snakes, tiger snakes, common brown snakes and several species of lizard are doing very well here, but there's nothing new to report, except the lack of a Southern Bell Frog. Or two. Two would be good.

Bear in mind that this is not a shy frog. It is not inclined to hide. This is a frog that basks in sunshine, out in the open. It is the one frog at risk from high levels of ultraviolet radiation. Diet? It eats other frogs, so there is no shortage of dinner. The creature is fixed in his mind as he walks the river's reaches and haunts the dams – that pale green mid-dorsal stripe, the large black spots, the exquisite turquoise thighs. The tadpoles, large and pink with yellow fins. His ears are tuned to its loud growling call that never comes.

In addition to this depressing situation, it's almost a fortnight since he wrote to Alice Kinnear and there has been no telephone call. The only other Kinnear in the region, a J. Kinnear, has been struck off his list. No connection to any Alice, said a woman, adding that she believed there were Kinnears at Coolabarradin who had been there for many years. Mamerbrook, she thought. But are they his Kinnears? And if not? What then?

If Alice is not here in the southern Riverina, she could be anywhere in Australia. Anywhere in the world. He'll have to advertise in the papers, as Robert suggested.

Anyone knowing the whereabouts of . . . It will blow it all wide open. Whatever 'it' is. He wants a resolution. He wants to know what it is all about. Is the rose really just a simple act of gratitude? Why, then, did Henry emphasise again and again the need for caution?

Lying in his tent listening to the sounds of the night, Thomas ponders the mystery of it. If a rose-grower gives a rose, does it mean more, or less, than when someone else gives a rose? He chews over the possibilities, frustrated and worried about blundering in and 'damaging the innocent'. It's fascinating to him, the idea that Henry might have had a secret love. Would the suspicion of it still be a threat to someone's peace of mind? A source of jealousy after fifty years? Unlikely, he thinks, but it's possible. The last thing Thomas wants is to bring trouble to anyone. He likes a quiet life. If only there was someone to advise him.

Anything to do with frogs, and Thomas is your man. It's only with people that he doesn't seem to have the right instincts.

Poor Thomas. He has no idea what he is bringing to Alice Kinnear.

Is it a rose? Or a time bomb?

Tick. Tick. Tick.

34

They've sent him home without even the badge of a heart attack to pin on his chest. Possibility of a minor stroke is all they will commit to. Blink and you miss it. It isn't enough. It isn't going to save him. Minor stroke! Ignominy, as far as Dobie is concerned, but he's giving serious consideration to the possibility of another one, to soften his reception at the farm where Bel and Pete await him.

There's no doubt he will be made to pay for his actions, in one way or another. It is apparent in the grim line of Pearl's lips when she comes to collect him from hospital. She doesn't even offer to take his bag. Dobie gets into the car, pointedly leaving it sitting on the pavement. She has to climb out again and swing it into the back, which she does with great force, slamming the door. When she settles herself into the driver's seat, he sighs and half-closes his eyes, sees her look across at him. Ha! Let her worry. Let her feel guilty. Miss Pearl-In-Charge. We'll soon see who's making decisions on the farm and in the meantime, give her enough rope . . .

Throw them all out, Dobie. Let them go. You can manage without them. More trouble than they're worth, the lot of them!

It's the Brecken again, making mischief inside his head.

Go away, he tells her silently. Haven't I got enough problems? A shiver runs through him. He sees himself alone at Mamerbrook, sitting up in bed with his newspapers, as the poplar suckers grow into thickets, the thickets into forests, hiding the house from the world. Thick spiderwebs shroud the windows. Thistles and kangaroos overrun the paddocks. All the dams run dry and the wild ducks build their nests and fly unchallenged. The river gums seed and soar and the bridge falls, year by year, piece by piece, back into the river.

It's a constant battle, he thinks sadly, as though he alone is responsible for the heroic task of maintaining order. Dobie Kinnear, vanquishing the witches of the night, taking on, single-handed, the dragons of loneliness, arm-wrestling the gods for a living from this land. And he's done it, hasn't he? Despite his father's lack of faith in him and the Brecken's mind-poisons, and all the people he loves who leave him. Look around! He's done it, despite them all. Give him his due. Don't tell him any other stories, because he doesn't want to hear them. Don't tell him what he's done wrong. Not ever! What does it matter in comparison with what he's achieved, what he's overcome? Minor stroke or not, he's still Dobie Kinnear, and the world owes him.

Hah! he thinks. When I go, it won't be in that place with its nutters and nurses. I'll go with my boots on when my time comes, even if I have to fix it that way myself. But in his mind, that time is indistinct as a shimmer of heat rising at the end of a long straight road and even though he's driving straight towards it, lead-foot, it never seems to come any closer.

Look at Alice. Her life. If she'd known it was going to end so soon, would she have lived it differently? Made other choices? Even after the worst had been confirmed, she refused to believe it. It was a long time, the waiting and the failing. It was a long time, and in no time at all, she was gone.

His own mother had no warning, haemorrhaging on the operating table during an operation for some woman's ailment. Dobie only has to close his eyes to hear again the muted echoing of that hospital corridor, and to feel the hard grip of his father's hand around his. One minute he is trotting fast to keep up with Alistair's urgent stride, then suddenly he is released and his father is not there. After a time, a tall nun appears and bends down to Dobie, taking both of his hands in hers. She whispers that his mother has gone to Jesus. She says that his mother is no longer suffering any pain, and hadn't woken up because Jesus called her. She just slipped from one kind of dreaming into another, the nun tells the child, who for years afterwards, dreams his mother as a kind of sleeping beauty, waiting somewhere, amidst the smells of ether and disinfectant, to take him in her arms again, if only he can find her.

Alistair had a quick death. Died with his boots on. Dobie had found him. Crushed when the supports beneath the machinery he was working on collapsed. He was younger when he died than Dobie is now. No time for preparations or regrets. No time to worry about how his farm would survive in the hands of his son. Or how his son would survive. No last words. What would he have said anyway? 'Take care of Mary for me,' likely as not.

Mary Brecken had gone quietly. Not a word of complaint when the stroke came; a hand at her breast, a crumpled fall, a poppyseed cake in the oven. One second she was there, the full force of her, and the next, a small and broken thing lay on the kitchen floor. He was free, and alone.

He'd picked her up and laid her on the bed that she and his father had shared. She was feather-light. Empty. He took the cake from the oven and turned it from the tin on to the wire cooling tray, just as she would have done. It was faintly disturbing to him that the cake, newly-baked by her hands, stood cooling now, as she was. He ate it all, slice after slice, and was still sucking poppyseeds out of his teeth when the doctor arrived to certify her death.

If she'd known the stroke was coming, would she have baked the cake? Or would she have chosen another way to fill the hours of her last afternoon? She'd have baked the cake. He's sure of it. She'd have chosen to die doing something she enjoyed. Baking a cake for Alistair's only son, who hated poppyseeds.

And here he is. Dobie Kinnear. But there's no Alice. No sons to train up. He's sabotaged every hope of grandchildren to satisfy the practical needs of his life. There'll be no more Kinnears from his line. It's a deeply melancholy thought. But at least there's Pearl, his own flesh and blood. And there's the farm. It continues to grow and produce, year after year. He will grow old here in comfort, with his daughter at his side. Things could be worse. Why, I might have lost her to a snake, he realises suddenly, having forgotten about Pearl's bit of excitement in the midst of his own worries.

He needs her as his ally now more than ever. She'll come round eventually. The worm might have turned but she's still on the hook. They'll be watching him, all of them, looking for signs. The trick is not to panic. He needs time to work out what's in his own best interests, time to get his strategies straight. He's still determined to get a new manager but in the short term it's best that he keeps his head down and stays out of trouble.

'Where'd the snake get you?' he asks.

'Leg,' says Pearl.

'But where on the farm?'

'River paddocks.'

'What was he doing out there, your Sir Lancelot? There's no hay out there.'

She shrugs. 'Bloody good luck, I suppose.'

Bloody miracle, is what he's thinking.

'Did you get him?'

'Who?'

'The snake.'

'No. One bite and he took off.'

'One bite was enough, was it?'

She ignores him.

When they arrive at the farm, Dobie takes his time getting out of the car and allows himself to stagger a little under the rapturous onslaught of Blackleg. At least someone's glad to see him.

'I'm going to lie down, Pearlie,' he tells her, with a weak, tired smile that she resists. 'I'm not feeling the best. Would you mind bringing the papers in for me? And perhaps some chicken soup. Yes, I think I could manage that. And some crusty bread. And biscuits? Or cake, if we have any?'

He's going to ground but there's no need to starve, is there?

35

Thomas, coming quietly through a patch of scrub, looking and listening for his beautiful, growling frog, stops
short. He can hear singing. A thin, high sound, a disem-
bodied melody without words, resonating with so much
sadness that the hairs rise on the back of his neck. The
song grows louder; the singer approaches. She's coming
towards him along the levee bank. It's going to startle
her when she sees him, but how can he avoid it? Perhaps
she'll go straight past without noticing? He keeps still as
a lizard, almost holding his breath. The song stops. The
woman turns and comes down the side of the levee bank
towards him, as if she'd known all along where he was.

'Hello,' she says. 'I've seen you around the place.
Seen you looking for things. You looking for snakes?
Lizards?'

'Hi, no, frogs, actually.'

'Frogs? Lots of frogs around here,' she says. 'I'm Bel.'
She sits on the river bank and he comes out of the scrub
and, rather hesitantly but sensing the invitation, squats
down beside her.

'I'm Thomas,' he says. 'It's just one frog that I'm looking for.'

'Just one?'

Is she teasing him?

'It's called the Southern Bell Frog,' he says, and he describes the frog to her – the green stripe, the turquoise thighs. 'Have you seen one like that? It's endangered. Might even be extinct. I can't find it. Listen, it calls like this: Crawk- crok – crok – crok.'

Bel's face lights up at his serious, passionate entreaty and the low growling frog call.

'I know it! There used to be hundreds of them round here. My kids used to call him the growler. Such a noise! I still see them now and again when I'm out walking, but not so many now. What happened to them? The herons, is it? I've seen him out in the open, sunbaking. Weird that, isn't it? A frog, sunbaking. I told him – you'd be better off under a log somewhere, frog. Doesn't pay any attention to me though.'

Thomas is beside himself with excitement. 'Where? Where have you seen them? I've been searching for days. I haven't heard a single call. Where can I find one?'

'What do you want him for?'

'Just to look at, to photograph, to count them. Nothing else. I won't take them away. I won't hurt or disturb them. We're trying to save them. They're endangered.'

'Endangered,' she repeats, thoughtfully.

'This research work I'm doing is backed by CSIRO and the University of Canberra.'

'And who will use your research?'

'Well, various groups, but only in the best interests of the frog, I promise.'

He hopes.

She's silent for a minute or two, thinking.

'The last time I saw your frog, maybe a couple of months or so ago, I was about a couple of miles over that way. Swampy land behind a river curve. Just keep heading in that direction and when you're close enough, they'll tell you where they are, if they like the look of you.'

Thomas is almost speechless with gratitude and impatient to take off in the direction she's indicated. It's going to take him further into Mamerbrook territory but what can they do? Shoot him?

'I can't thank you enough for this,' he says. 'I'll let you know if I find them. Do you live around here?'

He sees the shutters close behind her face, the eyes darken. What is it? What has he said?

'Don't you worry about that,' she tells him. 'You go off and save your old frogs. It was nice meeting you.'

'Oh, you too,' he says fervently, and as he pushes back into the scrub, she takes a short cut home. When Pete finishes his work today, she'll have to be ready to go with him to the Kinnear homestead, to say what has to be said. How nice to be a frog-man, wandering in the bush, in the riverlands. Does he know how lucky he is, she wonders? But then, who does?

36

Dobie is propped up in bed, a bedraggled grey rodent in a nest of crumpled crosswords and spilled newspapers. Can't go on like this. He's bored out of his mind. He's going to have to dig his way out and face them all soon. Pearl's no fun. Unbaitable and preoccupied, she brings his meals on a tray, kicking the balls of newspaper out of the way, saying little, not even inquiring about his health. He's watching her carefully. Something inside her has sharpened, crystallised. Some knowledge of herself? Or worse, a decision, perhaps? There is a briskness in her manner. A suggestion of authority and assurance. It doesn't bode well. Time to shake things up around here, he thinks, before they all get too complacent. There are no messages from anyone. No cards. No phone calls. He might as well be dead for all the impression he's making.

So what's the plan, Dobie?

Plan?

'How are those two thousand wethers?' he asks Pearl.

'They're fine. Chris brought them up to the sheds

ready for crutching. Shearers were due yesterday. They're late again.'

Chris? Who the hell is Chris? Is this something he's forgotten? Better not let her see that.

'How's he shaping up, Chris?' he says casually.

She shoots him a warning look that he counters with blank innocence.

'Everything's fine, Dad. You just stay there and build up your strength and don't worry your head about the farm.'

Well, he's asked for that, playing the invalid.

She sniffs once, twice, wrinkles her nose. 'You might think about taking a shower today. Unless you'd rather I gave you a sponge bath?'

Oh yes, like that's going to happen in a month of Sundays.

As soon as she's gone, he wriggles out of bed and pulls on a pair of trousers. Bugger the shower. He'll shower when he feels like it, not when he's told to. What is he? A child?

There's one important thing that has to be done before it flies out of his head again. He can see Pearl pegging washing on the line. In the kitchen, he finds an empty envelope. Wesfarmers. That will do. He tears it in half, turns it over and after a moment's thought, he licks the stub of the pencil and writes, *Pearl, remind me to tell you about advertisement for new farm manager. Much trouble here today. Can't go on like this.* He finishes off the note with a D.

Now, where to put it? Somewhere she won't look too often. Should he tuck it up there on the broad curved window ledge of the magpie moon? No. She'd never find it. He lifts up the long lace tablecloth and throws the paper under the dining table. She'll find it there, if she ever sweeps the floor. It's been a while since she's done that, evidently. He looks at it, worries for a moment. She might think it's just a bit of rubbish ... will she even notice it? Well, at least he can say that he told her, with his hand on his heart. Now, time to get out and about. No doubt the place is going to pieces without him to keep an eye on things. God knows what they're doing. He tucks his pyjama top into his trousers and goes to find out.

Over at the woolsheds, Pete hears the ute start up and sees the vehicle cross the track to East Paddock. He knows that it's Dobie, up and about at last, doing a tour of the farm, looking for fault. He spits into the dust, eyes on the receding ute.

Pearl's right. Everything's fine. You wouldn't credit it, would you? Dobie's driven right around the farm and can't find a single thing to criticise. He's going to have to front up to Pete with no ammunition at all. It's enough to make his hands shake. Driving towards the shed, looking for his manager, listening for his voice on the radio, Dobie reminds himself that Pete hasn't been to see how he is, hasn't given him any kind of an update. That's a pretty poor show. Perhaps he can open with that, and get him on the back foot? He pulls up by the diesel tank, wondering where to try next. I could put a call over the radio for him, he thinks. I could summon him. But he doesn't quite have the nerve.

He turns off the ignition and stares through the window at nothing, his mind running through all the possibilities of a meeting with Pete. He has to out-guess and out-manoeuvre. He has to come out on top. It's not going to be easy, given the position he's in right now. He doesn't even know if anyone has applied for the manager's job. Pearl might have been turning them away at the door. Hoards of applicants. He wouldn't know. No one's said a word to him. Do they think it's all going to blow over? Pearl, of all people, should understand that he can't back down now.

'Can I help you?'

Jesus! Can't abide people creeping up like that.

'You can start by telling me who the hell you are.'

The young man grins under the shadow of his hat, not at all abashed.

'I'm Chris,' he says, holding out a grimy hand. 'Chris Tillman. Just started here. Working the sheep. Pleased to meet you. Actually, we met before, some time back. I came to ask you about the pig-shooting. You're Mr Kinnear.'

Dobie sticks his arm through the ute window and shakes the offered hand in a reflex action. That face, it's vaguely familiar. Pig-shooting? And then he remembers, he'd told the boy no. There were sheep in the paddock.

He'd had a flashy looking red ute and an eager, frisky pup in the back. Dobie had been worried for his stock, and the fire risk, with a young hoon tearing about in the long dry grass.

'Good to put a name to the face,' he says, relieved that his brain hasn't let him down. 'Working the sheep, eh? You'll be working with me then.'

'Nah, I'm working with Alex and Pete. Good to see you again. Got to go. Shearers are on their way.'

Good to see you again! I've just been dismissed, thinks Dobie, outraged. They've written him off already. Replaced him. A new man, working the sheep with Alex. See what happens when your back is turned? Treachery. All his suspicions are justified, and in the deep reaches of his mind ancient insecurities begin to stir again, scenting daylight. He puts the car into gear and drives off purposefully but at the track junction he stops, utterly bewildered, not knowing which way to go. There's nothing for him to do here.

Nothing at all.

37

The old bridge was built by Dobie's father, Alistair. Right now, it's spanning about seventy feet of water, rising in a gentle arch to twelve feet above the river. Its weight is supported by red-gum piles set into the river-bed. The bridge surface is made up of sturdy boughs, cut to size and laid side by side. There are large gaps now, places where the old logs have fallen or broken, through which you can see the water. On each side, and running the whole length of the bridge, is a double line of long planks laid end to end. They are warped, see-sawing, with bolts sprung here and there. This is the pathway that Dobie keeps to as he crosses to the centre of the bridge. The structure itself, curving and creaking, sighing and quivering, seems a thing of nature still, the great piles linked by hawsers to their living counterparts on each river bank.

Thousands and thousands of terrified sheep have trotted and stumbled over this bridge on their way to the lush pasture of the back country. Tractors and trucks once crossed on these planks, but not any more.

A broad, flat concrete bridge, upstream a little way, takes the farm traffic these days and every year the old wooden arch sinks further into the background, dappling and fading amongst the river gums.

No one will find him here.

No one is looking.

Dobie stares up at the sky.

Just you stay in bed and don't worry about the farm, she said.

Oh yes, you'd like that, wouldn't you?

It'll be power of attorney next, no doubt.

Three bright green lorikeets fly past him, swerving left and disappearing amongst the trees, untroubled by his presence.

How did it come to this? When did it all begin to slip from his grasp? It was those ewes, he thinks. Leaving them without water. His whole body shudders in rejection of the thought. It is impossible – impossible! – that he would have chained shut the gate to the dam. He knows that a new manager is sure to hear the story and will reach his own conclusions about Dobie's competence. Judged and damned and disbelieved, everywhere he turns. And what use is a sheep farmer who can no longer look after his sheep?

The radio in the ute crackles loudly. Dobie can hear the voices from where he stands on the bridge.

'You on channel, Pete?'

'Yeah, Alex. Get that bin out to Number One, will you? You can clear up on that side today, if the ground holds. I'll be over at the sheds with Chris if you run into any trouble.'

'No problem.'

The sky is silent. The gum leaves hiss and whisper.

No problem, Dobie. Everything's fine.

Without you.

His mind curls in on itself, goes looking for places to hide. Beneath him, the brown water flows on and on.

'Over here, boy.'

It's his father talking. Dobie reels in the memory, fixes it in time, and allows himself to slide alongside. He's back in the big floods of '35 again. Uncomfortable images that have begun to recur in his dreams and daydreams, rippling outwards from a stone sunk long ago. Water over the levee banks. The house, sandbagged on its tiny patch of raised ground. Animals arrive like an invasion force. Mice and rabbits, roos and lizards, frogs and snakes . . . his father is busy with guns and traps. Can't let them starve to death. Dobie is, what, eight years old? He wears a blue flannel shirt with the sleeves rolled up, like his Dad's sleeves. Too-big grey shorts held up with brown braces. He feeds crumbs to the quick grey mice, watches them running in and out of clothes in his room, jumping from drawers, racing across the pelmets. Outside, milky water lapping against the verandah posts and all the garden shining like glass. The Brecken's there, wringing her hands about the water that is still rising, the carcasses.

'The smell,' she wails. 'Get them out of here, for heaven's sake.'

And there's the wooden dinghy from the big dam, tethered to the verandah. Dobie and his father have been loading carcasses into it and making trips out to where the current is running, the boat riding low. They throw the load into the water, to be carried away, and then row back for more. The Brecken waits for their return with little piles of broken bodies: mice from the traps, tiger snakes and red-bellied black snakes chopped into pieces with her long-handled shovel.

On one trip, heaving a limp joey into the boat, the boy Dobie feels warmth from its body through his shirt. There's a tiny movement, a twitch, then no more. Is it alive? No. But he puts the animal where he can see it in the boat. He keeps an eye on the little, unspoiled face, the sweetness of it. The scent of blood on his hands and his shirt. He works quietly, concentrating, all his senses taut and testing the air for any sign of, or opportunity for his father's approval.

When they have stowed as much as the boat can safely carry, Dobie climbs in. Alistair props the rifle clear of the water and rows away from the house. The boy sits looking back at his home over his shoulder. How strange it all is. How unfamiliar. A calm brown lake as far as the eye can see with all the paddocks lying beneath and mighty trees rising up through it. The diverging ripples behind the dinghy form a perspective on their home and it is beautiful, this house that his father built for Hannah Dobie, floating tenderly on the waters in a fragile enchantment.

Alistair is busy making the boat fast to a bough when the joey jerks violently by Dobie's foot. He half-turns when Dobie rises, thinking they've snagged on something. The current is fast and the water much deeper here, close to the true river.

'I've got it,' Dobie cries, diving for the gun. Kill it clean, he prays. Get it right first time.

And then the unbelievable happens.

Alistair screams, 'Don't shoot!'

Shocked, Dobie lowers the gun and looks up at his father.

'What the hell do you think you're doing, boy?'

'The joey's not dead, Dad. You always say don't let an animal suffer . . .'

They are both standing, keeping balance with difficulty in the rocking boat, facing each other across the tumbled corpses.

'Oh,' says Alistair, holding onto the bough of the river gum, struggling to keep the boat from swinging into the current, 'so you were going to shoot the roo, were you?'

Ribbons of menace curl through the air between them. What is it? What has he done wrong? All the glad effort of the day withers inside him. He feels an urgent need to pee.

'Yes,' he says.

'You were going to shoot the roo?' Alistair repeats, shaking his head.

'Yes, Dad. I'm sorry.' And he is sorry, truly sorry, but he doesn't know what for.

'What's underneath the roo, Dobie? Tell me that, boy.'

Without waiting for an answer, he bends and begins one-handedly to toss carcasses out of the rocking boat. Dobie stares miserably at the joey, now lying still, and at the curved boards of the boat beneath the animal. The boat! He might have shot right through the bottom of the boat. Sunk it! Maybe even drowned them both.

Alistair doesn't mention the incident again. Dobie never forgets it. It was that little shake of the head that Alistair gave, and all it said.

On the bridge, Dobie realises that he is holding his breath. He lets it go in a great sigh. He was eight years old, for God's sake. What did the man expect?

It can take a long time to forgive yourself.

And then there's the big picture. It's not just a matter of taking aim and – wham! You have to look up and look around. What lies beyond the target?

'I have to make this right somehow,' he mutters to himself. I'll call a meeting, he thinks. Get everyone together and let them know that I'm back at the helm again. Have to sort things out with Bel and Pete, whatever it takes. We were a team, before this. We were a family. I have to make it right.

The boat may be rocking, Dobie, but the boat is all you have. It's taken seventy years for the lesson to come home to him.

When he enters the house, Dobie hears voices that stop when the screen door squeaks behind him. They're in the dining room. He comes round the corner cautiously, sticks a head through the doorway. They're all sitting at the table. Slowly, their faces turn towards him. The gang of three. Pearl, Bel and Pete.

'Come in, Dad,' says Pearl. 'I went to get you when Pete and Bel came round but you weren't in your bedroom.'

Come in? Come in? He's being invited into his own dining room!

Stay calm, Dobie, you might have lost the initiative but don't lose your temper as well. Remember. Got to get things back on track. Show them who's boss, but with understanding, with tolerance. No chinks. No weakness.

He stands straight in the doorway, looking at them with what he judges to be an expression of polite inquiry on his face.

'A meeting? That's good. I've been waiting for an update, Pete.'

He's got the tone right. Stern, yet encouraging.

Pete says nothing, stares at the tablecloth.

Dobie comes into the room, pulls out the chair at the head of the table and sits down, ready to preside, ready to be magnanimous, to forgive and be forgiven.

It's her face that does it. The expression. Suddenly, he sees what Pearl is seeing. What they're all seeing. The three days' grey growth on his chin, the white hair sticking up in disarray as if he's just lifted his head from the pillow. Unwashed, unshaven and wearing his pyjama top tucked into old moleskin trousers.

Oh yes, Dobie, that's showing them who's boss.

Pearl drops her eyes, gives a little shake of her head, a tiny shake. Barely noticeable really, that shake. It slashes him like a stiletto. It opens him from chin to navel and his guts, red and purple, spill out into his old hands. He's holding himself together, but only just.

'Excuse me, would you?' he says, and stumbles out of the room, trying to keep his bursting heart inside his chest.

Pearl comes to him after a little while. After an age.

He's lying on his bed with his eyes open when she knocks at the door softly and comes in without waiting for a reply. She sits on the edge of his bed.

'They're leaving, Dad. They just came to tell me. Pete's got another position. Bill Fenman was on the phone to him the second he saw your advertisement. Told Pete he could name his price, just about. Pete told me he'd thought about it for a while but they just couldn't go on like this. I tried, Dad. I talked to them both. Promised them more money. Got him to hire another man to help with the workload.'

She spreads her hands in front of her, empty of solutions. 'It wasn't enough, apparently. It was the insecurity, Bel said. That it could happen after all the years they've been here. Pete just couldn't handle it.'

The words hang in the air, threatening to spill over into explanations, accusations.

'When?' he asks.

'End of this week. They've got the removalists coming. They didn't waste any time. Pete said there's no point in staying once your mind's made up. You're crazy to think you can treat people like that, Dad. You can't. Not good people. Not bad people. Why don't you ever stop to think about the unhappiness you cause? Their life is here, in this place, with us. I can't imagine what it will be like without them. They've been a part of it all for so long.'

She says nothing else. Just sits there on the edge of the bed, looking down at her hands. He thinks she may be crying but he can't see any tears.

You've got what you wanted, Dobie.

Except that you'd changed your mind.

Well, it's done now.

'I'll handle it, Pearlie,' he whispers. 'I'll handle it. I promise.

38

Pearl wakes and for a few minutes her mind is a void. Nothing. She's used all her resources to no avail. Disaster falls where it will – when her father has a hand in the matter. She has to fight a great weariness of spirit simply to get out of bed, and completely dismisses any idea of breakfast. He'll be around out there, somewhere. She can't bear the thought of seeing him. Not this morning.

There's work to be done. There's always work to be done. The farm doesn't take care of itself. Accounts have to be paid today. Late, but better late than never. Phone bills wait for no man. An $11 charge for late payment? Who the hell do they think they are? She spreads out the paperwork on the desk. What absolutely has to be paid? What can wait?

She gets the cheque book out of the drawer, smoothes the two-page statement from Coola Cellars, spoiled by rain. There's something stuck to the back of it. A letter, also rain-spoiled, the paper stained and curling. The single sheet inside has merged with the small envelope. She'll never get it out. Her first impulse is to throw it away, but she doesn't. They don't get many letters here. It's been handwritten. Curiosity drives her to peel the layers apart, the paper tearing at every gentle tug. A wash of blue ink is mostly all that remains of the writing, part of a word here and there, a pale blossoming of watercolour that once said – what? From the multitude of scraps laid out on the table, she pieces together two things. A mobile telephone number that she doesn't recognise, and the single word: budwood.

Budwood? she thinks. Budwood?

How very odd.

39

Three spoonbills startle and rise with a rush of broad white wings from behind a stand of saplings. Dobie turns off the motor. The birds settle about twenty feet away on a mudbank. All three of them stand the same distance apart from each other, facing the same way and motionless. Like a paper-chain of spoonbills, he thinks. Those queer bills pointing straight out in front of them, upriver. The tableau holds for two minutes, three minutes, but Dobie has given up looking for signs. Signs are everywhere and he doesn't like any of them. With an elegant dipping motion of their long legs and a corresponding movement from the heads, the birds resume their slow, methodical foraging.

Dobie puts his arms up on the steering wheel and rests his head on them, turning slightly to keep the spoonbills in his line of sight. Their beauty quietens his spirit. With an eerie but familiar tingle of privilege, he acknowledges this, the other life of his land, busy going about its own cycles of growth and decay, birth and death.

Truth is, he's exhausted, but he daren't be caught

napping at home. Not since he promised Pearl that he'd handle things. Here you are, Dobie, running your own farm again, and how does it feel? Not so good? You don't work in a district for as long as Pete has without the community making up its mind about you. Pete had kept to himself but he'd always had the respect of the men. They knew he could be counted on to pull his weight. They're all behind him. Sometimes, from the corner of his eye, Dobie catches a glimpse of himself as they see him, and no, it's not so good. Hostility surrounds him, implacable, drumming the air with ominous wingbeats, and no one says a word.

They could take advantage if they chose to. It's easy for a sullen attitude to translate into slack work practices. What if they know about his habit of parking the ute in quiet places, not easily overlooked?

(They do.)

What if they've seen him with his arms leaning on the steering wheel, head propped on them as though he's looking for a lamb, or maybe counting a mob, when really he's a million miles away and dreaming?

(They have.)

He's sure the smokos are getting longer and the unexplained absences more frequent. He can't be everywhere all the time. No doubt Pete knows what's going on but he's busy with his packing and won't lift a finger to help. Might even be encouraging it. You'd think, after all the time they've spent together . . .

No, you wouldn't, Dobie. You blew it.

His eyes follow the river upstream, in the direction the spoonbills were pointing, to a bend some distance away where an enormous gum tree straddles the water. He catches his breath, leans closer to the windscreen. Is someone there? Sitting amongst that sprawl of tree roots? Is that a figure or a trick of the light? Slowly, the form resolves itself. It's a man, in clothes the colour of river gum bark, silvery-grey, cream and tan. He's sitting on a huge tree root, one leg high, foot braced, knee bent. Is he balancing a fishing rod, or sleeping, or just staring into the water? It's impossible to tell at this distance. He looks peaceful enough. Is it one of the farmhands? Too far away to be sure. If it's not, he's trespassing, whoever he is.

I ought to cross the river and see what he's up to, Dobie thinks. I ought to fire the shotgun off and frighten seven kinds of shit out of him, lazy bastard. Kipping out there when honest men are working. But these thoughts are just the sad echo of an old bravado, and even as he thinks them, he knows it. The figure, so still, so much in harmony with its surroundings, seems to have emerged from the other life of Dobie's land – the wild life, the secret life, uninvited but mostly welcome, mostly cherished.

40

Thomas isn't fishing and he isn't sleeping. His almost magical stillness is required by his proximity to a long-necked turtle that is balanced on a floating log wedged amongst roots at the river's edge. The turtle is completely covered in mud. Excellent camouflage. If it hadn't been for the perfect curve of the shell, he might have missed it altogether.

Thomas can sit still for a very long time. He's had plenty of practice. Some people find it unnerving, his capacity for silence and stillness. It's as though you go somewhere else, one woman complained. As though your body is there but the rest of you has gone walkabout.

How to explain the fine tuning of all his senses, the energy that such a level of reception requires, and the peace that flows from it to every cell in his body? How can anyone understand that state, or compete with it? Sooner or later, that turtle will move, and Thomas is determined to see it. His brain processes the distant noise of a car engine and dismisses it. There are always vehicles coming and going invisibly around here, or unseen machinery starting up. Sounds can drift a long way on these plains. He doesn't even raise his head at that noise but the next sound that he hears makes him jump uncontrollably, shattering his composure and almost toppling him into the river. It's a loud barking call followed by a series of short grunts. It is coming from a small lagoon to his left and behind him.

Crark – crawwark – crok – crok – crok.

It's unmistakeable. It's the growler, in person. The Southern Bell Frog. Here and now.

Where?

He begins to extricate himself carefully from his position amongst the tree roots. It's vital that he makes no sudden movements, no noise. As he gets his balance, peering through lignum and saplings at the lagoon, the frog continues to call as if beckoning him. There's a splash from behind him. He looks around, just in time to see the widening ripples that mark the turtle's dive into the river.

Story of my life, he thinks.

But there is the frog, sitting pretty on a piece of rotting wood in a patch of sunshine. It's a male, he's almost sure. The females are much larger. He crouches, untangles his binoculars from around his neck and wriggles forward on his belly.

'Hello there. Do you come here often?' he murmurs beneath his breath. 'Hope you've got a couple of lady friends tucked away somewhere.'

The frog is silent, soaking up the sunlight. If he's the

last Southern Bell Frog in the world, he doesn't seem too worried about it.

Thomas eases himself into position for a long watch, avoiding an anthill, determined that nothing short of an earthquake will disturb this vigil. In a second, his world has changed. For Thomas, life is now bright and surprisingly perfect. Everything is possible once again, even, perhaps, the finding of Alice Kinnear. It may take a little more time, a little more patience, but that, he feels, will be no hardship now.

Very gently, he moves one hand to his pack, feeling for his camera without taking his eyes off the frog. He locates it and, at slow intervals, begins to draw it from the pack, every movement a stirring and then a settling, a leaf floating on the air, a twig turning on the water. His breathing is light and measured. Only his eyes convey his delight. This is what he has been waiting for, longing for. Look at him. Happy as a child.

You just know something awful is going to happen.

It does.

His mobile phone rings, shrilling out through the riverlands, and as he makes a grab for it, the Southern Bell Frog disappears.

41

Bel is in her garden.

With earth, you make a garden. With wood, you make a house. With hearts, you make a home. I have made our home here. Raised two children here. And now we have to leave.

She runs a fingernail under the white paint that is flaking off the kitchen windowsill. Through the window she can see the round shape where the clock has hung on the wall. The afternoon sun will continue to shine through here until even the shape disappears.

For a while, after Pearl had come apologising, begging them to stay, Bel had allowed herself to hope. A tiny chink of hope, through which she could see their life unfolding here in her cottage by the river, as surely as it was meant to do. And so she hadn't rung Sara or Daniel and asked them to come home. She's thankful for that now. At first, she could only think of Pete, how he had shut himself off from her, and how their children might reach him in that place where he was stoking his anger. But Daniel, she realises, would have been a far more explosive factor. Just as likely to go after Dobie Kinnear with a shotgun when he heard what had happened. No. She's glad she hadn't called them earlier. And when Pete accepted the new job, he came out of the dark place and held her and spoke to her about the farm they would go to, and then he rang Sara and Daniel and told them the news as if all along it had been his decision to leave.

Better that way. Better not to trouble the babes, she agreed. They have enough problems setting up their own young lives without having to worry about the two of us.

She has packed away the material side of their lives in sturdy boxes, each one labelled so that she'll know which room it belongs in, when they arrive. She has cleaned the house as though it had never been cleaned before, scrubbing the floors, washing down paintwork.

'Why do you bother?' Pete asked.

She doesn't know, only that it must be done.

She remembers coming here, seeing it, the first time. The manager's cottage, adjoining another, smaller, cottage where the shearer and his wife had lived for years until he retired and they went north. My house, she thought. It stood under blue sky, facing open golden pasture, with a shadowing backdrop of greens, browns, cream and silver – the river red gums. There was a garden of knee-high straw, with a drunken fence; weatherboard walls with peeling paint, a green tin roof and a red brick chimney, and it was all hers.

Privately, watching herself going about her tasks, getting everything ready for their departure, she considers the possibility that she is suffering from shock. Her head is full of windy spaces through which voices echo and images from the past shift in and out. Time has the inconsistency of dreams. There is Daniel on the garden swing, a lean three-year-old, already sure of his charm. There is Sara, Bel's little shadow, with her miniature basket on her chubby arm, collecting beans from the vegetable patch, chattering happily to herself. Bel thinks about this daughter of hers, so beautiful that she makes her father shy. She is almost overwhelmed by the need to have her close. Both children had offered to come and help. Better that they come when the new place is ready, she told them, trying to sound bright and hopeful, knowing she couldn't deal with their nostalgia as well as her own. When she's had time to get things organised, they can come, she said. No need to worry. Everything here is under control. And it is, isn't it? Every little last thing organised and under control. Except for this blustering gale in her head and the ragged gaps that grief has left in her heart.

On her knees in the vegetable garden, she takes up what she can. She packs a box for Pearl too, tomatoes, sweetcorn, three kinds of beans, bunches of basil, sage and parsley, knowing that Pearl can come and help herself to this garden once they've gone, and knowing that she won't. She packs away her gardening tools and the labelled brown bags and jars of seeds with which she'll start their new garden. She has cuttings wrapped in damp newspaper. They are from her own garden and from the homestead garden too, taken from all the plants she cannot bear to leave behind. Some will set new roots, some will wither and rot. The household items are packed except for last-minute essentials. Pete is sorting out which tools are his and which belong to the farm. He wants nothing of this place to travel with them, but she will have her plants. Their dogs will come but the chooks have to stay behind.

'Those old girls won't travel well,' he'd said firmly. 'Leave 'em to the new people. If they can find anyone crazy enough to work here. Best we have a fresh start with chooks, when we get there.'

She hadn't argued. What was the point? He was right. He is right about all of it. They have to leave. She understands this, and wonders when belief will bite. When she takes a last look at the river? When their home is packed into the removals truck? When they turn out of the driveway for the last time?

Is she strong enough, for that kind of pain?

She will have to be.

She takes the last bucket of scraps over to the hens. They bustle around her legs, clucking and protesting. Oh, the sweet babbling girls, who will they chatter to when she is gone? Who will gather their eggs and keep them safe from fox and snake? Who will bring them scraps and fling their corn? Who will tend the yellow flowering eucalypt that needs just so much care and no more? Who will have the benefit of this soil, turned and made richer, year after year? Who will water these seedlings? Who will keep the cockatoos from the peaches and apricots? Who will sit by that window and look out over the rosy paddocks as the sun sets? Who? Not Bel.

She knows little about the house they are going to. She hasn't asked. Good or bad, it makes no difference. She will make a home of it, in time.

'There's a garden,' said Pete, who'd had a look over the property. 'It needs a bit of work. Looks like no one's done anything in it for years.' He knows she'll be happier with this, preferring it to an established garden. Someone else's garden. 'And there's a real river, not like this old creek. Trees everywhere, Bel.'

Are they river gums, she wonders? So beautiful that it squeezes your heart sometimes, in a particular combination of light and shadow, just to look at them.

The new place is two hours north of here. Drier country. More sheep. No rice. No more wading through mud to fix up channel breaks and check on the water leaking over the stops. He's pleased about that. As soon as he made the decision, it was as if he'd sent his soul on ahead of him. Bel can feel its absence. What else can she do but pack?

'You'll love it, Bel,' he promised. 'It's a great house. Not falling apart like this old place. Plenty of room for when the kids come to stay. You'll love it every bit as much as here. More.'

Everything about the going is good to Pete. He can't get away fast enough now.

'Give me time,' she said. 'It's going to take a little time.' It doesn't mean you forget. Or forgive. She is relieved that Pete doesn't seem to be planning any grand gestures of revenge. She couldn't bear that. He knows it.

She leaves the box of vegetables and herbs just inside the farmhouse door where the Kinnears will be sure to find it. She's chosen a time when she knows she won't be spotted by Dobie or Pearl, unable to bear the thought of seeing either of them again. Imagine the need to be distant and courteous, when your mouth is full of bile and your mind blasted by treachery. She didn't see it coming. Snake in the grass. She couldn't trust herself not to rage and weep, if she saw them now. It will be a long time before they get anyone else here who will leave them boxes of good food. Let that fact sink home with every mouthful, she thinks. Let them come to understand a little more each day, what they have lost and what they have done. It is enough that we are going.

That night, as Bel slides back the bathroom window to let in cooler air, a small gecko freezes into immobility on the outside of the flywire. This is an old game. The gecko has been here all season, feasting on moths that come flickering at the glass, attracted by the light. It is about five inches long from its mouth to the tip of its tail, with a creamy, translucent belly. It moves its head slightly to the left, lifts a front foot that looks like a tiny, splayed hand. Bel gently scratches the wire beneath its body with her fingernail. The gecko freezes again, becoming both gecko and symbol of gecko. She scrapes softly at the wire beneath the gecko's throat, along its belly. The gecko moves its head around at each vibration. She taps at each of its feet in turn. The gecko makes its way slowly to the top edge of the window. The graceful, curving tail, hanging over the edge, is the last she sees of it.

How can it be? she asks, with her face upturned to the moon and her dry eyes closed. How did I get it so wrong? How can we be leaving this place where I thought I would live till I die?

42

Without headlights, under the stars, it's difficult to see the difference between the dirt road and the land that lies at each side of it. On the bends, Dobie slows almost to a stop, peering anxiously through the dirty wind-screen, trying to define the path he should take.

Suddenly, he's home. The shed and the garden are filled with parked cars. There's no room for the ute. Right along the river track, and stretching back down the driveway, cars gleam in the moonlight. The house is full of light and shouts and laughter. People every-where. It's like a big family party, women with babies in their arms, toddlers outstaring each other at knee level, young children tearing about, shrieking with excite-ment. Plates, piled on tables and chairs and the floor too, bear evidence of leftovers, and indicate that these people have eaten well. Wine bottles stand on every available surface. The cupboard where the glasses are kept is empty, its doors ajar.

The noise of their voices, the laughter, the background music – it's all too much. It's giving Dobie a headache.

He pushes his way through the jostling crowd to his bedroom, and stops. Someone else's clothes have been tossed onto his bed, a pair of runners discarded by the door. The bedclothes are rumpled. Dobie opens the wardrobe. It is filled with clothes. Not his.

'Excuse me!' he calls to a passer-by. 'What's happening here? Who's been sleeping in my bed?'

The man who answers is in his early forties, entirely unfamiliar to Dobie.

'Have you paid?' he says, and turns away to continue a conversation.

Dobie tries another person, and another. He can't make them understand. Some regard him with indifference, others with mild amusement. They look at him in distaste when his manner becomes agitated. Send each other meaningful glances. *Who IS this funny little man?*

They are all at ease in this company and enjoying themselves. He is the interloper here, in his own home. He tries again, shouting this time.

'But where do *I* sleep?'

No one answers. They watch him covertly, with curiosity and without pity.

Dobie goes from room to room, looking for someone who knows him, someone who can tell him what's going on. In the living room, a woman wearing a tight leopardskin dress is sitting in his chair. She has one brown leg raised, resting on the other knee, and she is carefully paring calluses from her foot with a tiny silver knife. He watches as she lifts a piece of skin from the sole. She looks up and shrugs.

'What can you do?' she says.

It's the hitchhiker. The woman he drove all the way to Swan Hill. She doesn't recognise him.

Dobie backs out of there, alien and lost. Summoning all his courage, all the inner conviction of himself as a smaller kind of hero, but a hero nevertheless, he raises his voice above the clamour and roars, 'Doesn't anyone here know WHO I AM?'

The party dissolves and he wakes, sweating and distressed.

43

Thomas is on the road again. He's been into Coola, ostensibly to pick up supplies but the truth is, his nerves are too jangled today for fieldwork. It was that phone call from Robert yesterday. It should have been so simple.

Turn off the phone.

(Oh, good idea, Thomas!)

Take up your position again. Listen. Wait for the frog to call again.

That's what should have happened.

Instead, in the shock of the moment, he'd pressed the button to take the call. But it was too much for him. Frog here. Frog gone. Was he devastated or delighted? Apoplectic or pleased? He couldn't speak. Robert's voice in his ear. The turtle had gone, the frog had gone, and Robert, unable to get any response from Thomas, had gone too.

Turn off the phone. Take up position. Listen.

No. I don't think so.

You idiot, Thomas.

I've never made that mistake before.

See what happens when you get your priorities confused?

I left the phone on in case Alice Kinnear rang me. It might have been her.

Stranger things have happened.

The road takes him closer to the Mamerbrook driveway and his hands tingle with a nervous flashback to the near-accident he'd had here with the old fool. Today, a big van is pulling out slowly onto the road. A & R Removals, it says on the side. A Ford ute, with two kelpies barking madly in the back, follows the truck out of the driveway and then accelerates noisily and overtakes it. Thomas, wide-eyed, gives panic a free rein. Oh no! Oh hell! What's going on? Is it the Kinnears? Is it the long-necked turtle story all over again? Not if he can help it. He swings the car into a screeching U-turn and follows the van.

They go right through Coolabarradin and leave it again on the northern route. Thomas is dithering, can't make his mind up about what to do. Is it the Kinnears? He can't just keep following them. They might be going to Queensland, for all he knows. On a long, straight stretch of road, he overtakes the van and squeezes the station wagon in between it and the ute, earning himself a loud blast on the horn from the van. He flashes his headlights at the ute and keeps doing this until the driver pulls up. Thomas parks behind him and gets out. The removals van slows, then roars past as Pete sticks an arm through the window and waves the driver on.

'Sorry,' says Thomas, smiling frantically. 'Sorry to hold you up.'

'What's the problem, mate? Something wrong with our ute?'

'No. No. Nothing like that. It's just . . . that farm you've just left . . . I thought . . . I was wondering if you might be the Kinnears?'

Pete spits out the window, just missing Thomas's boots.

'Who wants to know?'

'Oh. Look, I really am sorry to be such a nuisance. I wouldn't ask if it wasn't important. I mean, I wouldn't have stopped you like that . . .' He takes a deep breath. 'My name is Thomas Hearne and I'm looking for a woman called Alice Kinnear. My father was a friend of hers, I think.'

It's an odd conversation to be having on the roadside in the middle of nowhere. The big removals van is already out of sight and Pete is impatient to catch up with it.

'Can't help you, mate.' He puts the car into gear.

'Pete.' The woman beside him leans forward, a hand on his arm.

It's Bel.

Thomas is so relieved to see her. 'I found the frog,' he says, 'just like you told me. He's still there.'

She gives him a brief, tired smile but responds only to his query about the Kinnears.

'Have you asked at the farm, about Alice?'

'I couldn't raise anyone when I visited. I tried ringing too, and writing. No luck. And when I saw the truck, I thought it was the Kinnears, moving away. You're not the Kinnears, are you?'

Bel is thinking. If they've had a letter and not answered, it could be because they don't want any part in what he has to say. It's not her business. Pete's as jumpy as hell. He wants to get back on the road and put many long miles between himself and Mamerbrook. She keeps a gentle pressure on his arm. If this man's followed them all the way from the farm, it must be something important.

'I'm Bel Jenkins,' she says. 'This is my husband, Pete. We're going to another farm, north of here, but the Kinnears are still there, at Mamerbrook. You won't meet Alice Kinnear though. She died thirty years ago. I'm sorry.'

Pete closes the window, cutting off Bel's goodbye, and guns the ute, leaving Thomas standing by the road in a cloud of dust.

That's it then, he thinks. That's an end of it.

44

'Robert, it's me. Yes, I know you rang yesterday but I was in a bad reception area. Couldn't get a clear line.'

'Well? How's it going out there? Have you found Henry's mystery woman?'

'I've tracked down Alice Kinnear. She's dead. Died thirty years ago.'

'Oh, thank god for that!'

'What?'

'The rose is mine now. Right?'

'Looks like it might be. We'd better talk about it when I get back. Don't do anything with it yet, will you?' He's not in such a rush to sign off on Henry's quest. Robert's assumptions prick at him. That rose might be one of the greatest achievements of Henry's life. Had the old man spent long moments daydreaming of a time when he himself presented Alice with the rose? And had courage failed him, or loyalty to Nora overcome those desires? Such a lot of effort, years of effort, to produce this gift. For a customer? A friend? A lover? Am I to give up so easily?

But what else can be done?

'All that time you've wasted, chasing around Woop Woop or wherever you are. You might just as well have done what I suggested in the first place. Saved yourself all that trouble.'

'I've been working too,' Thomas reminded him.

'Oh yes. How did it go? Find any frogs?'

'I did, as a matter of fact.'

'There was a bit in the paper last week – something about the last known male Spotted Tree Frog. Think I've got that right. A ranger found it a while back in a national park and brought it in. I thought of you. The article said it produced six hundred offspring in a short period of time. Not a bad effort. Mel cut the article out for you, in case you missed it.'

'I know about it, but thanks anyway,' sighs Thomas. There's one ranger who didn't have his mobile turned on.

'Earth-shattering work you people do out there. With your frogs.'

'Yes, Rob,' says Thomas dryly.

'Tell you what, how about I get Mel to cook up a storm? In honour of Henry's rose? Are you all done up there?'

Is he? He hardly knows which way is up.

'As far as Henry is concerned, I'd have to be. There's really nothing else I can do.'

'And frogs?'

But Thomas knows he couldn't be still long enough for fieldwork. He's full of a queasy dissatisfaction, and the excitement of the hunt, which has kept him moving along since the meeting with Sheila Mulraney, has vanished.

There should have been a discovery.

That's what happens on quests. You make a discovery, and something changes. Something is transformed and nothing is quite the same ever again. It isn't supposed to be like this . . . trotting back to Robert with the rose.

'Dinner sounds good.'

'How about tomorrow evening? Give Mel a bit of time to plan something special. Can you be here by then? We can drink a toast to the old man. And his rose.'

And Alice Kinnear, thinks Thomas.

'I suppose I can be there. I can pack up camp today and leave after breakfast in the morning.'

'Don't sound so excited about it.'

'Sorry. It's just . . .'

'Anticlimax. I told you it was a crazy thing to do. See you tomorrow then.'

Thomas almost hangs up, when it occurs to him to ask (for no reason that he can determine, when he thinks of it later), 'Hey, Rob, that rose of Dad's, does it have a name?'

'Of course it does. He named it after himself. I always thought that was a bit weird. Must have been feeling pretty pleased with himself at the time.'

'He called the rose Henry?'

'Not exactly. He called it Henry's Pearl.'

Tick . . . Tick . . . Silence.

You miss a turtle's dive, you lose a frog, or two; you make an assumption, or two; you spend a lot of time smelling the roses, and what's it all about? What does it all come down to, in the end? The world of Mamerbrook turns and turns under the black magpie moon. Stories rustle in empty rooms, drift into corners, unheeded. You win some, you lose some, and the best laid schemes of mice and men oft go awry, don't they, Henry? You can only throw it all into the pot and hope for the best.

As Alice said.

Thomas cuts the connection. Pearl Kinnear picks up her telephone and dials the mobile number written in blue on a tiny scrap of paper.

Budwood? she thinks, not for the first time since she found the letter. Budwood?

She has to know why.

45

Is that the greatest achievement of Dobie's life, sitting in a cafe in Coolabarradin, drinking her second cup of coffee?

Pearl drove into town early and walked down the main street and then right around the shopping centre. Three times, she strode around the pretty park with its central lake and fountain, then down onto the river track and back to the main street again. It doesn't take long to do this town. She's the only one in the cafe now except for the girl behind the counter and an old man studying the racing form guide who has the look of a permanent fixture. She orders another cappuccino. It won't help her restlessness or quieten her anxieties but she can't just sit here staring out of the window. She's already half-regretting the impulse that led her to ring that mobile number.

'Pearl?' he cried, when she told him why she was ringing.

'Pearl!' he said again, when she confirmed who her mother was. He seemed to be experiencing a private epiphany.

(He was.)

Apparently her mother and his father had known each other a long time ago.

'May I come to see you, and explain?' he'd asked.

'I'll meet you in town,' she said, wondering at the excitement in his tone. A pleasant voice, light and precise. Slight trace of an English accent. Educated. She pictured him in pinstripe, with a goatee. She checks her watch. Still too early, but it won't be long now. And then what?

A man pushes through the door. Tall and bearded, with a distracted air. Something familiar about him. He sees Pearl straight away, sitting alone at her table. She offers him a tentative smile.

'Thomas?'

How scruffy, she's thinking. No one to iron for him. A sudden image of her mother tugging at the collar of Dobie's shirt. *You can't go out looking like that! They'll think nobody loves you.*

'Ah. It's you,' he says. 'You're early too. How are you . . . Pearl? Thomas Hearne. It's very good of you to meet me.'

He grips her hand, smiling and smiling. Pearl!

Think, Thomas. Go softly.

Oh, but she is so like Henry, with that round face and fair hair, it takes his breath away. The same nose. The eyes aren't Henry's though. Fine eyes, watching him warily even as her lips form the smile.

Where to start?

At the beginning, Thomas. At the beginning. Don't

start with supposition and assumptions. Don't frighten her off.

'It would have been hard to refuse,' she's saying. 'You were so mysterious on the phone.'

'Yes. Sorry about that. I wanted to see you. I needed to see who you are. It's not . . . the phone, you know? So inadequate for this sort of thing.'

This sort of thing?

He's still shaking her hand.

He's a little crazy, isn't he? But who isn't?

She extricates her hand, gently.

'I didn't know about you,' he says. 'I didn't know.'

He takes a few moments to regain his composure, breathing in and out audibly, his chest rising and falling as he gazes at Pearl with soft hazel eyes through floppy locks of greying sandy hair, like a twilight creature peering hopefully through the undergrowth.

He has no idea how irritating this is.

What is the matter with the man, she wonders?

'Won't you sit down?' she says. Best manners to mask a rising agitation.

It's coming isn't it, Pearl? You can feel it. Good news or bad news?

'My father knew your mother,' he tells her. 'He was a rose-grower. He died a few months ago. His name was Henry Hearne.'

'Oh!' says Pearl. Then 'Oh!' again.

The signature on the letters in Alice's rose book. *Henry Hearne.*

How odd, she thinks. How interesting.

She relaxes. Just a bit of ancient history after all.

Thomas pulls out a chair, folds his long legs under the laminex table and tells Pearl Kinnear the story of Henry and his roses, about the tape he made for Thomas, and the special rose that Henry created as a gift for Alice.

'He said, "Tell her it's for the budwood."'

'Budwood.'

'Yes.'

'But this is extraordinary. How wonderful. Why would he do that? It's not something you do overnight, on a whim. It takes years to breed a rose.'

It's there, teasing amongst the shadows. The idea.

Now you see it; now you don't.

'He must have been very fond of her,' she says hesitantly.

'Well, yes, I think so.'

'I found some letters from your father,' she says. 'To my mother. She had a scrapbook for her roses and she kept his letters there. In one of the letters, he asks if he could visit her. Alice. My mother.'

Thomas rubs at a reddening patch on his neck. 'I'm sure he did visit her.'

'Yes. There's a photograph . . . I think I may have a photograph of him.'

'Medium height, thick build, floppy hair like mine, except that his was fair? A big round face?'

'Yes, I think so. The photo was taken at Mamerbrook. My home. My mother wrote on the back of it. Budwood.

And something else. Henry's White Rambler, it says, and Budwood.'

'Henry's White Rambler.'

'Yes. Sounds like a rose, doesn't it? There's a rose in the photograph, behind him.'

He seems about to respond, but no words come.

'What is it?' she asks. 'What's the matter?'

'Ah, the rose . . .'

'Yes?'

'Not the rose in the photograph. I mean the special rose that Henry created . . .'

'For Alice.'

'Yes. Look, there's no easy way to say this. I think we need to be careful not to jump to any conclusions, not to, ah, make any unwarranted assumptions, but, the rose . . . it's not as if there's any indication anywhere that my father ever knew you . . . unless perhaps there's mention of you in his letters? Did Alice . . .'

'No, there's nothing about me. The letters are all written before I was born. A long time ago.' She laughs ruefully.

He frowns.

'The rose . . .'

'What about it?'

'He called it Henry's Pearl.'

A space opens up; the known world falls into it neatly and disappears, never to be seen again. The space closes.

'Pearl?' says Pearl.

Thomas nods.

'But . . .' she says, feeling suddenly threatened.

He looks at his hands. Pearl lets her gaze drift to the window but her mind is working furiously to find an explanation. It's ridiculous. A coincidence, nothing more.

'Henry's Pearl is a beautiful name for a rose,' she says. 'They may have discussed it over the budwood. Likely characteristics and so on. No doubt my mother remembered the name later, and took a fancy to it. Don't you think so?' she urges Thomas.

'It's possible,' he says, reluctantly, restrained only by the fear in her voice and by his father's warning. *It's so easy to damage the innocent.* Wait till Robert sees her, he thinks. He won't believe it. The likeness.

Oh my god! Robert! Mel's dinner!

He'll need rotor blades to get there on time now.

'Look, I'm sorry but I have to go. Something I arranged before you rang. It's a sort of family celebration.'

There'll be even more to celebrate now.

He grins at her and she notices that he is younger than she'd first thought. There's a gleam of the boy in that face still and this is why she smiles, despite her tension.

'Pearl,' he says aloud. 'Pearl.'

'Oh don't start that again,' she says. 'It's all right, really it is. You've given me more than enough to think about.'

'You've got my mobile number. Please call me. I'd be happy to come back and see you again, if you want me to. It's just that I'm having dinner with my brother and his wife in Kerrimuir this evening. It's a long drive. He, er, has certain expectations . . . God! I'm so sorry about this.' He scribbles on a napkin. 'Here's my number again. Don't lose it, will you? And here's my address. Oh, and my email address too.'

'I'll call you. I promise.'

Maybe.

'It's probably best if you have a think about all the . . . um . . . implications first. It's not just a rose, you see. Henry's Pearl. It's new. A new creation. There'll be the issue of releasing it to the world, promoting it, distributing it. A whole business comes with it, really. Robert said it's worth money.'

'Money?' Pearl leans forward.

'Quite a bit probably. Rose-growers everywhere are always after the latest new thing, and this one is a real beauty according to my brother, and he's the rose specialist.'

'Good heavens.' Money. Freedom?

'One option you might like to consider is to hand over the business side of things to Robert, for a percentage of the profits. He still runs the very same rose nursery that Henry developed. You must come and see it. Henry created the rose, but Robert has taken care of it. You might like to keep the family connection going?'

Oops. He hadn't meant that in quite the way it came out.

She's looking at him with one eyebrow raised.

Say nothing, Thomas. You'll only make matters worse. You've done your best for Robert. Planted the seeds. You can go to dinner with a clear conscience, at least. And you've done your best for Henry too.

'But what sort of money are we talking about?' she wants to know.

Thomas shrugs. 'There's no point asking me. I haven't a clue about roses. Frogs are my line of work.'

'Frogs? Really? Frogs?'

(Here we go again.)

'Yes. Look, you'll need to talk to Robert. But give me a chance to smooth the way for you. You're going to come as a bit of a surprise to him. Robert . . . I . . . well, neither of us expected you. I've been looking for Alice, you see. Anyway, there's no rush for a decision about this. Now you know. That's the main thing. Now we've met,' he looks right into her eyes, pauses, 'and we'll meet again, won't we?'

'Oh, I'm sure we will. Yes.'

'I'd like to get one of the roses to you as soon as possible,' he says. 'There are several plants of course, but I'd like you to have one here with you, while you're thinking about the whole story. Shall I send it to the farm? To Mamerbrook?'

'No, not to the farm,' she says quickly. 'There's quite a good nursery just outside town. Arbor View, it's called. Will you send the rose there? I can pick it up. And I'll have another look at Henry's letters to my mother. See if there's anything . . . But they're all about roses, I'm sure. I can get copies of them for you, if you like?'

'Thank you. I'd like that. Another piece of the puzzle.' But he knows it's not necessary. Henry's quest is at an end. Thomas has found what he's been sent to find.

'Did your father leave anything . . . was there anything that my mother wrote to him?' she asks.

'No. Nothing. Robert and I hadn't heard of Alice Kinnear until very recently. Oh, I'm sorry,' he says, seeing in her face how much she wanted the letters that Alice had written.

'It's fine. Don't worry. You'd better go. I'll call you. Don't ring me at the farm, will you? My father can be a little . . . difficult. And thank you again for taking the trouble to find us. He must have been very special, your father. I wish I'd known him.'

So do I, thinks Thomas, already on his feet, bracing for the race down the highway. Pearl gives him her hand. He takes it and, leaning down to her, he kisses her very gently on the cheek.

'I'll send the rose for you. You take good care of yourself, Pearl Kinnear. Call me if you have any questions, or if anything comes to mind, or . . . whatever. Call me. I'll see you again, very soon, I hope. After all, you m . . . might be my s . . . s . . . s . . . s . . .'

Sister.

Later, when Pearl is driving home, she remembers that Thomas came to the homestead on the day she pruned the oleanders. The white station wagon. She'd hidden from him. How odd that seems, now. How close she came to missing him altogether. A latent tenderness raises itself, sniffs the air and finds an ample target. Thomas Hearne. He could do with a woman's help, she decides, sensing his vulnerability, with no idea that Thomas has been running as hard as he can from just such impulses all his adult life.

How sad that Alice will never know that Henry Hearne created a rose especially for her.

And named it for her daughter?

You might be my sister.

Oh my goodness!

It's too ridiculous. It's making her stomach churn. With all the excitement, she's forgotten to have lunch. Did she have breakfast? This morning feels like a week ago. She fiddles in the glovebox with her left hand. Somewhere . . . somewhere . . . ah! There they are. Toffees. Caramel and chocolate. They should fill a gap. She pops one into her mouth, and then another one. And another.

Up ahead on the horizon, a grey plume of smoke hangs in the air. Dust, she thinks, but only for a moment. It's rising too straight for that. Smoke then, but a long way off. A few miles further on, as she takes the bend by Warra Creek, she looks again and her interest sharpens. By the time she takes the next bend, the plume has thickened into an ominous stain. Her heart is thudding. It can't be. It can't be! She floors the accelerator. She's miles away still, too far away, but she knows where the smoke is rising from.

'Mamerbrook!' she hawks into the radio past a mouthful of toffee, its sweetness closing off her voice. She tries again. 'Mamerbrook! Fire at Mamerbrook! Is anyone on channel? Please? Fire at Mamerbrook!'

46

'Lucky,' says Marjorie, Gerard Ettie's plump and grey-ing wife, her face streaked with soot.

'Lucky,' says a man whose name Pearl can't remember.

Lucky, they all agree, that it wasn't the homestead, that there was no one inside, that the trees didn't catch, that it didn't spread to the woolshed . . .

But Woolshed Cottage is gutted, its dry old timbers reduced to ash and blackened rubble. Only the brick chimney and hearth are still standing. Bel's pretty white weatherboard, built alongside, is also partially burnt and blackened, corrugated iron lifting from the roof. Take your eye off the place for five minutes and look what happens.

Pearl knows most of the faces milling around her and they all know her. There's a bustling of goodwill and purpose, through which she wanders distractedly. The fire is out. The place was insured. No loss of life or limb. Lucky.

'Thank you so much,' she says, to anyone and every-one. 'Thank you for your help. Thank you for coming.'

As word of her radio call spread, they had come with water tanks on their trucks, from neighbouring farms and far paddocks, with hoses and buckets and consolation. It's the way of things, out here. She had listened, speeding towards Mamerbrook, as Ian Finnegan picked up her call and other voices came on air, one by one.

'Don't you worry, Pearl. We're on our way.'

'Pearl? Alex here. I can see the smoke. I don't think it's the homestead. It looks to be farther over, from where I am. Might be Pete's place . . . Ian, the river tanks are full. We can use those.'

'Meet you there, Ian. Water tank on the truck.'

'Pick me up at the junction, someone. I'm on the tractor.'

'Don't you worry now, Pearl, we're coming.'

'I see it, Ian. On my way there now.'

Within five minutes of her radio call, alone in her car, she was surrounded by camaraderie. Pearl's community, for better or worse.

Now, people are beginning to drift away. One by one the vehicles take off. A couple of men in yellow jackets are still prodding and poking in the ruins, checking that nothing's going to flare if the wind blows up.

Thank god Bel isn't here to see this, Pearl thinks. The state of her beloved house would break her heart. And where is Dobie? She can see his ute down the track, parked in the shed. The truck is there too. He must be over at the homestead. But why didn't he hear all the radio calls or smell the smoke?

'You want to take a look at something, Pearl?' It's Ian Finnegan.

He jerks his head in the direction of Bel's house. She follows him through the white front door, still unmarked except for two handprints and a few dark smudges. He goes into the main bedroom. It is undamaged and empty but there, right in the middle of the floor, is a pair of boots. Her heart jolts. They look like . . . they are . . . Dobie's workboots. They've got those green paint splashes from when he painted the chookhouse last spring. Ian sees fear sweep across her face.

'Oh hell, Pearl, don't go thinking that. I'm sorry. I didn't think. I don't know where Dobie is but he wasn't in Woolshed Cottage, I promise you. No question of it. And I've just checked right through here to make sure the rest of that roof isn't going to come down. He's not here. I just thought it was odd, the boots. So tidy, in the middle of the room like that. Like a joke, or a message or something.'

Ian's voice reaches her through air that is thickening and curdling, long sonorous syllables of reassurance, the voice slowing, almost stopping. Is she dreaming? Is she? Did she fall asleep in the cafe? Did she dream Thomas Hearne and Henry's rose? Has she dreamed the fire, the boots?

No. Not dreaming.

The boots are there, empty of Dobie, in the empty room. Their surreal presence chills her. Where is her father?

'I'd better go and find him,' she tells Ian.

Sagging with weariness, she turns away. No need now to summon up an expression of bright gratitude. There's no one to see it. No need to keep her voice light and sensible. There's no one here to listen. The help received from her neighbours has cracked a great reservoir of need in her. Successive waves of fear and self-pity crash against the poor flawed substance that holds them back. Pearl's sanity. Tears swell and drop faster and faster, and she begins to run towards the homestead, a blundering, heavy woman, crying too much to see anything except the ground in front of her feet, stumbling up the dirt track as fast as she can.

They collide by the sheds, Pearl running blind, away from the burnt house, and Dobie, with his cheek grazed and his right eye swollen shut, running towards it. He falls to the ground at the impact, badly winded.

She's killed him! Breathless, she drops to her knees beside him and shakes him by the shoulders. 'Dad! Dad!'

He groans.

Not dead.

'Anything I can do to help here?'

Pearl looks up. A large figure, with curly hair and broad shoulders, comes between her and the brightness of the afternoon sun. Who *is* this man? The Archangel Gabriel?

Pearl begins to laugh.

'It's not really a habit of mine, rescuing people,' says the onion man, apologetically.

She can't stop laughing, hiccoughing giggles with tears streaming down her face.

He crouches beside her to assess Dobie's injuries.

Dobie groans, pulls himself into a sitting position and throws a lucky punch that glances off the big man's chin as Dobie falls over again.

'Hey! Steady on there. I'm only trying to help.'

Dobie screws up his good eye and squints at him.

'Where is the little sod then? Give me half a chance, I'll fix him. He should have fried in the place. Should have gone up with the rest of it. Bastard.'

He coughs, winces. The air is full of the smell of burning and hazy with smoke.

'It's gone, hasn't it?'

'Just Woolshed,' says Pearl. 'We can fix up Bel's place.'

It will always be Bel's place now. They both know that.

'Did you see him? Did you get the little bastard?'

They have no idea what he's talking about.

'How about we get you both inside,' suggests the onion man, 'and we can sort it all out from there?'

He holds out his hand and hauls Pearl to her feet. She puts a hand to her hair, pulls her shirt straight.

'What about them?' He nods in the direction of the two men turning over debris at Woolshed Cottage.

'Oh, they'll want to get back to their own farms, I expect. There'll be time for thanks later, and lots of beer, no doubt. There's no rush. We'd do the same for them. They know it.'

Dobie, down on the ground, clears his throat loudly. Why the hell are they standing there chattering when he's been beaten to a pulp?

'Going to leave me sitting out here all afternoon, are you?'

The onion man grins. Together they get Dobie onto his feet and support him back to the house. He's been punched in the ribs and stomach, as well as his face. Walking is giving him a great deal of pain but anyone can see that there's no point offering to carry him. Battered, bruised and bewildered, there's still a certain cockiness in the set of his old shoulders and the carriage of his head.

Pearl bathes the graze on Dobie's face and makes him hold a packet of frozen peas on his swollen eye. He assures her that there are no broken ribs.

'It's just bruising. Stop fussing, woman,' he tells her, enjoying it immensely.

The onion man is in their kitchen, hunting through her cupboards for tea, milk and sugar. He carries in steaming mugs on a tray and hands them out. Dobie takes a sip, curses when he scalds his mouth. He's bursting to tell his story but he wants them settled and paying attention.

'It was that young Chris,' he says. 'I had him working down by the river pump, mending a channel break. After half an hour or so, I thought, I'll just nip back and see how much real work he's doing.'

Pearl stifles a groan.

Dobie continues. 'I had a feeling about him, the first time I met him. He had a shifty look about him. I would never have hired anyone like that,' he adds, virtuously, daring anyone to challenge him.

'When I got within sight of the pump, he wasn't there. I had an idea he might be taking it easy, hiding out in Woodshed Cottage, so I crept up the back steps and pushed open the door and there he was, leaning back against the wall, with some magazines spread out on the floor in front of him – filthy stuff! – and his cigarette balanced on the windowsill – I remember seeing the smoke rising while he . . . anyway . . . you can imagine what.'

Telling them, he's incensed all over again. In Woolshed Cottage! And Dobie paying him good wages to get a job done!

'Take it easy,' warns Pearl. 'We get the picture. What happened next?'

'I fired him, that's what. Told him to get into the truck and drove him straight up to the sheds. Get your stuff, I said, and get off my property. Told him I didn't want to see his face here again. And how am I supposed to get to town, he asks, when my lift isn't due till the end of the day? I told him I couldn't give a damn. You can walk, for all I care, I said. Just get your hide off my land right now. And that's when he hit me. Whoompf! One, two, three times!'

Dobie tries to swing his arm to illustrate the punch but it hurts his ribs too much.

'The bastard,' says Pearl. 'Chris Tillman.'

Dobie remembers. 'I went to school with a Tillman. Thought that name rang a bell. Might be his grandfather. He was a bastard too.' He looks down at his hands. 'Just wish I'd managed to get a punch in before I went down, you know. Anyway, I must've been out cold for a while. When I got to my feet, there was bedlam and smoke everywhere. I came around the corner there and you ran straight into me and knocked the life out of me. I think you did more damage than he did!' he says to Pearl indignantly.

'And then you arrived,' he says, turning to the onion man, who's sitting quietly beside them, taking it all in. 'I'm Dobie Kinnear, and this is my daughter Pearl. What's your story then?'

'Well,' he begins, 'I've come to pick up a load of hay to take over to Todmorden for my brother but it seems as though every time I get here, there's another catastrophe. Last time, it was a snake bite and a mercy dash to the hospital. I still haven't managed to load any hay.'

'So you're the bloke who rescued my daughter? I've been wanting to catch up with you, sir. We are in your debt. Pearl,' he waves an imperious arm in the direction of the dining room, 'bring out that bottle of single malt whisky and some glasses for us. Bugger the tea.'

She knows better than to suggest that malt whisky might not be the best idea after the shock and the beating he's taken.

'Would you like to stay for dinner?' she asks the onion man, thinking to take advantage of Dobie's good humour. 'And we've plenty of rooms here. You don't have to worry about drinking and driving home. You're welcome to stay. And then tomorrow I can show you where the hay is stacked, if you like?'

'I wouldn't want to put you to any trouble,' he says.

'Trouble!' roars Dobie. 'After what you've done for us? Nothing is too much trouble. Stay. Unless you have a little woman to get home to?'

'No. No little woman,' says the onion man.

Aha! says a voice in Pearl's head. Full alert.

'That's that then,' says Dobie, tossing back his whisky and holding out his glass for a refill.

Ten minutes later, he's slumped on the sofa, fast asleep.

'It won't be any trouble,' Pearl assures their guest. 'I'll take a casserole out of the freezer and defrost it. I can have it ready in less than an hour.'

He looks across at the old man and lowers his voice. 'You know, a guest for dinner is the last thing you need after the trouble you've had today. I'm grateful for the offer, but I'd like to take a raincheck, if you don't mind. You look exhausted. How about I take myself off home and you run yourself a hot bath and relax?'

It's true then. There are men like this on earth.

'I think you're right,' she smiles, wondering at the relief she feels. Must be getting old, Pearl.

But too much is happening. Too many things, too quickly. She can't get a grip on any of it. Her whole life is whirling. I may spin out over the garden and into the evening sky, never to be seen again, she thinks, keeping her feet firmly on the floor. And who can I talk to? Not Dobie.

Thomas?

Yes. Now there is Thomas, and Robert, and once there was Henry, too.

Astonishing thoughts.

'Do you think you should call the police, and tell them what's happened here, with the fire?' asks the onion man.

'I don't know how Dad will feel about that.'

'It may have been deliberately lit.'

'That's true. I'll see what he says when he wakes up. You'll come and visit soon?'

'That I will. I have a load of hay to collect, remember?'

'It seems ridiculous, but I still don't know your name.'

'Mannie Eidelson,' he tells her. 'At your service.'

Jewish? thinks Dobie, surfacing for a moment but keeping his eyes shut. He doesn't look Jewish.

47

Pearl covers Dobie with a blanket and leaves a lamp lit so he won't be too disoriented when he wakes up on the sofa, which he does, in the early hours of the morning. It's still dark outside. He knows exactly where he is and remembers every detail of the day before. What he forgets is not to move. He straightens his legs without thinking, and the pain makes him cry out. Hell's bells, what's a man to do? He's bursting to go to the toilet. It takes him five minutes to get up off the sofa and another ten to hobble to the bathroom.

The house is still, the silence absolute, but something has changed. What is it?

Mannie Eidelson.

A frown touches Dobie's face, makes him wince.

Would you like to stay for dinner, she said. *You don't have to worry about drinking and driving home.*

Pearlie?

There was something in her voice. Beyond gratitude.

He'd heard their soft chatter as he floated in and out of sleep. *You'll come and visit soon?* she said. The nuance there. The hope.

What can you do?

All these years of plotting and manipulating. Is this what it comes down to? Sir Onion Farmer turns up on his white horse, saves her life and carries her off. Is that it?

Not if Dobie Kinnear has anything to do with it. Not after all these years of guarding her and keeping her safe.

Keeping her safe?!

Well . . . keeping her here.

Is it the effect of the malt whisky, or the over-excitement of the day? Lying in bed, he allows himself the rare comfort, half-memory, half-fantasy, of Alice. Her slender body and cool, soft skin, the small hard curve of a hip bone, the ripple of her ribs. Oh, how fragile she was, how strong he felt with Alice in his arms. And anything was possible.

'You're the one, my only one. You're the stars in my eye, the moon in my sky . . .'

My only one, she murmured.

The passion they shared! Too good to be true, she'd say, laughing, ducking her face into his shoulder, embarrassed by her own hunger for him.

Too good to be true.

For a long time, they had the world to themselves. Just the two of them. They planned for children, tried for them, god knows, but eventually Alice had resigned herself to the fact that it wasn't to be.

'Can't have everything,' she whispered, stroking him.

314

'Who needs children?' she'd say, joking. 'I'm waiting for my husband to grow up.'

'It's all right, Dobie my love. We have each other.'

'*You're the moon in my sky . . .*'

And she would kiss him and kiss him, to make it better. The wonder of it was that they hadn't had fifty children. But it didn't make it better. Not for Dobie. There had to be a child. There just had to be. And then, one summer morning amongst the roses, she'd told him.

'It's happened, Dobie. We've done it! Just imagine,' she said, serious for once, as they both gazed in disbelief at her still-flat stomach, 'I'm growing a child.'

Pearl.

48

It's past seven in the morning and birds are calling all over the garden. Even from her bedroom, Pearl can smell the after-effects of the fire. The acrid fumes had crept into every corner of the house. She props herself on one elbow remembering all the events of the last couple of days, frowning when she thinks of Chris Tillman. Had he really set fire to the cottage? Something will have to be done.

She goes through into Dobie's part of the house, following the sound of his rumbling snores to his bedroom. When she peeps in on him, he's lying on his back with his mouth wide open and his poor bruised face all swollen on one side. He will be so sore and stiff when he wakes. Better that he sleeps as long as possible. He's been up for a bite to eat during the night, she notices. There's a telltale line of crumbs leading from the biscuit tin in the pantry. It reminds her that she promised herself to write an advertisement for a housekeeper. She won't weaken. Not now. She won't back down and she won't ask permission. And she won't tell him about it until it's there in the paper, right in front of his eyes. The winds of change have blown right off the Beaufort Scale at Mamerbrook. Might as well ride on the back of them while she can.

An hour later, she is sitting with Alice's rose book, lost in thought. The book lies open at the design for the garden bed outside her own bedroom. The incongruity of that yellow climbing rose, Emily Gray; the odd combination of plants. She jumps when someone raps at her window.

She peers through the net curtain. Who on earth . . .?

She peers again. She can't believe her eyes.

It's Dan. Her first reaction is a flood of irritation.

Interesting.

Should she answer the door or hide until he goes away? Can't do that now, Pearl. He's seen you through the window. Blast him. How strange, that he should turn up without ringing first – and this early in the day.

Dan knocks again.

'Pearlie?'

There's something meek about that voice.

She opens the door.

'Pearlie!' he says, arms held wide and a great big smile. 'I was in the area. Thought I'd pop by and see how you're getting on. Heard you had a fire here yesterday. Everything okay?'

Pearl, still in her dressing gown and without a bolstering mask of make-up, is annoyed and looks it.

'Everything's fine, thanks.' She tries to smooth a lock

of hair that's sticking straight up over her ear. 'I wish you'd rung, Dan.'

He misunderstands her. 'Missed me, have you? I've thought about ringing a few times, but didn't get around to it. Busy. You know how it is. Still, I'm here now. Aren't you going to ask me in, Pearlie?'

She steps back, unwillingly. One more thing outside her expectations. One more shake of the kaleidoscope that is Pearl's world.

'You weren't yourself, the last time I rang, Pearlie. Bit out of sorts, were you?'

Where has this plaintive tone come from? This isn't the Dan she knows. Suddenly, she understands. You didn't like getting the brush-off from me, did you? You didn't ring before turning up because the last time you tried that, I didn't want to play. You're here to stake your claim again, make sure I haven't wriggled out from under your foot. What's wrong, Dan? Not finding it so easy anymore? Women not beating a path to your door? Not panting for the touch of your big belly and the taste of your brown teeth? Well, well . . . She cannot feel the slightest surge of that sexual need that has kept her running to him for so long.

Her watchful silence is making him uncomfortable. He looks around for something to hang a comment on, sees the rose book open on her table and ambles across to it.

'I'm quite fond of roses,' he says, hoping to break the odd tension, 'but I haven't the time for gardening. Beth takes care of that side of things.'

318

Ooops. Slack of him to mention his wife here. This is not going the way he'd planned but he knows how to put things right. He's about to turn to Pearl, his hand already lifting to touch her, when something on the page catches his eye. He stops.

'Hey! That's clever, that is.' He's pointing at the rose bed design. 'See?'

She looks down at it.

'See what?'

'They spell a name,' he says. 'The first letters of the roses on that side. It's your name. P. E. A. R. L. That's great. I like that.'

'Yes,' she agrees, holding his eyes with hers, willing him not to look down at the page again. 'This book was my mother's. She was a great one for roses.'

She picks it up. How calm she is. You wouldn't think that the book is almost leaping from her fingers.

'Dan, why don't you pop into the kitchen and make us both some coffee?'

She desperately needs to be on her own with this, because she can see what he hasn't yet noticed – that there's another name there.

Dan is confused. Shouldn't she be making the coffee? But she probably wants to brush her hair and put on some lipstick so she can look her best for him. Nothing worse than a woman who lets herself go, is there?

At the door, he pauses. 'Er, what about your dad?'

Funny. That's exactly what Pearl is thinking.

'Dan, be a darling. Just go and put the kettle on. Dad's

still asleep. He had a rough day yesterday. I'll join you in a minute. There's just something I have to do first.'

He goes off, reassured; the old magic is still working.

Alone, Pearl spells out with her finger the names that the two-part rose bed gives her.

Honorine de Brabant   Peace
Emily Gray   Emily Gray
Nuits de Young   Amelia
Rosa Mundi   Reine des Violettes
Yolande D'Aragon   Louise Odier
Souvenir de la Malmaison

Here it is again. First from Henry and now from Alice. Got the message now, have you, Pearl?

Tick. Tick. Tick.
Oh, Dobie.

49

Dobie's eye is healing well. The swelling has gone down and the graze on his cheek has almost disappeared but there's a hollowness inside him, spreading, as though he's dissolving from the inside out. It's an old enemy. Fear.

Pearl's been at him to press charges against Chris Tillman for the fight and the fire.

Fight? Hah!

There it is. The voice. The ongoing commentary inside his head that's giving him permanent indigestion and confusing him.

He can still feel the shock of the blows vibrating through him, the casual, brutal strength behind the fist, the utter abuse of that power. It shouldn't have been possible. No one but his father has ever raised a hand against Dobie. He warms his spirit with visions of what he would have done if Tillman hadn't caught him by surprise, imagines himself at the head of a posse of furious farmers riding over the Riverina plains, tracking down a cringing, terrified Tillman and then stringing him up.

Ah! listen to him shrieking for mercy . . .

There ought to be consequences.

*You know perfectly well, if you'd had your strength,
you'd have thrashed him – no thought of laying charges.*

That voice again; it's twisting his brain into pretzels.
Is he getting a conscience? At his age?

If he lays charges for the attack, won't it be because
he was too old and feeble to fight back?

Jesus! thinks Dobie, pushing open the back door.
Give me a break.

He bends stiffly to pull on his boots, winces at the
bruising on his ribs. Blackleg jumps at him from behind
and his heart knocks hard in the split second before he
realises it's only the dog. He gets his balance, gets his
breath, pulls his hat straight, and the two of them troop
slowly across the lawn towards the ute. Time he took a
closer look at the damage to Bel's place. Just as well they
haven't got anyone needing it straight away.

Pearl is convinced that Tillman started the blaze.
Revenge because Dobie sacked him. Dobie hasn't
argued with her but the voice in his head thinks otherwise, presenting him again and again with the image of
curling blue smoke rising from a cigarette balanced on
the windowsill.

Is it true? Did I hustle him out of there before he had
a chance to grab that cigarette? Did I?

You know what that means, don't you?

The fire was all my fault.

Why not? Seems like everything else around here is!

So how can he lay charges, not being sure?

He goes into Bel's house, feeling its desolation and remembering sadly the fresh gingham curtains and the rainbow rag rug. The stench of smoke and burnt cables still hangs in the air. No whisper of Bel's voice. No crackles of Pete's easy authority over the radio. Too late now to be sorry, Dobie, for anyone but yourself.

Most of the rooms are untouched by the fire. The damage is mainly in the roof. Looks like they can get the place back into shape pretty soon. He walks into the main bedroom, rears back as though he's been slapped. Christ! Is he dreaming? He looks over his shoulder for a clue, or a hovering stepmother. Anything. What the hell is going on? Is that a pair of boots?

(It is.)

My boots?

(They are.)

Why are they here?

There's no answer to that.

He looks around again apprehensively before he picks them up. Is it a trap? A joke? Is he being watched? He turns the boots this way and that. He knows perfectly well what they are. He just doesn't believe in them. He puts them on the floor and walks away. It's not that they're unwearable – a bit damp, that's all. And they were his favourite boots, comfortable as a pair of old slippers. But entire centuries have passed since those boots disappeared. It would be like walking around in a dead man's shoes, he thinks, with a sudden rush of goosebumps. Perhaps, when he leaves, they'll disappear again, like a trick of the light?

(They don't.)

He struggles with himself. Goes back in and looks down at them. Just a pair of boots, after all. He wriggles his feet into them, bracing himself against the wall. There! Waste not, want not. He carries his town boots home.

50

The sun rises through the pale dawning of a Thursday morning, long fingers of yellow light stretching over the well-watered lawns, the sleep-shrouded trees and shrubs of Mamerbrook. Creeping imperceptibly outwards and upwards, the yellow light climbs the trunk of the river gum that stands, eighty feet high, beside the house. It warms the bark, quickening the dark hanging ribbons of leaves and stirring three hundred roosting sulphur-crested cockatoos, who wake with raucous astonishment.

Magpies and butcher birds toss their warbling notes across peaceful paddocks where those small mammals who have survived this night's excursions nestle down in the safety of the deep earth. Sparrows, finches and thornbills set up a twittering and a chattering. Down by the river, fifteen stately night herons fold their cinnamon wings close and settle behind the green drapes of the willow trees to sleep away the day.

By a small lagoon that was once a part of the river's flow at the farthest extent of a curve, a large frog emerges from under a rotting log and, as the sunlight touches her exquisite turquoise thighs, she growls once, twice, three times for her eggs in the still water, for the warmth of the waking world.

Out and away over all the flat pastures of the plains, the fingers of light spread, touching the grasses and shrubs with blue-greens, browns and palest gold, pouring into a casual arrangement of dry grasses built by a small, round, speckled brown bird.

Behind the walls of the farmhouse, where daylight has not yet penetrated, Pearl stirs from her sleep on the rising tide of cockatoo calls and gets ready for work. The farm is beginning to recover its rhythms. The men appear to be working hard under Dobie's supervision. Alex Wenham is taking on more responsibility and doing good work on the rice header, something that would have been Pete's job in normal times. These are not normal times, but somehow, they're managing. As yet, no one has applied for the manager's position.

Pearl agreed to do the morning sheep run one day, when no one else could be spared to do it, and now she does the run every day, reporting over the radio if she needs help moving injured or flyblown stock. She's not imagining the increased respect in the voices of the men when they respond to her calls. They see the old man out there too, doing more than his share of the work, and they won't be shamed by him. They've all heard the gossip about Chris Tillman and they are unanimous in their condemnation of anyone who would raise a hand against an old farmer. It will be a cold day in hell before Tillman is welcome anywhere hereabouts. And Dobie, to his amazement, finds that he is supervising a team that knows exactly what needs to be done.

There's loyalty for you.

At last.

What a season it's been, thinks Pearl, swinging on the steering wheel to bring the truck around parallel with the water channel. What god did they offend? Is it safe now? Is it over?

Not yet, Pearl.

Not quite.

Whenever she gets a minute to herself, and that's not often with all the extra work, Pearl gets out the rose notes again. She's worked her way through from the front to the back, examining everything. The other rose bed designs yield no clues or names. They are exactly what they seem to be – plans for rose beds. She has studied the letters from the rose-grower, Henry Hearne, Thomas's father.

'. . . it would be marvellous if you could see your way to inviting me . . .'

She finds the photograph of the man, taken outside this house. The photograph that had been tucked away (now she comes to think of it, secretly, safely, tucked away) in Alice's jewellery box. She will keep it there, she decides, together with the garden plan that spells out the name of the rose, and the letter from Henry in which he asks Alice for permission to visit. What was it that Alice had written on the back of the photograph?

'Henry's White Rambler.'

Not the name of a rose. The name of a man and a rose.

And 'Budwood'.

For the budwood, Thomas had said. This was the budwood stock that Alice had given to Henry. The White Rambler. She's sure of it.

Pearl turns the photograph over.

'Hello, Henry,' she says softly. 'Am I Henry's Pearl?'

Oh, Alice!

Oh, don't blame me!

51

Dobie's out in the paddocks surveying his territory, trying not to think about the return of his boots. He's wearing them but hasn't quite managed to shake off that creepy feeling. Where have they been, all this time? Sometimes, you're better off not knowing, and that's a fact. Just another one of life's mysteries. Like women, he thinks bitterly. How could Pearl, who has everything she wants right here, even begin to contemplate leaving him for some onion farmer? Ha! See how much vodka she can bring home on *his* earnings. The brother down in Todmorden still hasn't got all of the hay that he's paid for. Mannie must be delivering the damn stuff one bale at a time, it's taking so long for the stack to go down. She's been seeing him and she hasn't said a word to her father about it. She's slipping away. He can feel it like a draught between his shoulder blades, the downrush of air from a wingbeat. A gust of loneliness.

'You seeing a bit of Mannie, are you?' he'd ventured at last. 'Getting serious, is it?'

Oh, but she resented that. His questioning her. She bristled.

'I like his company. His conversation. There's little enough of that around here.'

'He's Jewish, you know.'

'So?'

She doesn't understand. He has to know.

'But is it serious, Pearlie?'

'Serious? What do you mean? We have a cup of coffee together now and again.'

'Oh, for god's sake! Is it *serious*? Will you be going out to dinner with him? Going to dances? Getting engaged? Getting married? Going on a bloody honeymoon?'

Going?

He has to know.

'How would I know? I've only just met the man,' she says, and then adds slyly, hopefully, 'I might.'

They'll need watching, the pair of them. He'll have to see that she doesn't rush into anything, make any rash decisions. The worms curl in his mind; the voices croak and chatter. What kind of a house would an onion farmer have? What kind of a future can he offer Dobie's daughter? There must be something useful around a farm this size that the man can do? Perhaps I should make him an offer, he thinks. There must be some way I can stop her from leaving.

He slows the ute down, squints through the windscreen.

What in hell's name is that man doing over there, with the binoculars?

Dobie pulls up, close enough to call through the window.

'G'day. Help you with anything?'

'I'm not trespassing. I'm on public land.'

Now what's he got to be so defensive about?

'True, but it's my land you're looking at. A man can ask, can't he? What am I missing?'

He keeps his tone genial, casual. He watches the stranger weigh up the consequences of replying, as if wondering whether he needs to get Dobie on side.

'I'm a birdwatcher,' he says.

'Oh yes? I know a bit about birds myself. We've got a lot of them round here. What are you looking for?'

The man has a brief inner struggle with something, an excitement, a secret. He keeps it to himself.

'Oh, you know, whatever turns up.'

Here? thinks Dobie. By the side of the road, in the middle of nowhere, on my farm? You've come to watch birds here?

And suddenly, it's granted to him in a vision of perfect clarity, the awful truth – what this man has come for, and the many hundreds who will follow him. The letters that will arrive from the Departments of this and that. The contractors who will come to fence off part of his land. The inspectors who will hand over his rights to twitchers and greenies, all because of a shy little speck-led brown bird: the Plains Wanderer.

There's only one way the word has got out. There is only one man who knows, as Dobie knows; only one man who cares, as Dobie cares, that the little birds have been flourishing here at Mamerbrook.

Pete.

A quiet but effective revenge.

52

Pearl, staring through the kitchen window at the sky, is seeing only Henry Hearne's face in black and white. Caught up in the fascination of herself with another father, another family, another story. It's possible, she thinks. But then again, it is not possible. It is ludicrous. The idea that she might not be Dobie's daughter?

Who, then?

Who am I, without my assumptions?

What do you want to believe, Pearl? What do you need to believe?

She begins to look more closely at herself. At what she has achieved. What she has allowed. At what she has become.

And – oh! the utter impossibility of any conversation on the subject.

Dad, do you remember a rose-grower coming here...?

Dad, did you ever know a man named Henry Hearne?

Dad?

And if there is a flash of fear or anger behind his eyes, a glint of recognition, or the sudden, forced composure that would tell her that she's on to something – what then? It has the power of dissolution, this thought. She doesn't like it.

Better the devil you know, eh?

Hell's bells, one father is enough to deal with.

But the thought won't go away.

Look at all the lines winding out from that one clue that Alice left for her to find. Look at all the possibilities, all the implications. And look up.

She showers and puts on make-up sparingly, taking some time with her hair. In an hour's time, an applicant for the housekeeper job is coming to be interviewed. The only applicant. Looks like there isn't going to be a rush on for a housekeeping job on a farm way out of town. Pearl has promised herself she won't be too finicky. It isn't as if she has to like this person. She just wants the work done. By someone else.

Later on, she's going into town on a special errand. And Dobie has a doctor's appointment for his quarterly injection. She can run him in there, as long as he's behaving himself. I'm not going to put up with any more crap, she thinks, and knows that it's true.

According to her letter of application, the woman sitting in front of Pearl has first-aid qualifications and some experience caring for old people. She's older than Pearl had thought. A bit grim and bony. She can't imagine asking this woman to clean out the chookhouse.

'As I mentioned in my letter,' the woman says,

'I require weekends off. No exceptions. I always stay with my sister in town at the weekends and I don't know how she'd manage without me. She's a good deal older than me and not in the best of health. And then there's gardening. You have a very large garden here.' She looks out through the dusty window.

'Oh, yes,' says Pearl, relieved that the conversation is taking a positive turn. 'We do like our garden. Do you enjoy them? Gardens?'

'I like to sit in them,' she replies. 'Not that I get much time for that.' She sighs and looks down at her hands. 'We do what we must, but it isn't easy.'

Pearl thinks it best not to respond.

'And the cooking? How many meals a day will you require? I hope you have no objections to the occasional frozen supermarket meal? I can't be cooking all the time, especially not with such a large house to keep clean.' She looks around the room doubtfully, as though it might, by itself, prove too great a challenge to her capacities.

'And beds. I don't do beds. Too dangerous for the back at my age, you know. The old gentleman you mentioned, your father? He's not . . . infirm, is he?'

'My father's fine,' says Pearl indignantly. 'Still doing a full day's work on the farm. Wonderful really, at his age.'

And it is. But she hears an echo with that irritating question mark in her head.

My father?

How it fractures her awareness. The world before the rose notes, and the world beyond. Only the essence that is Mamerbrook remains unchanged, untouched.

To dispel the feeling, she quickly suggests a tour of the house. In the dining room, the woman looks pointedly at all the surfaces that need to be dusted, at the dirty streaked windows.

'Well, slate tiles are easy enough to sweep, I suppose,' she says, looking at the floor.

'They have to be polished, once a month at least, to bring the colour out,' says Pearl firmly. She has already made up her mind.

The woman sniffs in disapproval, twitches at a corner of the lace table cloth and looks beneath. They both gaze in horror at the crumbs and fluff-balls of dust, and what looks like a squashed grape smeared between two tiles.

'Something under there,' says the woman, standing back for Pearl, who, blushing with shame, goes down on her knees to retrieve part of an old envelope with scribbles on the back. She stuffs it into her pocket. Enough is enough.

'Thank you so much for coming,' she says briskly, rising to her feet.

'I can't start for two weeks, I'm afraid. I have obligations.'

'Oh. I'm sure you understand that we have other applicants to see. We'll be in touch. Very soon.'

'I see. Other applicants.' A likely tale, her face says.

Pearl is beyond caring. She wants the woman out of the house.

'Thank you for coming,' she repeats.

'You will find a great dearth of good quality, honest candidates. People such as myself,' the woman warns, her thin lips curling in dissatisfaction.

'I'm sure you're right, and it was very good of you to come all the way out here. I have your details. We won't be long in making our decision. You can see how we need help.'

'I can indeed,' she says, with another disparaging glance at the room. 'I hope for your sake that I am still available when you do call.'

Pearl hadn't expected to be pleased when their only applicant takes off in a little blue Mazda and high dudgeon, but she is. The house gives a quiet shudder of relief. Dust, everywhere, reclaims its territory. The garden relaxes and draws another breath. Blue wrens flit in the undergrowth, unaware of the shadow that has passed. Oh well, she'll just have to run the advertisement for another week and see what it brings. She leaves the letter of application on the kitchen bench, so Dobie can see that she means business, this time.

Dobie's inspecting the sandwiches she's made for his lunch. He's lost weight over these last few weeks. Picking at his food like a sparrow and shrinking into himself. His cheeks hang in veined pouches and his neck is scraggy and grey-looking. Pearl has noticed, at

336

moments when he believes himself unobserved, a cloud behind his eyes, of uncertainty or bewilderment. She wonders uncomfortably what it means. He looks tired too, all the time, though he still won't admit to it.

Tired? Me? Never felt better.

He's had a shower this morning without her nagging him. His sparse white curls are tousled and clean. He's wearing an old jumper, also clean, but inside out, with the label showing at the back. She has an unexpected urge to give him a hug, but resists. He might die from the shock. He is frail, this man, she realises.

And too old to change myths mid-stream.

How can I ever ask him about the rose-grower?

You can't. Leave him his stories. Let him believe what he wants to believe.

But I want to know.

You do know.

Yes.

But does he?

It hits her then – all the effort that has gone into deceiving this man, Dobie Kinnear. Protecting him. Keeping his illusions safe. Keeping the secret. Alice, writing the code in her rose book. Henry – the long years spent developing, tending and naming his secret rose. And Thomas, prowling about, knocking at doors, waiting for a chance to deliver his message to the right person.

And now it's up to me, Pearl thinks. Well, I can keep a secret too.

Dobie is reading the letter of application from the housekeeper. He holds it up to the light from the window, peers at it, mutters an incredulous expletive.

She braces herself.

'I told you I'm getting a housekeeper, Dad.'

'Jesus Christ! You didn't take her on, did you?'

'She was too gloomy. Wouldn't do this, wouldn't do that. I thought we could do better.'

He sags visibly against the bench-top, in relief.

What is it now, she wonders?

Dobie has read the letter three times and it still says the same thing: Veronica Brecken-Holmes. Brecken! Another Brecken is about what he can expect, the way things are in his life right now. But what are the odds against that happening? The name cropping up again after all this time?

Now that he knows he's safe, he wishes he'd taken a peek at her. She might have been related to the old witch herself.

'What did she look like?' he asks, trying not to sound interested.

'Oh, you know, respectable, judgemental, boring, ordinary. With a chip on her shoulder. A grudge against the world.' Pearl shrugs.

Yes, he thinks, that's how they always look.

53

When they get to the doctor's, there's no one else in the waiting room. Dobie can't remember ever being here without other people. It feels ominous. There isn't even a receptionist behind the high desk. The phone rings, unattended. Might be somebody dying on the other end. He's fidgety and irritable, not looking forward to another prodding from Dr Li. Pearl crosses her legs and buries her nose in a magazine. All right for her.

A woman appears from the corridor, heavily pregnant, flushed and triumphant.

'Oh, I know,' she's saying over her shoulder through a broad smile, 'you can't expect anything else at this stage, can you? But it won't be long now. I'm glad you're here though. Wouldn't want to go through it without you.'

And following her into the reception area, scribbling notes in a manila folder and saying, 'That's very kind of you, but you'll be perfectly all right you know, with or without me,' is Dr Macnulty.

Dobie's heart gives a great bounce. She smiles at him,

recognising him, and his heart is doing a polka now. Steady, boy.

'Mr Kinnear, how are you today?'

'Still here,' he says, joyfully. Shyness steals over him as he shuffles over to her and follows her down the corridor.

'Had a new fellow in here last time I came,' he says, his voice thickened with emotion.

'Yes. Dr Li. It was so good of him to fill in for me at short notice. He's very nice, isn't he?'

Dobie beams at her, nodding. 'Oh yes, good young chap, but you know . . .' He lets it hang in the air, the understanding that Dr Li might be good, might be brilliant, but he isn't even in the same paddock as Dr Macnulty.

She doesn't volunteer information about what took her away and that's how it should be. She's a complete professional and she's giving him her full attention. Concentrating on him. Dobie Kinnear. His health and welfare.

'You've lost a bit of weight,' she says.

'Feel all the better for it,' he tells her. He's not going to volunteer information either. Is he a weakling then, to blab about the many trials of his life – a fire and a beating, a stroke (minor), desertions and treachery, and a daughter whose thoughts are elsewhere and drifting farther away each day? No. But he wants to. Oh, how he wants to. To lay his head on her breast and murmur everything into the sweet confidentiality of that starched white coat. He gives himself up to the pressure of her hands, and feels something lighten inside him, as a thick cloud will glow with the sun behind it. He's in touch with reality though. Just. She's a good, kind woman. He's an old man getting a cancer shot.

But it's nice, all the same.

It's enough.

Pearl, waiting for Dobie, shifts her position to get comfortable in the straight-backed chair and hears a crackling in her pocket. She pulls out the envelope that had lain under the dining table for heaven knows how long. Dobie's handwriting. Another one of his scribbles.

Pearl, remind me to tell you about advertisement for new farm manager. Much trouble here today. Can't go on like this.

It's the note that Dobie said he'd left for her! Oh dear god. He really had tried to tell her. And she hadn't believed him at all. The poor old bugger had been lying there in hospital and I just walked all over him, she thinks. I trampled him. I didn't even give him a chance to tell me his side of the story. Oh Dad.

She's awash with guilt.

Again.

Dobie seems a little unsteady when he stands up after the injection. Dr Macnulty has to take his arm and walk him through to reception.

'I'll just put your paperwork through,' she says. 'Gillian's got a migraine and Margaret's away in Canberra on holiday, so I'm all alone today. Bear with me, won't you?'

Only until the sky falls, he thinks, deserting reality for warmer climes.

There are two more people in the waiting room, besides Pearl. A woman about the same age as Pearl and a girl of seventeen or so. The girl is looking at the blue-washed wall, bored. The woman's face is gaunt, as if eaten away from the inside. Cancer. He knows that look. Lived with it. She hasn't got long. And here's Pearl, ruddy and plump, rising to greet him with her arms outstretched as though she's about to hug him. Funny expression on her face. He dodges her, still mindful of housekeepers and her plans to leave him.

In the car, she asks if they can stop off somewhere before heading home.

'No problem with me,' he says, warily.

'If you're sure that you feel all right, after the shot.'

'Never felt better.' Not for a long time, anyway.

'I'd like to call in at the nursery and look at some roses. We can have a coffee there too, if you like.'

'Would have thought you've got enough roses.'

Roses? Coffee? What's this then? Is she going to make some kind of announcement?

They walk past lines of dusty bottlebrush and ti-tree, the dark green of camellias and weeping ficus, pots of lavender and rosemary, into the sheltered, sunny heart of the nursery where a few wrought-iron tables and chairs stand, surrounded by flowers.

She orders a vanilla slice with her coffee and he has plum cake, moist and sticky. He's nibbling away at it for the sake of appearances but not really enjoying it. He's trying to gather his wits, so he'll be ready for whatever it is that she has to say. He won't crack. He won't give her the pleasure of a reaction. He's quite determined about that.

'Dad,'

Here it comes.

'I owe you an apology,' she says.

Eh?

She takes a crumpled envelope from her pocket and smoothes it on the table in front of him. His handwriting. Ah! The note. She found it then. He's to be exonerated, is he? Might get some mileage out of this.

He picks it up. Frowns, taking his time with it. He turns it over and looks at the front. Sees with a sudden tremor what Pearl hasn't noticed – that the postmark on the envelope is dated the month after his collapse. Should have checked that, Dobie! He crumples it up and tosses it into a litter bin.

'Best let bygones be bygones, Pearlie,' he says, casually enough. 'I'm not one to hold a grudge.'

'I'm sorry, Dad. Really I am. I don't know where my head is sometimes. And you've had all this trouble, all the worries of the farm, and Pete, whatever he did . . .'

Yes, well, better not go into that one.

'So is that what we've come here for?' He's still begrudging. Still thinking about her plans to leave him.

'Not really,' she admits. 'I'm here to pick up a rose I ordered. I'll pop over and see them now.'

If she's going to leave him, he's not going to hear about it today it seems. He watches a trail of ants around the base of a lavender pot. Throws them a crumb from his plate. In no time at all, she's back. Hugging a plant to her chest. Bit of a glow about her.

'We can go now, if you've finished,' she says.

'Doesn't look like much of a rose,' he says, grumpily.

'No it doesn't, but there are buds here, lots of promise.'

'Lots of aphids, more like.'

Pearl, arms full of her very own rose, lets his baiting blow right over her.

'Where are you going to put it?'

'I'm going to make a garden bed in front of my bedroom windows. So I can see it every morning when I wake up.'

It's a way of connecting, she thinks. A way of honouring them both, Alice and Henry. It isn't going to hurt anybody. No one will know the significance of it, except me.

Henry's Pearl.

The garden bed will be Alice's design, but with an extra, very special rose included. She decides to ring Thomas to tell him that Robert Hearne can handle the business side of Henry's Pearl and have his share of the profits from it, on condition that the story behind the rose never comes out. It's the only way she can keep Dobie safe.

I'll have my roses, and a share of the profits too, she

thinks. I'll have the story and everything that spins out from it. It has changed everything. It has changed me.

Dobie doesn't speak. He's thinking about Alice, drowning in Alice and gratitude and the sweet, heart-breaking smell of roses is all around him. *So I can see it every morning when I wake up.* Pearl isn't going any-where. She isn't like everybody else. She isn't going to leave him after all.

'I'm going to put a couple of climbers in,' she's saying. 'Do you think you could knock up a bit of a framework for me? To run the roses up? Nothing too heavy.'

'Yes,' he says, 'I'll put something together for you. Something delicate-looking but strong enough to take the weight.'

'Perfect.'

'Last time I made a frame for a climbing rose it was a bit of lattice I put up on the western wall, for your mother. Feels like another lifetime.' The image is grow-ing stronger in his mind as he speaks. 'It was for a white rose. That was a rambler too. She loved it, your mother did. Couldn't get enough of its perfume. Good budwood, she said it was. Sturdy and reliable. Good budwood. Funny, what you remember. Such a long time ago.'

Pearl, holding her breath, sees the black-and-white image of a man standing in front of a rambling rose on the western wall. The stories are brushing against each other, in their own way, in their own time. The secret is still safe.

When Pearl doesn't respond, Dobie assumes that he's

moved her, mentioning Alice like that. He doesn't talk to her about Alice. He doesn't talk at all about Alice. He's never shared Alice with anyone.

After this, he's so quiet during the drive home that Pearl looks over to see if he's fallen asleep, but he's gazing out of the window at the long years, as they unfold across paddocks and pastures, by creeks and irrigation channels, and over the wooden bridge with its white palings. His face is more peaceful than she's seen it for a long time.

Nearly home, Dobie. Nearly home now.

The dog is barking and leaping up at his side of the car when Pearl pulls in.

'What's up, Blackleg? What's wrong, boy?'

The damn dog is all over him, trying to tell him something. Dobie can hardly get out of his seat. Pearl is the first to see the battered little yellow car parked beside the house. What now?

'Visitors?' she says.

'I'm going to have a nap. Bit weary,' he tells her quickly, thinking about government inspectors and little brown birds. Pearlie can handle it.

A voice rings out over the lawn.

'Hello, I hope you didn't mind me letting myself in to wait for you? I wasn't sure about the dog, you know? And it was a bit on the warm side in the car.'

The visitor is standing behind the flywire door. She can see them, not realising that they can't see her. Pearl doesn't recognise the voice and Dobie doesn't believe it.

The woman comes out onto the verandah, a hand shading her eyes.

'Who the hell is this?' says Pearl, under her breath, as they approach.

'I saw your advertisement,' the woman calls. 'I did have your number once, but I lost it.' She smiles, right at him. 'You know how it is.'

She's got blue jeans on with a white T-shirt and a lightweight jacket, red as pomegranates, with the sleeves pushed up. No leopardskin in sight.

God! thinks Dobie, shedding years as lightly as the petals from a blown rose, you wouldn't be dead for quids, would you?

54

Catherine Nunan is the name of the new housekeeper at Mamerbrook.

Temporarily housed in the guest room, she will be taking up residence in Bel's place just as soon as she and Pearl have it ready. Thirty-eight years old, born and raised in Adelaide. Ex-schoolteacher. No current husband. No children. Apparently strong and healthy. Apparently sane.

She's a curiosity all right.

'I'd rather be honest with you from the start,' she said to Pearl. 'I'll guarantee you six months' work, but after that I might want to be on the move again.'

Whatever she's running from, she might not find it so easy to leave this place, thinks Pearl, who knows.

'How are you with chooks?' she asked.

'Cleaning out from under them or wringing their necks? It's all fine by me,' said Catherine.

It was a done deal.

Dobie, listening behind doors, dreams of apple pies and roast chicken, rice puddings and the little tarts with marmalade inside that Alice used to make for him. He's taken to hanging around the kitchen after breakfast, hoping for a glimpse of his goddess. Pearl's onto him. She's given Catherine a later starting time. No fool like a old fool, she thinks, half annoyed, half pitying the way her father behaves when Catherine is around. Can't take his eyes off her. Sly glances at her breasts, and that goofy smile on his face. If Catherine has noticed, it doesn't seem to worry her. I'll have to watch him, Pearl thinks. I don't want him scaring her away. The sooner she moves into Bel's place, the better.

How Catherine's bustling vitality lights up the old homestead, banishing uncertainty and flustering the ghosts. The windows sparkle behind fresh clean curtains. Even the world beyond the glass seems imbued with a new energy and all of the cobwebs are gone.

Pearl had got the whole story from her, about Dobie's lift to Swan Hill and the job offer. Months ago, he'd tried to hire a housekeeper and said nothing to his daughter about it. Can you believe it?

Pearl can't.

There's no point, she concludes, in trying to understand people. You just need to know enough to get them to do what you want. That's Dobie's philosophy.

Careful, Pearl.

She dreamed about Mannie Eidelson last night. His boxer shorts, blue silk with little black ducks, were hanging from her bedhead. His arms held her close and when he nuzzled her neck and murmured a question, his breath smelt of green apples. His chest was big and warm with curling fair hairs. The rest of him was big and warm too. She kissed him in a frantic panic of energy. Forty years of yearning went into that kiss and he was man enough to meet it head on. She woke with the smile of a woman fulfilled, and carried it all through breakfast, but only on the inside.

55

Dobie has just woken from his nap. His mouth is so dry that his tongue is sticking to the ridge behind his top teeth. His right hand is clenched around the crossword that he's screwed up into a ball. Dammit! He hasn't finished it yet either. He uncurls his hand with difficulty.

It's mid-afternoon. Couple of biscuits or a slice of that supermarket fruitcake with a cold beer would go down well. He hauls himself out of bed and plods towards the kitchen, head down, watching his thick socks hit the slate floor one after another, pad, pad, pad . . . and only looks up when he hears singing.

He flattens himself against the wall (just in time!) and creeps sideways towards the kitchen door. Peering around it, he sees her. His hitchhiker. She's kneeling on the floor, lovely round bum pointing straight towards him as she rubs polish into the slates. He watches her strong arms going round and round and round. Her blonde curls are tied back off her face. Dobie holds his breath. She turns, bringing her cloth around under the ledge where the bench meets the floor, and stops singing.

She's seen him!

He ducks back.

She calls out, 'Hello there.'

He peers at her from behind the door.

'I thought you were a dream,' he explains.

Catherine doesn't miss a beat. 'Not me,' she says. 'I'm real enough. Nobody's dreamed me up.'

'Oh. Good. Er . . .'

'Do you want to come in? Probably better if I get you something. This polish can be a bit slippery under the socks until it dries out properly. What would you like? Cup of tea and a bite of cake? I often get peckish around this time too. I'll bring you a tray out to the verandah, if you like.'

Dobie sits, waiting for her. He's dreamed her in that kitchen so often that sometimes, waking, he forgets that she lives here now, at Mamerbrook. When she comes out with a great slab of homemade butter cake and a mug of tea for him, he's just so damn pleased with himself he could burst.

This is how it started between Mary Brecken and his father, all those years ago. The Brecken came to the farm to keep house. Cooking and cleaning – that's what she was hired for. But look where she ended up. Warming his father's bed with her own skinny body.

You never know, do you?

Miracles can happen.

No wonder he has a goofy smile on his face.

Holding on grimly to patterns of past behaviour, Pearl is having trouble establishing the desirable social distance between herself and Catherine, her employee. This is an employee who asks questions, even personal questions, and assumes there will be answers. *Did you grow up here? Live alone here, do you? With your father? No other family? Never been married? What do you do with yourself in the evenings? What do you do for fun?*

Fun?

She shows a cheery disregard for Pearl's reticence and is so content within herself that Pearl begins to find excuses to work alongside her at various tasks. Just for the pleasure of it. It seems churlish, after that, not to answer the questions. She is wary, but she is warming up. Those solid defences, so carefully constructed over a lifetime, have become a bit of a nuisance, haven't they? Against what, precisely, is she defending herself?

Look at her, jumping up and down to see over the top of the barricades, to a land where friendship grows.

Hello? Hello? I'm here. I don't know how to play, but I want to. Really I do.

But you can't let them see that you're needy, Pearl.

Can you?

The two women have been cleaning Bel's place. Making it liveable again. Pearl stands and arches her back, stretching the kinks out of it.

'There. That should do it. Now we can move some furniture in and make a home for you.'

353

'I won't need much,' says Catherine. 'Just the basics.'

But there is so much furniture at Mamerbrook that isn't used, isn't needed. Pearl finds the basics and adds rugs, curtains, bedding, towels, a little bookcase and a coffee table.

'Oh! These are lovely,' Catherine tells her. 'Are you sure you won't miss them? I can manage with any old things.'

'Nonsense,' says Pearl, puffing a bit under the weight of a rolled blue carpet. 'This is your home, for as long as you're here. You'll want to be comfortable.'

'You are very kind, to go to so much trouble.'

'It's nothing,' says Pearl. She's having fun. She's filched the standard lamp from Dobie's sitting room. He never uses it. He does all his reading in bed these days. She plugs it in and switches the globe on and off, to test it. It will make the small room very cosy.

As they drive household items across the garden and through the orchard in the ute, Dobie watches them from behind the water tank. Pearlie seems to have taken a shine to Catherine. Looks like half the contents of the bloody homestead are going to end up at Bel's place. She's trying to settle her in, he knows. She wants her to like it here. Wants her to stay. I could make her comfortable, given half a chance, he thinks, as their laughter reaches him through the trees and the afternoon shadows grow longer all around him.

'Thought I might go into town tonight,' says Catherine. 'Have a meal at the pub and catch a movie. Want to come?'

'Yes,' says Pearl, stamping both feet on the flare of inner protests. 'I'd love to. That'd be great.'

'We can get some popcorn,' says Catherine, 'and those little ice-creams with the chocolate coating.'

Pearl agrees, laughing.

Defences?

What defences.

56

Mannie Eidelson often visits the farm, tapping on the kitchen door, calling cooee if he can't see Pearl. He'll have a coffee with her, sometimes a piece of cake, and pass the time of day.

And that's all?

That's all.

'So what's with the big guy who comes around?' says Catherine. 'Are you and he –'

'No!' says Pearl.

Not for want of trying though.

She can feel it when he looks at her. It's there in the shy compliments, the gentle courtesies he offers. She knows he's interested but it never seems to go anywhere. He's happy enough leaning against a fence, watching the sheep or gazing into a sunset for hours on end. But if he wants Pearl Kinnear, he's going to have to put a bit more effort in. She's worth it.

'Why don't you invite him for dinner?' Catherine suggests, after Pearl has hinted at her frustrations. 'I could cook up a feast. All you'd have to do is choose a good wine, light the candles and leave it in the lap of the gods. If that doesn't put a spark in him, nothing will.'

'I might,' says Pearl doubtfully, preferring the dinner invitation to come from him. Is she being courted or not?

She has rung Thomas Hearne and told him she's sure they can come to some arrangement that will include Robert. She is tempted by the idea of running her own rose business, but she knows she wouldn't make a go of it without expert help. The thought of a partnership is intriguing. They must get together and talk. Secretly. She wants to get to know the Hearnes a little better and learn something about Henry's life too. It's only the thought of Dobie that holds her back. How to build a closer involvement with them, without the risk of Dobie discovering the meaning behind Henry's gift?

The garden bed has been marked out beneath her bedroom windows and Henry's Pearl will be settled into the good earth of Mamerbrook as soon as the season turns. She has ordered two of the yellow climbers, the Emily Gray rose, but cannot bear to have them stretching up in front of the windows, blocking her view. She will have them in the same order, spelling out Alice's last message to her, but with a small amendment to the design: Dobie's trellis, fixed to the wall of the house. The climbers will frame Pearl's windows, not blind them.

The rose, Henry's Pearl, residing temporarily in a

large, black pot, its buds opened to fragrant full blooms, is a small thorn in her understanding of Alice.

Mother?

What happened?

Was it just a bit of fun? A fling? Or had Alice fallen in love with Henry Hearne? But how could she do that to Dobie? Was she lonely? Was Henry Hearne a passing gift from the universe? A moment of comfort in a hard world? One chance?

Where is she to find an answer to these questions? There's no one she can ask.

Choose a story, Pearl.

Whatever you have to believe, to get by.

Maybe I will do something about Mannie, she thinks. He did ask for a raincheck when I invited him to dinner after the fire. I'll give him a bit of a push and see what happens.

57

Catherine is cooking a roast because Mannie Eidelson is coming to dinner.

'He looks like a beef-and-three-veg man to me,' she said.

At Dobie's special request, there will be a pineapple upside-down cake for dessert. He has begun to work his way through a list of food that he'd long resigned himself to enjoying in memory only. A concession has been agreed to, in return for this blessing. A small price to pay.

Mannie arrives a little late but all spruced up and with a bottle of Cabernet Sauvignon tucked under one arm and a bunch of white carnations in his hand. That shirt cost a bit, thinks Pearl, exclaiming over the flowers. She's only ever seen him in his working clothes. He looks good in dark blue with his broad chest and big kind face. She feels a little shy suddenly.

When she invites him to take a seat at the table, Mannie chooses the chair where she usually sits, so she takes Dobie's seat across from him. The winds of change are still blowing strong at Mamerbrook. Who is she to spit into them? Let Dobie deal with it, she thinks, annoyed that she hadn't found the courage to ask her father to eat elsewhere tonight. But looking into the face of another man, and sitting in her father's chair, the scene takes on bewildering dimensions, as though time has slipped and she's been granted a moment of her own future. The post-Dobie years. Disoriented, she presses her fingers into the lace tablecloth, reassured by its texture, the hard cedar beneath it.

Catherine brings the meal in. 'I'll be messing about in the kitchen for a while,' she says. 'Don't mind me. I just want to get this cake cooked and turned out and then I'll be off. Mr Kinnear says he'll have a tray in his room. He's a little tired. He says you're not to worry about him.' And from behind Mannie's back as she sets down his plate, she winks at an astonished Pearl.

So here is Mannie at last, large, genial, entirely comfortable and very pleased to be here. Pearl, serving him extra slices of beef, remembers the boxer shorts, and blushes. There isn't much small talk, but that doesn't worry either of them.

Later, after the beef, he asks her, 'Have you never wanted to leave here? Never wanted to travel the world or live in a city?'

'A city! No thanks,' she says with a shudder. 'But leave? Can't say I haven't thought about it.' How to explain that the years when she might have been strong enough, selfish enough to get away, were the years after her mother died. How to explain her promise to Alice, to stay? She can't even explain it to herself. And hasn't it been the perfect excuse never to risk anything. What? Pearl Kinnear? Deliberately turn a corner without knowing what lies ahead? Only on the sheep trails, well within the confines of Mamerbrook. Until Thomas came. Such a little life it's been, and where have all the years gone?

Mannie, sensing that he's touched a nerve, calls out to Catherine.

'And another fine woman in the kitchen there. All alone too, are you?'

'All alone and thankful for it,' she counters.

He shakes his head, pretending dismay. 'I can't understand why no one has snapped you up before now.'

Is he talking about me, or Catherine, Pearl wonders?

The excitement she felt earlier is threatening to leak away and she's aware of the quiet tug of melancholy. But, hey, who's got time for that? There's a quest here. Neither frog nor prince, but the man who saved your life. What are you going to do, Pearl?

Whip those horses.

Next to her plate is the squat, fat-bellied salt shaker. She runs her index finger down the curve of its cool surface. She has shapely hands with perfectly oval fingernails. Has he noticed? She raises her eyes to his face but Mannie is watching in eager anticipation as Catherine arrives with their plates of dessert and a jug of cream. And it isn't the dessert that he's appreciating.

Pearl narrows her eyes.

'Catherine, why don't you get yourself a glass and join us?' she says.

If Catherine is surprised by this, if she would prefer to go home to her cottage, she nevertheless responds to the subtle insistence in Pearl's tone.

Mannie pours her a glass of wine.

'You grow onions, don't you?' says Catherine brightly, in an attempt to dispel the slight awkwardness that hangs over the table.

'I do. Only the main commercial varieties though. Nothing exciting. I was telling Pearl earlier about an onion called Tawny Red that's so sweet you can bite right into it like an apple. But the seed is expensive and the market for these lesser known varieties is practically non-existent. No outlets. If the supermarkets don't want it, you just don't grow it.'

'Couldn't you get a little bit of seed?' asks Catherine, thinking of the dishes she could create with sweet onions.

'I might, for you,' says Mannie, including Pearl in this, but too late. Oh, far too late, Mannie.

'You haven't lit the candles I put out,' says Catherine.

'When I was young – it was a Jewish household, you understand – the woman of the household lit the candles at Shabbat dinner, every Friday evening. So much food my mother used to prepare. Places set for family, friends and neighbours too.' He describes the noise – everyone talking at once, shouting each other down. The warmth and laughter he recalls is reflected in his eyes.

Pearl thinks about her lonely dinners with Dobie

grunting and the wine bottle emptying too quickly. 'It sounds wonderful,' she says, and then feels irritated at the wistfulness in her own voice.

'It was sometimes. Not always. Families, eh? We got out of the habit of it as I grew older. No one had the time to spare. Everyone had something else to do, somewhere else to be.'

Dessert is finished. The wine bottle is empty. The conversation falters again.

'I'll be off now,' says Catherine. 'Thank you for the wine.'

'Time for me to turn in too,' says Pearl, gratified at the surprise on their faces.

'I'd better be making a move myself,' says Mannie reluctantly. 'Early start in the morning.'

Well? You have to dig in the worms if you want roses, don't you, Pearl?

'Mannie?' she says, sweetly. 'Would you mind dropping Catherine over at the cottage? Save her a walk in the dark?'

'Oh, there's no need for that,' Catherine protests, sure that the evening should be ending differently.

'I'll be happy to do that,' says Mannie, not sounding happy at all.

For Pearl, it's only a pinprick of bitterness that she isn't ten years younger with round breasts and slender legs like Catherine's. So soon assuaged that she almost relents, but she's had a good teacher when it comes to strategy. The best.

'Go on, the pair of you. I'll clear up in here,' she says as the three of them cluster awkwardly by the door. 'That was a wonderful meal, Catherine. Thank you. It was so much better than anything I'd have come up with. Mannie . . .' She leans forward as if to kiss him but at the last moment turns her cheek to his lips and then hands him his hat. 'It was good to see you. We must do this again. I've got out of the habit of being sociable.'

Never really had it, she thinks.

Bit late now.

But who knows, maybe Thomas will come here to dinner. Maybe even Robert? Maybe, just maybe, she'll ask Mannie back, and light the candles next time too.

And whatever will Dobie do then, poor thing?

Sit in a barn and keep himself warm and hide his head under his wing?

She sighs. Mannie feels this and hesitates, looking for some sign of encouragement, but she is gazing at the stars, not at him.

Poor thing.

This is fun, isn't it, Pearl?

Much more fun than she'd had dancing to Dan Woods' tune.

I've moved on, she thinks.

It's true. But to what?

Did Henry Hearne once sit at that table with my mother, she wonders, raising her arm to wave and smile as Mannie's car drives away with Catherine in the passenger seat.

Dobie hears the car drive off and he can't work it out. He'd given Pearl every chance tonight, leaving the two of them alone like that. He'd felt sure that one of them would make a move and confirm his darkest suspicions. But there is the car, driving away, and there is Pearl at the kitchen sink. An early end to the evening. He can't decide if what he's feeling is relief that Mannie has gone, or disappointment at being wrong. He settles on a mixture of the two. Has she blown it, he wonders? Has she said something to put him off.

What? Isn't my daughter good enough for a bloody onion farmer? He'd better watch his step if he's planning on coming around here again.

58

There's a woodshed at the bottom of the garden, but the garden at Kerrimuir Roses stretches a long, long way from the house and this shed has never been used to store wood. Henry Hearne built it many years ago, setting into its walls the hinged windowpanes that you could swing out to take advantage of any passing breeze, or shut tight to trap the winter sunshine.

Here, on the high wooden stool, Henry would sit at his potting bench patiently grafting and seeding, potting up his budwood, and dreaming. It is Henry's shed, and always will be. It is the birthplace of Henry's Pearl.

Robert has installed large glasshouses on the other side of the house, modern affairs of aluminium, glass and shadecloth with overhead watering systems and temperature control, but it is to Henry's shed that he comes to sort his budwood, as if he might find, trapped within the old boards, a touch of the generous magic that Henry brought to life, a whispering charm to guide his own fingers to the right decisions.

Today he is sitting on the old wooden stool, eyes

on the window and the roses beyond it but his gaze is inward. Henry's audio tape has finished playing. The portable cassette player clicks off. With the slight rounding of those shoulders and the greying hair, yes, it might be Henry sitting there, pondering for two hours or more as the sun moves overhead and the budwood stems lie scattered and forgotten on the bench.

At last Robert gives a little shake of his head and chuckles. The very idea that Henry's Pearl is a real person. Amazing. A person! That Henry would . . . the old rogue! Who'd have thought he had it in him?

Robert had wanted to write to the Kinnears as soon as he heard. Some kind of a welcome was in order, he felt, presenting the background of his own skills and making it clear that he has played an important part in bringing Henry's Pearl to its rightful owner. Mel thought it was a good idea but Thomas cautioned patience. She'll call us when she's ready, he said. Let's not rush things. She'll need some time to take this in.

Thomas told him that Pearl (Pearl! Just imagine.) had agreed to a joint arrangement, involving Robert in some way, but that she hadn't worked out any of the details yet. It went some way to soothing Robert's grievances about losing the rose to . . . but not to a stranger. No. The rose is staying in the family, isn't it? This is the fact that has finally overwhelmed all other considerations. Robert, who has inherited Henry's gift for making the best of things, for finding happiness in small occurrences and unexpected ways, is utterly astonished by the news that he has a sister. A half-sister out there somewhere, who loves roses. Henry . . . the crafty old devil. Robert shakes his head again and laughs quietly to himself till tears come to his eyes. And the tears won't stop.

Old Henry. You never really know them, do you? The joke of it, the glorious joke of it. Henry's way of bringing them all together as soon as he himself was safely out of the way, beyond criticism, beyond judgement, beyond questions. Robert, scrabbling for a handkerchief, no longer sure if he's laughing or crying, has so many questions, so very many questions he'd like to ask Henry.

Yes, a great joke, this is. A real pearler. No doubt the old man is laughing his socks off up there, wherever he is.

Can you hear him, Robert?

Oh yes.

Good one, Henry.

59

Catherine invites Pearl to dinner at her cottage.

'A thank you,' she says, 'for all the extra trouble you've gone to. Helping me furnish the place and everything. Let's have some wine and sort the world out. Two girls letting their hair down.'

'I'll come on one condition,' says Pearl. 'That you let me bring the wine.'

'Bring lots of it then, and I'll make up a casserole that your father can help himself to.'

He'll have conniptions, getting his own dinner, thinks Pearl, not without a touch of glee.

Dobie is not thrilled by this turn of events. He watched Pearl cross the garden with her clinking cardboard box. He knows she's going to have dinner with Catherine. No one has invited him. Nobody wants him. Nobody cares if he lives or dies, leaving him here, all alone. He wanders around the house forlornly, without appetite for the meal they've left for him. Some daughter, he thinks. She couldn't give a damn. He shivers suddenly.

The place is vibrating with emptiness.

Listen.

What is it?

But all he can hear is his own loneliness resonating in the empty rooms.

Come on now, he warns, giving himself a mental shake.

Get a grip, Dobie.

There's your dinner, there's the television. She'll be back. You know she will. But he can't settle to anything and goes from room to room, as if he's moving through the very moment (so often imagined!) when she's left him forever.

He meant to go straight out to the ute to do a paddock check before sundown. He meant to. Really, he did.

But look at him.

There he is, peering around the door of Pearl's room, snooping. What's he looking for? Clues to her future? His future? Something that will give him an edge, and banish this shameful fear. Nobody cares. He isn't consulted. He isn't informed. He isn't included. Somehow, all his power, his authority, the hold he had over her – it's all slipped away. He wants it back. He wants . . . something.

Clothes lie discarded on the bed. Tubes and bottles and make-up pencils scattered on the dressing table. Looks like she was in a great rush to be out of here. The air in the room is sweetened with the perfume she wears sometimes. It is feminine. Foreign territory. The tiny bottle is there, by the mirror. 'Joy', Jean Patou. Joy in a bottle, thinks Dobie, scornfully. Wouldn't that be some-thing? His eye is drawn to the marquetry jewellery box, sitting there just as it had when Alice was alive. Time wavers. Just for a second, it is his room, their room, he is coming to bed, to Alice.

Dobie! Boots! cries Alice in horror, so that he actu-ally spins around, guilty as charged.

But there is no one to see if he walks on the carpet in his old boots.

Nobody here but you, Dobie.

What now?

He stands by the jewellery box, looking down at it, stroking the timber that Pearl has waxed to a soft lustre. Knows how to look after things, Pearl does. He'll say that much for her. There's a book beside it: *Sally Mer-chant's Guide to Having a Meaningful Menopause*.

It doesn't mean a thing to him.

Is it a clue?

His hand hovers over the book. For a moment it seems as though he will flick through the pages, but then the hand moves back to the jewellery box. He opens the lid, and the last hope of his life flies up into his face and disappears for ever.

60

Dobie pulls up at the track junction to watch the sun set as he has done for more years than he cares to remember. Loose, rippling diagonal bars of cirrocumulus stretch across the blue; fish-scale clouds already turning yellow, orange and pink. There'll be a mackerel sky, when that glowing half-dome of the sun drops below the curve of the earth. A beauty.

Going, going . . .

Gone.

A V-formation of ibis flap slowly across the softening sky as the evening cacophony rises. A shrieking, trilling, cawing and croaking. A multitude of voices: cicadas, crickets, frogs and birds. The mad jungle whoop and cackle of kookaburras down by the river. Hymn to the long day's ending. Kangaroos bound cautiously one by one from the river scrub out into the open paddock to mingle with Dobie's sheep. One, two, three . . . he counts forty of them. Thieving buggers. I'm just a caretaker for kangaroos, crows and kookaburras, that's what I am.

The sky is luminous now, draining colour from the land so that the eye is drawn inescapably upwards. Dobie watches for a few more seconds then puts the ute into gear. Just a couple more paddocks to check and then he can call it a night. The men are long gone. There's Bel's place, lit up already, Catherine and Pearl well down their first bottle, no doubt. He can see the homestead too. No lights there.

Funny how things can turn in an instant. All those years worrying that Pearl might leave him, all the energy poured into strategies to make sure she didn't, and as soon as he discovers that she's staying, planning her garden beds, well, then he loses her forever. She's not his Pearlie. She's not his at all. He's just the caretaker and that's all he's ever been.

Three little pieces of paper. A letter to Alice from a rose-grower named Henry Hearne. An old garden plan of roses – a ring drawn in fresh ink around the first letter of each rose. A black-and-white photograph of a man, vaguely then horribly familiar, as Pearl's features seemed overlaid on his face. Three things. The only three things that she keeps in the jewellery box. Her treasures?

Here comes Alice.

Just look at her.

Glorious. Hand on her belly, in the rose garden, as she tells him she is pregnant.

Something inside Dobie uncurls, twists and rears; a nightmare of doubt suppressed for half a century; his own damn dark *knowing* of this thing, never aired, never healed.

There are no miracles, and nothing is perfect.

Not even Alice.

She's not yours, Dobie.

Shake up all the pieces.

Go on. Give them a good shake.

And what have you got?

All that it takes for Dobie Kinnear to vanish.

He replaced everything carefully. Shut the lid. His body felt extraordinarily light, as though he was barely making contact with the ground. What was it now? His life? What had it been? An illusion granted by the grace of Alice? Permission to believe?

Alice?

Not his Alice.

How long has Pearl known about this?

Pearl, who is staying.

How to have everything, and nothing.

What a lucky man you are, Dobie Kinnear. What a lucky, lucky man.

He's already put Blackleg on the chain by the kennel, so he won't have to fumble about with it in the dark later. The dog whined when the ute pulled away. Never did like being left behind. The ewes in the dusky back paddock are grouped peacefully beneath the huge old black box tree. They don't even lift their heads when he drives slowly past them, counting automatically, checking to see how they look. The evening star appears as he's making his last turn on the top bank of the big dam. It's been dry inside there for weeks now since they turned off the irrigation water. The ground has baked and opened in huge cracks, wider than a man's arm. A tumble of saltbush, blown on a whim of air, rolls across its dusty surface. Then he sees her. An old ewe. He stops the ute. She struggles. Tries to get to her feet but she's either too weak, or caught. He can't leave her. There's no one he can radio for help. No manager to come out at all hours to do his bidding.

Just you, Dobie.

He looks at the ground, at those cracks. It ought to be solid enough, but the width of them . . . if he got the ute stuck down there, he'd have a long walk home. Be easier with the ute though. He could haul her into the back of it. That would be the simplest thing, but . . .

Think, Dobie.

I'll go down and take a look at her. Maybe if I get her on her feet, she can limp out of here on her own. The ewe bleats at him, stirs briefly before falling back on her side. I'm coming, he croons. Steady on there, old girl. We'll sort something out, between the two of us.

He gets out of the ute, feels a teasing lick of a breeze across his face and looks up at the bowl of the darkening sky. The cloud has thinned and the last flare of the sunset has gone. It's time for stars now. The earth is turning. Every living creature on his land is going about its business, knowing its place, and for the first time in his life he is separate, outside of it all and isolated from it. Grief threatens. Grief for himself. Has his whole life been nothing but a sham of pity? Are there no memories he can depend on? He swallows. Turns suddenly and looks behind as though someone has tapped him on the shoulder. No one is there. Even his ghosts have abandoned him. The world is lonely enough to make a man howl.

He cautiously lowers himself down the bank in a half slide, half scramble, braking hard with the heels of his boots. He pictures the dam filled with shining water as it has been, as it will be again, and all the black swans and ducks, crested grebes, and even terns, he's seen here. Pelicans making those wide, lazy turns above the water. How often has he sat here, watching? How many days in a life? Listening to the wavelets, their miniature crests of coffee froth lap-lapping against these steep clay banks, soothing the heart and mind.

The light is fading rapidly.

Should have brought the torch from the ute, Dobie. Or put on the headlights? No point going back now. Probably better off without, he thinks, knowing how a sudden beam of light can cause distortions, shape-shifting in the landscape. He's tired to the bone and wants to go home. Home. No consolation there; just a bed to fall into. All his consolation has been stolen away. But sleeping, he might forget for a while.

One more time the ewe makes an effort for him and then she lies still. His eyes are on her. His voice reaches her. Low, reassuring sounds he doesn't even know he's making. Help is on its way, old girl. Hang in there.

He's a couple of yards away from her when he goes down, twists and slips, knocking all the breath out of himself.

Good one, Dobie. That's a real help, that is.

Why can't he get up?

It takes some time for him to work out what's happened. His right leg has gone down into the cracked earth to mid-thigh level. He grows angry, irritated at his own stupidity. Snakes, he thinks. Living in holes in the ground, curling up in the deep, dark cracks, and coming out at night to hunt. Christ! He can almost feel them slipping over his boot, sliding up his trouser leg. He struggles fiercely, heaving his body, leaning sideways, forwards, backwards, the muscles of his old arms bursting and straining, but he can't find the leverage, or the strength, to free himself. The ewe looks at him mournfully, her little eyes catching the last of the light. See?

Dobie renews his struggle, refusing to believe in this idiotic predicament. Eventually, exhausted, he stops, his body sprawled forward, one hand outstretched as though in a last attempt to reach the ewe. The old Akubra had tumbled from his head when he fell. He can see it but he can't reach it. Fear rises, blurring his vision, and his heartbeat is fast and erratic, hurting his chest. Ah! the pain. He has never known, never imagined, such pain. Then, a clear, cool space and no pain. I need my hat, he thinks. He could weep, for his hat.

Time stops. The earth grows soft beneath him. The sky above, no longer day but not deep night, not yet, is a source of great comfort to him. He is a younger man again, walking his acres with head tipped back, dizzy with moon shadows and Alice. He puts a shaking hand to his face and inhales her. Alice. Runs his fingers through her hair and hears her voice. *You're the stars in my eye, the moon in my sky . . .* He croaks the words aloud, singing along with her. Images come to him. The crepe myrtle tree in full blossom at dusk, the rich pink of its petals seeping into the evening sky. Mutt as a pup, all floppy ears and huge trusting eyes. Pearl, tiny puckered mouth at Alice's full breast. The innocence of it. A great cry rises in him then, and bursts from him, an explosion of agony, sparking tongues of white fire into silence. He is unheard, and lies still. There is starlight in his hair and on his skin, see! there, on the back of his hand. The purity of it troubles him – so hard and white, merciless.

A cold voice warns: Don't count your chickens . . .

What? he thinks. What?

And finally he understands.

So this is it? This is how it happens? But . . .

He is breathing starlight now, drowning in starlight.

He closes his eyes.

It seems to him that he can hear water. The lapping of wavelets under a summer sun. But no, that isn't water. It is a softer sound, wings, pushing the air on a down-beat. Shuh . . . shuh . . . shuh . . . He feels the breeze of the bird's flight against his cheek, a whispering touch of feathers.

'Hurry,' says someone, not far away.

'I've been waiting such a long time,' says another voice.

Where are they? Why can't he see them?

A mopoke calls, down by the river. Three times, the mopoke calls. High above Dobie Kinnear hangs the magpie moon, the invisible blackness of the bird around a white crescent blaze, the cock of the head, the glance from a star-bright, inhuman eye, the downward sweep of dark feathers.

What does it mean, Alice?

Anything you want it to, Dobie my love. Anything at all. Nothing matters anymore. Not grief, not envy, not pride, not laughter, not love, not knowing . . .

And Pearl?

Nothing now, Dobie.

You're the one, my only one . . .

Nothing.

61

Three miles away as the crow flies from where Dobie lies, Pearl is sitting in a creaky cane chair on the back verandah at Bel's place. At her feet, a mosquito candle burns like a votive offering. She's thinking about secrets, the power they bestow, and how they can set you free.

Catherine is sitting on a cushion on the back step, inspecting the stars through her empty wine glass. 'So peaceful here,' she says. 'A person could get used to this.'

Pearl smiles. 'All the times I've thought about leaving here, and then you get a night like this one. I don't believe I could breathe anywhere else. I'm so used to the space, and all this,' she says, gesturing towards the paddocks. 'I take it too much for granted.'

'But that sunset tonight! You could never take that for granted.'

'Sometimes, you know, I forget to look.'

'I won't forget,' says Catherine dreamily. 'Every day I'm going to stop what I'm doing, just for a few moments, to watch the sun set here.'

She's going to stay, thinks Pearl. She's hooked all right.

Catherine fills her own wine glass and passes the bottle to Pearl.

'Good, this,' says Pearl.

'Mmm.' Catherine thinks she's referring to the wine.

'No. This. You and me, talking. Being here. I haven't done a lot of this sort of thing. More used to being on my own, you know. Apart from Dad of course.'

'How old were you when your mother died?'

'Fourteen. It was cancer.'

'Must have been very hard on you, losing her when you were so young. What was she like?'

Pearl draws a deep breath and considers Alice. 'She was warm and funny. Terrific sense of humour. And generous. She had a great deal of dignity and a strong sense of what was right and what was not.' She pauses, remembering Henry, but goes on, 'And she loved roses. She kept a big scrapbook about her roses, with pictures, garden designs, so many details.'

And so Pearl tells Catherine all about Alice's rose notes, omitting only the story of Henry's Pearl, for that is her own story.

'It sounds gorgeous. You should get it published. People all over the world are crazy about roses. Just imagine!'

'Oh, I don't think . . .' says Pearl and then she stops.

Just imagine.

Pages and pages of rose bed designs, perfumes described, characteristics of growth and blossom, colour variations, companion planting, pests . . . and exquisite illustrations of all the beautiful old roses. Not only Alice's designs, but Pearl's knowledge too. Yes! And what about tips on growing better roses, from Robert Hearne, the rose-grower of Kerrimuir (oh, she can see it all!). And Henry. All those letters to Alice. All about roses. I could include extracts, she thinks. Henry's advice. We could share the profits, Robert and Thomas and I. We can use the book to promote the new rose, Henry's Pearl, but without telling the story. Without ever telling the secret.

It is beautiful.

It is perfect.

It is (she is absolutely certain of it) the way ahead.

'You might be right about that,' she tells Catherine, who has stepped into the garden to see the crescent moon.

'Not a bad idea at all,' Pearl says, more to herself this time. She can't wait to start. I'll ring Thomas first thing in the morning and ask him to set up a meeting with Robert.

'What will you call it?' asks Catherine.

'*Alice's Rose Book*.'

What else?

Some time later, Catherine brings out a platter of cheeses with biscuits and fruit and sets it on an upturned crate.

'Lovely,' says Pearl gratefully. And she's not just referring to the cheese.

She looks out beyond the verandah, beyond the garden where overlapping shadows shift and promise one thing and then another, confounding expectations. Her gaze drifts across the paddocks lit pale in starlight, down to the thicker darkness that is the line of old river gums where the river runs silver tonight, and she blinks back sudden tears because her heart is brimful and bursting with happiness. Salvation lies here, she thinks.

Close.

Close enough.

Tonight, as the black magpie moon rises over Mamerbrook, where all of the trails begin and end for Pearl, she could forgive anybody anything.

Even Dobie.

Nearby, a mopoke calls out three times. Once for the past that is gone, once for the glorious present, and once more for hope of the future.

Change coming, says Mary Brecken.

A big change coming, says Alice.

But no one is listening anymore.

Pearl turns ideas, images, conversations, slowly in her mind, turns and turns and turns. Mamerbrook Farm, *Alice's Rose Book*, Mannie's slow and gentle smile, Henry's Pearl and Thomas Hearne, and all her beloved roses. Pity anyone who doesn't have what Pearl Kinnear has, she thinks, and knows it to be true. Breathing in deeply, she throws her arms wide in all that space, spreading her fingers, reaching and spinning and dancing into her own future, her own time, at last.

EPILOGUE

1955

'Come on, sit over here beside me. If we're going to do this, we're not going to manage it at this distance. You are sure you want to do this, Alice?'

'Oh yes. I wasn't sure, until I saw you. I felt, from the letters, that you were the sort of man who might do, but one can never really tell, from letters. But I feel quite sure now. If you don't mind, Henry?'

'Mind? Eh, lass, why would any man mind? Look at you! There's men'd give their right arm for one kiss . . .'

'Henry . . .'

'I know. It will change everything, won't it?'

'Yes. There must be no more letters. No contact at all. I won't risk his happiness for our friendship.'

'One letter, Alice. There must be one last letter. I'll have to know if it works. You'll have to tell me. I mean, it mightn't work, the first time. You might need a second visit. Ah! At least that's made you laugh. You need to relax, you know.'

'I think you're a bit of a rogue, Henry Hearne. You're taking this very well.'

'Now that I'm over the first shock of it, I am.'

'I'm beginning to wonder if you don't travel around the countryside offering your services to poor women in need. Perhaps the rose nursery is just a cover? Perhaps you spend a day each week at a different farm, asking for budwood to build up your rose stocks?'

'Not me. One of nature's gentlemen, I am. Besides, the way I recall it, you asked me. There's no one else I'd be doing this with, I can assure you. I like a quiet life, I do, and I love one woman. Oh damn! Sorry. I didn't mean to make you cry.'

'No, no. I'm fine, really I am. It's just, I wish it didn't have to be this way. You know, Henry, I feel it in every fibre of my being that I can have a child, just as I'm sure that after all this time I'll never have one with Dobie. But he's the only man for me.'

'Well it's very hard on a chap, seeing you like this and knowing we won't ever meet again.'

'Or write.'

'Don't worry. I'm a man of my word. Come on now, relax, look around. There's no better place on earth to do this than in a rose garden, Alice. And it's a happy thought, that I'll be growing new stock from all those budwood cuttings we've just spent the morning gathering. I'll be gone before nightfall, but I'll have a little bit of you with me always.'

'And if all goes well, I'll have a little bit of you.'

'If all goes well.'

'It has to, Henry. I can't take a risk like this twice. It

nearly killed me, having to ask you, having to explain. One chance, that's all I ask. One chance to make it right. Or not. And they must be protected, always, your wife, and Dobie. They must never know. Promise me.'

'I promise. You took my photograph though. That's risky.'

'I know. But I have to have it . . . for the future. I'll keep it safe.'

'I hope he knows what he's got, with a woman like you.'

'He's the light of my life. He'll be back tomorrow night. He's away up north, buying merinos. I didn't plan things this way. He made his arrangements, you made yours. One could see it as a gift. An opportunity not to be missed.'

'The secret is safe with me, Alice, as long as I have your word. One last letter.'

'You'll destroy it of course.'

'Naturally. Now, you're absolutely positive that no one will catch us at it?'

'Absolutely positive. Not today. Today we're safe.'

'Well, come over here then. You're not shy, are you?'

'Haven't the time to be shy. I'm nervous though.'

'Me too. Can't remember when I've been so nervous. Hope it doesn't spoil the performance.'

'I'm sure it won't.'

'I've never had any complaints.'

'Oh, you are terrible! Heavens above. Henry, what are we doing?'

'Making a baby, I hope. Feeling better, Alice?'

'Yes, I think so. Oh look, Henry, you've got rose petals in your hair.'

'Just another perk of the trade.'

'Cheeky . . .'

Mamerbrook Farm

October, 1955

Dear Mr Hearne,

Just a short note to let you know how well the budwood took. A strong and sturdy addition to the garden. Pearl.

ACKNOWLEDGEMENTS

I am fortunate in my friends – kind, honourable people who have given me much support and encouragement. I want to thank Kerry Willcock and Clint Hinchen for the front door key to a palace by the sea in which to write; Peter Bishop of Varuna for belief when it was most needed; Cate Kennedy for tapping me on the shoulder one day and generously rekindling that belief; Lyn Tranter and Nikki Davies; my fabulous three – Julie Watts, Ali Watts and Belinda Byrne – and everyone at Penguin Books; and the Brooksby family, particularly Eric, Ruby and Angus, without whom this book would not have been possible.